The
Secret
Ever Keeps

"Accomplished and assured fictional debut."

ForeWord

"Learning the truth about yourself doesn't necessarily make you happy," Jake Eastland says. He should know. At ninety-three, he contemplates his life as a bootlegger and a thug, a tycoon and a killer with regret, not for the crimes he's committed, but for the family he's never known.

All that changes when Laurel Kingsford shows up on his doorstep. A dynamic young woman with a distinguished background in oceanic research, Laurel retreats to the only place she's ever felt safe following the loss of her job, her life savings, and her fiancé. A genteel old inn overlooking Lake Ontario's southern shore, the Twice Told Hotel was where Laurel spent idyllic childhood summers in the company of her grandmother, Jean. Jake Eastland built the Twice Told in 1940 and it was where he, too, retreated after his marriage to a society gold digger named Jean ended. Obviously, Jake and Laurel have much in common. They should: unbeknownst to Laurel, Jake is her grandfather.

Tirrell ... craft(s) a high-seas thriller replete with expected elements—killer storms, sabotaged equipment, and a race-against-time quest for sunken treasure—plus one stunning twist: said treasure implicates George Washington in a devastating political scandal.

If such cloak-and-dagger intrigue isn't stimulating enough, Tirrell throws in not one, but two, romantic triangles for good measure. This is an ambitious plot for a first-time author to navigate, but Tirrell does an admirable job of making it all coalesce by endowing his character-driven narrative with a romantic sensitivity and his intricately-crafted story line with a riveting focus. It is Tirrell's rhapsodic description of Lake Ontario's tortuous shoreline, however, that lends the novel its authenticity and allure: "horizontal slabs of black-tinged slate...devoid of life, beautiful in its raw wildness. And yet something more, some darker tension seemed compressed within, as if the place held its breath and waited."

Tirrell's multigenerational saga segues effortlessly between the internecine wars of Prohibition-era rum runners and the insidious perfidy of modern-day fortune hunters. Learning the truth about her connection to Jake's notorious background may not make Laurel happy, but it does make for an accomplished and assured fictional debut.

■ Carol Haggas./ForeWord

"Captivating and utterly engaging."

"**The Secret Ever Keeps** is a rollicking ride on the choppy waters of Lake Ontario. Like the Ancient Mariner, Jake Eastland is compelled to tell the story of his misdeeds—a story that includes romance, smuggling and murder. Tirrell writes with authority and confidence; he is truly in command of this ship! Wonderful!"

Garth Stein, author of *How Evan Broke His Head and Other Secrets*, 2006 PNBA Book Award Winner

The
Secret
Ever Keeps

A NOVEL

Art Tirrell

KÜNATI

THE SECRET EVER KEEPS

For information, contact Kunati Inc., Book Publishers in both USA and Canada.
In USA: 6901 Bryan Dairy Road, Suite 150, Largo, FL 33777 USA
In Canada: 2600 Skymark Avenue, Building 12, Suite 103, Mississauga, Canada L4W 5B2,
or email to *info@kunati.com*.

FIRST EDITION

Designed by Kam Wai Yu
Persona Corp. | www.personaprinciple.com

ISBN 978-1-60164-004-8   LCCN 2006930185
EAN 9781601640048   FIC000000 FICTION/General
Published by Kunati Inc. (USA) and Kunati Inc. (Canada). Provocative. Bold. Controversial.™

http://www.kunati.com

TM—Kunati and Kunati Trailer are trademarks
owned by Kunati Inc. Persona is a trademark owned by Persona Corp.
All other tradmarks are the property of their respective owners.

For my sisters,
Sally, Barbara, Patricia, and Jennifer

Acknowledgements

Without Novelpro, J.R. Lankford's wonderful critique list,
the skills needed to tame this story would have remained beyond reach.
Critiquers Pattipeg Harjo, Michael Jensen, Jilla Lankford, Gloria Piper, Don White,
Paul Jacobsen and Jerry Cohen; polishers Chris Hoare and Paula Jolin,
and the other Novelpro members who contributed chapter critiques.
John Raby for the prototype Bruce B. Longley, Chris Rotunno for Coast Guard detail,
Corky Nesbitt for the grain elevator plans; outside readers Rebecca Fay,
Donnie Mandurano, Jean Rotunno, Bonnie Sapka and Garth Stein;
editor James McKinnon. And my daughter Cayleen,
whose open heart and belief in others helped me
finish one page of life and begin another.

NEW YORK CITY

September 8

Laurel Kingsford flinched when the door of her office banged open and Jerry Garcone cruised in. The wisp of concept she'd flirted with all morning, the breakthrough solution to one of the most difficult problems her design team faced, disappeared from her mind.

She'd been Jerry's mentor in the firm since he came aboard three years earlier. He should know better than to barge in like this by now.

"Sorry to disturb you, IQ, but Nick wants to see you in his office ASAP. Want me to tell him you'll be up after you powder your nose?"

IQ again. The nickname had settled on her because she was so bright, the guys in the management clique said, but one of the other women on staff had whispered the truth. It stood for "Ice Queen."

"No, I'll be along as soon as I can save my work and shut down the system."

It was totally unfair, she was warm and open with everyone, but she was in New York to build a career, not catch a husband, and she turned down social invitations from male employees, Jerry among them. The nickname had been her reward, and it stuck—even after she and Rob became engaged.

Jerry maintained a friendly manner in her presence, but he was too ambitious for his own good. No way would she trust him alone with Nick if she could help it, not when everyone expected the new head of the fuel cell project to be named in the next few days.

Tom Everett, retired project head, had recommended her as his replacement and rightly so. She had the qualifications: six years in fuel cell engineering, two as team leader, several summers of deep-sea research with the National Oceanic and Atmospheric Administration at Woods Hole, and a love of everything nautical. She planned her summer vacations around one NOAA field project or another, and they always invited her back.

The job was hers. She was comfortable with that, but experience had taught her the importance of guarding her flanks. Her breathing accelerated. Could this be it, the formal announcement?

Jerry peered over her shoulder at her screen. She glared and he stepped back. "Okay, see you up there." He didn't bother to close the door when he left.

Five minutes later, Laurel left the elevator on the twenty-fifth floor and entered the reception area outside Nick's office. For the past weeks, she'd taken care to dress more formally, to be ready, if and when the announcement came. Today's suit set off her eyes, and didn't disguise the fact that she was young and trim, even if in her own mind she was too tall, and her figure less than eye-popping.

Nick's receptionist smiled. "Go on in, Laurel, they're all there."

All?

With a sudden sense of foreboding, Laurel entered the division head's office. Opposite the entrance, a bank of windows extended from knee height to the ceiling. Outside, Manhattan enjoyed another warm early September morning.

Nick Zaia's desk dominated the center of the room and he stood when she entered. Marianne, Laurel's friend and head of the Propulsion Project, was present too, and so was Jerry Garcone. Jerry wore a suit she hadn't seen before, of very good cloth. She hadn't noticed downstairs. He wore it well, along with a huge grin. Beside him, Marianne did not look happy. Her eyes flashed a warning.

"Ms. Kingsford. Good. Come in, please."

Laurel's sensors went to full alert. Nick always called her by her nickname. He came around the desk and offered his hand. He was tall and fair-skinned, with curly black hair and wide blue eyes. His outward demeanor was open as they shook hands.

Nick went to the windows, where he looked out for several seconds. Then he moved back behind his desk. He didn't sit, or invite anyone else to.

"I didn't expect you to get up here so quickly, Ms. Kingsford, but now that you're here, you might as well hear it from me." He shuffled papers on his desk while he shifted from foot to foot then looked up at her.

"I've just accepted Marianne's resignation as Propulsion Project manager…" His eyes were unreadable as they bored into Laurel's. When she did not react, he went on. "We've named Jerry Garcone to replace Tom Everett as head of the fuel cell project. Management decided a fresh approach, a new attitude, would be good for the department."

Laurel was struck mute. They couldn't leapfrog Jerry over her. She was senior on the design team, practically carrying the whole project on her shoulders. Jerry didn't have a prayer of handling the job. Had Marianne quit over the news? Until now, she'd been the only woman in a leadership position in the company, and Laurel's strongest ally.

"But… I thought…" she tried, but the words wouldn't come.

Nick seemed emboldened by her confusion. "I know Tom recommended you to replace him, hon, but we felt the program would be more stable with a… with Jerry's hand on the tiller." He stepped around to her, seemed genuinely sorry to have to deliver the news, and placed his hand on her shoulder. "You're a great asset for us. I just hope you can see your way to working under Jerry. We need you to keep producing the same high-quality work you have all along."

The truth came with his choice of words, the way he'd been about to say "a man's hand on the tiller." A heat began in Laurel's neck and rose upward over her face. Marianne out. The ally she'd counted on. It was all lost. How could she face the other team members, the other female employees? She trembled, shook his hand from her shoulder and stalked out the door, her body stiff and shuddering.

"Laurel, wait!" Marianne called. "Don't…"

On the elevator down to her floor, Laurel fought back tears only until she reached her office. When the door closed behind her, the dam burst and tears flowed so thick she stopped trying to wipe them away. Tears of indignation, not sorrow; resentment, not remorse.

She booted her computer. She might cry when things like this happened, but she could still function. They wouldn't get the innovations she'd conceived for the fuel cell, the ones she'd anticipated being asked to develop. Technically, they might be the property of Forrester NA, but they could hardly prosecute her for stealing something they had no idea existed.

When the system was up, she tapped in her code words and stuck a CD in the drive. Two minutes later she'd burned the contents of her personal files into the disk.

She pulled up the operating system and typed in the instruction, "FORMAT C:\". After assuring the mainframe that she really, *really* wanted to reformat her hard drive, which would result in the irretrievable destruction of all data there, she typed the final "Y" and waited as the routine got under way. Ten minutes later, her hard drive was fresh as a newborn baby. Deleted files? What deleted files?

Just in time too. Moments after she removed the CD, her system went off and the screen went black.

The bastards were making sure she didn't do anything irrational while she was angry, like quit and take work papers with her, exactly as she'd just done.

Let that bushwhacker Jerry Garcone stew in his own salsa.

All she could think of was getting out of there and getting home to Rob. Rob would know how to help. He would comfort her. She pulled the liner from her wastebasket and emptied its contents on the floor, then cleaned out her desk. When she finished, she pulled her keys, employee ID, parking passes, and even her unused lunch tickets from her purse and threw them on their desk.

She'd given this company the best of herself, her abilities and talents, her spirit. not because it was a way to make a living. It was much more, a demonstration to them, as well as to herself, of her value as a person.

It was exactly eleven forty-five when she left her office, carrying a half-filled trash bag and the disk containing solutions to problems her design team didn't know it had yet. Not much to show for six years of hard work, hopes, and dreams.

She ignored the stares that escorted her to the exit.

There would be other jobs. She'd quit without notice, so there'd be no money other than the refund of the retirement contributions she'd made, but they would manage.

Laurel turned the key and pushed the apartment door open. "Hello! Robbie. I'm home early," she called as she entered the hall. Rob had been busy today. He'd finally picked up the half dozen pairs of footgear he usually kicked off and then abandoned in the entryway. About time.

She went into the kitchen and put the plastic bag of belongings on the table. "Are you home, honey? I've got news."

Well, maybe he hadn't been so busy after all. The breakfast dishes were still piled in the sink. Maybe he'd gone out job hunting. That would be good news.

She entered the living room, on the way to the bedroom and the first wrong note sounded. The home entertainment center, which included TV, VCR, stereo, CD player and tape deck, was missing.

Her hand went to her throat and a chill spread. "Rob! Rob! Are you all right?"

She whirled a complete circle. Looking for what? An intruder? She ran into the bedroom.

"My God!"

The drawers of Rob's dresser were on the floor, empty. On the vanity, her jewelry box was open. She went to it and quickly pawed through. She didn't have much of value. She sighed with relief. Everything seemed to be there, except the small case she'd jotted her access codes and passwords in—the computers at work, the cable company. She'd probably neglected to put it back last time she retrieved a forgotten password.

A needle of dread lanced her, stealing her breath. She *had* put it back, she remembered clearly, after recording the codes to access her accounts on line, the ones the bank had just set up two weeks ago.

She reached over and booted her computer. In less than a minute she had her accounts on the screen. The funds from her savings account had been moved to her checking account ten days ago. The day after that, a check for virtually her entire balance had been paid to the account of someone named Andrew Pierce.

She sat on the unmade bed. The sheets were cold, unwelcoming. Her mind reached for understanding. Rob's closet was empty. Everything of his, his guitars, his hobby kits, everything was gone.

He'd betrayed her. She sobbed and fell backward onto the sheets. It would be too late to reverse the transaction. The money would be gone. He'd left her nothing, not even a note to say, "I'm sorry."

THE TWICE TOLD HOTEL

MEXICO POINT | Southeastern End of Lake Ontario

Those whom God wants to punish for the sin of selfishness, he first makes lonely then curses with long life.

Jake Eastland, six generations removed from his Revolutionary War ancestor Joshua, knew from bitter experience how empty such an existence could be. At ninety-three, alive but seeing no reason whatever to be happy about it, he frowned as the arrival of the hotel elevator disturbed his reverie. A moment later the doors opened and Sheik Carroway, longtime manager of the hotel marina and sometime friend, stepped out into the vestibule of Jake's penthouse apartment.

Sheik waved a registration card. "The desk asked me to bring this up. Only one new guest today, Jake. A young woman. They put her on the second floor."

With a dismissive movement of his fingers, Jake indicated the table beside his chair. The hotel lost money after Labor Day and he didn't much care. A year earlier, at his villa in the Swiss Alps, death had handed him its calling card in the form of a cerebral event. After seventy years out in the world, he hadn't come back to revamp the hotel's business plan.

He'd come home to die.

But Death refused to cooperate. Time dragged on. He imagined himself suspended in a kind of living purgatory from which he could not escape until life had exacted retribution for his many failures and misdeeds. One year would not be nearly enough.

Sheik, a robust man in his sixties, with a shock of white hair and watery blue eyes, dropped the card on the end table beside Jake's chair and crossed the room to the expensive exercise bike near the windows.

"The log still says 614. You do your exercise today?"

"Promise me it'll kill me. I'll ride till I drop. Otherwise, tell me again why I should bother."

Sheik came over and plopped down in the chair opposite Jake. "Come on, Jake. Don't talk like that. You're lucky. You get around good, you still got all your marbles, and you're rich as Croeseus. What more do you expect? Hard-ons?"

Jake's mood lightened. He had to suppress a smile. "I own Croeseus. Got him in a trade with the Rogala boys in 1945. Money isn't everything, bub."

"Maybe, but when you don't have any, like me, it's a hell of a long way aheada' whatever comes second." Sheik threw a worried glance Jake's way. "You're down again. You been takin' the happy pills doc gave you? He's gonna be here again tomorrow, you know. He'll be pissed if you ain't. That means he'll yell at me, not you."

Jake made a face. He'd thrown out the pills. Nothing to live for was one thing, voluntarily turning yourself into a zombie, another. He motioned in the direction of the lake.

"Any nibbles on the Whaler?" He'd amused himself by selling off his personal toys. Only the twenty-two-foot Boston Whaler remained.

Sheik nodded. "Oh yeah. Almost forgot. Guy offered twenty-nine for it. I told him I'd talk to you. It's ten thousand under the market, Jake. Three years ago you put twenty-five into new engines alone."

"Tell him I'll think it over."

Sheik braced his hands on his knees and pushed himself to his feet. "Okay, Jake. I gotta get back downstairs. Don't forget to ride the bike. Five miles a day. Keep your ticker runnin' good."

Jake let his gaze rest on the instrument of torture Sheik referred to. Its handlebars obstructed the view from where he sat.

He made as if to rise. "Okay. Maybe I'll take myself for a spin right now."

Sheik's expression said he didn't believe a word of it, but he went to the elevator without comment. The moment the doors closed, Jake fell back into the armchair, eyeing the remote control of the TV. The numbness of having nothing to do but waste himself watching television came over him, just as it did every day. Eventually, from desperation he'd turn the thing on. But not yet.

The blue of the registration card caught his eye. Reaching, he scooted it closer and flipped it over. Adjusting his glasses so he could see through the reading lens, he held the card to the light.

On the first line, the guest had printed her name: Laurel A. Kingsford.

Jake's heart took off on a run of extra beats and his hand trembled so violently the card slipped from his fingers.

Laurel. It couldn't be *that* Laurel. It just couldn't be.

Ten hours later, at nearly three in the morning, Jake had yet to sleep. Outside, wind swayed the trees. Light from the parking lot below cast nervous patterns through them onto the ceiling of his bedroom, adding to his wakefulness.

Beneath his fingers on the rumpled bed lay the blue registration card of Laurel A. Kingsford.

His only living heir. His granddaughter.

She thought he was dead.

Not surprising, considering that after her mother died and her grandmother took custody, the poor kid spent her formative years tucked away at one boarding school or the other. Hard to learn much about your family when you're only allowed to visit on holidays and vacations. By then, he and her grandmother Jean Gamble had been divorced thirty years, and Jean had been through a string of other husbands.

Jake's chest ached as remembrance, amplified by the shadows fretting on the ceiling, overrode his effort to suppress it. From the very day his daughter Saundra came into the world, he'd been pushed to the outside of her life. After the divorce from Jean Gamble, she'd vowed that so far as Saundra was concerned, Jake no longer existed.

By then, she had a good start on the girl. She countered his court orders with her own, fought him to a legal standstill, turned away every attempt he made to visit as the girl came up, all the while filling the child's mind with poison.

He'd vowed it would be different with Laurel, but business intervened like it always did. He let things slip, and Jean pulled the same tricks she'd done with Saundra all over again with Laurel. Before long, he'd lost his chance with his granddaughter too.

Jake focused on the shadows moving on the ceiling, his mind straining to find order where none existed. Some things, like the movements of trees in the wind, were beyond his control. Not the girls, though. For their sake, he could have done more, a lot more, to counter Jean's malicious influence. But he hadn't—how long would it take to pay retribution for that?

Now it was different, though. Now he could make it up to her, be the grandfather she'd never had. Laurel—his granddaughter who thought he was dead and had been taught to hate his memory—had taken the room for two weeks. But two weeks wasn't enough, he needed more time. He'd have to be careful about telling her, not blurt out the truth, win her over slowly, wait until just the right time, let it happen naturally.

He'd have to find a way to involve her in something, get her to stay longer, then, when she was ready for it, he'd reveal his secret.

Did he dare, after everything? Did he dare?

Shore smells wafted through the open windows with the cool September air; driftwood, drying seaweed, life and death. During lulls in the wind, the slosh of small waves came too, slapping as they tripped in the darkness and rode up the land. Tiny pebbles rubbed a chorus as the water moved them, swoosh, shuuu, the sound longer as the water receded.

He closed his eyes and took a deep breath.

His only granddaughter.

Could it really be sixty years since the night he first learned he had a daughter? With a flush of shame, Jake remembered. Not all the things Jean told young Laurel about him were necessarily lies. Come right down to it, most were probably true. His failures went back a long way, all the way back to that day in June of 1925, the day he killed his mother.

JUNE 1925

A plume of dust at the far end of the lane signaled the arrival of a visitor. Jake shaded his eyes. A gasoline buggy, but that's all he could tell. It was still half a mile off, moving so slowly on the rutted track its own dust caught up to it.

He frowned at the approaching cloud. Bad news came unannounced a lot more often than good. He'd hoped to find a way to turn things right side up before the papers came. What a fool he'd been. Lost the boat, and now the house was next.

Two years earlier, he'd talked his mother into putting the last of her savings into a fishing boat. From the beginning, nothing went right. The boat had too deep a draft. He had to fight just to get out of the inlet. The fish did not run. They barely scraped by on what little he earned. Then a freak storm drove him ashore. About all he'd been able to salvage was the nets.

Last week he'd traded them to Joe Zaia for a beat-up model T. Zaia lived a few miles north on the Salmon River at Port Ontario. He swore the Ford ran great.

He lied. On the car's running board, the major components of its generator lay disassembled. So far, Jake had replaced the head gasket, rebuilt the water pump, and installed new universal joints on both ends of the drive shaft. Now, the generator. The thing had yet to run for more than a few hours.

After five minutes, a brand new model T bumped over the planks that bridged the dry stream fifty yards off and came to a stop next to Jake. It didn't appear too new anymore after three-quarters of a mile of ruts and dust.

In the middle of a large white and silver six-pointed star on the driver's door was the word 'Sheriff.' The driver unlatched the door and stepped out, brushing at the sleeves of his shirt.

The sheriff was a big man, fortyish, two hundred and fifty pounds at least and tall, near six and a half feet.

He tipped his hat. "Hello, Jake. Is your ma to home?"

"Yes, Sheriff Graybill, she's in the house."

The sheriff nodded, went to the house and knocked on the screen door. Receiving a response, he pulled the door open and went in. Several minutes later, he came back out. The screen door slapped closed behind him with a different, emptier sound. His eyebrows were crunched together, like he didn't care much for his job just now.

He tipped his head toward the house. "You might want to go in and see to your ma."

He bent and spun the crank. The engine caught on the first turn. He got in, backed up, and with a short clash of gears bounced away toward Route 104.

Jake Eastland watched the law get smaller. He sat on the running board and began to re-assemble the generator. It ground on him the way honest folks like his dad caught nothing but bad breaks while the shysters and cheats always seemed to crawl their way to success.

"No!" he said aloud, resolve forming deep inside. "I'm not gonna' *be* like that, not gonna' *lose* all the time."

His words echoed against the side of the silent house. He put the part down. Entering his mother's house, the place his family had settled generations ago, he wiped his feet and took off his cap, the habit so ingrained he didn't think about it. He passed through to the back where the kitchen faced the shore of Lake Ontario. Outside, the high water mark was thirty feet below and a hundred yards away.

His mother stood at the white porcelain sink, facing away from him, slicing potatoes. Illness had kept her inside, almost from the day of the storm, and again today she hadn't put her hair up.

Once a rich, gleaming brown, it was now gray and hung straight down, its natural wave absent as if defeated by gravity. Life, and the grinding struggle for survival, had stolen its luster. Only a few dark strands remained to hint of former glory.

His throat contracted and his eyes filled. Crossing the room, he stepped up behind, put his arms around her and hugged her.

"Oh, Jake!" She broke out into full-fledged crying, spilling words between huge sobs. "...what I'll do if... lose the place... know what else... I'm so..."

His eyes found the sheath of papers on the small worktable to the left of the sink.

The top page bore the heading "Notice of Foreclosure" in inch-high block letters.

He hugged her harder, rocking her side to side a little, lost in his own thoughts, not noticing at first the way she sagged against him.

There was one thing he knew about. He prayed it was the answer. Every once in a while, when he was in the area and the lake smooth, he'd been able to negotiate the difficult entrance channel to Sandy Pond and sell his catch to Tony McBride at the Wigwam Hotel.

He'd heard whispers. A man could pick up a hundred dollars in a single night, if he had the guts and the right friends.

He took a deep breath. He would get the model T running. Then he would pay Tony a visit. He was willing to do whatever it took. He'd make the payments. His mom could live in peace.

She was heavy, all her weight on him, and still. Too still.

"Mom. Are you okay?"

Her head fell to the side.

He touched her neck, searched for the pulse. The reassuring pressure was not there. He carried her into the sitting room and put her in a chair. She couldn't do this. Not now. He would get the goddamn money.

"Mom, don't. Please breathe! I'm sorry I lost the money. I'll get it back, I promise." He fell to his knees and hugged her.

"I'll get the money, Mom. We'll never be poor again. Never. Please wake up. I'll do it, Mom, I swear."

More than seventy years ago, and Jake remembered pleading with his mother like it just happened a minute ago.

He traced the outline of the card on the bed beside him. Such a simple thing, the touching of pen to paper, yet it changed everything. He was no longer alone, no longer empty, and he had *everything* to live for.

Jake's heart made an extra beat. He had to smile in the darkness. Surely death wouldn't come calling now, before he had the chance to try one last time. His heart began another of the arrhythmias that came almost daily. Sometimes they made him dizzy. He'd regarded them as a nuisance.

But now, in the darkest hours of the night, with so much unfinished business, he began to fear them for the first time.

TWICE TOLD HOTEL

Laurel picked a table in the lee of the building, where she'd be sheltered from the breeze off the water and warmed by the bright morning sun, dapples of which peeked through the vines on the trellis edging the veranda behind her.

Last week, flattened by the suddenness of multiple disaster, she'd decided to come to the Twice Told Hotel. It was the favorite summer place of her childhood, and even though she was a relative stranger now, as close to a home as she had anywhere.

After Labor Day, things at the little hotel were quiet, rates were low. It was the perfect place to be alone, make plans, and gather herself for a new start.

Whatever it would be, it needed to happen soon. The refund of her retirement money hadn't arrived, and she had less than a hundred bucks in her wallet. Thank God the credit cards were still in her name.

Six years of hard work, her hopes for family, career, all of it gone. Even after a week, it still seemed like a dream.

Why had Rob done it?

What did it matter? Gone was gone. Like castles in the sand, none of the towers she put up stood very long. She sat straighter. Moping wouldn't help. Think about something else. Anything.

Movement drew her attention to the dining room entrance. The screen door opened, old-fashioned hinges twanging, and an elderly gentleman stepped outside. It was Mr. Eastland, the man who lived in the fourth floor penthouse, a newspaper tucked under his arm, a cup of coffee on a saucer in his hand.

He was a tall old guy, big-framed but with no extra flesh. She'd seen him several times and they'd begun to exchange greetings.

He stopped, breathed the fresh morning air and surveyed the wide veranda with its stamped tin ceiling, green-carpeted stairways, and varnished mahogany railings. He glanced her way, squinting at something near the mouth of the Little Salmon River behind the nook where she sat.

His gaze lowered, found her, and he smiled and came toward her, paying close attention to his coffee.

"Company?"

He seemed a sweet old guy. "Sure, Mr. Eastland, the more the merrier."

Mr. Eastland liked to wear flamboyant shirts, and this morning's was no exception, clashing red and yellow swirls of color. Other than the shirt, he dressed conservatively. Gray chinos fit his trim figure, and his shoes were expensive looking, probably Italian.

She pretended to shield her eyes. "Whoa! I should've worn my shades."

He turned this way and that, allowing time to appreciate the full grandeur of his shirt. His white hair touched his shoulders in back. She wondered whether it had been dark or light. Light, she decided. His eyes were large for his face, wide and expressive, a rich blue with azure highlights. They were his best feature, and kind, his eyes were kind. Some part of her trusted him from the start.

"Proud of myself," he said as he put his coffee and newspaper down and sat opposite her at the table. "Managed not to spill more than half on the way out. I'm not as steady as I used to be."

"You seem pretty steady to me, Mr. Eastland. You don't look all that old, either."

"No? How's ninety-three sound? Born right here at Mexico Point in nineteen-oh-five."

"You're joking. I thought you were probably in your seventies."

"I wish!" He sipped his coffee. "You have any idea what it's like to be this old?" He gazed at her over the cup, and one corner of his mouth curved a bit, giving his face a droll expression. "This hotel's been here sixty years, and I had it built, started it in nineteen thirty-eight, when I was thirty-three."

"You're the owner? That's incredible—my grandmother came here every summer for years. I wonder if you knew her."

His hand stopped in the act of lowering the cup. He stared at her, his expression intense. "Maybe. What was her name?"

"Jean Gamble."

His eyes seemed to take on a deeper blue and look straight through her, as if some invisible scene played in his memory then he blinked and nodded and put the cup down.

"I hardly ever visited myself—too busy—but sure, Jean Gamble. I remember her." He reached for the newspaper, and when he spoke again his tone was different.

"Well then, let's see what's happening while we wait for a waitress to show up."

Before she could formulate a single question he'd opened the paper to the financial page, slipped on a pair of glasses and tuned her out.

Darn! He'd gone from warm to distant in seconds. Something she said? Lately, she couldn't do anything right. She looked away, over the varnished railing, out to the water.

From the nearby shore, Lake Ontario rose to the horizon, majestic. Out there the cries of gulls rode the soft morning breeze, but the part of her that responded to the wild serenity of the place, the way everything balanced, was not free to receive its gift this morning.

She reached for the sections of the paper Mr. Eastland had discarded. He didn't notice. He was reading the stock market report.

Jake Eastland was *not* reading the stock market report. He hardly saw it. His heart still raced. Jean *had* loved the Twice Told, tried to get it in the divorce. He'd bought her off by offering lifetime guest privileges, and she'd taken full advantage, arriving each season complete with entourage. Mentioning he'd built the place was a mistake. He'd barely allowed himself to meet Laurel and she'd already come too close to the truth.

He agonized; tell her, or deceive? If he told her, she might get up and leave and he'd never see her again. Why take that chance?

He glanced at his granddaughter from under lowered lids. She'd be in her late twenties. She had Jean's eyes, green as emeralds, but larger and wider, and sandy brown hair just like his had been. She kept it short, combed straight back. With her lack of makeup she looked almost boyish. Some would call her plain, but to him she seemed perfect.

Jake folded the paper and dropped it on the table. "What about your parents? Do they live nearby?"

Her face fell and she shook her head. "My parents are dead."

"Any brothers or sisters?"

She blinked several times rapidly. "No."

An idea jumped into Jake's head, and he came within an inch of blurting it out. Instead, he tapped his chest, "Say! Aren't we a pair? I don't have anyone either…"

He stopped, on the verge of asking her to call him Grampa. His soul needed to hear it at least once before he died.

He made fists with his hands and pressed them against his chest. "Why don't we do first names? You call me Jake, and I'll call you Laurel."

She peered at him and slowly smiled. "Okay… Jake." She paused, swallowing. "You know what? I feel like I've known you a long time."

"It's a deal, then." He held out his hand and they shook on it.

Back in the penthouse, in his northeast corner office, Jake touched a key and waited while the dialer called Allie King's private line at The Big ONE, Inc. in Manhattan.

It rang once. "Allie King speaking."

"I'm surprised to see you in this early, big shot."

The connection was good. Jake heard the quick intake of breath before Allie yelled, "Uncle Jake! It's great to hear from you. Hey! Did you see what we did with Syman Rubber last week?"

Allie was the son of Albert King, Jake's former Comptroller and longtime friend. With Jake's forty percent stake in Ampanco, the world's largest shipping line, for a cornerstone, as well as good-sized chunks of two major airlines, Allie had picked up right where Jake left off. He'd called him "Uncle Jake" since childhood.

"Probably made them an offer they couldn't refuse, right? What'd the stock do?"

Allie laughed. "We almost never break bones anymore. Did it smooth, just like you taught me. Stock's up six on the deal. I think we'll see twice that before it settles in."

Jake wasn't very interested, a first for him. "Good work. I never thought making money would bore me, but it's starting to. I want you to do something for me, Allie."

"Sure, Uncle Jake. Name it."

"I want to change my will, name a new principal beneficiary."

The pause at the other end was almost brief enough to indicate a total lack of concern.

"Okay. Let me put the tape on so legal will be sure to get it right." A click in the line. "Okay, go ahead, Uncle Jake."

"I've decided to leave my estate to my granddaughter, Laurel Kingsford. That means I no longer plan to liquidate my assets and distribute them to charity. Of course, everything else in the will stays as is."

He sensed Allie letting go of his breath. Jake's will treated him well.

"That's a huge change, Uncle Jake. Are you sure?"

"Yup. I should have done it a long time ago. She's my only heir, you know."

"Okay. Legal will take care of it right away. I'll have notaries there tomorrow afternoon for your signatures and the witnessing. Shouldn't be any problem at all."

After a brief hesitation, Allie said, "How come you're doing it now, Uncle Jake? I thought the Gambles didn't want anything to do with you."

Jake visualized Laurel. "They didn't. But this girl is different. She's staying here. I think she's more like me than she knows."

Allie's laugh made Jake hold the receiver away from his ear. "Staying there. That I'd like to see! If I could get clear I'd bring those papers up there myself, just to get a look at her."

Jake hadn't mentioned concealing his identity from Laurel. Allie worshipped him. It wouldn't do for him to know his hero had feet of clay.

"You stay put. I'm not running a circus up here."

The enthusiasm left Allie's voice. "Okay, Uncle Jake. I was just... All right. I'll get things rolling. Bye."

Jake put the receiver down. He felt bad enough, withholding the truth from Laurel. Now he had a secret from Allie too. Ninety years, and deception still came easy as breathing. Who was he kidding about reforming himself? He didn't deserve Laurel. He hadn't changed a damn bit.

LAUREL

The days grew cooler, and Laurel wore a sweater to breakfast in the morning. Close to the shore, fall came later than inland and the big oaks, maples and beeches that populated the vicinity were in the first stages of colors, though September was nearly past.

Jake had arranged for her to have one of the bungalows behind the hotel at a very low weekly rate. She'd collected several letters of recommendation. Soon it would be time to begin the big push to find another job. Meanwhile, the pension plan money had arrived and she had enough cash to stay a while if she wanted.

She drew a line through the last of the employment ads in the Sunday paper, took a bite of her cherry Danish and sipped her coffee. The sweetness of the Danish made the coffee taste even better.

Everybody needed engineers, but none of the ads listed deep-sea research, or six years in marine fuel cell design, as desirable qualifications. None of the ads listed experience coping with a sexist boss, either. She would've smiled, except it wasn't all that funny.

Several Forrester suppliers were located in California, two she'd worked with in San Diego alone. The West Coast, that's where she needed to be. She had contacts there, people who knew her work. It'd be a great place to make a new start. She decided to do it and the decision behind her, she felt better. She swallowed the last of the Danish and licked a gob of jelly stuck to her finger.

"Hey there, good lookin'!"

She looked up from the paper, smiling. Sheik Carroway, Jake's friend and manager of the hotel marina, headed for her table. Sheik was a round, happy-go-lucky widower with a jovial air and an expressive way of speaking. This morning he wore a ratty-looking knitted sweater to ward off the chill.

"Hi, Sheik. Where's Jake?"

Sheik wore a yellow-gold wedding ring on his left hand. He waved in the direction of the penthouse. "He's still up there, tryin' to use up the entire supply a' hot water. I never seen anybody stay in the shower so long. I got tired of waitin.'"

He poured himself a large glass of orange juice. Although as far as she knew his right hand worked fine, Sheik used his left to do everything. He gulped the juice. "Ahhh. Hits the spot." He slapped the empty glass down. "Hey, anything interestin' in the news this morning?"

"There's a piece on the grain elevator over in Oswego. I guess it's going to be demolished."

Sheik gave a disdainful flick of his wrist in the direction of the newspaper. "They started yesterday. I was there."

"I like engineering stuff like that. I'll have to drive in and see."

Sheik laughed. "There's plenty a time if you don't get to it today. They're gonna hafta' hit the old dame a lot harder than they did yesterday if they want anything to happen."

"I don't have much time. I've decided to go out west, to California. I've got to get a job, get started again."

His face fell. "Aw."

"What's the matter? You look like I just kicked you. Aren't you glad for me?"

This time his hand hardly moved. "Sure. Sure I am. It's just… I was gettin' used to havin' you around."

She liked Sheik, but she needed to be more than an ornament. She eyed his sweater. A large, ragged hole gaped in the left armpit where the seam had given out.

"Why don't you bring that sweater over to the cottage later? I'll try to patch it up for you before I go." She was probably the only woman in a hundred miles who knew how to pick leeches for bait, overhaul a marine carburetor, and also mend a sweater.

Sheik's watery blue eyes went wide. "No kiddin'? Could ya' really?"

"You think someone like me wouldn't be able to?"

"Yes." Sheik's brows pulled together in momentary confusion. "I mean no. No! Not at all." Sheik ran his hand over the fabric. "It's just, I love this sweater. My wife made it for me. Cripes, I'll bet it was twenty-five years ago." The yellow of the gold in his ring stood out against the maroon wool.

To their left, the screen door slapped. Jake came toward them. She could tell when he'd just come from an exercise session: his color would be high, and his long hair wet from the shower.

Before Jake made it halfway to the table, Sheik blurted the news. "Jake, Laurel's leaving us. Going out to California."

Jake stopped, a strange expression on his face for a moment. Then he continued his approach as if nothing had been said.

"I swear," he said as he took a seat, "the devil himself invented that exercise bike. I hear him laughing every time I sit on it." He fanned his face with his hand. "About the only thing I can remember being harder was fishing for whisky, and I was young then."

Laurel perked up. "Fishing for whisky?"

The wrinkles etched into Jake's face gave it character, and his wide blue eyes, deep-set amid wizened seams, sparkled with life. They showed the kindness, as usual, but now he almost seemed to gauge her interest.

"Yeah, back during Prohibition a lot of smuggled whisky ended up abandoned in the lake."

"Cool." Laurel leaned closer, intrigued. "Prohibition was during the Roaring Twenties, right?"

Before Jake could answer, Sheik pushed his chair away from the table and stood. "I'm gonna go inside. Too much fresh air makes me cough." Sunlight flashed as he gestured. "Besides, I heard the whisky stories a hundred times already." He winked at Laurel. "I'm warnin' you. Get him goin' and you might be here all day."

Jake rolled his eyes at Sheik's retreating form. "Let's see, where was I? Oh yes. Nineteen-nineteen through nineteen thirty-two. Those were the Prohibition years."

"But why did they fish for it? I don't get it."

"Some carried the booze in sacks. If the Coast Guard came snooping, they'd tie them all together and put the stuff over the side. Later, they'd come back and try to fish it up. But a lot stayed lost."

Laurel loved the water. She was well trained and had plenty of bottom time in submersibles. On the other hand, SCUBA diving was not her long suit. But the thought that there might be contraband on the lake bottom fascinated her. If finding some meant using SCUBA, she had enough training to do whatever was needed.

Jake went on. "Sometimes there wasn't time to look. It was supply and demand. You had to keep the stuff moving. I know where a big load sank that nobody ever looked for. It's in shallow water, too. It's been seventy years, but I bet some of those bottles are still intact."

She sat forward. "How do you know where it is?"

He grinned and held up his hands. "Threw that load overboard with my own two hands."

"Because the Coast Guard was after you?"

He leaned closer, and she did the same. "Uh huh. That was some night, all right. I was a raw kid then, just starting out in the smuggling business. It was my first trip."

JUNE 1925

Jake Eastland used his hands to brace himself as his new boss pulled the throttles back. The roar of the engines faded to a murmur and *Mis-Behavin'* lost way and squatted deeper in the water. At two in the morning, the moon had set. Jake could see a few yards, no more.

"Okay kid, this is it. We get caught with this stuff, we cool our heels in jail, so from here on in, we've got to be dead quiet, eh?"

Jake nodded.

"Good. Now, get the pipes and put 'em on like I showed you."

Jake felt for the L-shaped metal tubes on the floorboards near his feet. With no forward movement, the boat rolled in the small waves. He found one, then the other and made his way to the stern where the exhaust pipes of the idling hundred-eighty-horsepower Packards rumbled and gurgled, alternately submerged and lifted out of the water by the passing waves.

He lay on the fantail deck, reached down over the sloping transom, and slid one tube over the end of an exhaust pipe. Holding it tight, he rotated it ninety degrees. It locked in place, directing the exhaust gases and cooling water downward into the dark water. He repeated the process. This time, when he twisted the tube downward the sound of the engines disappeared, muffled by the water.

"Good work kid." Bruce Longley slipped the Packards into gear.

Mis-Behavin' was thirty-five feet long, with a low-slung, sleek profile. In the right conditions the Packards could propel her at upwards of thirty knots, fast enough to outrun any Coast Guard vessel. She had an open cockpit, her only protection from the elements a foot-high V-shaped windshield and a shoulder-height cuddy cabin forward. She was built for speed, not cargo.

Nevertheless, tonight she carried cargo, a very valuable one. Rows of burlap sacks filled with whisky lined the interior of the boat, one hundred cases in all. Bruce Longley paid thirty-six dollars a case wholesale. Each of the dozen quarts brought seven dollars in the US, or eighty-four dollars a case. He'd clear almost fifty dollars a case. Tonight, he stood to turn over a cool five grand.

Jake felt more than saw the looming presence of the fifty-foot cliffs at Nine Mile Point. He'd been here dozens of times, swimming or fishing off the rocks.

He heard something. Or had he imagined it?

He held his hand up toward his boss. "Shhh!"

Bruce shut down the engines and they both listened. Nothing. Then they both heard it, the rumble of an exhaust.

United States Coast Guard Picket boat CG2207 carried a thirty caliber Lewis machine gun, but could produce only twenty-four knots in a flat sea, significantly slower than many smugglers. Still, she experienced a great deal of success in the Oswego area, due primarily to the skill and perception of her commander, Bosun's Mate Marvin McKean.

Tonight, running without lights, McKean idled along near Nine Mile Point, a favorite rendezvous of rum runners. A few minutes earlier they'd heard an engine. His bowman made his way aft to the cockpit.

"I lost 'em," he said through the open window.

McKean motioned to the engineer. "Kill the engine."

The engine sighed to a stop. The night settled on them, the only sounds the soft sigh of the night breeze rustling leaves atop the nearby cliff and the slap of water against the hull.

"Drop the small hook, and be quiet about it."

"Aye, aye skipper." His bowman felt his way forward in the darkness, picked up the twelve-pound navy anchor and began to lower it. In spite of his efforts at silence, the chain rattled.

McKean winced. If a rum boat hid out there, they'd heard it too. He held his breath and waited.

Urrmp, Urrmp, Urrmp. The sound of a big engine being cranked came through the darkness. It caught, and another one cranked. Twin engines. His jaw clenched shut in a grimace. A rum runner for sure.

"Get that hook up," he yelled. He grabbed his engineer by the arm and pushed him aft. "Crank the engine, quick." He stepped to the spotlight and flipped the switch. A spear of brilliant light stabbed the darkness. There! Two hundred fifty yards away, a black boat moved, leaning steeply into a deep gash of water as it turned hard and headed away from shore, and them.

"I need spark!" his engineer yelled. "Throw the lever."

"Damn!" The Chief leaned in and switched on the magneto. The engineer cranked once, twice, and the warm engine fired and rumbled into life.

"Anchor's aboard," came the call from forward.

"Let's move!" The chief kept the light trained on the black boat, now almost a mile off.

⌒⌒⌒   ⌒⌒⌒

"This one won't start!" Jake yelled above the noise as *Mis-Behavin'* rushed through the dark. "I've cranked it a hundred times." Only one engine. Not good with a load as heavy as theirs.

"Maybe it's flooded. Wait a minute or two." Bruce had to yell against the roar of the wind. "I could have given it too much choke."

Fifteen minutes. The spotlight seemed a little closer. Bruce knew nice hiding places on Henderson Bay, but first they had to get around the point. Thirty minutes. The picket boat had definitely gained.

Bruce grasped Jake's shoulder and pulled him close. Despite the buffeting wind and movement of the boat, Jake heard every word.

"If they get within range with their machine gun, we'll have to surrender. Take those pieces of twine I showed you this morning and tie the bags into two chains. We might have to dump them. Put the salt buoy in the second batch. I'll try to get us into shallow water for that one."

Within five minutes Jake had the sacks on the port side tied in a long chain then went to work on the starboard row.

"It's done," he yelled. "Where's the salt buoy?"

"Good work, Jake. In the cuddy cabin under the port bunk. Hurry up, they're

gaining."

Jake secured the float to the string of sacks, making sure the line would run free when released.

In the glare of the floodlight, he saw Bruce grin. This was going to cost his boss a bundle and the man was having fun. He liked something about that.

Bruce's voice was harsh. "Okay. Toss the port side load over."

Jake lifted the first of the sacks and dropped it overboard. The first pulled the second and third over the rail. He jumped back, fortunate not to be caught in the tangle as the sacks were sucked over the transom and into the dark water.

Half empty, they developed a decided list but gained speed. Jake could see Stony Point light ahead. They needed just a few more minutes.

Aboard #2207, Chief McKean clenched his fists as he saw the load go. "Ready with the ought-thirty?"

His gunner worked the action and the sound of a round being chambered answered him.

"Put a few rounds over his head."

"Aye, aye sir."

The Lewis rattled. Within ten seconds a dozen tracers arched over the bow of the black boat. Without warning, it turned hard to starboard, escaping the cone of light.

"Hard to starboard. They're headed toward shore. We've got them now."

McKean swung his light, but with the angle of the turn and the boat bouncing around on the waves it was half a minute before he found his quarry again. "There! Put another burst over him."

The Lewis rattled again. This time, the black boat responded by slowing, veering to the left. Frantic activity came from the waist.

The Chief screamed, "They're dumping the rest of it! Close and board at once." Grabbing his megaphone he called across the narrowing gap, "This is the United States Coast Guard and we are about to board you. Stop what you are doing and put your hands up."

His words did not halt the action aboard the black boat. A minute later, two men straightened and raised their hands.

"Sure Cap'n," one called across the twenty feet of water separating the two boats. "Come ahead. Too bad you were a little too noisy tonight, eh?"

Marvin McKean slapped his hand on the cabin top. "Damnation!" He glowered at the smugglers. The older of the two gazed back at him, a dapper looking sort, five-seven or so, with an open smirk which now spread itself across his face. The other, a boy of about twenty, was half hidden behind the older man.

"Step out where I can see you, boy!"

The boy flinched then slowly straightened, his shoulders went back and he stepped into the light. McKean knew the look of a hard man when he saw it.

"Board them. Get names and home ports, and if you find as much as a drop of whisky, we'll be towing them in yet."

TWICE TOLD HOTEL

Laurel could hardly contain herself. This was the kind of adventure she'd always wished she could experience. "God, Jake, that must have been exciting. What happened to the second engine?"

A gentle breeze made dots of sunlight dance on the distant water. He watched for several seconds before answering.

"We found a faulty check valve in the exhaust manifold. Water backed up into the engine because we were moving when I cranked it."

"You had to turn them by hand?"

"Oh yes, no fancy self-starters until a few years later. Heck, now I can start our Whaler's engines by remote control."

She leaned closer. "The hotel has a Whaler?"

"Sure. A twenty-two-footer. Fantastic boat. Best money can buy. Darn thing hardly gets any use. Too bad."

She might have a use for it. With her connections she might be able to wheedle the use of a side scan sonar, and scuba gear.

"Wouldn't it be great if we could find some of that old whisky?"

Jake's smile faded. "Sure, but I'll never do it, and with you leaving to go out west, there's nobody who cares enough." After a pointed silence, he gestured toward the lake. "Besides, whisky's nothing compared to the real stuff out there." He said this softly, but nothing could disguise the intensity in his voice.

They stared at each other, she waiting for an explanation, he with an unreadable expression.

"What real stuff?"

His eyes burned bright. "What if there was a storm more ferocious than any other before or since, and a ship, a very old ship, went down in that storm, not far from Stony Point? There's a legend around here says it happened just like that, way back at the time of the Revolutionary War. And they say that doomed ship carried treasure."

"You can't be serious. Lake Ontario isn't exactly the Florida Keys.

How would treasure find its way to the bottom around here?"

"I told you. A storm."

Laurel shook her head. "I'm sorry. Without some kind of solid evidence, I'm afraid I find the idea very hard to believe."

Slowly, his expression tightened. "Fact is, I *know* it's true."

Something in his voice stopped her. "What makes you so sure?"

"Because my great-grandfather, I don't even know how many times removed, was the only survivor."

She shook her head. "You must realize how impossible that is, Jake. I mean come *on*, during the Revolution this was a frontier. Nobody had gold. They used salt for money."

Jake started to respond, then his expression changed and his brows furrowed. He put his cup down. "Sorry, I shouldn't have said anything. It's just a family story. No one outside knows about it."

"Oh, please! Don't do that to me. You have to tell me."

He shook his head. Even his mouth gave no hint of his mood. He fished through the paper and pulled out the financial section.

Miffed, Laurel crossed her arms over her chest. Every time he said something interesting and she wanted to know more, he picked up the damn newspaper and clammed up. This time, he wasn't getting away with it. She had an idea. She smirked a little as she thought it over.

"Jake?"

He stopped reading and looked over the paper at her.

"How would you like it if I called you Grampa?"

He warmed, walking right into it. "Sure. That'd be okay. Why?"

"I don't know. I'd love to, but somehow," she gave an exaggerated sigh, "I just don't feel like a member of the family."

After several seconds the corner of his mouth tugged upward in that way he had and his eyes softened. He'd tell her the rest now. Warmth spread through her. The feeling surprised her.

"How'd you like to see his grave?"

"H-His grave?"

"Sure. If you're gonna be part of the family, you need to learn all about us. Might as well start at the beginning, right?"

OSWEGO HARBOR

Michael Marvin McKean had never been to Oswego before. The McKeans were Coast Guard, though, and Oswego the oldest port on the Great Lakes. Naturally, the family had history here.

The reality of the place was not so different from the pictures he'd seen from his great-grandfather's day. The huge grain elevator still stood on the West Side of the river, derelict now. The Coast Guard station had been moved from the East Side to the west, and the East Side docks filled in to make room for the Port Authority Terminal.

Mike wasn't Coast Guard himself. Not anymore. Oswego was just another place and this, even though a Sunday, just another workday.

Satisfied that he understood what he'd be seeing underwater, he pushed the drawing aside and stepped toward the stern of the thirty-six-foot workboat. Black rubber flippers made his movements awkward, semi-comical as he stepped over the transom onto the dive platform.

He dipped his facemask in the green water, cooling it so it wouldn't fog up once he was under. After half a minute he dumped the water and pulled the mask on, settling the faceplate. Holding it in place, he stepped off the platform and let himself sink fifteen feet.

Not so long ago, he'd commanded a Coast Guard vessel assigned to drug interdiction off the coast of Florida. Now, due to his indecisiveness at a critical moment, his wife and unborn child were dead, he no longer had the command or the career, and he made his living as an hourly employee of A. A. Harris Inc., marine contractor. When the air bubbles created by his plunge cleared away, he swam along the pier toward deeper water to begin the inspection.

At eight hundred fifty feet long and a hundred forty feet wide, the pier pointed to the north like an extended finger with a squared-off tip. Two-thirds of the way out stood the monolithic grain elevator.

He switched on his light, illuminating the horizontal timbers that formed the face of the pier. From the drawings, he knew each would be twelve inches square and between sixteen and twenty feet long. At seven-and-a-half-foot intervals on every other layer, the butt end of a timber appeared in the wall, part of the box-like structure, or "crib" that held the outer face in place.

They'd been submerged almost eighty-five years, yet they weren't rotted at all, a phenomenon peculiar to fresh water: no oxygen, no rot. In the next forty-five minutes he inspected half the length of the pier. When he returned to the workboat, Carl Benz, the Port of Oswego Authority foreman, was waiting. In his forties, of average height and weight, Carl had a ruddy complexion and curly blond hair.

"How's it look down there?" he asked as Mike slipped off his tank and lifted it over the transom of the workboat.

"Like the thing was built yesterday." Mike kicked his flippers off. "This side is solid as a rock."

"That's good." Carl indicated the giant crane behind him. "We don't want anything moving under that sucker." Demolition of the grain elevator had begun the previous day. "Hey, it's almost 12:30, want to get some lunch?"

"Sure, if you're buying."

Carl snorted. "What've you got in that tank? Laughing gas?"

Mike grinned. "Okay, you're calling it. Where do we go?"

"Up the street," Carl pointed up West First Street toward the business district. Officially, First Street ended at the base of the pier where they stood, but for years it had been possible to drive onto the pier and out to the extreme end where one would be, literally, in the middle of the harbor.

Fifteen minutes later, as the waitress took their order, Mike noticed a striking woman in a crisp blue Coast Guard dress uniform step out of a vehicle across the street. She and two similarly dressed male companions, a petty officer and a seaman, crossed the street and came into the cordoned-off area of the cafe.

She stood at least six feet with ample breasts and full hips. Blond hair pulled back on sides and top, pinned into a vertical roll against the back of her head, gave her a Scandinavian look. The insignia high on her left sleeve bore an eagle over a pair of crossed anchors plus three white chevrons and a rocker.

Mike blinked. A chief bosun's mate! He'd never heard of a woman rising that high in deck division in all his years in the Coast Guard. Deck division did the physical work of operating and commanding Coast Guard vessels, as opposed to the other divisions, most of which stayed safely ashore.

As her group approached his table, the chief glanced his way and their eyes met. She raised her eyebrows and flashed him a thousand-candlepower smile. It went through him like a thunderbolt.

It had been a long time since he'd so much as glanced at a woman, but her magnetism pulled, and his eyes followed her. She caught him at it. Smiling, she raised her eyebrows, twice.

Carl gaped. "What was *that* all about?"

Mike's fingertips tingled. "Our eyes happened to meet."

"More like a small nuclear event, bucko." Carl grinned. "Man, would I like to get my hands on that."

Mike smiled. Carl stood all of five foot eight. "That one'd mess with your head, little guy. You'd never get it up for your wife again."

Carl laughed, "Hell, I already *got* that problem. What would I have to lose?"

By four o'clock Mike had finished the preliminary inspection of the pier. In the morning he'd drill the core samples and do the videotape. He peeled his wetsuit down to his waist and stood on the dive platform, relaxing the way he liked to after a dive.

He couldn't. Without Mary, things that once fulfilled him—the warmth of a late season sun, working on the water—were of no value.

"Fuck it!" He reached over the gunwale of the boat, flipped open the cooler and grabbed a beer. He pulled the tab and raised it to his mouth, taking a big swig. It gave no pleasure whatsoever.

A drunk puts the thief in his mouth to steal his pain, but there was nothing Michael Marvin McKean could put in his mouth, or in his veins, to exorcise the demon that lived in his soul, slowly eating it from the inside out. He knew. During the past two years he'd tried them all.

And the thing that depressed him most was the knowledge that tonight, alone on this lonely boat, he would think about it again. He put the beer down and reached into the ice chest for the bottle of Jack Daniel's. He unscrewed the cap and took a big swig. The whisky went down cold and hot and smooth all at the same time. There. This time he tasted something.

LAUREL

The cemetery lay two miles west of the hotel, close to the water. A grove of slender white birches lined the shore, providing shade and blocking much of the wind off the water. A peaceful place, small, maybe two hundred feet wide by four hundred on the lakefront. A good place to be buried—if you had to be dead.

All the stones were old, some upright but most flat on the ground.

Jake pointed at the row closest to the birches. "They're the oldest."

In that row, the inscriptions were nearly illegible from wear, especially those at the western end. She went to the furthest marker. "This would be the first, then. The first person buried here."

"Probably."

She brushed away a layer of accumulated sand to reveal the inscription. The chisel marks were faint with age. All she could make out were the words "Louis-Char" and the numerals "XVII," and the date 1812.

She looked up at him. "Louis something. I can't make out the last name."

Jake pointed to the next stone in line.

"That one's Joshua. It isn't the original marker. Someone in the family must've had this stone made later."

Laurel brushed the surface of the stone.

Joshua Eastland
b— d 1812
Thys man lived life avain,
searching for six legs of chain.
To the place where riches sleep,
came the fearsome devil seicuhe,
and now the secret ever keeps.

Laurel read the verse aloud, "…came the fearsome devil sy-say…"

"It's pronounced 'seeche'. You know what a seiche is, don't you?"

Now that he'd pronounced it, she remembered reading about the phenomenon. "Something about the atmosphere and rapid changes in water level?"

He nodded. "Right. Unique to the Great Lakes. Boats at anchor go aground, or lift their moorings and float away. The currents they cause are unbelievable. If you happen to be swimming, forget it."

Shuddering at the thought of being caught in such a situation, Laurel read the inscription again.

"What do you think the verse means?"

He gazed in the direction of the birches. Finally, he said, "I always thought it might be a kind of warning. Always told myself I'd find out some day. Never did."

Wind swirled, seemed to whisper as it brushed her hair. Laurel pulled her jacket closer, no longer hearing the waves trip down on the stony shore, or the occasional gull's cry overhead, only the wind, and the faint lisp of… what?

Again she let her fingers touch the gray surface of the gravestone. It was rough, etched by long, hard winters and hot summer suns, and at one corner bright green moss grew from a diagonal crack. Fallen leaves and bits of dirt already encroached on the area she'd cleared.

What did you see, Joshua Eastland? Six lengths of chain. What do they mean?

A new gust swayed the grass around the stone, moving the fallen leaves. For an instant, beneath their skittering, a voice whispered, but before her mind could focus, the words were swept away, out over the water, and except for the rustle of birch leaves flashing pale undersides in the stand of trees, no sound remained.

But she'd *felt* something.

Laurel stood, brushed dirt from her hands, filled with a sense of having experienced something deeply personal. "Have you ever told anyone about him," she lifted her eyes and met his gaze head on, "who wasn't a member of the Eastland family?"

He went so long without answering she almost thought he wouldn't.

"No." His hesitation gave the word finality.

"He's here, Jake. And he knows I'm here. He wants me to find his treasure, I can feel it. But why? I'm not family."

The deep shadows at the corners of his eyes lengthened, and his eyes were warm as he rested his hand on her shoulder. "I'm the last one. When I die, the story will go with me if I don't tell someone. I guess he wants it to be you."

His face changed. "My grandfather called her the *Ontare*. He used to say she was lost the night the wave came down the lake."

"The wave?"

"Yes, just like a tidal wave." He rubbed his forehead, thinking. "The story claims the earth shook, so there might have been an earthquake. I think it's pretty much died out now, but when I was a kid, the Onondagas told a story about how every tree, everything, was knocked flat as far as a mile inland."

Laurel couldn't imagine how big a wave would have to be to wash as far as a mile inland. "How long ago did it happen?"

Jake pointed at the gravestone. "Must have been around the time of the Revolution, because that's when Joshua lived. I don't know if any of it's true, or if it's just a story."

Laurel touched his arm. "You're just full of them, aren't you? How many more stories do you have tucked away?"

Grampa Jake's eyes fell away, as if her question pained him somehow. He kicked at the tufts of grass beside the stone. He'd done that before, gone off by himself into some secret place in his mind, like there was something there he wished he could change.

He glanced her way, his expression a bit sheepish. "Probably a few too many. They're not all…" he searched for the words, "…not all so easy to tell."

Laurel's breath caught. There it was, the way to help him. She'd encourage him to tell his stories. Eventually the hard ones would come, they'd talk, and he'd be freed of their burden. Excitement surged.

They'd hunt for the treasure together, it was the kind of adventure she'd dreamed of—But wait, hold everything! She'd just made plans to move to California, to make a fresh start. That move represented stability and the ordered world she knew. She couldn't just toss it away less than an hour after she'd decided because of some wild story about a shipwreck.

Jake broke into her thoughts, "Too bad, you having to leave right away. It's only the twenty-fifth. Lots of good diving weather left."

"I can't, G-Grampa Jake." It was the first time she'd spoken the word aloud. It didn't feel bad at all, saying it. "I've got to take control of my life again, get back to the business of making a career. That's the sane thing to do."

He accepted that, nodding, the corners of his mouth edging down a bit, then he turned and made his way toward the hotel Blazer.

She studied Joshua Eastland's grave one last time. She couldn't stay, but maybe after she initiated the California job search she could do some research on Mexico Bay and the *Ontare*. It couldn't hurt to see if there had ever been any shipwrecks in the area.

OSWEGO HARBOR

Chief Bosun's Mate Charlene Stone's second-floor office offered a fine view of the grain elevator pier, but not much else. A workboat had tied up opposite the entrance to her anchorage. A man stood on the dive platform suspended from its transom, his feet awash as the boat rolled in the small swells. He seemed familiar.

She pulled her binoculars from their case. Careful not to smear her eyeliner with the rubber eyecups, she tightened the focus. It was the hunk she'd seen at the restaurant yesterday. He had to be at least six-three, with the square-jawed steely-eyed look of a man who'd faced hardship and kicked the shit out of it. He had a dark swirl of hair on his chest. Nice. Most of the types she saw in the weight room shaved everything, probably even their pubic hair, the losers.

His body, at least the part she could see above his peeled-down black wetsuit, was well developed, entirely acceptable for a quick tumble. Probably in town for a day or two, three at most. Six weeks had passed since she'd last…

She let go and breathed again. She had to be careful, couldn't let her appetites rule her. She had a certain status now, a certain social position. She couldn't be caught balling the locals. It could undermine her authority and jeopardize her career.

This man, on the other hand, would be perfect.

She'd worked hard to get where she was, steamrollering male competition where she could, sleeping with the enemy when she couldn't. Certain of her superiors, those lucky enough to be in a position to help her career, knew from happy firsthand experience to what lengths Char Stone would go in order to further her career.

She liked men, and she liked sex. That made it easy for her. Except men, taken as a group, were pathetic. She'd never met one who could outdo her.

Char put the glasses back in their case. She left the office and went down the stairs.

"Whaley!" she yelled as she reached the ground floor.

The Bosun jumped to his feet behind the OD counter. "Aye, Chief."

"I'll be on the grain elevator pier if I'm needed."

Whaley delivered each word with metronome-like precision. "Aye, aye chief, on-the-elevator-pier."

She pulled on her slicker, left the station and headed out onto the long pier. The man lounging on the dive platform of the workboat watched her approach.

She kept it casual, let him know he could relax. "Morning."

"Morning, Chief. What can I do for you?"

"Nothing official. I saw you working from my office," she indicated the upper floor of the station behind and to her left, "and I wondered what you were up to."

"Inspecting the pier. That's a forty-ton crane out there."

"You ex-military?"

He deadpanned her. "What makes you think that?"

"I can tell. The way you stand, your hair. Navy?"

He shrugged as if it didn't matter. "Coast Guard. It's a family thing."

She nodded, digesting the information. "Your outfit local?"

"International—I'm employed in the US, but I work out of Niagara-on-the-Lake on the Canadian side. By the way, my name's Mike, Michael M. McKean."

"Stone." Char tapped the cement with her toe.

"This pier is quite a piece of engineering. Have you seen the specs, Chief?"

"No. You have a print?"

"Yeah, it's in the deckhouse. Why don't you come aboard?"

He offered his hand. Not really needing to, she took it and stepped down to the gunwale and then to the deck of the workboat. Once aboard, facing him, Char experienced a tremor of excitement. He had several inches on her. A two-count passed before she released his hand.

He pulled on a t-shirt and followed her into the small deckhouse where he spread the scrolled drawing over the small chart table, holding it open with his hands. "Here they are. See? They used sawn timbers to build the walls. Each timber was a foot square. Imagine how much that size lumber would cost today."

She leaned closer, almost touching him. The U-shaped outer frame of the long pier had been formed with timber cribs, sixteen feet square, backfilled with bowling ball-sized rock. "What kind of wood?"

"Hemlock."

She studied the print. After a few minutes she tapped the drawing. "Impressive."

"It is, isn't it, Chief?"

"Charlene." Her eyes challenged his from a foot away. "My friends call me Char."

"Do I qualify as a friend?"

"I'm not sure… Maybe." She let her eyes drop to his chest then raised them again, re-engaging his. If he'd said "Let's" just then, her thermometer would have said, "Go."

Char forced herself to focus on the diagrams. "If the wood hasn't rotted, the only other danger is the fastenings could rust through." She pointed to one on the drawing. "Have you checked them?"

"Can't. No way to get at them. They're countersunk into the face of the wall."

She touched the drawing at the north end of the pier. "You could check a few of these. They'd probably be representative of the rest." The timbers there were lagged together by bolts, no doubt to help hold the corners together.

He straightened and signaled his approval.

"Good one. I think I'll be able to get a wrench on one and pull it to inspect it. Now I'm the one who's impressed."

She faced him, inches away. Did she dare? Why not? She had nothing to lose. "The least you could do in return is buy me a drink."

She held her breath.

"I'd love to, but I came in on the boat. I don't have a car here."

"I'll pick you up later. 7:30 sound good?"

"Yeah, 7:30 sounds good."

"Okay, see you then."

Back in her office on the second floor, Char picked up her phone and dialed Washington.

"Lieutenant Andy Anderson please," she said when the phone was answered. Ten seconds later he came on.

"Andy, It's Char Stone. How are you, big guy?" She kept her voice light. Andy was a former lover. Useful to her—not so useful in bed— but very good for her career. He congratulated her on her promotion.

"Thanks Andy, I still can't get over it myself. Andy, I need a little favor... Oh, you are *so* bad, Andy... Of course I'll do one for you too. Any time, baby." She crossed her eyes and made a face. "There's a guy who says he's ex-Coast Guard applying for a diving job with a local outfit," she lied. "I told the owner I'd see if I could get a peek at his service record, you know, see if there's any goblins there... I know, but just this once? ... C'mon, be a buddy, hmmm? For me?"

She shot her clenched fist toward the ceiling when he said "Okay." She gave him Mike's full name.

While she was on hold, she put the call on the speakerphone. She was standing by the window watching the first of the rain blow in when the line clicked and he came back on.

"Char?"

"Go ahead."

"You got yourself a good guy there, Char." She could hear papers rustle in his hands as he spoke. "Michael M. McKean. He came into the service out of the Academy at New London, active duty '83 through '96. Rank at time of discharge, hmmm, Captain. Decorations and commendations, a bunch of 'em. Wonder why he quit? Wait... here it is. Resigned in 1996 after a board of inquiry found no reason to press charges after a shootout with Colombian drug runners off Miami resulted in the death of two of his crew members."

He paused. "Wait a second. Oh, Jesus. No wonder he quit." Even on the intercom she heard his voice change, become sympathetic.

"He was secretly married to one of the victims. She was pregnant at the time of her death. Oh shit. She only had three months left on her enlistment."

That had to be the pain she'd seen in him. Hopeful thoughts followed her new knowledge. She needed a good lay, sure, but a long-term relationship—with the right guy—wouldn't be bad either. This guy had the look. She could be good for him if he'd let her. It could *work* for them.

She pushed the lovely thoughts away, forced herself back to the present. First, she needed details. Then she could plan how to help him. "What schools did he have?"

"He's a trained diver, had the whole shot, went through the Navy school. And there's the usual Coast Guard stuff."

They made small talk for a minute. "Thanks, Andy, you've been a big help. I'll see you around, guy." She switched off the speakerphone. This could be the one, she just knew it. Tonight, she'd have him all to herself. She already knew what she'd say:

Yes. Yes. Yes

TWICE TOLD HOTEL

The rain promised by the morning's dark overcast arrived just before noon. Jake heard the rattle as a powerful gust threw the first large drops against his windows and the panes flexed in their frames. He loved the raw power of the elements, always had, and it was no accident his penthouse offered a good view of the incoming weather. He crossed to the windows to watch.

It was a good day to be inside, a favorite old sweater warming your bones, but also the somber, moody kind of day when your failures seemed greater and your successes, measured against the grand span of time, miniscule.

Out on the lake, large combers ran in from the northwest, green-cast shades of dark gray, many topped with curls of white. The rain made diagonal streaks on the glass. Soon, the view would blur.

The sound of a vehicle broke into his thoughts. Down in the parking lot, Laurel stood on her porch and watched a UPS van leave. He would lose her soon and it distressed him more than he'd imagined possible. Sure, she'd been interested in his story, fascinated. Why not? He'd practically laid the bait at her feet. She hadn't bit.

No, she'd set a different course. The wrong one, he knew, but it was her life, not his. She seemed to be having a hard time with her sense of self-worth. Handing over his money before she found herself would be the worst thing he could do to her. With ten tons of found money plastered over her existence, she'd never manage to face down her problems.

This morning at breakfast she'd been withdrawn, barely responding to his attempts at conversation. Anybody else's grandfather would find an excuse to sit down, see if he could help, not stand off at a distance and throw money at the problem.

He was so used to protecting himself that way, keeping everyone at arm's length, he had no idea how to begin. Had he thought changing his will would somehow earn her love through osmosis? Clearly, all that money would destroy the person she was now. No matter how much he hated appearing indecisive, he had to change the will back.

He swung away from the window and pushed the speaker button of the phone on his desk. Then he touched Allie's number and listened to the familiar tones. A ring, another, and the receiver picked up.

"Allie King." Allie sounded different on the speakerphone.

"Jake here."

"Uncle Jake! Hey, twice in three weeks. Everything all right?"

Jake hesitated. He'd changed his will the first time on a whim and almost immediately had second thoughts. What would Allie think now?

To hell with that. "Remember the changes I had you make in my will?"

"Sure. They were okay, weren't they?"

"Yes. But I think I acted too quickly. Maybe we'll do it later."

Allie whistled, the sound tinny in the loudspeaker. "Jeez! You want me to switch it all back?"

"Get the notaries back up here. One other thing."

"Shoot."

"What do you know about a naval architecture outfit name of G.A. Forrester? Do we have any 'ins' there?"

Jake heard papers moving on Allie's desk. "Wait a sec, that name sounds familiar." Allie put his hand over the mouthpiece and said something to someone. The delay lasted more than a minute.

"Uncle Jake? My assistant found them. Let me see… wholly owned subsidiary… Oh! Hey, they're Ampanco! That makes it easy. You want to know what color toilet paper they use, no problem. What do we need from them?"

"Laurel used to work there."

"I thought she wasn't talking about her past."

"She cashed a company check. Get hold of personnel over there. I'm gonna have a talk with her boss."

"Jeez, Uncle Jake. Is this anything I should know about?"

"No. It's personal. Go ahead and take the rest of the day."

What good was money if you couldn't buy what you wanted *when* you wanted it? Allie knew what he'd been told to do: apply money, get results.

The phone buzzed. Jake opened his eyes. Outside, the growing storm stripped leaves from the trees in large wet handfuls, sent them scuttling past his windows. He checked the time. He'd slept for an hour.

Allie's voice came through the speaker. "I decided to call first. I'll send the contact details by fax."

He heard Allie shuffling papers. "Let's see. Her supervisor was a guy named Nicholas J. Zaia. His title is Division Manager for Design."

Nicholas Zaia! The name echoed from all four walls of the room. Jesus!

"We did a quick rundown on him. He's forty-four, unmarried. Hmmm, that's strange. Forty-four and never married?" Allie slowed and Jake heard his chair creak. "I'll have them look into that. Where'd I leave off? Oh, yeah, RPI '78, BS Mechanical Engineering, honors. Nineteen years in the field, seven with Forrester, four in current position…"

Allie had more, but Jake didn't hear. The Zaias were bitter enemies. Twenty years ago he'd tried to make amends, given a promising kid named Nicholas Zaia a leg up through an intermediary. Look at the result. Maybe Laurel had let some fact about her past slip. Maybe Nicholas Zaia picked up on something in her employment application. Maybe he slowly sabotaged her career, held her back, then forced her out.

She'd have been better off with me dead.

Jake pressed a hand to his chest, trembling from a surge of self-loathing. Even things done with the best intentions ended hurting the ones he loved. Would the world escape the curse of Jake Eastland only after everyone who'd ever come in contact with him was dead and in the ground?

Through the sheets of water cascading down his window, Joe Zaia's face appeared as it had been that night in the Hotel Comfort in 1926. And Estelle, he could see Estelle too, at the moment their eyes met for the first time. If only he could go back and live that time again.

"Uncle Jake. You there? Talk to me."

Jake's mind wanted to go on, rehash the entire story, the whole wild ride. The memory usually came in the wee hours, on nights when he couldn't sleep. Never had it happened in broad daylight.

"Yes. Just thinking about something. What did you say?"

"Hell, I ain't reading it all again. It's six pages. I asked why you want all this so fast. I don't hear from you for months, then all of a sudden you're changing your will back and forth, and digging up information about some guy named Zaia. What's going on?"

"Do a workup on Zaia."

"Okay. I'll get them going on it. Uncle Jake, you take care of yourself now. I'm worrying."

"Don't. I'm okay. Everything is okay." Jake touched the button, severing the connection.

Outside, the rain swatted the glass harder.

DOWNSTAIRS

Laurel stood on the screened-in porch of the bungalow and watched the parcel service leave with her laptop. Yesterday, after returning from the burial plot, she'd been eager to get it going, but it had refused to boot.

It was cold and rainy, a dull, brooding morning with a dark, low overcast. Her mood fit the day. She'd awakened with a headache and hadn't been able to eat much at breakfast.

Grampa Jake's story, the eerie feeling as she knelt by Joshua Eastland's grave, her excitement over researching the lost ship, the clash of emotions—whether to go west or stay put—then not being able to make progress toward either, left her feeling tense, suspended.

The van disappeared. She went inside and kicked off her shoes, stretched out on the sofa on her back, and contemplated the ceiling. After a bit, her eyes drifted shut and she dozed. She came awake with a start when someone tapped on her door.

"You in there, kiddo?"

Grampa Jake.

"C'mon in." She spoke louder than usual to make sure he heard.

The door opened and he peered in.

"You decent?"

"Yeah. C'mon in, I'm just lying down." She sat up and patted the seat beside her.

He stood his umbrella in the stand and sat on the sofa, facing her.

"What's going on?" she said.

"I got to thinking... I figured it might be good to have a little talk, just you and me."

She tensed. "About what?"

He gazed at her. "About you, I guess. I'm worried for you. You seemed... distracted... at breakfast."

She prided herself on her pragmatism, but lately the tiniest thing could set her off. She averted her gaze and blinked away tears. "I haven't done a very good job with my life, G-Grampa Jake."

He touched her hand where it rested on the cushion beside her. "I don't know about that. You seem fine to me."

The tightness built in her throat and her voice wavered. "Yeah. Real fine." Any more and she would choke.

"Feel like talking about it?"

All at once the injury to her sense of worth became too much to hold in any longer. She pressed her hand to her chest.

"I was up for a promotion I deserved, but they didn't give it to me. Instead, Nick, the division head, passed me over and promoted my assistant. A junior man I mentored. No way could I hold my head up after that."

She strained for control but her voice faltered. "I... I walked out." She choked out the rest. "That same morning, my fiancé stole my savings and disappeared. I swear! I'll never trust another man as long as I live."

Tears rolled down her cheeks, all the more copious for having been so long repressed.

Grampa Jake slid over, pulled her close and embraced her, cradling her head between his neck and shoulder.

"Now, now then. It'll be all right. You're not the first one who's lost a lover. After a while, it'll be all right." He said it over and over, almost humming the soothing words as he patted her shoulder.

She looked up and studied his face. What little light there was in the dim room seemed almost to spring from his eyes. Strangely, his words did make her feel better. He'd loved and lost, too. Each time he said, "It'll be all right," she could hear in his voice that it would be.

She pulled some tissues from the box on the stand next to the sofa, wiped tears away, and leaned into him.

"I *have* made a mess of my life, Grampa Jake, almost right from the start. Something's wrong with me."

"Hush! There is not. You can't let yourself think like that." He hugged her harder.

"Come. Now!" White petticoats flashed as he forced her to stumble along behind him.

Jake started after them. A hand grasped his shoulder from behind.

"Hold it, Jake. That one's trouble," Bruce said. "That's Joe Zaia's daughter. I didn't recognize her at first. Him, I'd know anywhere. He runs booze, too. He's got his customers, we've got ours. Don't go stirring things up."

"I know him," Jake cut in. "He gave me a skinning on a trade last year. I owe him one." Jake looked toward the ballroom. "Besides, she's begging for it. I'm going to ask her to dance."

"You do, and you're liable to find yourself out back with your guts on the ground in front of you." Bruce shook his finger for emphasis. "Those Dago's don't like anybody messing with their women."

Jake believed him, but the girl was hot for him, and he owed Zaia a screwing.

In the ballroom, the band struck up a fast number. Jake clamped his jaws together and entered the large, dimly-lit room. Spotlights illuminated a rotating mirrored ball on the ceiling, casting hundreds of tiny spots of light that moved over the floor and the dancers. Seated people lined the walls.

He circulated. Halfway up the hall he spotted her sitting between an obese old woman and a girl of twelve or so. On the other side of the old woman sat a young man about his own age. He stared at Jake through slotted eyes. Joe Zaia was nowhere in sight. Jake stopped in front of the older girl, and extended his hand.

"May I have this dance?"

The girl glanced at the old woman, then at the younger girl whose eyes had become round as dollars. She took his hand.

Immediately, the old woman broke into a shrill stream of Italian and tugged at the girl's hand. The girl pulled away and fired a string of words back at the old lady, silencing her. Then she turned back to Jake and pulled him out onto the floor.

"I am Estelle Maria Zaia." She had a soft, throaty voice. "I am happy to dance with you."

"Jake Eastland. Pleased to meet you."

Many on the dance floor were dancing the Charleston, the newest rage. Jake and Estelle giggled at each other as they tried without success to emulate the better dancers. Then they caught on a little and for the next minutes whirled around as if possessed. Jake wasn't very good. Neither was she. It didn't matter.

The band segued into a slow number. Jake held up his arms and she stepped into them, their bodies not touching as they danced. He was several inches taller. Estelle's eyes flicked up to his.

"You have-a the most beautiful eyes," she said at last.

This might be easier than he thought. "Thank you, Estelle. I think you're beautiful."

She moved closer until their bodies just touched.

"You live here, Jake-a Eastland?"

He found himself exaggerating his words, as if it could help her learn the correct enunciation. "I live at Mexico Point, and you live in Port Ontario."

Her eyes lit up.

"I see you before, last month." She slipped a little further into his arms. Her face was freshly scrubbed, smooth.

Holding her was intoxicating, made him feel like he was falling. "Will you be here again next Saturday?" His voice wobbled, embarrassing him. She noticed and smiled. Pursing her lips, she flashed her eyes.

"You come, I try..."

"*Estelle Maria!*" The deep male voice boomed through the dance hall, shocking the dancers into immobility. Estelle froze in his arms, her eyes dismayed. Even the band petered out and fell silent.

"Some other time we see about you and me, Jake-a-Eastland," she whispered, squeezing his shoulder. She turned and hurried to where Joe Zaia stood, swaying, his fists clenched. The man was drunk. She gave him a wide berth, her head lowered, and the other two women hustled her from the room.

Joe Zaia motioned to the young man who'd stared at Jake earlier. "What you do? Sit there? I din' say she dance-a with him."

The young man glared at Jake, who remained in the middle of the now-empty dance floor. The girl's brother stood a little taller and looked heavier than Jake, maybe a year older. He stepped onto the floor. "What you think you gonna do, take her upstairs?"

That was exactly it, but Jake kept his voice calm. "I think we were having fun, dancing." His anger rose, he didn't like this person. He didn't like Mr. Joe Zaia either.

Zaia jabbed Jake's chest with the first finger of his right hand. "You no dance. You no touch." He shoved one time for each statement, pushing Jake back a half step.

Jake slapped the hand away and shoved his adversary with both arms, propelling him backwards several steps.

He held up his fist. "And you no touch me either, *dago*." He crouched, ready to receive the attack.

He didn't have long to wait. The immigrant boy screamed, pulled a wicked-looking stiletto from his back pocket, and lunged at Jake.

Jake was not new to brawling. He had only two chances against a knife: dirty fighting or surprise. No time for either now. It had to be a short fight or he would be cut to shreds. He calmly parried the knife with his arm and went for his assailant's balls as their bodies came together, receiving a mean cut for his trouble. But it was already too late. In close quarters, Zaia had the momentum and propelled Jake backwards until he stumbled and fell, carrying his attacker with him. Jake's head banged against the floor. He saw stars.

"Ahheeeiii!" Zaia cried, triumphant. He straddled Jake and brought his knife to Jake's neck, the point pressing against the skin, drawing blood. Blood welled from the back of Jake's arm. His head spun.

"Now, I'm gonna cut you." Zaia's son growled.

"Emilio!" Joe Zaia bellowed. "Not now!"

Jake's attacker hesitated, looked around at his father, then lowered his face until his mouth was inches from Jake's. "Next time, I make sure no audience. Then I cut you good." He pushed off on Jake's chest, got to his feet and walked away.

Exactly one week later, Estelle Maria Zaia followed her grandmother, mother and younger sister into the ballroom of the Hotel Comfort. The band had just begun to play and the room was not yet crowded. Without moving her head, she searched the room as she walked. No sign of him. She exhaled a sigh, worried. He could be in the bar.

A thought chilled her. *Maybe he won't show up at all.*

She hadn't been able to think about anything else all week. She tingled every time she thought about those eyes, and the way he made her feel, and oh, how much she wanted to have him for her very own. He wasn't Italian, and that would cause problems, but she didn't care. He was the most beautiful man she had ever seen. And now it was Saturday night again and she was shaky with anticipation, but he wasn't here.

Although she'd just turned sixteen, Estelle's hips were full and rounded and her breasts large and high. She was proud of them and made a point of standing very straight and holding her shoulders back so they'd jut outward at a saucy angle, bouncing as she walked.

She'd had sex with many men, by force, beginning at age thirteen, then later by choice. She liked it, but Italian men were rutting animals. She wanted love, romance; she wanted a man who would fight for her, risk everything for her. And she'd found him, was more than ready for him—but where was he? Damn!

Lucky thing Emilio had used his knife to hurt Jake Eastland last week. Her father was madder at him for being stupid enough to pull his knife in public than he was at her for dancing with a man he considered an enemy.

Her brother would never have confronted Jake if his father hadn't forced him. He'd sat there without saying a word when Jake Eastland asked her to dance. Jake had a strong, self-confident way. Emilio never did anything on his own. He was afraid. She knew it.

Her father entered the ballroom and came toward them. His bushy eyebrows lowered in a frown as he stopped in front of her.

He'd been to the gambling tent already. She could smell the alcohol on his breath. She hoped he wouldn't get too drunk. He liked to hit when he did.

"Boys ask, you dance, but rememb', leave-a room for the Holy Ghost between you." He waved his finger. "No coochee, coochee."

Estelle's sister tittered. He silenced her with a glare.

Estelle put on her most innocent face and lowered her eyes. "All right, papa."

"One thing more. Stay inside, you no go upstairs, capichay?"

The bedrooms were upstairs. Estelle felt a small tremor pass through her. What would it be like, to do it with Jake Eastland? She knew, on some level, she'd never be able to win him for her own any other way.

Jake and Bruce were in their room on the third floor. Bruce had spent the afternoon in Oswego having final alterations made on the hundred-dollar suit he'd just finished the final stages of donning.

Bruce frowned into the mirror. "If the Dagos are here again this week, you better make sure you cool it with that Zaia girl."

Jake exhaled smoke toward the ceiling. He'd been thinking about her all week, the way she smelled, the way she felt in his arms. She'd be here. He would try for all the marbles tonight. Let Joe Zaia swallow that.

In a way, he was sorry he had to treat her like that. She interested him, in a rough way. If it hadn't been for her father... He pushed the thought away.

"I'll ask her father if I can dance with her, let him know I want to show my respect."

"Good luck! I know those people. Their way of settling differences of opinion is seeing who can make the biggest holes in the other guy."

"I've dealt with him before." Jake ground his cigarette out in the glass ashtray on the nightstand beside his bed. "Tonight, I get even with the bastard."

Fifteen minutes later he left the screened porch of the hotel and made his way toward the lanterns marking the big tent the Italian men used to play cards, smoke, and drink while the women and children were in the ballroom. Wagons and vehicles surrounded it and he was not seen as he approached. He lifted the flap and stepped inside.

Conversation inside the tent ceased. Near him, the young man who'd attacked him last week stepped forward.

"I think you lost. Yes?"

Jake remembered his name. "No, Emilio, not lost. I'm here to see your father."

Silence in the tent.

To Jake's left, halfway across the tent, Joe Zaia slowly stood. He swayed on his feet, his hair mussed. A water glass half full of clear liquid sat on the table in front of him.

"You look for Joe Zaia?"

Jake stopped in front of him. "I came to ask your permission to dance with your daughter, Estelle."

Zaia stared at him for several moments, his face going dark. "You. I recognize…"

"You have a very nice daughter. I enjoyed her company, and I would like to dance with her again."

Joe Zaia put his hand to his jaw, blinking like he'd been poleaxed. Jake wondered what the clear liquid was. Wood alcohol?

"Okay, you dance, but no trouble," Zaia tapped his chest. "Or this time you deal with me."

The men around the card tables relaxed and sound filled the tent again. Emilio glared, his eyes cold, hard. Jake could see an enemy there. Be careful around that one. He backed out of the tent, careful not to turn his back for an instant.

By the first of September, six weeks later, the romance had reached fever pitch. They'd made love a dozen times, and she was his, body and soul. He'd had his revenge. Time to drop her and then laugh in Joe

Zaia's face. But something stopped him.

Another Saturday night, late, Jake pushed open the door at the bottom of the stairs leading up to the bedrooms and peeked into the hall. No one paid any attention.

"C'mon." He pulled Estelle's hand, and they left the stairwell and hurried toward the dance floor.

Just as they reached the middle of the hall, Joe Zaia stepped from the shadows and blocked the entrance to the ballroom.

Behind them, the stairwell door clicked shut. Zaia's eyes flickered to it. Not so drunk he didn't understand, his face flushed and his lower jaw pushed forward, the onset of rage so palpable it seemed he might explode into a million pieces any moment. Zaia lifted his hand and in what seemed like slow motion, crooked a finger at his daughter.

Estelle released Jake's hand and went to her father, back straight, head high. He gripped her by the arm and slapped her. The sound caused heads to turn.

"*Puta!*" He scowled at her disheveled hair, and slapped her again. "Go. I deal with you later." He shoved her toward the exit.

She resisted. "No! Nothing happen! Nothing!" Her cheek was bright red. "Leave him alone. I love him! Nothing happen, I swear."

He shoved her harder and she fell against the door. "I say you go." The impact pushed it open and she fell outside with a cry.

Jake took a step toward her, but Joe Zaia stepped in front of him. "I tell you no trouble. Then you do this behind my back. From now on, you stay away. You no see, you no talk. You try… I *kill* you. Capichay?"

Summer faded. Fall, and in its turn winter came and left. Estelle stayed with her man. Nothing, not even her father's threat, could keep her away.

She went to him every other week, knowing her family would never accept him, knowing how vulnerable her actions made her, knowing the names others used behind her back.

She lived for the light that came to his face each time his door swung open and he saw her again. Lived for the moment he would say the words that meant he would marry her. When she hinted, trying to steer his thoughts, he always said endearing things, but never *those* words.

Spring approached. Soon he would go back to the lake and his work and she didn't know when she would see him again. Her flow was a few days late this month.

"You love me, Jake? I make you a good wife."

Beside her in his bed, he didn't answer.

"Please, Jake, answer."

He moved closer, his mouth by her ear. "I think so."

She whimpered. "What you mean, think?" A tear slipped onto her cheek. Didn't he know? What if her period never came?

"It's all I know to say. I think about you all the time. When we're together, the time slips by too fast. But we're so different. What I'm feeling… I just don't know if it's enough."

She lifted herself on one elbow and put her hand on his. "Jake-a Eastland, I love you. I have a baby for you right now." She lifted his hand and put it on her stomach. Maybe that would make him love her. She didn't really think she had his baby. But she *was* a few days late. At that moment, if she could have willed it, she would have made herself pregnant just to win his love.

Jake stared at the hand pressing his into the warm flesh of her belly. The fingernails were uneven, several with dark crescents of dirt. Funny, he hadn't noticed that before. Maybe he was so used to those things about her, her accent, the way she dressed, her general manner, none of it registered on him anymore.

She took pains to be clean for him, he knew that, her skin always scrubbed and her hair fragrant, but how do you wash away a lifetime of ignorance?

Had she just said she was pregnant? The thought shocked him.

Could he be the father?

Of course, he could. But there had been others before him. Had there been others since? They saw each other every other week. Who had her dress up the rest of the time?

"You're pregnant?"

She laughed and tossed her head, black curls flying. "Not so fast, mister. We get married first, then pregnant."

Jake stared. He remembered why he'd started seeing her. He couldn't allow it to become more. She had a wonderful zest for life, and he loved her different sense of humor, her fun-loving nature. Her love for him was so honest, so obvious, it became almost impossible to tell her the truth.

Her mouth came to his, questing, and he forgot that he could never marry her, that no matter how hard she tried, she'd never be able to keep up, that she'd hold him back.

Not for the first time, it occurred to him that his actions were dishonorable, had been from the start. The understanding shamed him, but not enough to make him get up and leave.

The very next morning, Bruce called from Kingston. The ice was out of the Bay of Quinte and the runs to Belleville could begin again. Good thing. The network Jake had set up over the winter clamored for whisky, and the price had jumped another dollar.

For the rest of that spring and well into the summer, he didn't see her. Business boomed. He hadn't been home to his apartment in Oswego in months.

During those weeks away, he knew he wouldn't marry her, but the memory of her arms, her smile, her dark eyes, her oddly wonderful sense of humor, made knowing painful. The thought of her flashing those dark eyes, stamping her foot while she bawled him out for staying away so long, made him warm inside. His mind's eye conveniently expunged the bouquet of onion that clung to her, the hint of garlic. Those were part of her, and his mind accepted them.

For no reason at all, during a side trip to Kingston, he ordered a gift for her, a gold locket, engraved. During the week it took the jeweler to fashion it, Jake wondered what possessed him. He didn't love her. She wasn't good enough for him. Why, then?

He didn't know. Only that he wanted her to have it.

Then he had the locket, solid gold on a gold chain, cradled in his palm. He wasn't marrying her, not a chance. All he wanted was one more roll around. After, he'd give her the locket and kiss her goodbye.

You make me so mad Jake-a Eastland!

Tears trickled down Estelle's cheeks as she worked. Her grandmother watched, her head covered by a black shawl in the cool morning air. Estelle took her frustration out on the perch on her cutting board, slicing it open, the knife slipping with ease through the soft underbelly of the fish.

Wait till I see you!

His phone rang and rang but he never answered. When the chance came to visit her aunt in Oswego, she'd taken it.

At his apartment she knocked, then again, louder, not caring who heard. There was no answer, only silence.

Just a glimpse of him would be enough. Didn't he care about her even a little?

"Plenty other fish in the pond, Estelle Maria," her grandmother said, sad eyes old, disillusioned. "If one wiggles away, always another come along."

Estelle pouted, her lips pushed out in a moue. It *was* Saturday, and she'd been very good all summer.

Always another come along.

Like Angelo Spina. He always teased her about being afraid to date a real man.

If he only knew! Ha!

And Tony Piazza. She'd always thought Tony was sexy, though his wife had run off with another man. Maybe tonight at the dance she would let Tony take her outside, just for a minute.

What if Jake Eastland had another woman? The back of her throat tightened and she severed the head of the perch with a vicious stroke. She knew exactly how to deal with anyone who tried to steal her man.

She suppressed a sniffle and wiped the corner of her eye with her finger. Why don't you love me Jake-a Eastland? I love you the best I can.

Jake stepped onto the dock at the Hotel Comfort. In his pocket, a jeweler's box held the locket. Tonight, after they made love, he would give it to her. And then he would tell her.

This is goodbye? I love you Estelle, I want to marry you?

No! Not that. It *would* be goodbye.

She'd probably pretend at first that she didn't want to talk to him, but she'd melt as soon as he had her in his arms.

He entered the hotel through the side door of the bar and headed for the dance floor.

"Jake! Jake Eastland!" Tony McBride, the man who'd set him up with Bruce, waved from the bar. Jake owed the man a drink. They chatted for a few minutes then Jake excused himself with a promise to stop back later and headed for the dance floor.

Like a miracle, Jake-a Eastland appeared. Estelle saw him enter the hotel and go into the bar. It was a most inopportune moment. She'd allowed Tony Piazza to ply her with liquor, and they'd just come inside after half an hour in the warm darkness. Tony's warm kisses and skillful fingers had aroused her so much her body still vibrated.

When she saw Jake, she clutched her hands to her throat in a seizure of joy. A moment later, a half-intoxicated rage settled on her.

I'll show *you*, Jake-a-Eastland. You'll never leave *me* alone like that again. She pulled Tony onto the dance floor and slipped into his arms. Close, very close.

"Mmmm, hold me, Tony." She tilted her face up, her lips close to his. Out of the corner of her eye she saw Jake leave the bar, waving to someone. He came toward the ballroom. She stood on tiptoe and kissed Tony full on the mouth. It took him only an instant to kiss her back. She felt his hands slide down her hips, pull her tight.

When she checked again, many seconds later, Jake Eastland was gone. He had to have seen. He wasn't jealous at all.

"You beautiful like a rose, Estelle. Let's go for another walk," Tony whispered. "I gotta little more picker-upper." He patted his back pocket.

Jake Eastland didn't love her. Suddenly, she wanted to do the thing she hoped would hurt him most. She nodded at Tony. "Okay, let's go."

That night, after several more shots of whisky, Estelle Maria Zaia gave herself to Tony. She cried the entire time.

Jake stopped in the entrance of the ballroom. Right there, not ten feet away, Estelle stood on her tiptoes, deep in an embrace with an older man, kissing him the way she'd kissed Jake so many times. The man's hands slid over her buttocks, squeezing as he ground his body into hers.

For several seconds Jake forgot to breathe. Then, his movements wooden, he went to the exit, pushed the door open and stepped outside. There, in the cool darkness, he leaned face-forward against the building, resting his forehead against the siding, and tried to catch his breath.

Surprise and remorse came in waves. He had it completely wrong, she didn't love him after all, he'd been nothing but a fling for her. He wouldn't need to throw her away. She'd already done it for him.

He should be relieved. Why wasn't he? Why had his chest tied itself into such a knot? He tried to retreat, go back to where he'd been minutes earlier, but that person no longer existed. Nothing remained except the pain of knowing how much of a fool he'd been.

After ten minutes he could think a bit. That was when the anger began. It built in him, slow and hot. He had no plan as he opened the door and re-entered the hotel, only a need to confront, find out why. He went to the ballroom and scanned the dancers.

Estelle and her boyfriend were gone.

LAUREL

Grampa Jake leaned his head against the backrest of the sofa and closed his eyes. There had to be more to it. He wouldn't remember a youthful fling all these years later, not in such perfect detail, unless there was more.

Despite the distress he showed, the things he'd done diminished him in her eyes. She detested the way he'd treated the girl, and his motive for pursuing her. Only an insensitive, selfish person would deliberately seduce a woman to get even with her father. The betrayal of trust came too close to her own experience. She knew just how Estelle must have felt.

On the other hand, he could have lied about his motives, left the ugly parts out, but he hadn't. She had to respect that. From the look on his face right now, he'd paid for his mistake with years of remorse.

Her rationalization of his behavior came easily. She wanted to believe in him.

"You were young. People make mistakes."

He opened his eyes and regarded her coolly. "No mistake. I knew what I was doing every second." He hesitated. "I've never told anyone about Estelle. I needed to. Thanks for listening."

Despite her misgivings about what she might hear, he wasn't getting off that easy. "What about the rest?"

His gaze wavered, a sheepish look taking over. "What?"

"There's more, isn't there? More between Estelle and you."

His eyes fell, his shoulders sagged and his head went forward until the cords in the back of his neck stood out. "Yes," he said to the floor.

He slowly straightened and at last looked at her again. "But I didn't come here to talk about me. I came to talk about you, remember?"

She braced herself, not at all sure it was a good idea.

He studied her through narrowed eyes. "Tell me about your life with your grandmother. What did she think about you being a bit of a tomboy?"

Laurel flinched. He couldn't possibly know how sensitive a place he'd touched.

"She detested it. She only let me come home when there were no guests, or for a few weeks in the summer when we came here. She was horrid to me." She fell silent, memories flowing, then, "Did your grandmother love you, Grampa Jake?" The question was out before she knew it was even there in the back of her mind. He'd shared with her. Was that why she'd blurted it out? Did she want to do the same, prove that something was wrong with her, too, by revealing she'd never been good enough to deserve her grandmother's love?

He stared at her for what seemed like a long time before answering. "Sure. She was always hugging me."

Laurel held herself rigid. "I don't think mine did. I lived with her, but I can't remember her ever smooching or hugging me." The confession edged her closer to losing control. "Somehow, I did something to make her dislike me. I know I can't, but I wish there was some way I could go back and change things, make myself worthy…"

Jake clenched his jaws. Laurel had many of his physical characteristics, the wide eyes, the reedy build, and the complexion. Dammit, Jean, the one person who needed you to love her, and you couldn't bring yourself to do it? Was it because she looked too much like me?

Christ! Everything wrong in his granddaughter's life could be traced directly to him. Had some evil force brought her here so his money could finish the job of destroying her? Maybe he should get up and walk out, leave her be.

A heaviness draped itself over his chest. He breathed, trying to drive it away. No. Walking away would be a mistake. He'd been thrust into Laurel's life at a pivotal moment. He had to at least try. Try to be the kind of grandfather a girl could love.

She drew breath to speak. He touched her lips with his finger.

"Shhh. Things happen that we *all* wish we could go back and change. But no one can. Your grandmother loved you very much."

She dropped her gaze, looked at her hands.

It came to him that having outlived practically everyone else involved, truth, at least in this case, lay at his mercy. From this moment, Jean would be as he said—regardless of how she'd really been. With a finger, he lifted her chin.

"I know you're thinking, why didn't she *show* it. Well, sometimes you can't know the reasons for things, especially things like that. Good thing we had this talk."

She looked at him, her eyes puzzled. "It is?"

"I knew your grandmother a little better than I let on. She never came out with her feelings, always kept them hidden away." Jean had been plenty expressive, downright corrosive at times.

A note of hope appeared in Laurel's voice. "Is that really the way she was?"

He nodded, slowly. "Sad to say, she was the only person I ever knew I never saw smile."

The glow that came to Laurel's face rewarded him. Clearly, she wanted to believe. Even with her eyes red-rimmed and sore-looking, strands of hair sticking to her forehead, and no makeup, his granddaughter looked so beautiful he could hardly breathe. Funny how life had a way of surrendering its sweetest moments at times like this, right when you least expected them.

At the same time, the need to lie brought him down. Long ago, he could have done the right thing, stepped in after her parents died, been a real grandfather. Which was better medicine, a lie oiled with good intentions, or the truth, straight up, with no chaser? She'd had the oil. Maybe this would be a good time to tell her the truth about how he knew.

She hugged him. "I know you're probably just saying those things, Grampa Jake, but thank you anyway. I feel so much better, and there's no one else I really trust to talk to. My real grandfather was a horrible person. Grandma Jean told me he did the most unspeakable things, even murdered people, and all for money. All he ever cared about was himself, and money."

Her words impacted like a string of smart bombs. Jake's heart flipped a strong extra beat. Jesus! He'd been on the verge of telling her. His heart took off on the series of fluttery beats promised by the first, different this time, more in his throat than usual.

"Grampa Jake?"

"Uh huh."

"If I get hold of the equipment to search for that load, do you think we could use the hotel's Whaler?"

The arrhythmia ended as abruptly as it began and Jake experienced a resurgence of hope. He hugged her harder, wishing again he could tell her everything but he was further than ever from that. Maybe he'd never be able to, but so what? If she trusted him, maybe that was enough.

He let go and sat forward. "Yes, my young friend, I'll bet that can be arranged. You might even be able to convince me to show you the place."

LAUREL

Three days later, with Grampa Jake at the controls of the Whaler, they began the search. The temperature stood at eighty, unusually warm for so late in the season, and the air rushing past as the Whaler sped north held no hint of the coming season.

At the helm, Grampa Jake grasped the knobs of the throttles and pulled them smoothly toward him. In seconds the Whaler came down off plane. With no power on, their stern wave caught up and lifted the transom, giving a surge of forward movement while it passed.

Beside Laurel, Sheik clung to the siderail.

"Some piece a' equipment, ain't she? I almost feel safe out here in this one."

"What? You're the marina manager. I figured you'd be right at home on the water."

Sheik shook his head. "You don't hafta like big waves to run a gas dock or collect slip rents. Long as the water's flat, I'm fine. I can dive a hundred feet, go anywhere, no problem. But get me in a storm an' I don't know my left hand from my right." He held up his right hand when he said "left", then his left when he said "right."

Grampa Jake stood and sighted the land, looking back toward Nine Mile, then toward Stony Point a few miles north. He motioned with his arm. "Should be just about right in here."

Last night, the discussion over how to proceed had taken a decidedly circular form. Laurel had her ideas, Grampa Jake had his, and while each remained courteous, neither budged an inch. In the end, Laurel saw the futility of further discussion and agreed to do things his way.

Now she had little confidence but went ahead anyway. "Let's put the fish in, Sheik. Careful not to foul the props."

The sonar "fish" looked like a small torpedo, and contained a sonar array that could look sideways and create a three-dimensional image of the lakebed. Sheik bent to the task.

"Is it all right if we make a square search around this spot, Grampa Jake? We could make each leg a quarter of a mile."

Grampa Jake considered that. "Sure. Sounds good. We ought to find it pretty quick—if that equipment's any good."

Three hours later the sun passed its zenith and beat down on them in relentless waves. Not a breath of wind moved the air. They'd found nothing.

Grampa Jake's nose had a pink cast and his neck was red.

Laurel found his hat atop the control console and handed it to him. "Grampa Jake, please put your hat back on."

"Yup. Getting a little headache." He opened his water bottle and poured some on his head and the back of his neck, then put the hat on. He looked toward Mexico Point, then at Stony Point again. "Could have sworn we dropped it right in here."

Neither Sheik nor Laurel commented.

Grampa Jake let go of the wheel. "Okay! I can take a hint. How would *you* do it, Miss Smarty?"

Laurel gave him a good-natured shove. "Hush. Are you sure it was along this line?"

"Unless they moved Stony Point and forgot to tell me."

She entered their GPS coordinates into the chart program on her laptop then turned the computer so both men could see the display.

"Okay, this is where we are right now, approximately four hundred yards west of the rhumbline, the line drawn between Nine Mile Point, where the chase began, and Stony Point Light, your destination."

After some further calculations, she entered another set of co-ordinates on the map. She showed them the display again.

"This point is exactly two miles north of us on the same heading as the rhumbline. We could tow the fish and look toward shore along it, then move fifty yards in and go back the other way on the reciprocal heading. I think there's time to make seven or eight passes before we lose the light."

Sheik moved toward Grampa Jake. "Why doncha' let me take over for a while, Jake? You look tired."

"Since when can you do anything better than me?"

Sheik stopped in his tracks, his face flushing. "Aw. I didn't mean anything by it, Jake. I just thought I'd…"

Laurel stepped in. "I think he's right, Grampa Jake. Your face is beet red, so is your neck. You haven't been on the water in a while. Besides, we need you to work the surface when we find something. If you get sick, there'll just be the two of us. Why don't you take a break?"

Grampa Jake looked from her to Sheik, and back again. "All right. Take over, Sheik. I do have a little headache.

By 5:30 they'd searched an area two miles long by four hundred yards wide. They went home empty-handed.

As they walked from the marina to the hotel, Grampa Jake snapped his fingers.

"Wait! I know why we missed it. We ran in toward shore at the last minute. I forgot about that."

Laurel remembered too, now. From his story. "How long before you stopped?"

"A minute, maybe. I wasn't paying attention to the time."

"That could be a half mile or more at twenty-five knots." Laurel slipped her arm through his. "We'll need to look further in."

A little after one the next afternoon, Laurel stood at the gunwale of the Whaler. The sonar towfish had revealed an unusual projection on the bottom. If the lakebed hadn't been so flat otherwise, it wouldn't have interested her.

A small green wave loomed, splashing away as it contacted the side of the boat. She winked at Sheik. Inside the full facemask, he elevated his eyebrows in response, then made the sign of the cross, and stepped off the boat, one hand holding his facemask in place.

Grampa Jake was not with them, doctor's orders. Laurel hesitated: seventy-five feet to the bottom. No matter how many times she dove, the kernel of fear never quite left her.

She shook it off, breathed, closed her eyes from habit and stepped into the water, holding the new-style full-face mask in place as she plunged.

As she sank, the water shaded from blue-white to blue-brown amidst the bubbles. The familiar unpleasant slithering of water entering her wetsuit at the neck, wrist, and ankles began. When her initial plunge slowed, she bent and followed the anchor line down, hands in front as if diving, flippers on her feet providing the thrust. She exhaled and breathed. No trail of bubbles resulted, only a soft hiss from the re-breather apparatus.

The bottom appeared from the gloom. Little light penetrated to this depth, but she could see about twenty feet. Sheik waited near the anchor.

"Visibility's not bad," she said into the speaking cavity of the mask. She'd never used an underwater communicator before. Aaron Hoenig, her archaeologist friend at Woods Hole, had arranged for the gear— including the communicator—in return for her promise to hand over a few bottles of any whisky she found.

"Darn good," a fair facsimile of Sheik's voice answered.

She unhooked the dive light from her belt and clicked it on, illuminating the bottom in front of her. She scanned, exploring from right to left.

"There!" She pointed toward a small log protruding from the bottom about twenty-five feet away.

He swam toward the projection and hovered near the object, trying to minimize the amount of silt he stirred up. He touched it, ran his hands over the top, waved. "Come here," his voice was distorted but audible. His hand flashed in the light.

Laurel swam toward him. On the way, she spotted something on the bottom and stopped to take a look; a length of old chain, small diameter, encased in marine growth, both ends buried. Nothing there.

Sheik drew a circle in the water with his finger. "It's round, manmade."

Laurel looked closer. The object swarmed with marine growth, tiny brine shrimp, algae, and zebra mussels. Sheik scraped at it with his dive knife. Suddenly, she saw what he meant.

"My God! An old gun." Could this belong to the treasure ship? Was the gold somewhere close by? She had to force herself not to breathe too rapidly. She grasped the end and tried to move it but it remained firmly bedded in the lake bottom, with only two feet projecting.

She fanned the sand near the base of the cannon with her hand. A bloom of silt lifted, then edged away on a gentle current. She pulled the paddle-like silt wand from her belt and vigorously worked at the base of the cannon while Sheik did the same on the other side. They raised a large cloud and had to stop work until it drifted off in the current.

They cleared a depression several inches deep around the base of the cannon. Laurel began to fan again and something flashed in the glare of her light. She signaled Sheik to stop, and gently fanned the sand in front of her. There it was again. She reached down and moved the sand with her glove. A piece of glass peeked out of the bottom. She picked it up and held it for Sheik to see. It was clear, two inches by four and curved.

Sheik nodded vigorously and dug with his hands. Almost at once he produced another prize. A bottleneck!

They'd found an old cannon and booze as well, and maybe, just maybe, something much more important was very close. She checked her watch. They'd been on the bottom twenty minutes. If they didn't want to spend time decompressing they had to go up soon.

She showed Sheik her extended fingers and said, "Fifteen minutes."

"Got it." He bent to the search again, this time several feet away.

She adopted his technique and she too began to find pieces of broken glass. Almost seventy-five years it had lain here. Please, let at least one bottle be intact.

Sheik let out a yell, too loud for the system to handle and she couldn't make out what he'd said. He appeared out of the cloud of silt, holding an intact bottle full of brown fluid.

"That's it!" She pounded him on the shoulder.

In their excitement, time slipped past. They found three more bottles. Laurel checked her watch. They were now at forty minutes and would need to decompress.

She waved Sheik off and when the silt had cleared, took several pictures of the cannon from different angles, then fished in her dive bag for a marker and wired it to the snout. It could be activated from the surface and would permit them to easily return to the site.

They swam to the anchor line. Forty-five minutes meant decompress time of seven minutes at each fifteen-foot stop. They ascended to sixty feet and stopped, smiling and talking. Being able to communicate underwater went a long way toward allaying her fear. The simple ability to ask for help if she should ever need it made her feel a hundred times more secure.

Thirty minutes later, they surfaced. Laurel climbed the steps of the swim ladder and shrugged off her re-breather.

Sheik held up the mesh sack containing their find. "Boy, that voice system works great. Here, take this."

She grasped it by the neck and lifted it aboard.

"Careful now," he said. "We don't know how brittle that glass is."

He climbed aboard, his face flushed. "Whew, I gotta' siddown." He dropped his SCUBA and unzipped the front of his wetsuit. "That was a lot like work."

His face was red but his chest had normal color, so did his hands. "Are you all right, Sheik? Any joint pain or a stiff neck?"

"No, I'm just bushed."

"You did great. What do you think about that cannon?"

"Dunno. Nobody's ever found anything like it that I know of, and I been on this end of the lake all my life." His ring gleamed as he pushed his hair away from his eyes. "The sacks of whisky must of hung up on it as they drifted along the bottom. The currents can run pretty good out here."

It made sense. The sonar showed the bottom to be flat and featureless, except for the slight mound and the projecting snout of the cannon that had attracted her attention in the first place.

"That would mean they'll be draped around it on both sides, in the direction of the prevailing current."

"Yup. It probably runs south to north at this end of the lake."

She could hardly keep her enthusiasm at bay. "We'll need a pro. Somebody who really knows about working on the bottom. That gun will weigh a lot."

Sheik waved in the general direction of Oswego. "The Port Authority has a diver on the grain elevator job. Every morning he goes down to check the cribs to make sure they aren't being damaged by the demolition work. Maybe we could hire him to take a look."

"I hate to trust a stranger with something like this," Laurel said. "What if he tells people?"

"Whyn't you go in tomorrow and have a gander at the guy. If he seems all right, see if he's interested in a small salvage job, one or two dives at the most. If he is, bring him out to the hotel and we'll all have a talk with him, kinda size him up before we tell him anything important."

Laurel nodded. "I can't wait to see Grampa Jake's face when we show him what we found."

"I'll have to sweat rotgut out of him every morning for the next year."

She laughed. "I can hear him now," and sang, "Hap-py days are here a-gain..."

A FEW MILES AWAY

Romy Zaia considered the eastern end of Lake Ontario "his" territory, so he took a closer look when he spotted the Twice Told's Boston Whaler. He could see no one aboard, and a flag bobbed near the boat, a red square with a diagonal white line signifying divers in the water. Goddamn people over there had more money than brains. What were they doing anchored out here, five miles from Stony Point?

The Eastlands were enemies from way back. His grandfather Emilio had ranted about how an Eastland killed his father and caused him to lose his hand.

Today, Romy was headed to Canada to drop off the two hundred cases of cigarettes stowed in the cabin of his forty-foot workboat. He'd bought the boat for peanuts, salvaged it off the bottom after it sank in a storm, rebuilt the engines, the whole thing. It was slow, and ugly too, but solid work platforms were hard to find, and it was his most valuable possession by far.

His current speed would put him at Collins Point, Ontario, shortly after dark. Darkness was required because what he planned was not quite legal. In fact, the Canadian authorities considered it downright illegal. The cigarettes came from US government PXs, or post exchanges, and had neither federal nor state tax stamps attached, to say nothing of the import duty taxes the Canadian government imposed.

Romy stood to make a profit of fifteen dollars US per case, or three thousand for the load. In return, he risked jail time in both Canada and the US. He wasn't concerned. He'd made dozens of trips and never had a lick of trouble.

He recorded the reading on his GPS and searched for a landmark on the limestone bluffs that formed the shoreline at this end of the lake. Finding one, he sighted across the Whaler from his current position, and noted the compass heading. He needed one more sighting in order to triangulate the Whaler's position. A minute later, he had it. With the information he now had, he could put his boat close to the spot the Twice Told's Whaler now occupied. Maybe he'd stop on his way home and take a peek. Where there was smoke you could usually find a fire.

OSWEGO HARBOR

Mike McKean had plenty of time before his final dive. Good thing the demolition crew didn't work on Sunday. Last night, he'd had dinner at Char Stone's, their third date.

More important at the moment, the date made him late starting his nightly routine and it had been almost four A.M. before he finally got off to sleep, or passed out—whatever.

He stretched out on the afterdeck of the workboat, feet up. His head felt swollen now, but by noon or a little after, the effects would fade and he'd be a hundred percent.

Odd how his body had become used to the whisky. Now he needed a third of a bottle between dinner and bedtime or the price would be a sleepless night. The rest of the time, he was completely sober—except for days like this when something interrupted his normal routine.

"Excuse me. Are you Mr. McKean?"

Mike opened his eyes. A woman stood at the edge of the pier above him. She was lean, twenty-five or so, with sandy blond hair the sun had bleached out. Unremarkable, except for a spot of blush in the middle of her cheek that made her seem familiar somehow. She wore a blouse and slacks, with leather shoes.

He stood and moved closer, until her knees were roughly at eye level. "Yes, I'm McKean. What can I do for you?"

"I have a short job. It involves one, maybe two dives in seventy-five feet of water on the open lake."

It was the twenty-eighth of September, late in the season. Tomorrow was his last day on this job. He was ready for a few months on layoff.

"What's the job?" He asked to be courteous, knowing he wasn't interested.

"I'm sorry... I'm not able to give details just yet, but—"

Mike's head throbbed. "If you can't tell me, send the person who can.

I'll talk to him." It was hard to think straight this early. He started to turn away.

"Excuse me. You didn't allow me to finish, *Mister* McKean. Or is this the way you treat *all* women?"

Her words sliced through him like a shiver on a winter morning. He stopped, faced her again. Her eyes flashed emerald darts.

He held up his hands in surrender.

"Okay." It couldn't hurt to listen. "Go ahead and finish."

The woman stared down at him, lips pursed. When she spoke again the emotion present earlier was gone.

"My friend wants to talk with you about the job. He's older, in his nineties, and he's been ill, so he couldn't come in person. He sent me to see if you were interested, and if so to bring you to him."

"I see. Sorry about that, before." He motioned toward where he'd been standing.

She didn't defrost a bit, and her tone reflected the chill. "It's two thousand an hour, bottom time. Are you interested or not?"

Damn good money.

His logical mind said, "Illegal." Still, there was something about her and he wanted more time to figure out what.

"I might be," he heard himself say.

"Are you free now?"

"All day."

"Good. I'll drive you. The car is over there." She pointed toward a new Chevy Blazer with the words "Twice Told Hotel" on the door.

As the woman drove, Mike surveyed her from the corner of his eye. Her skin was smooth and clear. He could detect no makeup, but a hint of scent drifted his way. Woodsy.

He liked it. "Is it all right for me to know your name?"

"Laurel Kingsford."

"We're going to this Twice Told hotel?"

She glanced his way, then back at the road. "Yes. It's about twelve miles east, at Mexico Point."

Mike took care not to exhale in her direction. Alcohol could stay on your breath longer than you thought. He remained tense and they drove the rest of the way in silence.

The hotel lay at the end of a private drive, right on the lakeshore, a solid four-story structure of dark brown brick with muted green trim. She pulled into a parking area along the west side and parked in front of a row of small bungalows adjacent to the main structure.

There was an entrance on the side, but she led him to the front where a wide, carpeted stairway led up to an equally wide veranda. They went up. The veranda offered a great view of the lake, and just to the far side, the mouth of a good-sized river where it emptied into the lake

"Hey. This is a nice spot."

"Yes. Mr. Eastland built it during the Depression when so many men were out of work." Her voice carried a note of pride. "Have a seat. I'll go see where he is." She indicated one of the all-weather upholstered chairs. Moments later she returned with an old man and introduced him to Mike as Mister Eastland.

"McKean. McKean..." Mr. Eastland repeated the name, staring off into the distance. "Somehow that name rings a bell." He shook his head, trying to place it.

"It might, for someone your age."

Eastland's gaze locked on Mike. "Why do you say that?"

"During the twenties, my great grandfather was stationed here in Oswego. He was in the Coast Guard."

The old man walloped the table with the palm of his hand. Everything on it jumped. "I knew it!" His eyes sparked with intensity. "I see him in you; Bosun's Mate Marvin McKean, the scourge of rum runners all over the eastern end of the lake."

Mike was proud of his family tradition, and pleased to meet someone who knew about it. "From what I've heard, he had a sixth sense, a gift for catching smugglers red-handed."

The old man laughed. "He was good, all right." He let his head loll back and closed his eyes as if in the midst of a fond memory. Then he sat forward and peered at Mike. "Let me tell you a secret." He leaned forward, motioning for them to come closer.

Laurel and Mike moved in unison. His arm brushed hers and they both flinched as a sharp discharge of static resulted from the contact.

"Oops," Mike joked. "We're electric."

She pressed her lips together without responding.

Mister Eastland said, "It was the first night I ran booze. I was just twenty. We were sneaking up to the shore near Nine Mile when a spotlight clicked on and lit us up like a Broadway stage. I swear, I remember the sound the switch made across the water before the light came up. The guy was just sitting there with his lights off, waiting for us like he knew we were coming." He pointed at Mike. "It was your granddaddy. He chased us up the lake to near Stony Point. We could only get one engine to start, so he caught up to us and we jettisoned the load."

Mr. Eastland straightened and looked around, as if checking for eavesdroppers, then leaned forward again.

"What if I was to tell you," his intense eyes locked on Mike's, "we want you to go down and retrieve what's left of that load? How'd that be for things coming full circle?"

The old boy was off his rocker. Mike gave an emphatic shake of his head. "Nah. No way any of it's still intact. What is it, seventy-five years?"

Mister Eastland tipped his head toward Sheik, who jumped up and hurried away. A minute later he came back with a bottle and handed it to Mike.

"Careful, Mr. McKean," Sheik gestured with his left hand. "That glass is real old. Might be brittle. We don't know for sure."

Handling the bottle as if it were a large egg, Mike held it up to the light.

"Go ahead, open it," Eastland said.

Mike grasped the cap and twisted. Bits of the edges of the metal cap disintegrated in his hand and a small rush of gas escaped the bottle. The rank-sweet odor of raw whisky filled the air for a moment before being wafted away by the afternoon breeze. He held the open bottle to his nose and sniffed.

He leaned his head away, wrinkling his nostrils. "Phew! It sure smells strong." He was used to the hard stuff, but nothing like this.

"Yeah, but the proof is in the tastin'," Sheik said, his voice eager. He slapped shot glasses down all around, and took the bottle from Mike. Holding it by its body, he filled four glasses to the rim, ignoring the embossed white ring. Putting the bottle down, Sheik raised his glass, extending it forward.

Laurel Kingsford lifted hers, poising it an inch or so from Sheik's. Her eyes met Mike's head-on. Was she challenging him? Mike raised his glass.

Mister Eastland said, "To my load of Corby's Special Whisky, and the divers who found it on the bottom yesterday. Bottoms up!" The four of them clinked glasses, sloshing not a little of the fuselious nectar over the edges. The old man placed his to his lips and threw his head back, tossing the shot into his mouth, swallowing. Sheik did the same. Laurel Kingsford belted hers down too, showing no outward signs of aftereffect.

Mike poured the raw spirits into his mouth and swallowed. Fire burned its way to his stomach. This was nothing like the aged Jack Daniel's he'd pampered his stomach lining with for the past two years.

"Aaaagh!" he gasped, clutching his throat. He could actually feel the stuff corroding a new passage through the walls of his esophagus as it migrated downward toward his stomach. How could they drink this garbage with so little reaction?

Eastland held his glass up and studied it.

"You know, Sheik, I think this one is a little bit smoother than the last batch we found." His voice was just a bit hoarse.

"No doubt about it," Sheik croaked. "My taste buds never lie, not about whisky."

"That's the worst liquor I ever tasted," Mike rasped when his eyes stopped watering and he could speak again. "Why bother searching for it?"

Silence, and a complete lack of movement around the table followed his question.

Eastland answered after a few seconds. "Sentimental value, son.

Besides, you get a taste for it after a while." He touched his throat beside his Adam's apple with his fingertips, as if feeling for the pulse. His eyes caught Laurel's for a moment. His cheeks and neck were pale.

"Who brought this one up?" Mike asked. As far as he was concerned, whoever had could go back and finish the job without him.

Sheik tapped his chest. "Laurel and I did. Laurel will be your dive partner after you join us."

Mike glanced at the woman, then at Sheik. Not much chance of him diving with a STROKE in *this* lifetime. STROKE was an insider term for a person who dives without proper knowledge or intelligence. Diving with such a person was even more dangerous than diving alone.

"How'd you find it?" He directed the question to Sheik.

"Oh. I didn't. I was just backup. You know, in case something happened. Laurel found it. She got this underwater radar, then she made up a grid and we worked our way along until we found the can…" He stopped, his eyes shifting between Jake and Laurel.

The woman's face didn't show anything.

This time he addressed her. "Side scan?"

She shrugged. Her cheeks had the same rosy spot he'd noticed earlier.

"Where'd you learn that technology?"

"National Oceanic and Atmospheric Administration. I spent two summers at Woods Hole during college. Since then, they've asked me to do a three- or four-week project with them each year. I make those my vacation weeks."

Oops. NOAA had their pick of the best. He squirmed in his chair. "They do great work there."

She gazed at him without comment.

Having failed to so much as chip her ice shield, he turned to Mr. Eastland.

"So, I take it you are the rightful owner, and the project is to bring up as much of the lost load as possible."

The old fellow didn't answer. He was locked in silent communication with Laurel.

Then she turned to Mike again, her eyes cold.

"Where did you learn to dive?"

Okay, she wanted bona fides.

"At the Navy dive school in New London. I went through the Coast Guard Academy."

"How long were you in the Coast Guard?"

He kept his tone matter-of-fact. "Twelve years."

Her eyes bored into his. "Why did you leave?"

"Personal reasons." He matched her gaze.

Her eyes flickered toward the old man. After several seconds, Eastland's head moved a fraction of an inch and he smiled at Mike. "Yes Mike, the booze is mine. That makes the dive one hundred percent legal, but the booze is just part of it. There's something else down there."

He lifted a book from his lap and tossed it onto the table. A Bible, covered in black cowhide, the edges of each page gilded reddish gold.

"Now, Mister Michael McKean, we won't ask you to break any laws. If somehow we do run afoul of the law during this project, this oath of honor won't be binding with respect to that part of our relationship. Please put your right hand on the Bible."

Mike blinked in surprise. A confidentiality agreement he'd expected. Two thousand an hour was serious money. But this? A Bible to swear on? Well, he would have signed an agreement. Why not go ahead and swear not to tell?

He hadn't touched a Bible since his early teens. The dimpled texture of the leather beneath his fingers brought back memories.

"Do you swear to keep the secrets we are about to share, and promise never to reveal them, or any others you might learn in the course of your work with us?"

There was more to this dive than whisky. What could it be?

"I swear."

"Good." Jake Eastland reached over and clapped him on the shoulder. "If you have half the pluck your great granddaddy did, you'll be plenty enough man for us." He dropped a packet of photos on the table. "What do you think of these?"

Mike opened the package and removed the photographs. They were underwater shots, taken with a flash from varying distances, of a branch-like object projecting maybe two feet from the bottom. One of them was taken with the hand of another diver extended next to it, adding perspective. He guessed the object at nine inches in diameter at the lakebed. There were several shots taken from directly above. These caused Mike to do a double take.

There was a definite roundness to the end. Whatever it was, it was man made. My God! A *cannon*! Had they found a wreck? His interest in the job quadrupled.

He scanned the faces around the table. "We'll need a sand gun and some high-capacity lifting slings. Let's see, this thing might weigh as much as two thousand pounds. We'll need a couple thousand pounds of lift… better double that."

"Why so much?" Sheik asked.

"There might be more than one down there. It must have been jammed or you could have brought it up, right?"

Sheik and Laurel exchanged glances. They both nodded.

"There could even be a wreck right there, beneath this spot, or nearby."

Laurel's voice carried a note of certainty. "There's no wreck there. The bottom is flat as a pancake all around the site."

"Good. That makes your find abandoned property. The Law of Finds says we can bring it up and it'll be ours. Let me see, we'll need…" He hesitated, feeling a bit awkward all of a sudden. "Just jump in when you have something to add." No one said a thing. Mike smiled at them and went back to building a plan.

Laurel drove the diver back to his boat. They'd decided to meet at the hotel the following Sunday. Meanwhile, she would acquire the equipment and materials he'd listed.

After a few miles, he cleared his throat, "Ah, M-Miss Kingsford. I'm sorry about getting off on the wrong foot like I did. I promise to work with you like any other pro."

She kept her eyes on the road. "Thanks for that."

His breath no longer reeked of leftover alcohol. He was handsome. So what? A silence began that stretched for the rest of the trip.

A woman waited near his workboat when they arrived. When she saw Laurel, her face darkened and her foot tapped the pavement. After they stopped, she approached Laurel's side and peered in. Then she spun on her heel and stalked back over to the workboat. She was a big woman, tall and wide but well formed, with the look of a body builder.

Laurel kept her voice neutral. "Your friend seems to be angry. You should have told me someone was waiting. We could have come sooner." The big woman had her hands parked on her hips. "Is she always this hostile?"

He gave a little shrug. "Beats me. I didn't know she'd be waiting. We've dated a few times." He stepped out of the Blazer, then stooped to look inside. "I meant what I said about working together."

She motioned for him to close his door. When he did, she put the car in gear and drove away. In the rear view mirror, she saw the woman approach Mike and slip her arm through his.

Sure, he was great looking, but as long as he showed up for work sober and did his job, that was all she cared about. For the rest, the weight lifter was welcome to him.

TWICE TOLD HOTEL

Jake watched as his granddaughter left to drive Michael McKean back to town. McKean. Now *there* was a memory.

Sheik went inside to use the facilities, leaving him alone on the veranda. No one in sight. Why not? Jake filled his shot glass to the rim from the bottle he'd thrown overboard that night in 1925, hoisted it between thumb and index finger, and threw it back. He actually enjoyed the harsh taste and the feel as it burned down his throat and dribbled into his gut like hot oil.

Two shots inside an hour. A strictly forbidden pleasure these days. Corby's Special, straight from Belleville on the Bay of Quinte in Ontario. The whisky made his gut warm and he sat back in the chair and let the late afternoon sun comfort him.

Sixty-seven thousand cases. That was how much he'd brought in after he left Bruce and went out on his own, more than anybody else at this end of the lake by far. Getting started was the hard part. If he lived another ninety years he'd still never forget the look on the face of—what was his name?—Sills. Yes, Sills, the sales manager at Corby's on the day Bruce introduced them the first time.

CORBY'S DISTILLERY

Belleville, Ontario | Fall, 1925

"John, I'd like you to meet my friend Jake Eastland. Jake, this is John Sills." Jake and Bruce were in the office of the Vice President in charge of sales for Corby Distilleries.

Sills extended his hand. "Pleased to meet you, young man." He wore a mildly amused expression.

Jake gripped the older man's hand and gave it a solid shake. "Call me Jake," he said with all the confidence he could muster. He'd dressed in his best suit and shoes for the occasion. Ten hundred-dollar bills were tucked in his vest pocket.

Sills sat behind his desk. "Yes then, have a seat Mr. Eastland. What can we do for you this morning?"

Jake fought to keep the eagerness out of his voice. "I'm in the import-export business. I'd like to establish a business relationship with you. I expect to be buying as much as five hundred cases, in time, I hope as often as three times a week."

Sills' eyebrows went up. "Well, now, five hundred cases." His expression conveyed amused incredulity. "You understand we require a deposit equivalent to the largest order you place with us?"

"I do."

"That comes to, let's see, yes, eighteen thousand dollars." Sills pronounced the numbers as if each were a battering ram.

Jake leaned forward and slapped his money down in front of the man. "I'll start by placing one thousand dollars with you and taking delivery of twenty-five cases of Corby's Special."

Sills sniffed. "Twenty-five cases is not large enough an order for us to consider on a factory direct basis, young man." He stood again. "I suggest you speak to a wholesaler. And now, if you don't mind…"

"Give the boy a chance, John," Bruce said. "Remember what you told me when I first started?"

John Sills hesitated. "As I recall, I remember thinking you'd be lucky to last two weeks."

Bruce said, "And then?"

Sills conceded the point. "And then you made yourself into one of my top customers."

He turned back to Jake. "Very well, we'll give you a try. Twenty-five cases against a deposit of one thousand dollars." He wrote a receipt. "A boxcar will be at the government dock at six tomorrow morning with your shipment. Just show this to the dockmaster." He held out a sales order marked 'paid.' "But mind you, if you don't at least double your order each time you make a purchase, the deal's off. Understand? You come back here again, you buy fifty cases or no sale."

Jake took the paper. "Thank you, Mr. Sills. I expect to see you again soon."

Sills had already turned his attention to the work on his desk. "Yes, yes. I suppose you do," he said without looking up. "Just remember the conditions."

On the way back to Belleville, Jake said, "What a pompous stuffed-shirt that guy is."

Bruce threw his head back and laughed, then clapped him on the shoulder. "Wait till you're buying five hundred cases at a clip. He'll kiss your royal red arse for you then. Eh?"

Two mornings later, Jake left the Belleville docks. He navigated with skill, staying in deep water, and proceeded at a speed of three knots through the Bay, heading down to the open lake. A person observing would have seen a fishing boat towing her nets, an everyday sight.

By six that afternoon he arrived at Indian Point, which marked the entrance of Prince Edward Bay, and later led to the open lake. He tucked into Prinyer's Cove on the north side of the point and dropped the anchor. There, he spent the night, safe from the elements.

Dawn produced another sparkling September day and he left the anchorage shortly after daybreak. By ten he'd skirted Main Duck Island and by three-thirty neared his destination on the U.S. coast. He'd chosen Catfish Creek, two miles west of Mexico Point, as his drop-off spot because a family Jake had known since childhood, and whose sons he had schooled with, owned the land. The farmhouse sat just west of the creek outlet, about two hundred yards from the high-water mark and visible from the lake. It made a perfect signal platform.

From a mile offshore, he inspected the house. The shades in the four upstairs bedroom windows were up, the all-quiet signal. Jake eased the boat toward shore until he found the sand bar in fifteen feet of water. He gunned the engine and dragged the net he towed, the net filled with bottles of whisky, up onto the bar.

He put the engine in neutral and dropped the anchor. The bow swung into the gentle northwest breeze. Moving to the gunwale, he put pressure on the winch handle until the gears cleared the stop pawl, flipped the pawl up, and let the winch handle rotate, releasing the net.

He moved to the fantail, untied the other end, tied the two ends together in a square knot, attached a small blackened cork tied to a piece of fishing line, and dropped the whole works into the water. The cork bobbed on the surface, marking the spot.

Jake hauled up the anchor, and when he had drifted clear of the net on the bottom, put his engine in gear and went home, his first load delivered without a hitch.

He'd done it! His plan had worked, he was on his way, never to be poor again.

The next day he met Slim, his buyer, at the Ferris Hotel.

"The load is ready. Twenty-five cases. It's on the sand bar just west of Catfish Creek. Look for a black cork float."

"Good. We're runnin' real short. This'll tide us over for a coupla days."

"Do you have the money?"

"Bet your ass. Got it right here." Slim checked the room through slitted eyes before reaching into his breast pocket. He took out a wad of cash and handed it to Jake. "Twenty-one hundred. It's all there."

A wad of bills an inch thick, fifties and hundreds. His heart going a mile a minute, Jake folded it in half and jammed it into his pocket. He'd just made a profit of one thousand two hundred dollars.

He stood. "Next load will be sixty cases. It'll be ready in a few days."

That night, when he counted the money, he was short fifty dollars. "The son of a bitch cheated me." He spoke the words aloud. That Slim had so little respect for him stung more than the loss of the money. Something had to be done about it right away.

When he left Mexico Point at four the next morning, rain kept him company and by the time he arrived in Belleville at noon, everything was soaked. He hired a hack and visited the distillery.

John Sills' secretary remembered his name. "Well, if it isn't Mr. Eastland." She stood as he entered the outer office. The sign on her desk said "Corinne." She had dimples in each cheek. "Mr. Sills is out today, but he has assigned one of our sales representatives to work with you. Why don't you have a seat while I page him?" She flashed her dimples at Jake.

So, Sills was handing him to some underling. Jake didn't feel in the least insulted. He wanted them to sell him the whisky, didn't give a hoot who did it, either.

Several minutes later, a young man in shirtsleeves strode into the room. Spotting Jake, he held out his hand. "You must be Mr. Eastland. I'm Walter Collins. Why don't we go to my office?"

Walter Collins led the way down the long hall. Jake waved goodbye to Corinne and followed. Halfway down, his host stopped and held his arm to the left at the entrance to his office. They passed through the doorway into a large room divided into four cubicles by moveable screens. A secretary sat in the common area of the four offices. Apparently, the workers in each cubicle shared the secretary, a male with a sallow complexion and receding hair.

Seated, Collins said, "Mr. Sills has asked me to handle your account. Are you here to make a purchase?"

Jake nodded his affirmation.

"Very good. Let's see here," Collins opened a ledger with little more than a few entries at the top of the first page. "Okay, you purchased twenty-five cases of 'Special Blend' three days ago. You'll need to buy at least fifty according to Mr. Sills' notes."

"I'll take sixty." Jake couldn't keep the quiver of victory out of his voice.

Collins did some quick math. "That works out to two thousand one hundred sixty dollars at thirty-six dollars a case."

Jake leaned forward. "How about a little quantity discount? The price at twenty-five cases was thirty-six dollars. What is it for sixty cases?"

"The same. It's government-controlled, you know."

"Oh!" Jake shook his head. "I didn't know. What about the hundred dollars I had left over last time? I deposited a thousand and only used nine hundred."

Collins ran his finger over the ledger and nodded. "You're right, of course. Please forgive me, I'm just seeing these numbers for the first time."

"When will it be ready at the siding?"

Walter Collins snapped his fingers. "Sixty cases? You can have that tonight. We keep a loaded car on the siding all the time."

For the first time in his dealings with the distillery, Jake's temper stirred. Sills had made him wait overnight, when there had been a car there all along. Without ceremony, he counted twenty hundred-dollar bills and placed them on the desk.

"That should leave forty dollars on deposit for the next load." He waited for his receipt and the sales order, thanked his new contact at Corby's, and left the office.

Two days later, he met Slim in the bar of the Ferris Hotel and received an envelope containing five thousand forty dollars.

When he counted it at home, it was short seventy-five dollars. Jake didn't mind. Two of the cases he left for Slim contained water, not whisky. That made them just about even.

He went fishing. For three days he sold his catch to a market on the Varick Canal, which ran along the West Side of the Oswego River, earning twelve dollars, and establishing his bona fides as just another fisherman. Then he made another run, bringing in a hundred and forty cases.

Whatever else happened, Slim got the message. This time, the count was spot on. Jake now had over eleven thousand dollars, a wad of cash several inches thick. If the plan continued to work, he'd soon be handling as much as forty thousand dollars two or three times a week. He decided to talk to Bruce about it.

On his next trip, he stopped in Kingston. Bruce wasn't in town but Jake hung around, figuring it wouldn't be long before he showed up. Late in the afternoon of the second day, he heard the familiar sound of his mentor's laughter. Moments later Bruce came bursting into the bar.

He pumped Jake's hand. "Jake! I heard you were in town. How are ya, kid?".

"Okay. I made three runs so far and not a sign of trouble."

Bruce's brows lifted in surprise. "Great! What's your secret?"

Jake deadpanned him. "It's still a secret."

"Aha! I knew it. You've dreamed up some new angle." Bruce clapped him on the shoulder with his rock hard hand. "Out with it."

"I've been watching the Coast Guard. They almost never go out in the daytime. They leave at dusk and patrol all night. I don't think they have enough men to patrol in the daytime too."

Bruce stared at Jake for several seconds, eyes narrowed. Then he shook his head. "No. You wouldn't be dumb enough to take it across during daylight. You've got to be doing something else."

"I wanted to talk to you about something."

"Oh? What's that?"

"I've got over ten thousand on me. I'm worried about getting robbed."

Bruce checked to see if anyone had overheard. "You *are* batty! For ten thousand bucks I'd knock you over myself."

"I don't know how else to do it. How did you?"

Bruce lifted his omnipresent fedora and scratched his head before patting it into position again.

"I don't know. Earl always handled that part of it for me." Bruce had worked for Earl before branching out on his own. "I know," he brightened. "Let's go talk to him. He lives a few blocks away."

Earl McCune was a tall, ruddy man in his sixties with a brusque way about him.

"I suppose I could, sonny. What's in it for me?"

The hostile overtone got Jake's dander up. "I'll be glad to pay for *good* advice. How much do you want?"

"What's it worth to you?"

"Fifty dollars."

"You sure you got fifty dollars, sonny?"

Jake reached into his pocket and pulled out a wad of cash.

"What's this look like?"

McCune's attitude did an about-face. "C'mon up on the porch, sonny, take a load off your feet, and put that away."

"My name is Jake, not sonny."

"Jake it is. Come on, boy. Fifty won't buy you all day."

Once they were settled, McCune tapped his pipe on an ashtray and fished a pouch of tobacco from his breast pocket.

"What you want to do is start a company to buy the whisky." He dipped his pipe into the bag to scoop up the fragrant blend. "Next, you have your buyers deposit their payments into the company account." He packed tobacco into the bowl with his thumb and pointed at Jake with the stem. "You have the bank issue a 'Teller's Check' in the amount of your transaction, and you pay for the whisky with that."

"Will the distillery accept that form of payment?"

Earl struck a match on the sole of his shoe and held it to the pipe. "They'll take all the teller's checks you want to give them." Puffs of sweet-smelling smoke emitted from his mouth.

"Later, when you have more money than you need for a load, have the bank issue a 'Letter of Credit' in an amount the size of your biggest purchase. You send it to the distillery. After that, the distillery will take your personal check. Got it?"

"Got it," Jake stood and stuck out his hand. "Thanks, Mr. McCune. You've been a great help."

"You forget somethin'?"

Jake dug in his pocket and came up with a fifty-dollar bill.

McCune clapped Jake on the shoulder as he fingered the brand new fifty. "Quite a lad you've got here, Bruce."

"If he can stay out of trouble." Bruce sounded worried.

McCune locked eyes with Jake. "Can you, son?"

Jake shrugged. "We'll see."

October arrived and with it the season of northwest gales. Jake did the best he could to pick good weather for his runs, but summer was over. Good conditions were far less frequent now.

This load, the full five hundred cases, would mark the breakout for Eastland Associates. If he could get it across the lake safe, he'd have forty-two thousand dollars, more than twice the cost of a full load. Afterward, for the first time, he wouldn't be risking every penny he had each time he crossed the lake.

Corby's, in response to demand from the many "exporters" operating from the docks in Belleville, had introduced cardboard cases, each with several three-inch holes, side, top, and bottom. The bottles came cushioned in excelsior and wrapped in enough lead to assure they wouldn't float. The cardboard held up well enough, even to several days of submersion, but with two-hundred-fifty cases in six nets, three on either side, the natural motion of Jake's boat would be dampened. If the lake should kick up while they transited the thirty miles of open water between Main Duck and Mexico Point, it would be slower to rise. Waves would come aboard. Breakage was also a factor. If it got too rough, even the wood shavings wouldn't prevent breakage.

Survival on the lake meant paying attention to the small things. Before he left for the run, he went over his boat inch by inch. He caulked every seam, sealed every hatch, and made sure the engine would stay dry no matter how much water came aboard. Next, he disassembled the bilge pump.

Good thing he did. The leathers were rotted. He replaced them. In its former condition, the pump wouldn't have lasted five minutes in hard usage.

Last, he recruited two helpers. Sean and Tom Neal were farm boys, both of them older than Jake, hungry for work, but green when it came to being on the water. Jake brought them aboard one at a time and showed them every piece of equipment on the boat, discussed its function, showed them how it worked and had each of them operate it. Tom, the oldest, had a knack for it all.

When he had satisfied himself they'd be able to function under normal conditions, they went across to Belleville.

The trip north proceeded smoothly, as did the loading, but during the run south on the Bay of Quinte, signs of change appeared; a slate-gray overcast slipped in from the southeast, and a sullen feel with it. The wind disappeared altogether. When they rounded Indian Point the lake surface to the south resembled glass. Weather might be coming, but if it held off a few more hours they could be safely home. Jake decided to make the run.

An hour later they cleared Main Duck·Island and entered the lake proper. The overcast thickened and it began to rain and then, in less than half an hour, the wind swung to the west and went from calm to a hard blow. Too soon, eight-foot waves sluiced aboard from aft the starboard side, washing the deck before draining through the scuppers.

Sean, the younger brother, turned a pasty shade of gray and found his way to the leeward rail, tossing his lunch over the side. He bent over for a long time. Afterward, Jake sat him down and gave him a blanket.

The waves stacked up until they were ten and twelve feet high. As each swept past, the deck went awash beneath as much as two feet of water. The boat couldn't lift her stern to the waves fast enough.

Jake grasped Tom's arm. "Go below and see how much water we're taking." Tom disappeared into the forward cabin. A moment later his head popped up. "Holy mackerel! There's water everywhere."

"Go aft and see about the engine compartment."

Tom returned after a minute. "She's wet, but not too bad yet."

"How many gallons, about?"

"Fifty or a hundred. It's splashing the engine when we roll."

Not good. The deck had to be leaking when the waves came aboard. There was still a long, long way to go.

"Get your brother on the bilge pump. Tell him if he doesn't pump fast enough, he'll need to learn to swim in about fifteen minutes."

A fierce gust tried to lay the boat over on its side, but the suspended whisky stabilized them, preventing the roll. Jake did not like the way that felt. Things could not continue this way. The wind would probably die around sunset. If he could hold position for a few hours they might be all right. He turned to port, intending to head into the waves so the higher bow could lift to meet them.

A yell came from aft. "Jesus! Look out!"

To starboard, a huge wave loomed.

Jake screamed, "Close the engine hatch."

Tom slammed the hatch and the wave tripped and broke, foaming right into the boat, pressing them almost entirely below the surface. Too slowly, the water drained away.

Through his feet, Jake felt the engine falter. There was no time. They were broadside to the waves, trapped. Another wave came aboard, not so large, but still dangerous. He fought his way out of the deckhouse.

Tom crouched nearby, holding on for dear life. "Tom, we're dropping the load. Get the salt blocks, quick."

Jake scrambled to untie the lines securing the nets to the boat. Tom ran forward, hanging on to the rail to stay aboard, returning with the blocks.

"Sorry, lost one. What do I do with the other?"

"Tie it to this net. Make sure it doesn't foul."

When Tom finished, Jake let the lines slide until they were sure to run smoothly then released them. With a snicking sound, both disappeared over the side. A hollow sensation yawned in the pit of his stomach. He'd just sent his breakout load to the bottom.

He smiled at Tom. "Pray the water is less than three hundred feet deep."

That was how much string the salt buoy held. Three hundred feet. The salt would dissolve in the fresh water. In a day or so the cork would float to the surface, marking the spot. Good in theory, but too many things could go wrong. Jake didn't want to think about them.

He found two reference points on the Canadian shore and wrote down the compass heading to both. Then he spun the wheel and headed south. With the load gone, the boat rode easily and the pump soon had her empty.

Slim Carroway waved his arms. "You lost the whole load? What about my hundred cases? Without the friggin' booze I'm outta business."

Jake tried to calm his associate. "There's no guarantees in this kind of operation, Slim. You know that."

"I'm sorry, Jake. I like doin' business with ya' but I'll have to take my business to that other guy from over Port Ontario way. He's been sniffing around, promising better prices. It's nothin' personal, Jake, it's business. He stood and headed for the door of the Ferris Wheel. "Sorry kid, see you around."

The slap of the screen door, and Sheik's reappearance, interrupted the stream of memories. A strong gust ruffled Sheik's fluffy white hair as he eyed the level of whisky in the bottle, then cocked an eyebrow at Jake.

"Okay, Hawkeye, so I had another snort. Sue me," Jake said.

"You know you ain't supposed to drink, Jake. That stuff'll kill you." Sheik touched the squat bottle, let his fingers trace the letters cast in relief into the glass. "On the other hand, nobody told me not to go ahead and tip a few if I feel like it."

He poured himself a healthy dollop, and after sampling the aroma of the liquid, held the shot glass to the light for several seconds, then touched it to his lips and downed it. The way he savored each moment lent the process an almost religious solemnity.

"Ahhh!" He plopped the glass down after the liquid was on its way to his stomach. "I'm gonna miss the taste a this stuff after I die."

Jake smiled. Sheik wouldn't be going anywhere for a while. He wasn't so sure about himself. He breathed the fresh air, savoring it. Inside the dining room, the tables offering the best view of the water were being set up for the few diners who would come. There would be a nice sunset tonight.

"You know, Jake, Laurel seemed different around that guy. You notice how straight she sat, they way she kept her hands in her lap like a kid at Sunday school? She hardly let out a peep the whole time he was here."

Jake *had* noticed, although her behavior hadn't really registered on him as significant. She usually had plenty to say, bossy almost. Today, she'd let him do all the talking.

"Yeah, now you mention it, I did. Why do you think she did that?"

Sheik tapped his ring on the rim of the empty shot glass, making it ring. Good crystal. "Maybe she didn't like the guy."

Maybe just the opposite. She thought men didn't find her feminine enough. Had he just witnessed his granddaughter's concept of "being feminine"?

That had to be it. She probably didn't even realize she was attracted to the guy. He watched as Sheik's fingertips inched toward the bottle of whisky.

"No. I don't think that's it. I think she *does* like him. I bet that's why."

Sheik's fingers stopped short of the bottle and he leaned forward, his expression serious. "I dunno if I like that. I think maybe the guy's a boozer. I smelled it on him when I first sat down."

"You sure?" Now Jake didn't like the idea either.

"It's like my father used to say..."

Sheik's father had kept a tavern for years. "What's that?"

"Booze on his breath 'fore noon, drunk all over again pretty soon."

At 2:15 Sunday afternoon, the fifth of October, exactly a week after he signed on to dive for Jake Eastland, Mike McKean slowed, changed lanes, and eased onto the off ramp leading to the Weedsport exit of the New York State Thruway. The day was cold and blustery. A steady rain had dogged him for the entire three-hour trip from Buffalo.

After paying the toll, he turned north toward Oswego. The leaves were beginning to change, and the further north he went the more color he saw in the surrounding landscape.

He hummed along with the radio, his passage barely stirring sodden leaves that had come to rest along the edges of the roadway. His initial enthusiasm for the project had given way to serious reservations: the season far from ideal, his fellow diver less than a friend. She'd said no ship, just the gun. If it was true, raising it would be okay. But if there was a wreck, he'd be breaking the law by taking anything off it.

What was it about Laurel Kingsford? In a flash it came to him: the spot of blush in her cheeks. Mary had blushed exactly the same way the first time they met.

Without warning, Mary's face appeared, ephemeral, present just long enough for him to see her fiery red hair, the points of red in her cheeks, but not long enough to… to reach out and touch. He blinked away grief that remained too ready, too near the surface.

The ache of living without her heavy on him again, he rolled down the window and a blast of wind and cold swirled into the cab, wetting his face and shoulders until he shivered. There would be no whisky tonight to ease his pain. He didn't like the fact that his drinking time seemed to be taking over as the center of his existence. It didn't really help in the long run, anyway. He hadn't had a drop since he met Laurel Kingsford. Not because of her, but because for reasons he didn't fully understand, he didn't want it anymore.

He closed the window, forced his mind to take another line of thought. The empty road stretched before him. For a long time the ache lingered in his throat.

Laurel lay curled up on the sofa in the bungalow behind the hotel, reading. The small fire she'd laid warded off most of the chill, but not all. She had her comforter, about the only personal possession she'd unpacked, and which she kept over the backrest of the sofa, spread over her feet and lower legs.

Her eyelids drooped. It would be so deliciously decadent to lie back and take a nice nap, right in the middle of the afternoon, a thing she could not remember doing even once during her years in New York.

Outside, a vehicle splashed through the puddles of the parking lot and nosed into a spot near her door. Curious, she got up and crossed the room. Standing on tiptoe, she peeked through the small window positioned high in the door.

Hard rain poured straight down, drumming against the roof of a black pickup. The diver, Mike, opened the door and climbed out. He wore a yellow rain hat, the type with the wide brim all around, and he spread a jacket of the same color over his shoulders before dashing across the lot toward the rear of the restaurant. He took the steps two at a time and disappeared inside.

She checked the time: ten after three, the quiet period between lunch and dinner. There would be a fair crowd in the dining room a little later on. Bad weather in the fall brought out the diners. She wanted to tell Mike about the equipment she'd located. If she didn't do something, she'd end up asleep and then she'd never get to sleep tonight. She decided to go across and get it over with.

A minute later she climbed the steps to the kitchen, shivering. The wind and rain had probably made a mess of her hair and drops of water slid down her cheeks. As she opened the door she heard the sound of a man laughing, Chef Marc, no doubt, making another one of his smutty remarks. She glanced into the kitchen. Sure enough, the chef stood there with Mike, a leer animating his face.

Laurel's stomach rolled. It looked like Mike was just like all the rest, only interested in one thing. She altered course in mid-stride, pushed through the stainless steel-clad doors and went into the dining room. She stopped, leaned against the back wall of the dining room, and took a deep breath.

Moments later, Mike came out. Seeing her he stopped and nodded toward the kitchen. "What's with him? Doesn't even know me and he's grossing me out with his stupid joke."

The angry tightness in her stomach loosened.

"Somebody should have warned you."

He was better looking than she remembered, more solid. A wild hair angled outward from his right eyebrow. She experienced an urge to stand on tiptoe and pluck it.

She motioned toward the bar. "Why don't we go into the bar and get something to tide us over until dinner?

The bar occupied the east third of the first floor, oriented north to south, facing the river and the hotel marina. A row of tall windows offered an unimpeded view of the entire basin. The space, done in rich woods and ceramics, had an air of well-used quality.

Mike put his spoon down and pushed the bowl away. "Delicious. The more I see of this place, the more I like it."

They'd taken a booth near the back, on the side away from the windows. She'd told him Jake Eastland wasn't really her grandfather, that she called him Grampa because they were both alone in the world and it made him happy.

She changed the subject. "How do you think we should go about it? The dive I mean."

He wiped his mouth with his linen and placed the cloth on the table beside the bowl. "If we want to do it right, we'll need to set up a big grid, say twenty-five yards by fifty, in the direction of the prevailing current. There is current down there, right?"

She nodded.

He flipped his place mat over, and on the blank side drew parallel lines then rungs connecting the two lines.

"We'll start at the south end and excavate each rung with the sand sucker. You've seen the technique?"

"Sure. Pinpoint the highest concentrations of debris and then concentrate there."

"Right. After that, whether we do or don't find some intact bottles, we'll go for the cannon. I'd say we'll need a day to a day and a half for the first part and another day to bring the cannon up."

"Will we use the re-breathers?"

"No. Nitrox. It'll give us the longer dive times we'll need." His eyebrows questioned, "You've used it before?"

"Yes."

"Good. I can't wait to get down there." Mike rubbed his hands together. "I haven't had this much fun planning in ages."

Grampa Jake entered the room and came toward them. "Hello there, Mike. I see you got here all right."

Laurel scooted over and Grampa Jake slid in beside her. She gave him a smooch on the forehead. "Mike got in about an hour ago. He asked if we have a dive boat. I didn't know if the Whaler would be big enough."

Grampa Jake clapped his hands. "Oh, no. Way too small. We've got something much better. Wait till you see her."

This was the first she'd heard of a second boat. "Where is it?"

"On the way up the canal from New York. Should be here tonight. First thing in the morning we'll go in and check her over."

She wasn't convinced. "Are you sure this mystery boat will be all right? We need the right equipment to do the job."

Grampa Jake waved off her concern. "Trust me. I have a friend who knows boats."

He turned to Mike. "Your suite is all set. You can bring your car around and the staff will take your bags up for you. Here's the key." He slid a card across to Mike. It was on a ring, along with a blue plastic number 3B.

Mike stumbled for words. "I—I didn't expect this. I made reservations in Oswego."

"Nonsense. We'll be working together. It's much better for you to be right here."

Grampa Jake's eyes were little more than slits. What was he thinking?

Grampa Jake went on. "I'll have the desk make a call and take care of that other reservation. Who's it with?"

She pretended not to be paying attention. She wouldn't mind him staying here. It would help keep his mind on business and off the body builder. The woman wore mounds of makeup. How could he be attracted to her?

She smiled when Mike said, "Day's Inn."

Monday morning brought another unsettled day; neither cold nor warm, the sky overcast but not threatening. At 7:30, Laurel, Mike, Jake, and Sheik arrived in Oswego.

Grampa Jake pointed. "There she is."

The berth where Mike had tied up his workboat was now occupied by a smart-looking vessel with a high prow and wide, fully enclosed deckhouse/control station with windows all around.

Laurel marveled. "Wow. You really do things right, Grampa Jake." She estimated the vessel to be sixty or sixty-five feet in length, and constructed of welded aluminum. The front windows of the deckhouse were fitted with two clear rotary disks to spin off rain and spray, one for each helm position, port and starboard. A two-foot high gunwale surrounded the low afterdeck, with scuppers cut at deck level to allow water that washed aboard to escape.

The entire hull had been painted black, and the sparse wood trim varnished to a dull sheen. At the square transom, a set of davits supported a wide dive platform, the base of which hinged at the waterline. Raised at the moment, it could be lowered by unwinding cables fed from the davit arms. Two other davit arms, one port the other starboard, were served by electric winches positioned nearby. A seventeen-foot Boston Whaler nestled in its cradle near the port side davit. It would be useful as a skiff.

Mike stepped on the gunwale and down to the deck, and she followed. He operated the deck key and lifted the hatch covering the engine compartment. Two shiny new Cummins diesels sat side by side in the spacious compartment.

"I'd make them to be eight hundred horses each," Sheik said from beside her. "This is a beautiful outfit."

Laurel nodded, wondering how Grampa Jake could summon a boat like this on a week's notice. He owned the Twice Told, a substantial property, but this was serious money.

As if he could read her thoughts, Grampa Jake stepped up beside her. "I own a few shares of stock in the company that owns her. I heard she was on the way up the canal. They're leasing her to an outfit in Thunder Bay for a big project up in Lake Superior in the spring. The lessee jumped at the chance to dock her free over the winter."

"How'd you manage free dockage?"

"I've got a friend on the Port Authority Board."

Laurel shook her head. "For a second, I thought it might actually be your boat."

Grampa Jake slapped her on the shoulder. "The bottom line is, long as we take good care of her and pay the bill for the fuel, the rest of it's free, courtesy of Ampanco."

Up at the bow, two large plow anchors were pulled tight into chocks, their chains connected to the dual electric windlass mounted on the foredeck. Inside the deckhouse a short stairway led down to a well-appointed forward cabin.

Sixty-five feet of solid, functional dive boat. Five million dollars at least. With this much boat, they'd be short on manpower. She'd have to bring that up.

She went aft and leaned over the transom to check the boat's name. The large letters were gilt-edged in gold: **Bruce B. Longley**

Wasn't that the name of the man Grampa Jake worked for back in the Prohibition years?

She straightened and turned to him. "May I ask how this boat you accidentally discovered was available happened to get this name?"

The blue in Grampa Jake's eyes got deeper when he was happy. "Hell, I wasn't the only person who knew him. Somebody else probably did too."

She parked her hands on her hips and glared at him. How dumb did he think she was?

When he saw her expression, the blue of Jake Eastland's eyes became even richer, and he turned on his heel and went into the deckhouse.

After lunch, they met to plan.

"Let's face it," Mike said. "With a boat like the *Longley*, we need more crew, and we really need four divers, two more than we have, to make this job go the way it should."

The same point she'd meant to bring up. But what did he mean two more to make four? They already had three. One thing she knew for sure, he wasn't squeezing her out of her own play. "Counting Sheik, we have three divers. Why do you say we need two more?"

Mike hesitated, then looked at Sheik. "Are you sure you're up to this kind of work, Sheik? It's your call."

Sheik's face ran the gamut from relief to disappointment.

"Jeez, Mike. Thanks for the chance, but I ain't. I barely made it through the dive with Laurel." He glanced at her as if feeling guilty, then back at Mike. "Besides, you need me topside, running the boat and so on."

Mike nodded. "Right. So that leaves Laurel and me. Where do we find two more divers who can also help as crew hands?" He scanned the others. There were no answers. His eyes met Laurel's. "Then, may I offer a suggestion?"

"Go ahead."

"I have a couple of friends, brothers. Maybe they'd be interested in a few days work. I'd be willing to bet they're both on layoff right now."

"Can we trust them?" Grampa Jake asked from beside Laurel.

"They're both square guys."

Laurel made up her mind. "Okay, go ahead and see if you can bring them aboard."

Mike pushed himself away from the table. "Good. I'd better get underway. I'd like to be on the water Wednesday morning."

He stood. "I'll call as soon as I know anything. Meanwhile we might as well start bringing stuff aboard."

After Mike left, Sheik spoke up. "I think we have the right man for the job. But I dunno, I ain't comfortable bringin' in strangers."

Laurel indicated the door through which Mike had just passed. "What do you think he is?"

Grampa Jake laughed. "A misfit among the misfits, you mean?" He put his arm around Laurel's shoulder and pulled her toward him, hugging her.

"Straighten him out, Laurel." Sheik said. The two men smirked. Laurel took one look at Sheik's expression, rolled her eyes and poked Grampa Jake in the ribs with her elbow.

"That's enough of that. Cut it out, both of you."

Laurel

Laurel waited while Windows loaded the gazillion programs she didn't need. At last it finished and she went online. She typed the URL for Infoseek and when the site came up, she typed "Ontare" and hit enter.

Quite a day. First the great dive boat, then Mike keeping his promise to work with her, and then for a nice little kicker, her computer back from the repair center. Since finding the cannon, she'd been champing at the bit to do the research on Grampa Jake's mystery ship.

The search results were garbage, nothing at all connected with boats or the water. The pronunciation was close to "Ontario," though, so she tried that. Jeez! Everything you never wanted to know about the province of Ontario, Canada, but not a peep about ships or shipwrecks.

She typed in "Great Lakes Shipwrecks." Voila! The fourth header on the list of hits was "The Great Lakes Shipwreck File 1679–1998." The site claimed to be the most complete and accurate list of losses of Great Lakes commercial vessels in existence.

She typed "Ontare" into the site's search box and was rewarded by a gaggle of partial information about Lake Ontario wrecks, none of it any good.

Below the search box were the letters of the alphabet. She clicked on 'O' and scanned the long list of ships whose name began with that letter. She counted ten "Ontarios" in all, and reviewed them one by one.

When she saw the final entry, a chill stilled her, and in its pall she read:

ONTARIO

other names : none

official no.: Royal Navy

type at loss: armed sloop warship, 22 gun

build info: 1779, Carleton Island
specs: "large"
date of loss:1780, Nov 1*
place of loss: 4.5 mi NE of Oswego
lake: Ontario
type of loss: Storm
loss of life:172-350
carrying: Soldiers, (gold, silver)

detail: She foundered in a blizzard/gale. A drum that washed ashore was the only trace of her. No two reports agree on the details. One source says she was carrying $500,000 in gold specie. She was reported at the time as being "too flat bottomed."
*also given as Nov 23, 1783.

Four and a half miles Northeast of Oswego, very close to where she'd found the cannon last week. A treasure ship and five hundred thousand in gold had to be worth zillions today.

Grampa Jake read the printout she'd made. "Says here she was a Royal Navy ship. That'd make her HMS *Ontario*. Why don't you try that?"

Laurel typed it into the search engine and brought up a list of seemingly unrelated hits. She tried again, this time placing periods between the HMS and producing one solid hit. It was a response by a man named Christian Van Derme of Calgary to a woman who'd posted a question to the Great Lakes Shipwreck Research Group. He seemed very knowledgeable.

She read aloud. "The Captain's name was James Andrews. Oh, oh. Calgary guy says the ship went down near Toronto. How would he know that?"

Jake patted her shoulder. "Take your time and read through it."

"He claims they found flotsam thirty miles east of Fort Niagara, and that seven bodies gassed up from the depths in July 1781, and that they were readily identifiable by their uniforms."

Van Derme claimed to have over a hundred pounds of research papers on the *Ontario*; including something he called "the Haldimand Papers."

She stood and stretched. "I don't know what to believe, Grampa Jake. Maybe it's a wild goose chase."

He leaned closer. "Keep looking. That guy might have a hundred pounds of research papers, but he doesn't have what you do."

"What's that?"

"A cannon. All we need to do is prove that cannon came off the *Ontario*. If we can do that, we'll have proved it's not those dead men who're full of gas; it's Mr. Christian VanDerme of Calgary."

She laughed, "You sure can turn a phrase, Grampa Jake."

"It's all part of the service." He moved toward the door.

"Grampa Jake?"

He stopped with his hand on the doorknob, a question in his eyes.

"Could I ask you for a huge favor?"

"You know you can."

Laurel braced herself, "I'm temporarily embarrassed. I—I mean, could I borrow some money until I get back to work? I'll pay you back really fast, I promise."

He laughed and came toward her. "I wondered what you were doing for cash after that boyfriend of yours cleaned you out."

"Maxing my credit cards with cash advances."

He put his arm around her and hugged her, then kissed the top of her head. "I've got a better idea. Why don't I hire you to take charge of getting those cannon off the bottom? How's five hundred a week sound? I'll throw in room and board."

What a relief! She'd be able to take care of the payments on the credit cards, and put something aside while at the same time concentrating on what had by now become a passion: salvaging the cannon and locating the wreck.

118 ■ ART TIRRELL

"That's such a great idea. I'll take you up on it, starting right now."

He hugged her again and released her. "I'll get you a cash advance in the morning. Meanwhile don't stay up too late. Remember, tomorrow morning we start bringing our equipment aboard the *Longley*."

JAKE

Jake left his granddaughter to her research, but her money trouble stayed on his mind. Back upstairs, he checked the time: eight-thirty. Allie deserved a little time to himself. He decided to call first thing in the morning.

He flopped into his favorite easy chair, parked his feet on the ottoman, and picked up the novel he'd been reading the night Laurel first arrived. The bookmark remained where he'd left it a month earlier. No wonder. Her presence stirred up so many old memories, the printed story paled by comparison.

He read for fifteen minutes, but his eyes grew heavy. It was too early to go to bed. He went to the kitchen and chose a good bottle of Cabernet. He poured a glass and carried it and the bottle back to the living room.

He turned on the television. A second glass of wine later, he turned the TV off.

No use trying to watch. He was more interested in thinking about Laurel… and ways to help her without her realizing it. Her initiative and enthusiasm pleased him. She became a different person when she had her mind on a goal.

So far, so good. McKean hadn't touched a drop of booze since he arrived. That was good. Maybe Sheik had it wrong.

The story of the Ontare had worked after all; kept Laurel from taking off for California. What was it about the West Coast that stirred the imagination of kids? Where did kids already there yearn to go?

Jake checked the time again: a little after ten. Shit. He had to do it or the night would never end. He flipped open the organizer on the table beside him and looked up Allie's home number. After three rings a woman answered.

"That you, Nannie?"

"Uncle Jake! Hello! How are you? It's been too long. You never come to see me anymore."

"I'm not running around like I used to. Time you came to see me for a change."

"You devil. You know I'd come in a second, but you work Allie so hard we never do *anything* together. Wait a second, here he is."

Jake heard a rustling as the phone changed hands.

"Don't believe a word she says, Uncle Jake. Hey, I'm glad you called. I would've called you in the morning. I got the preliminaries on that Zaia character."

In spite of his effort to stay calm, Jake's heart did a long series of flippy beats as the "Z" word passed Allie's lips.

"Go ahead."

"Yeh, Uncle Jake. I knew there was something off there, a guy forty-four years old and never married."

"A bachelor is a guy who doesn't make the same mistake once."

Allie chuckled. "Sure, but most of us do manage to make it at least once. This guy never did. His jib is cut high. Know what I mean?"

"You sure?"

"Yeah. He's out. And get this, his best friend is a character named Robin A. Flagg. No pun intended. Flagg's a pretty boy with a long rap sheet. Confidence schemes, extortion, that kind of stuff. Gay, but swings both ways. Anyway, this Flagg character's gig is professional women. He builds them up, then takes them down."

Jake tried to remember Laurel's ex-fiancé's name. Was it Rory? No, Rob. That was it. Rob. Short for Robin. The last piece fell into place and he had it: the connection to Zaia.

Damn! Zaia finds out about Laurel's background, he schemes to discredit her. He brings his buddy Rob in. Before she knows what hit her, she's demoted, broke, heartbroken and out in the cold.

Jake felt sick. "Okay, Allie. Good work. Let's get a complete workup on Zaia. And expand the investigation to include Flagg. Send me the final results when you get them."

"Okay Uncle Jake. You got it. What do I do then?"

"Let's wait to see what we get. We'll think up something appropriate when the time comes."

"How appropriate?"

Jake growled into the receiver. "No broken bones. Maybe they'd enjoy a few years in Bangladesh."

Allie laughed. "Is that all? I'll keep you posted."

Jake turned off the reading light and leaned against the backrest of his chair. In the near darkness, he stared at nothing. Chill air moved around him. He'd need to close the windows tonight, except the one in his bedroom. That one he'd leave open a little. He liked the air off the lake.

Slowly, his mind turned to the Zaias, how they'd threatened his plans and the steps he'd taken to defeat them. They still hated him for that. He turned it over in his head. Was there some other way, a way that would have avoided all the pain and hatred that followed?

The way he was back in those days, wanting it all for himself, he guessed not. They shouldn't have left their calling card. Without it, he'd never have known who to look for.

1926

Two days after sending the load to the bottom in the storm, Jake and Tom left Oswego well before dawn. A breeze would develop off the Canadian shore around eleven, ruffling the surface, making it hard to spot a floating object. The cork they would be searching for was small, the size of a tennis ball.

"I sure hope the float didn't get fouled on something," Tom Neal said, his face serious.

Jake glanced at the compass bearings he'd made when they dropped the load. "We're on course. If it's there, we'll find it."

Ten minutes later, they sighted the navigation buoy off Main Duck Island. He picked up the compass, held it at eye-level and sighted on the buoy. The bearing read twenty-four degrees. The number on his paper was twenty-eight. He had two references, one the buoy at Main Duck, the other Point Petre at the southernmost tip of Prince Edward County, visible to the northwest. Its bearing had been three hundred-sixteen degrees on the day they dropped the load.

In theory, all he had to do was maneuver until the heading to Main Duck was twenty-eight degrees then head straight toward it until the bearing to Point Petre matched what he had written down.

He motioned for Tom to come back. "Here, take the wheel. We're getting close. Slow down so I can take bearings."

Tom throttled down until they crept along, the engine idling. Jake smelled exhaust gas as the fumes drifted past, moving faster than the boat. He took another sighting. Almost. The navigation buoy was right on the horizon, bright red, about three miles away.

He took another sight. Exactly twenty-eight degrees. His excitement grew. They were close.

"Okay. Head right toward the buoy. Keep a straight course."

When Tom completed the turn, Jake took a bearing on Point Petre.

Three-thirty. They needed three-sixteen.

The bearing changed to three twenty-six, then three-twenty.

"Come on, baby, be there." Jake muttered under his breath. He searched the surface ahead then took another bearing. Three-sixteen.

"Stop here. We're very close."

The words were hardly out of his mouth when Tom hollered, "Jake!"

Fifty yards ahead, a cork lay on the surface, rolling a little in the flat water. "Whoa!" Tom yelled, pumping his arm in the air.

Jake grabbed a coil of line and quickly tied a bowline around the steel ring of a small white mooring buoy, tied an anchor to the other end of the line and put it all overboard to mark the exact spot.

"I'll take the helm, Tom. When we get close, pull the slack out of the string and see which way the load lies. Then we'll see what we can fish up with the grappling hooks."

Tom retrieved the cork. The string curved off toward the marker Jake had set. As slowly as possible, Jake edged the boat in that direction while Tom retrieved string. Finally, the string went straight down. "We're right over it. Two hundred feet, Jake."

Jake let the anchor go and Tom hand-lowered a three-tined grappling hook on a half-inch manila rope. When it was on the bottom, he went forward as far as he could, and in a slow but deliberate motion dragged the grapple along the bottom. Within a few feet it went taut.

"I feel it moving. I think we've got one."

Jake controlled his elation. "Put it on the winch. We'll grind it up to the surface so I can fetch the end ropes." At each end of the net, the individual strands came together to form a thick bundle, which in turn were secured by the long rope tails which had secured the nets to the boat. It took fifteen minutes of agonizing cranking to bring the nets awash. Half the load, two hundred and fifty cases, twenty-one thousand dollars, close to back under control.

Jake stripped off his boots and socks and pulled his shirt off. "Try to hold it there. I'll find the end ropes."

After emptying his pockets, he took several deep breaths and stepped off the fantail of the boat. Once in the water, he bent into a surface dive and pulled himself under.

In the crystal clear water he could see the entire net. It bulged with soggy cases of whisky. At about ten feet he ran into a layer of much colder water. Ignoring the shock, he went deeper. The grapple had caught two thin strands near the middle. They were stretched to the breaking point. He swam deeper until he came to the first end rope. He caught hold of it and dragged it up with him as he swam to the surface, no easy task because it was near fifty feet long.

His lungs burned as he cleared the surface and gasped for air. "Here's the first one. Secure it quick. I think the grapple's about to let go." He held it up and Tom caught it with the boat hook, pulled it aboard, and tied it to a cleat.

"The other one must be on the far side. Let me catch my breath and I'll get it." Two minutes later, Jake found the second end at a depth of only fifteen feet. He brought it up and, when Tom had the net secured fore and aft, Jake pulled himself back aboard.

With one side of the boat weighted and the other not, they had a distinct list. Would it be better to get what they had safe ashore or at least on the sand bar? Maneuvering for the second half would be tricky with the boat burdened the way it was. Besides, the spot was marked. They could come back in the morning and fish the other bag up.

Jake faced his helper. "We'll have a heck of a time maneuvering with this net, Tom. I think we should take it across and come back for the rest tomorrow."

Tom shrugged, "My ma always says half a cake is better than none."

Tom cranked the engine and they made their way back to their drop off point, lowered the load and went back to Oswego. By five o'clock they had the load ashore and safely tucked away.

At peace for the first time in days, Jake slept a deep and dreamless sleep. They cleared Oswego well before dawn again the next morning. All went as planned until they reached the spot triangulated so perfectly the previous day. The white buoy they'd left wasn't there. They re-triangulated and dragged the entire area, hoping some accident had caused the buoy to drift away.

No whisky.

A mile away they came upon a drifting marker float. The kind used to identify the owner of a net. The cork had an "E" burnt into its surface. Jake recognized his own work at once. The float was from one of the nets he'd traded to Joe Zaia for the model T.

Zaia had his load.

In Slim Carroway's office above the Purple Orchid, one of three Syracuse bars Slim owned, he jumped to his feet and held out his hand. "Jake! Damn, am I ever happy to see you. That thief from Port Ontario wanted twelve bucks a bottle. Shit, that's what I get at retail. Do you have any stuff?"

Jake took the proffered hand. "Yes. I've got a hundred twenty-five cases now and more on the way."

Slim's face fell. "I can't take that much right away."

"Last week, you were going to leave me because I couldn't deliver enough. This week, you can't move what I deliver. Make up your mind, Slim. How many outside buyers have you put together, anyway?"

"Six regular, two or three once in a while. I thought I could find more but I haven't been able to."

More likely hadn't tried.

Jake pushed his anger back. The moment he did he knew this was his next opportunity. How to grab hold of it, that was the question. "Okay Slim, how many cases can you take?"

"I can take a hundred."

"Tell you what. I've had losses, so until I make up for them the booze will be eight dollars a bottle. That's fair isn't it?"

Slim's face took on a sour expression, but he agreed.

Jake took the next step. "If you want, I'll handle the retrieval and delivery for six bits a bottle. How's that sound?"

This time Slim agreed faster. "It'll be a load off my back, Jake. That's the God's honest truth." He sat up in his chair. "In fact, I'll pay you up front." He swiveled and leaned down to the small safe chained to a stout steel post mounted in the floor. He opened it and removed an envelope. Licking his fingertips, he counted out nine thousand six hundred dollars, all in hundreds. Picking up a pencil, he did some math. He raised his eyebrows and hesitated, then sighed and counted out another nine hundred. "Ten thousand five hundred for a hundred cases, delivered."

"It'll take a few days to set up."

"No problem, Jake. No problem at all."

A conviction had been growing in the back of Jake's mind. He had this season, maybe next, to make his money and get out. Any longer and the law was bound to catch up to him. So he had to move volume. Volume required distribution. Distribution meant trucks. But he couldn't use somebody else's trucks to haul booze. It had to be a legitimate operation, a straight trucking company in every way but one.

Jake Eastland was going into the trucking business.

"See, Mr. Thayer? In return for a chance to haul your produce from the regional market, I'm willing to work for two cents a pound. That's less than half what you're paying now."

Jake stood on the walk outside the grocer's shop. On both sides were rows of fresh produce. "I know Thad Jones has been hauling for you for years. I'm not asking for all your business, just a little now and then."

"I need reliable service, not just price," the diminutive grocer said. "You're pretty young to be taking on a responsibility like this."

"Just give me a try. Let me bring something to you tomorrow. If I don't do it right, you don't pay anything."

The grocer had bought Jake's catch several times. "Okay. Tomorrow I'll need melons, twenty-five pounds, potatoes, two hundred pounds, and whatever fruit is available, as long as it's fresh and ripe. As much as a hundred pounds if the price is right." Jake jotted down each item as Thayer fired it at him.

"Yes sir, Mr. Thayer. We'll see you tomorrow morning."

Jake climbed into the secondhand van he'd purchased the day before for eight hundred dollars. Leaving the city, he bounced and jounced his way to Mexico Point and turned onto the track leading to the shed where the Neal's lived.

Dust billowed, and chickens scooted out of the way as he stopped in front of the house. Mrs. Neal, a lock of hair dangling over her tired face, came to the door. She wore an old cotton print dress. He tipped his cap, and threaded his way through the scrap-strewn yard to the front door.

"Afternoon, ma'am. Is your boy Sean around?"

"He went up to the point, fishin'."

"Thank you, ma'am." Jake tipped his cap again and drove off.

He found Sean at Nine Mile Point, fishing off the cliffs with a friend. He had two nice bass to show for his efforts.

"Jake!" he exclaimed. "What're you doing out here?"

"I came to offer you work."

The tow-headed young man held up his hand, palm toward Jake. "Oh, no you don't. You'll never get me more than ten feet away from land again."

Sean had a big Irish grin and Jake liked him.

"This is something different," he said. "Something I'm positive you can handle, you being a farmer and all."

"What do I have to do?"

"Drive my truck down to the Regional Market in Syracuse, buy some produce and deliver it to Thayer's grocery first thing in the morning."

Sean scratched his head. "Is that all?"

"Not quite. You'll run a delivery route for me, too. I'm setting up several runs. We'll move the whisky at night and sell the produce the next day. You'll make two runs a week. It'll pay thirty dollars a run."

Sean's eyes popped. "Thirty dollars a run?"

"Thirty dollars."

"When do I start?"

"Right now. Where's Tom?"

The seventy-five cents a bottle Slim Carroway paid to deliver his booze covered the entire overhead of Great Lakes Express, the name Jake gave his new enterprise. Because of this fact, Jake could undercut his competitors. The business grew by leaps and bounds. The produce he carried soon required him to put a second and then a third truck on the road.

The organizational load quickly became too much. He was in the trucking business, something he never wanted. He searched for a way out, but there didn't seem to be one.

"I've come to ask for work." Thad Jones stood in front of Jake, his eyes lowered. "First the Zaias out there at Port Ontario undercut me, then you started up. I can't keep operating at the prices you charge. Nobody could."

Jake squinted at the man. "Who managed your business finances?"

"I did. I've always been good with books and numbers. My wife helped too."

"How much did you earn when things were good, Thad?"

"Sometimes sixty dollars a week," the older man answered.

"And your wife?"

"Oh, I didn't pay her."

Jake thought it over for a second. "Tell you what, Thad. I like you. I'm sorry this happened to you. Here's what I'll do. I'll offer you three hundred-fifty dollars in cash for that truck of yours, and you and your wife come to work for me and run this business. I'll pay you seventy-five dollars a week plus three percent of the profits, and your wife twenty-five dollars a week plus one percent."

"You want me to run the whole shootin' match? A h—hundred dollars a week and a percentage? Oh, my God. I must be dreaming." Thad Jones fell to his knees, his hands clenched and held upward toward Jake. "Thank you, Mr. Eastland, thank you. I'll make it grow for you, I promise."

Jake felt like yelling at the top of his lungs.

Jones would find out about the liquor hauling. It was inevitable. But Jake was pretty sure the man would be willing to look the other way. Fifty-two hundred dollars a year plus a percent of the profits was a lot of money. The booze was Jake's end of the business. No records, no dispatch addresses, no bills of lading. He had it all in his head.

Now, only Joe Zaia remained. What to do about him? A remembrance of Estelle brought a twist of anger to Jake's chest. Another of the Zaias. Maybe his intentions hadn't been honorable at first, but they had at the end, and she'd spurned him.

And Emilio, Joe Zaia's son. He had a score to settle with Emilio.

Suddenly, he knew exactly what he needed to do. Thad Jones had said it. "I can't keep operating at the prices you charge. *Nobody could.*"

Joe Zaia put the coffee tin down and stared at his daughter through narrowed eyes. Sure enough, after a few seconds, Estelle moaned and bent over the sink, her hand on her belly for the second time that morning.

He wiped his mouth with his sleeve.

"Whatsa matter?"

The kitchen fell silent. No one met his gaze. She'd been sick almost every morning for two weeks.

"*Prego!*"

His chair scraped as he rose, grabbed Estelle's arm and pulled her around to face him. They stood in the middle of the kitchen, glaring at each other.

"Tell me *now*, who's the father." The vein pulsed in his forehead.

The girl screeched, "Yes! It's true. I'm pregnant. But I don't *know* who the father is." She looked at her mother. Her mother, eyes round, did not move, the back of her hand touching her lips.

Zaia slapped his daughter, his work-hardened hand impacting her face with a loud "whap", carrying all the force his hundred-and-sixty-pound body could muster.

"*Puta!*"

The force of the blow spun her around and she fell to the floor, knocking over a chair and bumping her head. She blinked, eyes unfocused. Only feet away, her mother wrung her hands and watched, helpless tears oozing from the corners of her eyes.

His rage peaked again and he kicked his daughter in the buttocks with the side of his foot, hard, moving her entire body toward the doorway.

"I no have a *puta* in my house. You have so many men you don' know the father, you get out, now." He kicked her again, moving her closer to the door.

"...my clothes..."

"Get out, *puta*."

Whimpering, she got to her knees and crept to the door. Outside, she fell forward, blinking in the bright fall sunlight.

Joe Zaia leaned forward until his mouth was a foot from his wife's face. "She don't come back in. You take her clothes out to her. When I come home, she better be gone. Capishay?"

He straightened, left the house by the back door, got in his truck and left. He fumed as he drove. What happened to the loving innocent girl she'd been? She defied him at every possible opportunity, and worse, shamed him in front of his friends.

He knew she went with men. He'd heard whispers. She'd been seeing Angelo Spina and Tony Piazza. Joe remembered catching her with the Eastland kid. Scared the shit out of him at least. He hadn't seen the kid since. Maybe he should have tried the same thing with Angelo and Tony.

Fifteen minutes later, Joe pulled over and stopped in front of Stevens Grocery in the village of Mexico. Mark Stevens had become one of his better customers, and his store a regular stop on the truck route Joe had established to sell his goods.

"Mornin' Mister S., got some nice fresh melons today," he half bowed as the grocer approached, his white apron fresh and clean. "Just ten cents each."

Stevens waved. "Hello, Joe." He wore rimless eyeglasses with a bifocal cut across the bottom of each lens. "I don't need anything today. Great Lakes Express was here an hour ago and I bought through the regional market in Syracuse."

He motioned toward a stack of several dozen melons. Even now a customer hefted one. Stevens leaned closer so as not to be overheard. "Six cents each—and I've been selling them for a quarter." He raised his eyebrows.

Joe had to move his melons in the next few days or they'd get overripe. "Great Lakes? Never hearda' them."

"It's a new outfit out of Oswego; fella by the name of Thad Jones runs it. Don't know how he does it. I never bought melons cheaper. Maybe next time, Joe." The grocer shrugged and went back to his customer.

Back in his truck, Joe remained hopeful. Maybe Mr. Ventra in Parish would buy.

Ventra didn't. Everywhere, it was the same story. The new outfit had beaten him to every single customer. By 4:30, he'd managed to move only a fourth of his melons, and to make matters worse, he'd been forced to meet his new competitor's price—which happened to be less than his own cost to grow and market. Joe Zaia didn't like losing money.

When his number one customer, Thayer's market in Oswego, needed nothing, his frustration peaked. He and Thayer stood under the awning in front, fruits and produce neatly organized on spacious tables all around. Thayer finished spraying a mist of water on everything, keeping his merchandise fresh and moist, and the street dust down.

"Who is this Great Lakes Express anyway?" Joe asked.

"It's owned by an energetic young man by the name of Jake Eastland. But he doesn't run it. Thad Jones went to work for him a while back. He pretty much runs the outfit. They're growing fast."

Jake Eastland! The same kid who'd fucked his daughter now trying to put him out of business. Before, it wasn't personal. Now, it was.

Thayer touched his arm. "Are you all right, Joe? Can I get you a glass of water?"

Joe knew his face could get red when he was angry. He forced a smile. "No thanks. Just thinking. You know where their office is? I go see."

Thayer gave him directions. Joe nodded. "Thanks, see you tomorrow, Mr. John."

Great Lakes Express occupied a large warehouse on the East Side of the river. Three trucks were backed up to the loading platform, all painted white with dark blue lettering over a wide horizontal stripe of robin's egg blue. Joe cruised past. One of the trucks was just pulling away. Crews were busy loading the others.

On an impulse, he followed the truck. It went east on route 104 and left the city. He was surprised when the driver turned onto 104A and then north on Route 3 a few miles later, headed right to Port Ontario, where Joe lived. At the Salmon River, the Great Lakes truck crossed the bridge, passed Joe's roadside stand and the boat livery, and headed north toward Watertown. Joe kept him in sight.

At six o'clock, an hour later, they reached the outskirts of Watertown. The driver ahead pulled off the road into a small cleared space and stopped. As Joe passed, the driver climbed down, stretching his muscles. Joe kept his eyes straight ahead. Half a mile down the road, he pulled over and waited. Half an hour passed. An hour. Darkness settled.

What the heck was the guy doing?

Joe's stomach rumbled. He hadn't eaten since breakfast and it was now after seven, well past suppertime. By seven-thirty the Great Lakes truck still hadn't showed.

Maybe he went back the other way.

At last, two pinpricks of light showed on the road behind him. The white truck rumbled past, traveling at normal speed. Joe followed without using his headlights. Two miles down the road, the white truck pulled into the parking lot of a combination roadhouse/restaurant. Joe eased to a stop and watched.

The driver disappeared inside. A minute later, he and another man came out and talked while they smoked. They came to some kind of

RCheck Out Receipt

Hayner PLD - Downtown Branch (HYNP-ZED)
618-462-0677
www.haynerlibrary.org

Friday, April 21, 2017 2:57:37 PM
TILLER, EUGENE

Item: 0003003511569
Title: Speakerboxxx [sound recording] ; Th
e love below
Call no.: CD YZMA OUTK SLB 042
Due: 05/05/2017

Total items: 1

You just saved $21.98 by using your librar
y. You have saved $21.98 since April 14, 2
017.

Thank You!

agreement and the driver opened the back of the truck, climbed up and disappeared inside. A few seconds later, he re-appeared and placed a square wooden case on the tail of the truck. A produce case, perhaps two feet square. The driver jumped down and together they lifted the case and carried it around to the back of the building, out of Joe's sight.

When the driver came back out, the case he carried was empty.

Booze! They were running booze.

The white truck moved on, but Joe didn't follow. He sat there for several more minutes, working it over in his mind. He knew Jake Eastland ran whisky in from Canada. Great Lakes Express was a front to distribute the stuff. He delivered the liquor at night, probably sold the produce on the return trip.

Joe remembered the load he'd salvaged last year. Sweet. Very Sweet. Here was a chance to pick up another thousand or two. As he made his way back to Port Ontario, he thought about what he'd learned, and a plan began to form in his mind.

Sean Neal put his feet up on the armrest of the driver's side door, then rested his head against the passenger door and closed his eyes. This job was a cakewalk. There hadn't been a lick of trouble in the ten weeks he'd been doing the runs. He had a little under an hour to kill before it would be full dark and he could start his Watertown run.

He pulled the blanket higher. Near Thanksgiving the nights were cold. Beat the heck out of being on that boat, though. He remembered the agony of his trip across the lake with Jake Eastland. Now, he lay warm and safe in the cab of his truck. His brother Tom made the runs across the lake. He could have them.

Tom got a hundred bucks a trip, and he only made sixty a week. Keeping his feet on solid ground was worth it. Who needed the extra excitement? He'd take his twenty-four hour run—one night to sell off the booze, and the next day to sell the produce, his prices so cheap the grocers fought over who'd be first on his list of stops—over the danger of being on a boat anytime.

Then he'd have a day off before his next run took him to the Utica-Rome area. He repeated each route once a week.

A sound outside woke him from a doze. He yawned. Good timing. Nearly full dark. He heard it again, right outside the door of the truck, a scratching noise. He sat up and looked out the passenger window.

A face stared in at him, lit by his dash lights. He jerked away from the window with a gasp, his heart standing still. As he did, the man standing on the running board pointed a gun at him through the window. Flame spit from the muzzle and the window imploded with a crash. A thousand shards of splintered glass filled the cab of the truck, sluicing into Sean's flesh in a deadly torrent. But the glass didn't kill Sean Neal. The bullet that passed through the exact middle of his forehead did that.

From the moment news of the hijacking arrived, settling the score became Jake's top priority. He tried a make-up run. It failed. He heard from several sources; the Zaia's had whisky and were selling it cheap.

Strong men accept responsibility when things go wrong. He treated Sean's death as a legitimate business expense, paid for the funeral, and even though he considered her a useless slattern, arranged a comfortable annuity for Mrs. Neal. On one level this made him feel better, but on another, deeper one, did nothing to correct the main problem; Zaia still had Jake's property.

God help him, he couldn't let it be the end. If he didn't get even, the Neals would never forgive him. More than that, he'd never forgive himself.

Okay, Joe Zaia. An eye for an eye.

At six in the afternoon, seven days later, a brand new white Ford truck with a stripe painted the same shade of blue rumbled past Joe's roadside stand at Port Ontario.

Zaia and his son Emilio watched from the shadowed interior.

Jake Eastland didn't give up so easy. It looked like they'd have to teach him another lesson.

He sneered at Emilio. "Don't be so scared this time. Remember—no shootin' unless he shoots first."

Because Emilio panicked, Joe's plan to steal both the truck and its cargo then repaint the truck and either add it to his own fleet or sell it went out the window. No way to do that with the cab full of blood and bits of bone.

"You go see Tony Piazza. I'll get Angelo and his brother. Tell them to be here at seven. This time we do the job right."

Jake pulled into the rutted rest area where Sean had been ambushed. He'd taken the run himself. No way could he ask any of the men working for him to take the chance. Not for sixty bucks a week. He'd come prepared. On seat beside him a thirty-eight caliber pistol sat nestled in its holster.

He waited for the light to fade.

At 7:45 it was full dark, and little traffic on the highway. The most recent vehicle had passed ten minutes ago. If the moon had risen, clouds blocked its light. A cool wind blew.

His eye caught a flicker of movement in the side view mirror mounted outside his door. He reached for the pistol beside him.

"Don't do that." The voice came from the passenger side, surprising him. He caught his breath. A masked man stepped onto the lower step and pointed a pistol at Jake's head. "Put your hands on the wheel. Both of them."

Jake hesitated then obeyed. A second man approached the door, stood ten feet away. He had a pistol too. A scarf covered the lower half of his face.

The first man motioned with his pistol. "Get out. Lie on your face."

When Jake lay spread-eagle on the ground, a vehicle approached and entered the rest area, backing in until its loading door came a dozen feet from the rear doors of Jake's Ford.

"Get the keys, open 'er up, hurry," the second gunman called.

Jake's guard pulled the keys from the ignition and tossed them back. Two men left the second truck and waited near the cargo doors, shotguns cradled in their arms.

The masked bandit pushed the gun into the small of his back. "Get up. Go to the back. Move."

Jake got to his feet and moved toward the rear of the truck. The second man had the padlock securing Jake's cargo open. He grasped the large handle, releasing the latch prior to swinging the doors open.

The instant the latch cleared, Jake's men hiding inside shoved the doors open, slamming them into the bandit, propelling him backward into the two with the shotguns. The floodlight inside clicked on, bathing the bandits in light. Gunfire erupted.

At the same moment, Jake spun, his forearm contacting his guard's weapon, pushing it to the side before the man could react. When he did pull the trigger, the bullet missed, and Jake smashed his fist flush into the hollow between his nose and eye.

"Ohhhh!" The bandit reeled backward.

Jake knew he had to keep his enemy off balance. He kicked at the man's gun hand and sent the gun flying then he charged, knocking him over backward. Jake straddled him and slammed his fist into the man's face again. The man moaned and went limp.

Jake pulled the scarf away. Emilio Zaia.

"You killed my driver, you scum. Only a coward would do it that way."

Emilio stared up at Jake.

Jake brandished his knife, pushed the button. It snicked open. He held the point to Emilio's throat. "Did you do it?"

Tears came to the other man's eyes and he swallowed hard, nodding. "I was scared, accident." His right hand covered his eyes and he sobbed.

"Yeah? Let's see how trigger happy you are tomorrow." With a deliberate motion, knowing full well what the result would be, Jake slashed the razor-sharp blade across the back of Emilio Zaia's right wrist, just at the skin-fold.

"Aaaaiiiieeee!" Zaia clutched his wrist.

Shaking, Jake stood. The fight wound down. The four hard men in the back of his truck had come well prepared. Each wore a thick protective vest and carried an automatic weapon. They'd cut down two of the hijackers. The rest had fled into the woods.

Tom Neal motioned to Jake, and pointed his flashlight at one of the two bodies. He nudged the man with his foot. "I nailed this one. You know him?"

Jake stood over the prone form. The pain behind his eyes grew. "Yeah. It's Joe Zaia. We've tangled before."

"You won't be tangling again. He's deader than a doornail."

Jake let his shoulders slump. What began with a simple dishonest trade had now led to Joe Zaia's death and the maiming of his son. An eye for an eye. He had his revenge. It became possible to feel the pain of Sean's death, but Jake didn't permit himself the luxury. He made himself hard. The road ahead had been cleared of obstacles. That's all he cared about.

OSWEGO HARBOR

From her office, Chief Petty Officer Char Stone couldn't miss the surge of activity aboard the black boat. She pulled her binoculars from their case and trained them on the boat. One by one, she checked out the individuals.

With a jolt, she spotted Mike McKean. He was back in town! Char prayed for just one more chance with him. Since their dates she'd thought of little else. She'd played the perfect lady, all the while hoping he'd come to her, wanting him to seduce her so much she quivered every time their eyes met.

He hadn't.

At the memory, needles of annoyance prickled. He'd turned her down. She'd offered him the whole enchilada that third night and he'd turned her down flat. Underneath, she knew she'd pushed too hard. It was too soon.

She wasn't giving up. It wasn't about a lay anymore. When they were together she had thoughts, unfamiliar but nice thoughts about a home, children, the whole routine. With a man like him, there could be a real relationship.

Her binoculars scanned the others, stopped on the woman who'd been in the Blazer. Her! She clenched her jaw.

The woman handed Mike something and looked up at him. A chill spread through Char. The bitch wanted him. It was all there in that look.

Reason fled. Movements methodical now, she focused on the boat's registration numbers and wrote them down. She stood and left her office, taking the slip of paper with her.

Downstairs, she motioned to her favorite whipping boy.

"Whaley, run this registration number and man the cutter. We'll be going out at 1445."

Whaley reached for the intercom to order the boat manned. Char stopped his hand with hers. "No need for that. Just pass the word."

No sense advertising that they were coming.

Ten minutes later, Char in command, the forty-four-foot cutter approached the black boat tied up just outside the government anchorage.

At the last possible moment, Char caught hold of the reins of her emotions. She turned to her helmsman. "Seaman Hardy. We will not be boarding them at this time. Proceed past and out into the harbor for boat-handling drills."

Char's forehead broke out in droplets of sweat. Her entire body burned. She'd almost done something incredibly stupid.

Faces lifted aboard the black vessel as the cutter's bow, marked by the distinctive wide orange stripe of the Coast Guard, glided past.

Char seethed, passing within ten feet of the other woman, but kept herself under strict control. Her time would come. She could wait.

Aboard the *Longley*, Mike stepped to the rail beside the woman and waved.

"Morning Chief," he called. "Out for a training mission?"

Char didn't answer right away. Her face burned as she remembered how forward she'd been with him. What was routine for other men seemed wrong for him, made her feel cheap. She put her thumb to her ear and mouthed, "Call me," and nodded with a smile while avoiding the other woman's eyes.

The large diesel growled and a swirl of water came from its stern as the cutter moved off.

Aboard the *Longley*, Laurel said, "She wants you to call her? What about? It's not anything to do with us?"

"I told you we'd dated. We got along pretty well."

"I remember her from the time I dropped you off. I bet she thinks it's more than that."

The cutter disappeared around the end of the grain elevator pier. Mike turned to go ashore.

"One thing I know for sure," she said.

He stopped. "What's that?"

"We'll be seeing that Chief again."

LAUREL

"We should be pretty close," Laurel called from the Nav station aboard the *Bruce B. Longley* the next morning. "Let's see if we're close enough to pick up the homing beacon."

Grampa Jake sat at the port helm station, but Sheik, at the starboard, had control of the vessel. The morning light was dull, even though the sun was well above the horizon to the southeast. Later, after the sun got a little higher, a thermal breeze might develop and with it would come waves.

Outside, Mike sat with the new divers, talking and sipping coffee. The brothers were quiet, professional men, dark-haired and trim. She flipped the switch. Everyone in the deckhouse listened.

"Ping. Ping. Ping." A bearing appeared on her screen, followed by the distance to the coordinates. "There you go, Sheik. Head for it."

A half-hour later they'd pinpointed the beacon and set anchors over it. Jerry and Sam, the brothers Mike recruited, went down first to set up the grid. She and Mike readied the big lights and the suction gun.

"Are the compressor and generator ready, Sheik?" she said.

"Purrin' like kittens." He gave her a thumbs-up. "You got pressure and juice right now."

Beside her, Mike went in, tools hanging off every part of him. Holding her mask against her face, Laurel stepped off the platform into the water.

The light tiers and their negative buoyancy took her down in a rush. Mike, with his own load and the sand gun, descended just ahead of her. She saw lights first, and then the bottom came up fast. Jerry and Sam already had the south corners of the grid set and had disappeared from sight in the murk to position the final two corners.

Laurel opened the aluminum tripod legs and wrestled with the first light bar until she had it solidly footed beside the nylon twine that delineated the south end of the rectangle; she positioned the second set and switched them both on, bathing the lakebed in brilliant light. She could see the projection of the cannon about thirty feet away.

A minute later, Jerry and Sam swam into sight.

"Okay." Jerry's voice. The device pressed against Laurel's skull transmitted the sound through the bone and she "heard" him. "The corners are set."

The four of them went to work on the remaining rungs of the grid. Mike said, "I"ll fire up the gun. Why don't you watch for glass."

"Okay."

The sand gun created suction by introducing compressed air through a fitting about four tenths of the way up its length. The compressed air expanded and rose, establishing a powerful vacuum that caused water to be sucked into the lower end, or mouth.

A stream of bubbles gurgled upward and Mike jammed the maw of the tube into the bottom of the lake. It made a burbling, scratching noise. Seconds later a stream of dark sediment plumed from the exhaust of the tube and a trench six inches deep appeared. Mike dragged the tube along the nylon string–marked line and she followed. He covered half the width of the grid, but Laurel, hovering inches from the mouth of the device, didn't see anything significant.

He levered the tube off. "Going to the next rung," he said.

While he moved to the second rung five feet away, she checked her watch. They'd been down thirty minutes. Mike rested, allowing the current to clear away the cloud of silt dislodged by the gun.

Jerry appeared from the gloom. "Ah, we have eight rungs done." He signaled "up" with his finger, and said, "Can't see a thing with the silt."

Laurel saw the logic. If Jerry and Sam went up now, they wouldn't need to decompress and would be ready to go again as soon as she and Mike finished their dive.

Sam appeared along the far side of the grid, using it to navigate in the sand-colored murk. He and Jerry began to ascend.

Mike levered the suction on again. This time they covered the full twenty-five yards.

"Stop." Laurel pointed at the trench. The gun had uncovered a few links of chain atop a slight mound. "Looks like old anchor chain. I saw another length on my first dive."

Laurel checked her watch. The second tier had taken twenty-five minutes. They could do two, maybe three more rows before they had to go up. The chain wasn't important.

"No time to investigate now. Let's worry about it later."

Near the middle of the third rung, Laurel reached into the trench he'd excavated and lifted a round object, hefting it. She handed it to him, shining her flashlight on it. A two-pound lead sinker.

He nodded, "Save it."

They found the first shard on the fourth rung. Then, three feet from the cannon, the gun sucked up glass, a lot of it. There seemed to be a ledge of shards. "Move a foot south and dig there," she said.

Almost at once the gun sank to a depth of a foot or more. "Stop!" A bottle cap projected from the stack of shards. She grasped it and gingerly wiggled it loose.

Yes!" She held up an intact bottle for him to see. Mike nodded and worked to extend the trench along the edge of the pile of glass.

After several minutes, they had a curving trench that began just south of the cannon and followed the current "downstream" to the north. Mike moved to the other side. The pattern there was the same, a long parabola of debris.

By the time their bottom time ended, they had fifty intact bottles. They gave each other high fives.

Back on the surface, Mike fed the retrieval line into the sheave of one of the davits, took a few turns around the winch and set the bight into the self-tailer.

"Look what *we* found." He pulled the lever and activated the winch. The nylon line went taut and after a minute the net holding the whisky came awash. Everyone watched as it came clear of the water, swinging back and forth with the movement of the boat. Between the dark strands of netting, its amber cargo glistened in the late morning sunlight.

Sheik clapped his hand to his forehead. "Will you lookit that, Jake. It's a lifetime supply."

"Where was it?" Jerry said from the shade of the deckhouse.

Mike scribbled a quick diagram. "There's a projection from the bottom right about here. The nets must have caught on it as they settled to the bottom, and they laid over and around it like this." He drew two lines showing how the bottles had strung out down current. "When you go down after lunch, dig both sides, here and here." He indicated areas beginning just beyond the cannon and progressively further from it.

They relaxed for the next half hour, ate a light lunch and discussed the plan for the afternoon dive. At one, Jerry and Sam suited up. Minutes later they were in the water.

The small gas engines of the compressor and generator chugged away. Laurel sat at the Nav station, exploring the equipment, some of which she hadn't seen before. She found the cannon on the bottom, as well as the divers moving about.

One thing puzzled her. A hundred yards or so beyond the north end of their grid, another smaller reading showed.

"You have experience with mag gear, haven't you, Mike?" She beckoned. "What do you make of this?"

He leaned over her shoulder to see the screen. "What've you got?"

"I see our cannon right here, but I can't figure out if this is an echo or a genuine hit."

His head came very near hers as he leaned closer to the screen. "Mmm, no. That's a hit of some kind." He tweaked one of the controls. "It's long and narrow. I think it's worth checking out. We can do it after we get the cannon up." He straightened. "Nice catch." He squeezed her shoulder, lingering a few seconds, then let go and left the deckhouse.

He'd never touched her before, not even in passing. Or complimented her. Laurel's shoulder tingled. Her heart felt like it had shifted to somewhere in her throat. There'd been more to his touch than mere congratulation, the way his hand lingered afterward.

Laurel clamped down hard on her emotions. He'd done what any leader would do and here she was, reacting like he'd offered her an engagement ring.

By two, the brothers had five dozen intact bottles. They came out of the water after their decompress time, laughing and smiling, proud of their find.

Laurel congratulated them, then said, "Listen up, guys. That projection on the bottom is an old gun of some kind. Part of our plan is to bring it up."

Jerry shuffled his feet and raised his eyes to Mike. "So that's why we've got all the flotation aboard."

Mike glanced at Laurel before answering. "Tell you what, Jerry. Laurel spotted another object down there. You guys can be first to check it out."

Jerry didn't bother to consult his brother. "Deal."

Conditions were poor on the bottom. Mike and Laurel dragged the light stands closer, until sheer brilliance overcame the silt.

Mike stuck the sand gun into the bottom next to the cannon and threw the lever. In minutes a foot-deep trench surrounded it. Working the tool, he widened the excavation and deepened it to a depth of two feet, exposing four feet of the cannon's length. Laurel tried unsuccessfully to rock it back and forth. Mike jammed the sand gun down next to it while Laurel wiggled it furiously.

Mike levered the gun off. "Laurel," he wagged his finger at her. "Don't work so hard. You'll mess up your mixture."

"Okay."

He pulled a pry bar from his belt, jammed it into the loosened lakebed next to the cannon, and pulled on it as hard as he could. The bottom bulged for a foot or so and a crack appeared in the sediment. Mike handed the bar to Laurel and retrieved the sand gun. In a minute he had another deep hole. At the bottom, the dredge clinked against metal.

"There's something else here," he said.

Three quarters of an hour later they had the site excavated. There were three cannon. Two large guns lying breech to snout on the bottom. Pinched between them, wedged in place and back-filled by sediment, the smaller cannon.

"They had to have come down in a tangle to stay together like this," Laurel said. "But why here? There's no ship."

"Um... good question. I think we can finish up with one more dive." Mike checked his watch, tapping it for her benefit.

"Okay," Laurel acknowledged the time. "Better start up." They began the ascent, bringing the lights and the sand gun with them.

The weather held and by eleven the next morning, Mike, working with Laurel and Sam, had both large guns in double slings, and the floats ready to be inflated. The small cannon was free, too. He watched as Laurel attached floats to the line circling its snout.

Jerry appeared out of the murk, "Something there, all right. Can't tell what it is. Need the gun," he motioned. "Dig it out."

Mike signed OK. "Later this afternoon. Help us get these up."

Everything ready, Mike disconnected the air hose from the sand gun and brought it over to the first float. He held the tube inside the mouth of the bag and twisted the valve.

Air rushed into the float with loud gurgling sounds. The bag lifted off the bottom, straining toward the surface. He moved the nozzle to the second float, then the third and fourth. As the fourth bag filled, lift overcame dead weight and the gun rose off the floor of the lake for the first time in over two hundred years. Little by little, he added air until the bags began to ascend. As they rose, atmospheric pressure would decrease, causing them to expand and rise faster. He motioned for Sam to follow them to the surface where Sheik would need help getting the hoisting tackle on the gun to lift it aboard.

Minutes later, two more floats carried their prizes upward.

Mike closed the valve of the air tank. The stream of bubbles dwindled and ended.

Alone, he scanned the silent murk of the lakebed. This was it, the thing he loved. He, alone among men, had touched this part of the earth. He kicked upward toward the world.

On the surface, Sheik had the first cannon lassoed and suspended from the starboard davit, the noose of the cable looped and pulled tight under the gun's trunnion arms. As Mike watched from the swim platform, Sheik swung it aboard and lowered it to the deck.

Thirty minutes later, three growth-encrusted cannon safe aboard, the air bags and slings deflated and also aboard, the four tired divers relaxed, sipping hot tea, or in Jerry's case, coffee.

"What did you find, Jerry?" Mike asked, his feet up.

"Not much to see, just a small depression, but the metal detector liked it a lot," Jerry said. "It could be a chunk of iron ore but I don't think so."

"You guys check it after lunch. If it's anything, Laurel and I will come down and give a hand."

Mike studied her from the corner of his eye. He wondered how he could have thought of her as not quite beautiful. Even with her hair a tangled mess, and not a trace of makeup, she was.

❧   ❧

At 1:55, Sam broke the surface.

"Better bring the slings and bags back down, Laurel." His voice belied the excitement in his eyes. "We've found another one."

At the transom, Mike leaned over and swung two slings onto the swim platform. "You take these, Sam. Give us ten minutes and we'll bring down the bags."

The brothers wasted no time. By the time Laurel and Mike donned their gear and brought the lifting equipment down they had the slings under the new find. In minutes the floats were attached and inflated, and they all watched as the fourth find floated off toward the surface.

"That's it. We're done," Laurel grinned at them, nodding. "Let's go home."

Back aboard, Laurel stowed her equipment and went into the pilothouse to switch off the search gear. She glanced at the screen just as she pushed the mag set's power button. A broad yellow blip in the center of the screen seemed to flash as the screen went dark, probably an anomaly occurring when the unit was de-powered. They'd left nothing down there, so it couldn't have been an actual hit.

TWICE TOLD HOTEL

Although salvage law gave them full rights to anything found on the bottom, old guns implied a wrecked ship. Since 1987, it had been illegal to remove anything from the site of a wreck in the waters of New York State. Since there was no wreck where they'd found the guns, Laurel knew they were within their rights. At the same time, the less official interest they attracted, the easier life would be, so they brought their finds to Mexico Point under cover of darkness.

By ten they had their discoveries sequestered in the Twice Told Marina's aluminum-sided storage barn. Grampa Jake had long since retired to his apartment.

Sheik aimed the nozzle of the power washer at the gun they'd found last and squeezed the trigger. Mud, vegetation and zebra mussels flew. The surface cleaned, he rinsed the debris away and the three of them tapped and chipped at the more persistent scale until the dark gray surface metal near the trunnions, or pivot arms, lay exposed.

Laurel looked first at Mike, then at Sheik. "If there was a sinking, where's the ship?"

She studied the primitive weapon. "I keep going over it in my head, but I still can't figure how these guys got down there."

Sheik shook his head and Mike shrugged, not pretending to have an answer.

"What if there was a battle and the ship got hit and the cannons were knocked overboard in a tangle?" She paused, thinking about that. "Except it doesn't explain why there were three in the first bunch, then this one, two hundred yards away."

She touched the cold grey iron and slid her fingers along the uneven surface for several inches in each direction.

"What *were* you doing down there all alone, two hundred yards from your brothers?"

Sheik flipped the first of the light switches, throwing the back half of the interior into darkness. "I dunno, but I got enough sense not to stand here all night starving while I think about it."

Laurel didn't sleep well. With each restless movement of her body the grain of an idea grated, sand in an oyster. At last, she sat upright in the bed, in her mind's eye a flickering vision, a dark night, a fierce storm, a ship blown off course. Close enough to shore to hear the breakers, maybe shipping water or dismasted and under a jury rig. No matter, her captain needed to fight his way off that lee shore or the storm would wreck him for sure.

He gave the command to lighten ship. Bulwarks were flung open, ropes and tackle hacked away, the first two large and one small gun went overboard. A few minutes later another, then another and another.

In the dark-shadowed room she shared the agony of command with that brave captain. Somehow, she knew his desperate action helped, and the ship might possibly have escaped. But again, if the ship had indeed been the Ontario, it couldn't have or she wouldn't have found the report of the sinking, and Grampa Jake would have had no story to tell.

What would it take to prove her idea? Pulling on a t-shirt against the coolness of the night, she padded over to the desk, where she switched on a lamp and sat with a piece of paper and a pen, doodling as her mind extended her thoughts. At last she came to the only conclusion that made any sense.

Morning, October tenth. From the open window of her bungalow, Laurel noted an overcast sky and large seas cresting on the horizon. If conditions deteriorated any further, the lake could become a dangerous place today. A blast of cold air made her window vibrate and she cranked it shut.

At 8:30 she entered the dining room and made her way toward the veranda.

"Hey, we're in here," Grampa Jake called as she passed the bar. She stopped and backed up. Everyone was there, forced inside by the blustery weather.

In a far corner, the fireplace glowed. Welcoming warmth flowed from the room. Smiling, she joined them. Mike sat next to Jake so she slid in beside Sheik.

Platters circulated. Scrambled eggs with small bits of melted cheese and diced green peppers, short stacks of pancakes, bacon, breakfast ham, sausage. Laurel loaded up her plate.

A gust rattled the windowpanes. "Looks like it might blow today," Grampa Jake said as he finished a piece of toast and wiped his fingers.

Ten minutes later, Laurel put her cup down and pushed it away.

"I've got a few ideas I'd like to throw at you all. Mike, how about helping me clear a space so I can lay out this chart?"

The table cleared, she laid out a chart of the eastern end of the lake, orienting it so Grampa Jake and Mike viewed it right side up.

"I've noted the exact location of our find. The whisky and the three cannon were right here," she pointed to a small red dot she'd made, "give or take a foot. Now, the second find, the single gun, was one hundred and ninety yards almost directly north." She touched the tip of her pen to a spot close to the first, making a second red mark. "Here. Now, knowing that, two things come to mind. First, a line between these two points might indicate the ship's course, at least at that moment in time."

No one challenged her logic so she went on. "Second. I believe we'll find *other* cannon at approximately the same intervals."

Mike interrupted. "Why?"

"Because he was being driven onto a lee shore in a storm. Maybe his masts were down, or his sails blown to rags. He tried to lighten ship. That's why we found the guns so far apart and why we'll find others further north."

"How do you know he was heading north?" Sheik interjected. "He could have been headed south."

Laurel nodded, acknowledging the possibility. She'd thought it through during the night.

"I don't think so, Sheik. The ship was a mile, mile and a half offshore. If the storm had been a nor'easter, they would have been in calm water, sheltered by the land. Why throw your guns overboard in that kind of situation?" She paused, waiting while Sheik thought it over.

"Yeah, but what if the storm was from the west or northwest?"

"Why would a Captain sail south in such a storm, toward nowhere, when he could simply tack or jibe and run with the wind around Stony Point," she indicated the point on the map several miles north, "to the shelter of Henderson Harbor less than ten miles away?"

Sheik studied the chart. "Yeah, you got a point there."

Mike touched the chart. "I see how it could have happened. The ship goes off course for whatever reason. At last, they hear the surf and realize they're being driven onto a lee shore. Maybe it's the dead of night, or it's snowing or raining..."

"Yes!" Laurel's voice trembled. "That's it. They're desperate, they jettison the guns to try to stand off the shore, and they succeed, for a while, but then..." she made a series of red dots on the map, extending the course hinted at by the position of the guns they'd found, "... the land... comes... out... to... meet... them."

A new red dot followed each of her words, until the line reached the headland known as Stony Point. A simple row of dots, yet they hinted at a journey of desperation and fear, of heroic struggle no one present could really comprehend. And at last, they told of the loss of hope and the certainty of death. Iron men, those sailors, brave. They'd fought hard.

"Here." She almost whispered, touching the map, "is where I think we'll find our brave captain and his ship."

The silence stretched until Grampa Jake stirred, breaking the spell. He tapped the row of red dots. "Only way I can think of to prove it is to go out there while the lake is up, like today, and see if you can hear the breakers from there."

Mike jumped in, "Or, if the other guns are where Laurel thinks they are, it'd be easy to set up on the projected path and look for magnetic signals. It's pretty rough today, but the *Longley* could handle it."

He glanced at Laurel. "What do you think?"

"I've seen it worse."

"Me too. Let's do it."

Sheik spoke up. "If you don't mind, I'll stay here. I could use a day off. Besides, I don't do good in the heavy going."

It would be just the two of them.

They cleared the harbor at 12:10, breasting the larger waves stacked up just outside the mouth of the breakwaters. A low, fast-moving sky cast the water ahead in grays and blacks. Now and then an opening would appear in the cloud cover and sunlight lance down, spotlighting the whitecaps on the surface for a few seconds before disappearing.

Laurel headed north, taking the seas on the port bow. Occasionally, water came over and swept the decks, but for the most part the boat's motion remained easy enough.

"We're in a hundred and sixty feet of water," she said after five minutes. "The intervals are getting longer. I'm going to head east now."

Fifteen minutes later, Oswego lay low on the horizon to the southwest. Laurel touched the control console, moved the wheel smoothly, allowing the BBL to surf down the front side of a large roller. The wind had come up a good deal. She had the boat trimmed perfectly, running just a little slower than the overtaking seas, blunting their impact and lessening the effect of the wind.

She looked over at Mike. "I love this kind of weather, the sound of the wind, the whine of the rigging, the way spindrift comes off the tops of the waves. How about you?"

Mike could see she did: her face was flushed, animated, eyes alight. "Me too."

He watched her as she piloted the boat. A wisp of hair had escaped the green foul-weather cap she wore and fallen onto her forehead. His fingers twitched, ready to smooth it back for her, away from her eye, but she did it for herself before he could act, their eyes meeting for a moment.

She checked her course before looking at him sideways. "What?"

"I... I like the way you handle the boat." He wasn't quite able to say what he'd really been thinking, which was that right now, like this, she took his breath away.

She felt jittery, a little out of control. If they were forced to run into Henderson, they'd be alone all night. In spite of her best efforts to prevent it, she was attracted to him. Would he try...?

They arrived at the dive coordinates at two-thirty. The waves were very big now, and visibility down even further. The front had to be very near.

Mike had the helm.

"We're just about there," he said. The ceiling had dropped to two hundred yards and it was beginning to rain. "I don't think we'll be able to pinpoint anything on the bottom in these seas. I think we'd better just run into Henderson." He sounded disappointed.

Laurel had to agree. The anemometer read forty knots. "Hey!" She grasped him by the elbow, "Why don't we do what Grampa Jake suggested, see if we can hear the breakers?"

"Okay, I'll throttle down and you go outside and have a listen."

Laurel wrapped herself in her foul-weather gear, opened the deckhouse door and stepped outside. Driven rain found its way up her sleeves, under her waistband and down her collar, soaking her.

"Whoa!" she cried and grabbed, too late, at her hat. A gust claimed it and carried it several hundred feet before dropping it in the water. The wind shrieked through the antennas and exterior rigging, threatening to lift Laurel and carry her away as well. With the engines idling, the *Longley* fell into the trough of the waves and rolled.

She cupped her hand to her ear. There, under the fury of the wind, came the nearly continuous roar of surf, rolling in like endless distant thunder.

She had to fight to open the narrow door against the storm. Once she squeezed inside, the gale banged it shut behind her.

"I heard it! Let's get moving." She shivered her way out of the sodden gear. "I've got to change and dry my hair before I catch pneumonia."

She went down the steps toward the forward cabin.

Mike yelled after her. "I'm going to go ahead and run into Henderson. No sense beating ourselves up."

Just the thing she'd hoped would happen? Laurel wasn't sure. She stopped at the base of the companionway. Raising her voice, she said, "Okay."

Ten minutes later she'd changed and returned to the deckhouse. As they rounded Stony Point, the rain lifted and the sun peeked through a seam in the overcast.

Laurel gasped. "Take a look at that!"

Beyond the point, combers rolled in to the base of jagged cliffs, until the bottom tripped them at the last moment, causing them to break right into the base of the cliff. Huge plumes of water exploded, fifty, a hundred feet into the air. The unspent energy of each rejected wave rebounded, creating a cauldron of wild, undulating back-waves for hundreds of yards.

"I wouldn't want to get caught in there," Mike's voice broke into her fixation. "I doubt anything could survive that."

A stab of dread made Laurel shiver. If the wreck lay in there, they'd have to dive near those rocks. She shivered again. "Let's get out of here. This place gives me the *willies*."

After they rounded the head of Association Island and turned south toward Henderson, they came into the lee of the headland and the *Longley* settled into an easy motion for the run down the bay.

Mike eased up to a deserted pier in the town of Henderson, on the eastern shore of the bay. The marina was closed, the season long over. A few boats were still on moorings here and there, forlorn, but most had been hauled for the winter.

They worked together to secure the *Longley* for the night. Mike uncoiled the shore power cable, found an outlet, and pushed the prongs of the connector into the receptacle. He twisted, locking it in position.

"Okay, try it," he called.

Aboard, Laurel flipped a switch on the breaker panel and tried the 208V shore power system. It glowed to life. "Hey, we lucked out. They haven't turned off the juice yet."

Mike stepped back aboard, chuckling. "There's nothing sweeter than a free night at a commercial marina, and we've got the place to ourselves."

Laurel's cheeks warmed. "I'm going below," she stepped down to the cabin. "I'll see if I can find some wine."

She found a bottle of Chablis, and they ate in semi-style at the small dinette, splitting the wine. By seven, as dusk settled, the dishes were cleaned up and they took opposite ends of the settee built into the port side of *Longley's* cabin.

Laurel had herself buoyed up on pillows, facing him, feet tucked under. He had his legs extended, feet propped on the small table in front of the settee.

The radio played in the background.

Laurel let her magazine drop. After a minute their eyes met. She understood that by asking, she was telling him she was interested. She went ahead and did it anyway.

"Is there—anyone in your life?"

The question grabbed Mike and dragged him toward the pit. He blinked and tried to answer.

"There was, but…"

"Were you married?"

The mouth of the void opened wide. He could see the darkness inside. He managed one word. "Yes."

"What happened?"

Damn. She wasn't going to let up.

"She was kill..." his throat locked around the word.

"Oh. Oh! I... I'm sorry. I didn't mean..." She moved closer, the blanket still wrapped around her, rested her hand on his wrist and squeezed a little.

"Would it help to talk about it?"

The underside of his jaw clenched, constricting his throat in an all-too-familiar way. Suddenly, he was close to breaking down, and embarrassed, embarrassed that this woman could see him this way, see his weakness.

"We were in the Guard. I ordered her team aboard a suspect boat. There was a firefight. She didn't make it. It... It was my fault. I shouldn't have..."

She squeezed once, hard. "I don't believe it. Was there an inquiry?"

"Yes, it cleared me. But it didn't bring her back."

"Is that when you left the Coast Guard?"

He nodded slowly, dragging the back of his hand over his eyes. "I'm sorry. Every time I think about her, I crash."

"How about when you start feeling down, come talk to me."

He let his head rest against the cushions. "Thanks. I've got to pull myself together."

She let go his hand and stood. "I'm in the mood for tea. Want some?"

"Sure."

Laurel busied herself in the small galley. Less than two weeks ago, with Grampa Jake as her witness, she'd vowed never to let another man near her. Yet here she was again, thinking this one would be different.

She sat close to him, sharing the warmth of the blanket as they sipped the tea and talked, mostly about his life at first, his dream of living on the water, earning a living in some exotic way as yet undefined.

Animation returned to his voice little by little, creeping into his facial expressions, until he laughed once, and then, as though his laugh were a signal, she began to talk about herself.

"My mother died before my first birthday." She saw his face change as her words registered on him. "I always wished I could see her just once, talk with her, tell her I loved her."

She fell silent, resting her chin on her knees. Why do this?

"But I had Dad. Not having a female role model, I never knew what I missed. I grew up liking the same things he did. We sailed and fished and skied in the winter." She smiled at Mike. "I was the best player on the boys' hockey team for two years."

"No wonder you handle a boat like a pro. Where's your dad now?"

Laurel had to work to maintain the smile. "I lost him, too, when I was ten. There was a helicopter crash in the Alps." She wiped at her eyes. "Darn, now it's my turn. Anyway, for the longest time, I was mad at him two ways. One for not taking me on the ski trip, and the other for never coming home."

She had herself back under control. "My grandmother took me in. She shipped me off to boarding school in New York City, but I got to spend the summers at the Twice Told."

"Any special boyfriends?"

Why would that subject interest him? Unless…

"No, not then, I…"

But she'd hesitated long enough for him to misunderstand. "Sorry if I'm prying," he said.

"No, it's okay." She glanced at him, then quickly away. "I was about to say, something went wrong with me. I didn't have many friends. Not many people liked me." Laurel's lower lip trembled. She caught it between her teeth to still it, bit until it hurt.

"Laurel." He leaned closer, until his breath brushed the side of her face. "Thank you for listening, earlier. I didn't realize how much I needed to talk about all that."

He sat straighter, moving his head away so she could see his face, then put his hand over hers. "We could try being friends, you know."

She closed her eyes, afraid that if she allowed it and it didn't work she'd never be able to put her heart back together.

He let go of her hand. "It was just a thought. Think it over."

He stood and went to the forward bunk. "It's late. We've got to leave early if we want to be back before your friend from Woods Hole gets there. Let's get some sleep." He turned back the covers, got into the bunk, and switched off the light.

Laurel stretched out, pulled the blanket up to her chin and stared at the dark ceiling. Minutes passed, and the silence deepened. Outside, wavelets slapped the hull, and the boat moved ever so slightly in response. She felt much closer to Mike than she had that morning.

"Mike."

Silence, then, "Hmmm?"

All he wanted was to be her friend. "I'd like to be friends. I'd like it a lot."

Another, longer silence while her inner tension increased. When they came, the words were soft against the darkness.

"Okay. I think I would too."

The butterfly of tension in her belly relaxed and she breathed out. She felt just slightly shaky, as if she'd taken the first step toward something really good and wasn't quite sure how to continue.

ON THE LAKE

Romy Zaia put the SCUBA mouthpiece in and took a breath. Air flowed into his lungs from the tank on his back. He nodded to his deckhand, Nick. Joey, the helper, dumped the water from the facemask and handed it over.

The lake had calmed down a lot since yesterday's storm, but it still took an hour to get into just the right position. He was pretty sure he was right over the spot where the Eastlands had been diving.

The wetsuit he wore had seen better days; the seam under one arm had a small tear, and there was a hole in one knee, but his single tank gear was well maintained, in perfect operating condition, and he knew how to use it. He would have liked to have one of the new suits, but a guy had to make sacrifices sometimes. He had a woman, and a couple of kids, and it took just about everything he could bring home to keep them happy.

The tank would give him about twenty minutes on the bottom in seventy-five feet if he didn't exert himself too much.

He hooked the strap of the underwater light to his weight belt and held his mask in position as he dropped backwards into the water.

Water flooded his suit through the holes, numbing his knee and his side. Ignoring the cold, he pulled himself down the anchor line to the bottom. Visibility was about fifteen feet. He clicked the light on and scanned the bottom a full three hundred and sixty degrees. Nothing. Flat as a board, except for a shadowed area twenty yards away, a hole of some kind. He swam toward it and hovered overhead, ten feet up. A recess perhaps six feet square and three feet deep was cut into the bottom.

Puzzled, he scanned another full circle of the bottom. There were no other places like this one. As he aimed his light at the hole again, something sparkled against the far side: a piece of glass. He held it up, discarded it and shone his light against the wall, close this time, a foot away.

What the hell?

The neck and top third of a bottle projected from the gravel. He wiggled it and it came loose easily: a bottle of whisky.

Shit! Bootleg whisky. They must have found a stash.

He took his knife and dug more silt and gravel out of the side wall. In minutes, he had another bottle. He checked his watch; it was time to go up. He secured his find and prepared to leave. As he did, his light reflected off a different kind of item in the opposite wall. He moved closer. Two links of old chain lay under a yellow coin-like object. Could it be gold? He picked it up, ignoring the chain, and ascended.

When he was aboard, he showed the whisky to his men. He did not show them the disk.

That night, after his sister and her family were asleep, Romy used a magnifying glass to study it. It was smaller than a dime, and thinner, not quite round. One thing about it was unmistakable: it was dated seventeen-sixty. There was something down there. Something big, and old, very old. The whisky must have been jettisoned and caught on whatever it…

Treasure!

The idea was almost too much for him. He would watch everything they did, beginning first thing tomorrow morning. A chance to get even with the Eastlands didn't come along every day.

He could almost see his grandfather Emilio waving his wizened stump of a hand while he told his stories. Course, he was always drunk, so who knew how much of it was true?

Hatred of the Eastlands was part of being a Zaia, but the only person in the family who had a handle on what really happened was his cousin Nick. Nicky was smart as hell, had a big job in New York City. Secretly, Romy was jealous of his nose-in-the-air attitude, but Nicky knew the story.

The whole feud happened because the Eastlands were trying to horn in on Joe Zaia, his great grandfather. Naturally, Joe was forced to fight back, and the Eastlands killed him for standing up.

Romy put the medallion on the chest beside his bed. Nicky would be proud of him when he grabbed the treasure and beat old man Eastland all by himself. He decided to give Nicky a call and tell him what he'd learned. No. It was too late. He'd do it in the morning.

TWICE TOLD HOTEL

Aaron Hoenig, Laurel's archaeologist friend from Woods Hole, was a big man in his late thirties. In faded jeans, a bushy brown beard and with fingers thick as sausages, he resembled a lumberjack. The only external hint that he might be more than he seemed was the pair of rimless eyeglasses he wore. His area of expertise: nautical archaeology.

From a tool kit filled with picks, calipers, rock hammers and more, he selected a sturdy knife with a thick three-inch blade. This he pushed into the wall of solidified marine growth that filled the bore of the cannon they'd begun to clean.

The knife went in as if into butter. Taking pains not to gouge the metal, Hoenig cored the marine growth and wiggled until it dropped to the floor.

Ignoring the mess, he lifted a Dremel tool from its storage pocket in his case. It emitted a *wheee* like a dentist's drill as it reached operating speed of thirty thousand RPM.

Dust flew as he worked the rabid little tool back and forth until he had exposed the bare metal of the first few inches of the bore. He went to the tool kit again, this time for a magnifying glass. Holding it close to the surface, he bent to inspect the exposed metal.

"Hmmm." He slid the handle of the magnifying glass into his back pocket, lifted a set of inside calipers from the raised lid of his tool kit, and measured the bore.

"Just as I thought," he mumbled, looking around at Laurel. She, Grampa Jake, and Mike waited a few feet away, watching.

As if remembering his manners, Hoenig straightened and smiled.

"The bore is three point sixty-six inches. That makes it a six-pounder, and the bore is drilled, see." He pointed to the metal he'd exposed. They moved closer and bent over to see better. "You can see the tiny grooves made by the drill."

"Weren't all cannon drilled?" Laurel asked.

"Oh, no. The technology wasn't there until the late seventeen hundreds. Until then, guns were cast with core rods in place. After the metal cooled, the core was pulled out and the opening reamed to the right size." He patted the muzzle. "That means this guy was made sometime after seventeen seventy-three."

"Is there a way to pin down the exact date?" Laurel asked.

"Maybe. Most iron guns weren't dated or marked with the founder's name. I'm not sure about this one yet. Let's measure it." He handed her the end of his tape measure. "Hold it on the top of the breech ring."

Laurel didn't move. "I... I'm sorry, I don't know what the breech ring is."

"Shame! What kind of scientist are you?" Aaron joked, then looked at the others.

"Does anyone know the parts of a gun?" He polled faces. No one answered.

"How about a quick run through, then?" He rubbed his hands together, and touched the muzzle. "Anyone know what this end is called?"

"The business end?" Mike quipped.

"How right you are, Mike." All four of them laughed.

"Technically, this whole swollen area here at the end of the gun is the muzzle. It extends as far as the fillets," he tapped two raised rings of flat metal ten inches from the muzzle face. "It's upside down the way it's sitting now."

"We can roll it over," Mike said at once. "We've got it sitting on bearing races. I can do it alone." He demonstrated, rotating the big gun one hundred and eighty degrees.

"Very clever," Aaron said, beginning again. "Incidentally, the location of the trunnions, the arms that support the gun in its cradle, is one of the things that tell me this is a British gun. See how they're located below the midline?" He indicated the middle with his hand. "If you could see the bore inside, you'd see that the trunnions are centered on its lower level. The stodgy British were the last to raise them, even in the face of proof that guns were easier to point with the higher trunnions."

He moved nearer to the back end of the cannon and rested his hand on the widest reinforcing ring at the end while smiling at Laurel. "This is the breech ring. It's there to add strength and also to provide a collar for the Cascabel to fit into."

The dome-shaped breech end of the gun had a kind of knob protruding from the middle. Aaron indicated it with his hand. "This is the Cascabel. It was made from a separate mold, which was then fitted to the tube mold to form the breech of the gun." He touched the widest ring. "Measure from here."

Laurel held her end of the metal tape at the point he indicated. He stretched the tape and made a note on the notepad he carried.

"Now, we'll see if this fellow was a ship's gun or a landlubber." He bent over his notebook and did a quick bit of figuring. "Most likely from a ship's ordnance," he announced fifteen seconds later, slipping the notepad into his shirt pocket.

"How can you tell it's from a ship?" Laurel said. The fact tended to support her theory, but how could Aaron tell so easily?

Aaron turned to her. "Shore guns were almost always shorter than ships' guns. It made them lighter." He patted the gun. "By the time this guy was made, bore lengths of ships' guns were at sixteen times caliber, and shore guns fifteen times. It made them easier to lug around, I suppose."

Grampa Jake spoke for the first time. "You said the trunnions were one of the things that told you this was a British gun. What were the others?"

Aaron's hand stopped in mid-gesture. He nodded at Jake.

"Yes. Of course." He pointed to an area on the first reinforce. With the gun upright, they could see raised letters and a symbol. Laurel leaned closer. The symbol was an inverted "W" with two extra legs. Below it were the letters "G R."

"See the crown?" Aaron's voice was hushed. "It's George Rex, King of England."

There in the bright morning light, a distant time reached out and touched Laurel.

Aaron spoke again, this time looking at Grampa Jake.

"Your question got my head going, Mr. Eastland. I don't know why I didn't see it sooner." He traced the raised inscription with a fingertip. "By seventeen-ninety, the practice of casting guns with relief inscriptions like these had ended. Later guns were lathed and then engraved, rather than cast with raised areas that couldn't be turned in a lathe. They worked just as well and were cheaper. That narrows this gun down to between seventeen seventy-three, when the first solid-cast British guns were founded, and seventeen-ninety, when they'd just about stopped making them with relief castings. This gun was probably aboard a British warship during the Revolutionary War."

Laurel put her fingers on the spot where she'd held the tape measure. She'd noticed a depressed area as she held the tape in position. "Is this anything, Aaron? It looks like a carving of some kind."

The magnifying glass appeared from his back pocket.

"Good eyes! It's a maker's mark." Aaron knocked his tool kit over in his hurry to retrieve the Dremel tool. He finished and brushed away the last of the dust. He studied the breech markings, moving his head side to side in wonder.

They pressed closer. The words "BACON SOLID", and the code "C.18 q.0" stared back at them from across the centuries.

Aaron's tone went reverent. "This man was the first English founder to cast solid guns that proofed." He shook his head. "It's one of the very first ones. This find may be unique in the world. I've got to get into the archives and find out what ship it was on."

Laurel held her tongue. If Aaron came up with the same answer she had, it would strengthen her own conclusion. Besides, she hadn't told Mike there could be a treasure aboard and she was a little afraid of how he would react. She really needed to tell him soon. First though, she wanted to prove the treasure existed. Easy to say. So far, she had zilch.

They reconvened in the bar for drinks before dinner.

Aaron blurted his news the moment their waitress left. "The ship was H.M.S. *Ontario*. She was lost October thirty-first, seventeen-eighty, while on her way from Niagara to Oswego."

"What cargo was aboard?" Mike asked.

Laurel thought he looked very handsome tonight.

Aaron grinned. "Military gear and supplies. But there was a payroll, too. The manifest didn't say how much, only that it was sufficient to pay the garrison for a period in excess of one year. That wouldn't add up to a lot, but I'll tell you this much." Aaron tapped his finger on the table. "H.M.S. *Ontario* was new, and had a top notch captain and first officer, plus an experienced crew. It would have taken something special out there on your pond to knock those boys down. Your average gale wouldn't have been enough to do it."

Laurel thought about the poor souls who had run into "something special" and gone down with their ship into the cold black depths. A favorite passage leapt into her head. She spoke into the silence,

"'Now gentlemen, in their interflowing aggregate, these grand fresh-water seas of ours—Erie and Ontario, and Huron and Superior and Michigan—possess an oceanlike expansiveness. They contain round archipelagos of romantic isles. They have heard the fleet thunderings of naval victories. They are swept by Boolean and dismasting waves as direful as any that lash the salted wave. They know what shipwrecks are: for out of sight of land, however inland, they have drowned many a midnight ship with all its shrieking crew.'"

Mike said, "That's beautiful. What's it from?"

His eyes warmed her. "It's Ishmael. From *Moby Dick*." She looked around at the others, shy all at once. "It's always been one of my favorites."

"She's a poet but she don't know it," Sheik waved his left hand, fracturing the mood.

Laurel's eyes found Mike's and held them.

"What?" he asked.

Now that she'd decided to be friends, her feelings threatened to become much more than that. She felt one corner of her mouth curl in a little smile, almost like Grampa Jake's. It was an easy habit to acquire. "Nothing."

Laurel's back ached and she was discouraged. Aaron Hoenig's excitement over the guns had caught her up, but, Boolean waves notwithstanding, it was now ten o'clock and her research efforts had run into a stone wall.

After several hours on-line, she was no closer to proving a treasure had been aboard the Ontario than the day she discovered Grampa Jake's legendary ship actually existed.

She hit "tab" and the next letter came up on her monitor. Another of the voluminous Haldimand Papers, the personal papers of Frederick Haldimand who had served as Governor of Canada from 1778-1784.

Several earlier letters had made reference to H.M.S. *Ontario*. She'd even found a copy of the ship's manifest. But it indicated little of value to a treasure hunter. The passengers had been mostly soldiers.

The date of the latest letter caught her attention and she leaned closer to the screen. Nope, no good; written long after the ship went down. Her eye scanned it anyway and when she caught a reference to *Ontario* she read more carefully.

May 6, 1781.

"Dear Frederick, I am dismayed to learn of the disappearance of the brig Ontario. I saw her off myself. She was a fine ship. I must admit I feared for her when the earth quaked that night. Fearful it was, I assure you. I was thrown from my bed and our new home nearly destroyed. And then the storm right on the heels of the quake.

Most unusual. Many of the Indians camped nearby perished. They had no food and little shelter, poor creatures. How they will manage through the next winter I can not say.

Dear Sir, it has just occurred to me that the proceeds of the tax you levied on all shipping two years ago were aboard her. One day before her departure I saw it loaded myself, a black chest made secure with both padlock and chain. It took six men, one on each length of chain, to carry it. Must you now increase the levy to gain back what has been lost to the deep?

She had to read it twice before it fully registered. A black chest, six men to carry it! She jumped to her feet, so filled with energy the room could hardly contain her.

Mike! He'd be happy and surprised. She had their provenance. All that was left was to find the ship, and they knew right where to look.

It was just before ten, she could probably catch him before he went to bed. She reached for her windbreaker and slipped it on.

Jake turned out the lights, ready for bed, and crossed to the row of windows. He cranked two shut, leaving the third open just a little. Below, in the private lot behind the hotel, he heard a door close, and a few seconds later the sound of an engine. He stepped closer and peered down. Headlights came on and backup lights flashed. Mike's truck.

After Sheik's warning that Mike might be a boozer, Jake had a little talk with his hotel manager. If Mike drank, or used drugs, Jake would hear about it before it got done happening.

To date, Mike had not purchased any alcohol, except for a glass of wine with his dinners, since arriving at the hotel. He did not smoke, and the housekeeping staff had found no traces of clandestine imbibing, or any other substance use.

Jake crossed to his desk and picked up the phone. He tapped three pads. A minute later, Sheik answered.

"This better be good," Sheik sounded testy. "It's after ten."

Mike felt better than he had in a long time. During their night together, Laurel had helped him get past something major. At the same time, her closeness created a tension in him. He wasn't sure he could let go of Mary all the way yet. If he could be in neutral territory, just for a little while, it might help.

He left his room and went down to the veranda. There was no one around. Why not go for a ride, just for the heck of it? Maybe he'd run over to Oswego and have a beer. The only bar he knew was a place called the Ferris Wheel. He and Carl Benz, the Port Authority foreman, had stopped there a few times. Carl might even be there tonight.

He went around to the parking lot, pulled open the door of his truck and climbed in. He rolled the window down, fished around in the never-used ashtray for the key, found it, kicked the engine over and backed out of the lot.

Laurel had her hand on her doorknob when Mike's headlights came on, bright on her ceiling. Going out at this time of night? Had he done what the Coast Guard woman asked? Called her? Was he going to see her now? She peeked out in time to see taillights.

There was nothing between them, but after last night, after they'd shared those things, she felt a kind of bond with him, one she didn't yet have words for.

My God! What if he told the weightlifter what they were doing? Laurel could see it in her mind's eye, that woman plying him with liquor, pumping him for information, using sex to get what she wanted from him.

There was no kidding herself about that. The woman would do it, it would be too easy. Mike's emotions were at a delicate stage. There was no telling what he'd blurt out in the heat of passion.

She jammed her feet into her shoes, grabbed a coat, and went out to the hotel Blazer. His taillights were pinpricks in the distance when she reached the main road. He was headed toward Oswego.

She followed.

Mike found a stool and ordered a draft. When it came, he downed it in several gulps and planted the mug on the bar, signaling the bartender for another. He rested his back against the bar, one foot on the foot rail, his knee lifted.

The four-piece band hammered out a respectable cover of a seventies hit to a dance floor crowded with younger people.

Char walked right into him, straddling his raised knee. When she stopped, her crotch pressed square against his thigh. She leaned closer until her mouth was inches from his.

"Hi there, big guy. Didn't you see me wave?" She inched further up his thigh.

She wore tight-fitting jeans and a short-sleeved blouse. Her body was hot where it contacted his thigh. Warm dampness. In spite of himself, he was aroused.

A fast number throbbed.

"Let's dance." She wouldn't take no for an answer, pulled him out to the dance floor. She could really move her body. Mike noticed some of the younger guys eyeing her.

The number ended and the next began. A slow dance. Char raised her arms. He stepped into them.

"Ah yes," she sighed, hugging him as they moved. "I remember this. I'm jealous."

"Jealous? Of who?"

"That little twitch on your boat. Who do you think?"

"You mean Laurel? No, I..."

"Of course, dummy. She's after you. Can't you tell?" Char pressed closer. "I am too, but you never call. What am I supposed to think?"

She moved against him, promising everything. The beer he'd chugged hit him. His body answered. He tried to draw away.

"Don't," she whispered. "Let's just dance. I love the way it feels against my belly." They danced for several minutes, if you could call it that.

Char raised her mouth to his ear. "I want you, big guy. We can go to my place." She pulled him closer. "I'll make it special for you."

If he let it happen, maybe it would take some of the pressure off. He pulled her close.

hit him. His body answered. He tried to draw away.

Laurel passed the waterfront restaurants on the East Side of the river. Their parking lots were well populated, but his truck was not there. She crossed to the west side and made the sharp right on Water Street, parallel to the river.

Old City Hall and The Wheel faced each other across the one-lane brick-paved street. Both bars were crowded. Down by the river she spotted a truck with a Coast Guard decal on the rear window. Now what? Waltz up to him and say, "Oh, hi there, I just happened to be following you?"

She should leave. He was in the bar having a few beers, most likely alone, just needing some time away from the Twice Told. Her showing up would make her look like a fool.

Fool or not, she had to know for sure.

In the "Wheel," patrons stood two-deep at the bar. The small pool table was in use and at the long end of the room, the dance floor crowded. He wasn't at the bar. She scanned the dance floor.

No! He *was* with the slut from the Coast Guard. Her worst fear, the bitch had hold of him, and whatever she had in mind seemed well advanced. The woman said something into Mike's ear, at the same time grinding her pelvis into him.

The big woman wouldn't hesitate to go all the way with him. She was about to steal him before Laurel even got started. She felt lightheaded. She had to get away, get some air.

Outside, the night air had become cold. She leaned against the building and let her head rest against the brick.

It wasn't fair, he was hers. Even when she didn't really want to want him, she'd gambled everything on his friendship.

She heard his voice and turned away just as they emerged, arms around one another. They laughed and talked as they went down to the parking lot.

Three blocks from Char's condo, Mike changed his mind. He slowed, pulled into a parking spot, and stopped. In front of him, Char's brake lights flashed and she pulled over too, then backed toward him in the deserted parking lane.

He put the truck in park and got out. A hundred yards ahead a traffic light blinked and went red.

"What's wrong? Why'd you stop?" She'd left her car door open and he could hear the dinging noise. She tried to embrace him but he pushed her arms down.

"I'm sorry, Char. I'm just not ready for this."

"What? I don't believe it. What happened, baby? You were hot for it in the Wheel." Her eyebrows pulled together, making her eyes seem narrower. She put her hands on his chest. "Please, just try. I'll be so good to you."

He grasped her wrists, lightly. "There… might be someone else. I'm not sure yet. I can't do anything to jeopardize that."

A vehicle approached and flashed past, speeding. Mike recognized the Twice Told Blazer. The driver ignored a yellow light at the intersection and kept going.

Char jerked her hands away, her mouth partly open. "It's that bitch I saw outside The Wheel isn't it? She thought I didn't notice her there, spying on you."

What could she be talking about? Mike didn't have time to think further. Char got right into his face. "You tell her she better have a bodyguard along the next time I see her. And you, you *prick*, I'll get even with you if it's the last thing I do." Spittle flew from her lips with the word "prick", landing on his cheek.

She wiped the corner of her eye, pushed herself away and ran to her car, sobbing. She slammed the door. The transmission clanged as she forced it into gear and squealed away from the curb in a cloud of blue-grey smoke. At the intersection, the brake lights of the stopped vehicle flashed as Char passed it on the right and ran the red light.

Mike turned onto the lane leading to the Twice Told. What a night. He'd burned a tank of gas running the back roads. At first, thoughts of Mary jammed themselves into his head, riding up and over everything else. So many things he could have done differently; used protection the night she conceived; ordered her to stay home that day; assigned someone else to go aboard the drug boat.

Then, little by little, things Laurel had said at Henderson Harbor chipped away at the wall of guilt he'd put up. He began to see what she'd tried to get at. He couldn't have done any of it differently, especially that fatal day, and still stay true to the things he believed in.

Laurel had her problems, too. She'd shared them with him honestly, and for her they were every bit as serious as his were to him. He hoped he'd been at least a little help. He sensed the beginnings of something good for them, if they could both manage not to make any false steps.

They had no agreement, other than to be friends, and he remained free to see others. It was far too early for the intimate part, anyway. At the same time, he understood sleeping with Char would have been a mistake. God knew his body needed release, but he didn't want it with Char. If and when it happened, he wanted it to mean something.

At eight in the morning, there were few signs of activity as he pulled into the parking lot. Right now, he needed a shower and some coffee, in that order. Using the side entrance, he took the stairwell to his room.

An envelope lay on the floor near the door. It had the hotel logo in the return address corner. He opened it.

"*Mister M. McKean:*

Effective immediately, your services will no longer be required. Payment in full for services to date will be made via registered mail within twenty-four hours of receipt of your room keys."

Laurel Kingsford for Jake Eastland

Mike read the note again. Jake Eastland firing him? After all he'd done to help make the dive a success? What about Laurel, what about…?

Surprise twisted into pained rejection, then anger. She'd written the goddamn note. She had to be in on it. He went to the phone and called the desk. Mister Eastland and Miss Kingsford were out on the lake, fishing. They were expected back around noon. He slammed the phone into its cradle and pulled his suitcase from the closet.

Wait. On the lake, were they? Well, shit, they didn't have to fire him. He'd quit! He left the room and took the stairs two at a time. Outside, he double-timed to the marina and pulled the door open.

"I need the keys to a boat. Quick!"

Sheik dropped his feet to the floor and sat up in his chair. He didn't seem surprised to see Mike, or upset by the urgency in his voice. He waved at the wall beside him. "Sure, Mike. Take the seventeen-footer. Third key from the right."

Mike grabbed the key and turned toward the door.

"By the way, Mike."

Mike stopped, looking at Sheik.

"They headed west."

Laurel hadn't slept a wink. Good thing, because she'd completely forgotten her promise to go fishing with Grampa Jake this morning.

Grampa Jake pointed at the thermos. "Want some more coffee, hon? Maybe you need something to speed you up. You look like you're about to doze off."

Not a chance. They'd been out three hours. Her seat was

uncomfortable, and she was chilly, even in the oversized flannel-lined shirt he'd loaned her.

Laurel put her hand to her forehead. "Not now, thanks. I have a wicked headache."

In truth, second thoughts buzzed around in her head. How would she come up with another diver? She dreaded the thought of looking, and what if Mike didn't take being fired easily? What if he demanded reasons?

A corner of Grampa Jake's mouth twitched. He was about to tease her. He had no idea how much crud flopped around in her head at the moment. "I thought I heard you leave around ten last night. Hot date?"

She forced a smile and patted his hand. How would she explain? In the hard light of morning, what she'd done last night seemed less than logical.

The tip of his rod bent and the drag whirred. "Hey! You've got a hit." A reprieve. Just in time, too.

"Yo!" He grabbed the rod and lifted the tip. "Turn the motor off, hon. Feels like another good one."

They let the boat drift. Laurel started to feel a bit better. Being in the midst of nature calmed her. For several minutes they didn't speak, enjoying the silence, the small movements of the boat beneath them. Bits of seaweed kept pace as a gentle wind moved the water.

Time slipped. The lake turned navy blue and the sky piled high with immaculate white cumulus. Her headache faded.

Beside her, Grampa Jake stirred, "Somebody's coming out. It looks like the seventeen-footer." He pointed.

A boat ran straight toward them at full throttle. Her headache made a sudden comeback. She shielded her eyes with her hand. "Can you tell who it is?"

"Nope. But it won't be long before we find out. That boat can't run any faster."

Laurel had a pretty good idea. She should have known Mike wouldn't go away without a fight.

PORT ONTARIO

Sunday. The best day to reach Nicky. Careful not to disturb the medallion he'd found on the bottom yesterday, Romy reached into his shirt pocket and took out the slip of paper he'd written the number on. When he heard the dial tone, he touched each number on the chrome-plated keypad, making sure each tone was clear and distinct.

An automated voice said, "You have dialed a number outside this area code. Please insert one dollar and seventy-five cents for the first two minutes,"

"No shit, Sherlock," Romy mumbled. He plumbed his pockets and came out with a handful of quarters. He put six in the slot, one after the other. Nothing happened. He fed another quarter in. That one did it. After a series of clicks, a phone began to ring.

Out on the road a semi passed, followed by a string of cars. He hardly heard when the other end was picked up.

"Zaia residence."

Romy yelled. "Uncle Nicky, that you?"

"Just a minute," the voice sounded distant.

Nicky came on. "Romy, I can always tell when it's you calling. My roommate claps his hand over his ear like he's gone deaf."

Romy laughed. Nicky was the sarcastic type. "Hey, I can't help it if a truck went by just as he answered."

"You can get a phone right in your own house now, Romy. Lots of people are doing it."

"Hell with that!" Romy snorted and stamped his foot in the dust outside the gas station. "You have to pay 'em every month even if ya don't use the fuckin' thing. And by the time they get done sneaking taxes on… I don't even wanna talk about it. It oughta be free, just like TV. You buy the set, put rabbit ears on and there you go, all free."

Romy heard Nicky laugh. Of course he was just kidding. He couldn't call from there, his sister listened to everything he did. It made him feel good to make his uncle smile. "Hey, Nicky, you ain't gonna believe what I found out. It's about the Eastlands."

Silence from the other end, then a curt, "Tell me."

Nicky sounded different, harsher.

"The old man moved into the Twice Told about six months ago. I told you that, remember? Well, anyway, now they've got a big boat, I mean over sixty feet, and some chick is with him and they're lookin' for something. They got a whole team of people." Romy glanced to either side, and covered the mouthpiece with his hand. "I think there might be a shipwreck, maybe even a treasure."

Uncle Nicky didn't say anything for a long time. So long, Romy started to think the connection might be broken. He worked the hang-up lever on the phone's cradle. "Uncle Nicky, you still there?"

"Stop that! I'm here. I'm thinking. Give me a second, goddamn it."

After a few more seconds, Romy heard Nicky let his breath go. "Okay, now listen here, Romy. I'm going to tell you a secret. A real big secret. If you work with me on this, it'll mean money. More money than you ever dreamed of."

That got Romy's attention. He put a hand over his ear and turned away from the road, hunching over to hear better.

Nicky said, "What if I told you I know how to get that old bastard's money, all of it?"

"He's got a lotta money?"

"Jesus, Romy! Ah, never mind, take it from me, he's loaded."

"But how could we get it? He probably don't keep it around."

After another pause, Uncle Nicky said, "Listen close. Pay attention, Romy. You take care of things, and you'll never have to work again, okay? That woman is Jake Eastland's granddaughter. I thought I had her out of the picture, but she's a resilient little bitch. Good thing I checked the address we sent her retirement fund money to."

Romy scratched his head. What the heck was Nicky getting at? "I don't get it. What the fuck's that got to do with us?"

"If something happens to her, he won't have anybody to leave his money to. His will could be challenged by his other heir."

"An accident, no problem. But how does that get us the money?"

"Listen close, Romy. *I'm* the other heir. My father was Jake Eastland's son."

Romy tasted diesel fumes on his tongue. "But, that makes you his…" His mind couldn't produce the word.

"His grandson, that's right. I'm Jake Eastland's grandson. Illegitimate as hell, but still his flesh and blood, and he doesn't have a fucking clue. I can prove it. With Laurel Kingsford out of the picture, I'll have an almost perfect claim to his estate. I might even get it all."

Romy heard Uncle Nick chuckle. "You listen to me, Romy. You do your part, and pretty soon we'll get even for every rotten thing that bastard has ever done to our family."

INSHORE

Jake watched his seventeen-foot Whaler approach. At the last moment, the power went off and the Whaler squatted in the trough, showed the underside of its belly, and stopped, ooching forward as the stern wave caught up and pushed.

It was Mike, and he didn't look happy as he spun the wheel and deftly slid the craft around to come alongside. The two boats rocked in the leftover wake. Obviously, something had him upset.

Mike grabbed the gunwale of their boat and kept the boats from bumping.

His eyes bored into Jake's. "I thought you had more class, Jake. I'm really disappointed." His voice rasped as if under great strain. "The least you could have done is fire me face to face. I put a lot more into your job than I had to."

Fired? What the hell was the man talking about? Jake started to stand.

Before he could, Mike reached into his pocket and pulled out the blue key holder. "I just wanted to make sure you got your goddamn key back. You can have it right now. I don't take that kind of crap from anybody." He threw the key toward Jake's feet.

It bounced and hit Jake in the shin.

"Hey! What the hell…?"

McKean shifted his eyes and glared at Laurel for several seconds. He shook his head grimly then pushed off, put the Whaler into gear and jammed the throttle all the way forward. The engine revved, pulling the bigger boat toward its backwash, and as quickly as he'd arrived, Mike left.

Laurel's face was white and she looked stricken. She knew something.

"What just happened, Laurel? Did Mike just quit us?"

Her words came slowly. "No. I fired him. Last night. I meant to tell you."

"You fired him? What the hell'd you do that for? He's doing a great job for us."

"He… he left with that woman from the Coast Guard. I saw them together. I… I thought he went home with her."

Jake stared at his granddaughter. Her eyes couldn't hold his and she looked away. Jealous retribution, plain and simple. Would she compound her error by trying to make a bad decision seem plausible?

She stared after Mike, disappearing across the water. "I feel sick. I've made a mistake. A terrible mistake. Hurry, we have to catch up to him."

Jake started the engines. In a minute, they were headed for home at top speed.

The seventeen-footer bobbed at the Marina dock when they arrived, its engine ticking.

Sheik helped Laurel step up to the dock. "What the devil's going on, Jake? First Mike comes running in wanting the keys to a boat, then he comes slamming back, runs to his truck and leaves without a word. Now, you rock the whole marina with a two-foot wake."

Jake tossed up the bow line. "Laurel fired him."

Sheik gaped at her. "Wow. When you blow one, you blow it big. Mike was hot enough to melt the sidewalk."

"Yeah," Grampa Jake said, "and I don't blame him. You still got that recipe for baked crow, Sheik?"

Sheik smiled. "Makes it taste just like chicken, my wife useta say. Hafta look. Maybe I threw it out."

She had to apologize. Knowing made her stomach feel queer in a way she'd almost forgotten. She put her hands on her hips and faced them. "Okay, it was a stupid mistake. He'll have to stop at the *Longley* to get his gear. I might be able to catch him and see if I can get him to reconsider. Give me that key." She held out her hand to Grampa Jake.

"You better get your butt in gear," he said. "I don't think I ever had him give us a registration card. Did he tell you his address?"

"My God. No." Laurel ran toward the hotel Blazer.

Jake's stomach rumbled. Laurel had been gone two hours. The phone rang. "We have Mr. King on the line, Mr. Eastland."

"Thanks. Plug me in."

A click, then Allie said, "Hi, Uncle Jake. How's tricks?"

"We got a couple nice bass this morning. Tony's frying them up in his special batter."

"You've got the life up there. I can almost taste them."

"Say, Allie, have the preliminaries come in on our diver?"

"The McKean fellow? There was nothing to worry about. I mailed the report."

"Good. See if you can dig up a current home address."

"Just a second." Allie gave someone an instruction. "What'd you do, lose touch with him?"

Jake frowned at his reflection in the glass. "Yes, kind of. Laurel did something pretty immature. I don't know about that kid. By the way, where's the paperwork on my will? I asked you to change it back. I haven't seen it yet."

"Eeech! I completely forgot. I'll take care of it right away. Okay, here's McKean's mailing address."

Jake wrote it down as Allie read it off.

"Don't give up on her, Uncle Jake. From what I've heard so far, I think she's got the right stuff."

"I'm not so sure. She fired McKean because she thought he was sleeping with some woman from the Coast Guard. I hate petty stuff like that."

"Sure, but hey, we all make mistakes. Give her time to figure it out."

"What're you, her lawyer now?"

Allie laughed. "Let me come up there for a couple weeks. I'm missing everything."

"Get that will to me." Jake put the phone down. Actually, he wasn't that sure he wanted to change the will back anymore. Overall, Allie was right. Laurel wasn't doing all that bad. Still, he'd told Allie to do it and he didn't like changing his mind mid-stream. Time enough to decide when the paperwork showed up.

Down in the parking lot, a car door closed. He stepped over to the window. He watched Laurel enter the hotel. A minute later the elevator dinged and she arrived at the penthouse.

"I missed him." She came over and flopped down beside him on the couch. "I'm so sorry, Grampa Jake. How could I have let myself do something so stupid?" She held her palm to her forehead and closed her eyes.

"I thought the two of you were beginning to be a little more than friends."

She leaned on him. "I… we… I hoped."

He put his arm around her and gave her a hug. "You'll find him. He'll come back. With someone like you interested, he'd be crazy not to."

The curtains billowed and a wave of cool air invaded the room. Moments later, the light went flat as the sun slipped behind a cloud. Rain in the forecast again. Rain and cold.

She stirred against him, "I'm so tired of living with everything all tied down and in order. Sometimes I wish I could let go, let it just happen without worrying about it."

Jake stood and went to the window. Since she'd arrived and stirred things up, memories of the past plagued him. He plunged his fists deep into his pockets, her words still resonating. He'd felt that way too, long ago. He could have taken the chance, committed himself to Estelle. It might not have worked out, but the mistakes that followed with Jean would never have happened, and neither would the bigger, more devastating ones that came later on.

Behind him, Laurel said, "The day you told me the story of the storm. I had *such* a strange feeling. Like the ship existed, but only for

me. Going west was the right thing to do, but I didn't want to. The need
to stay here came so fast and so strong it scared me. I thought if I let
something so crazy catch me up, I might never be able to get control
again."

He turned away from the window. "A lot of people out there never
reach for the brass ring because they're afraid of what others will think.
If you want happiness, stop worrying about what other people think
and concentrate on doing the things you think are right for you."

Jake frowned, the king of unhappiness dispensing wisdom from his
flask of tears. He chided himself for presuming to give her advice.

He turned away, toward the lake again, looking out to the empty
horizon, then let his forehead rest on the cool glass.

He spoke into it, "Learning the truth about who you are doesn't
always make you happy."

His breath made a momentary fog on the glass. His throat felt dry
and he stopped to clear it. "Marriage did it for me. I didn't really know
until after I got married. Even then, I didn't admit it to myself for a long
time."

He stopped, a little shaky. This came too close for comfort to the
core of his failure. She didn't want to hear about all that, anyway. She'd
wrapped herself in the pain of losing somebody she'd started to care
about, and he'd been about to open a door closed a long, long time ago.
So long he wasn't sure he could handle opening it.

"What was her name?"

"Her name was Jean."

"Your wife was named Jean? So was my grandmother. What was her
last name?"

Another slip. Before he could mouth the lie, she skipped past the
question. "Tell me how you met her, everything. How old were you?
Where did you meet?"

Like a terrier after a bone, on the scent.

"Okay, let me think." He eyed her, the person who might in the not
too distant future inherit his entire fortune. How to start? She knew
about the booze. It would be safe to start there.

"January of twenty-nine, I'd just quit the booze running business. Things were pretty tight with the Coast Guard patrols."

"Did you make a lot of money smuggling?"

Slowly, he nodded. "Eastland Associates had three million dollars by the fall of nineteen twenty-eight."

More than seventy years had gone since that day and he felt the weight of every one.

Laurel gasped . "Three million dollars? I can barely imagine that kind of money. You were filthy rich!"

Seed money for the real moves. "It was a lot back then."

"How did you meet her?"

Jake smiled. "I moved into town. Her Aunt lived next door. She took a liking to me. Jean and I met one Thanksgiving when she and her mother came for the holidays. I was invited to dinner."

Laurel came to the window and stood beside him. "Love at first sight, again?"

From the way she said "again" he could guess her thoughts. He looked at her through the glass.

"I wouldn't say that. Not exactly."

NOVEMBER 1928

Jean proved an adept conversationalist and a source of knowledge about the cultural aspects of life. Her father owned a successful law office and apparently had tons of money. Her mother came from really old refined money. Clearly, Jake did not rise to the level of potential suitor. He was, however, adequate as a temporary escort.

"You really should put at least some of your assets into the stock market, Mr. Eastland," the young man seated next to Jake at the dinner table said. "I can practically guarantee your money will double in the next six months."

One of the things Jake liked about Jean's aunt was the constant flow of guests she brought to her table. This fellow sold stocks and bonds. He dressed in a well-cut three-piece suit, and his shoes were shined. He appeared prosperous, just as a stockbroker should.

Jake had given a lot of thought to the stock market. He'd attended lectures on the subject. Too many things he heard made him uncomfortable, and he hadn't bought any yet.

"Double? How do you justify that?"

The salesman put his fork down and leaned closer. "Look at the numbers. The market has jumped forty percent since this time last year. Stocks are going off the charts. Everybody's getting in on it."

Jake kept his voice low so as not to intrude on the other conversations at the table. "The Times says the construction industry will be off two billion this year. That kind of news hardly justifies a forty percent jump in the stock market, don't you agree?"

The salesman blinked, taken back. "I hadn't heard that."

Jake pressed his advantage. "Six hundred banks failed last year. Maybe that's another thing you haven't heard. More than half the people in this country live below the minimum subsistence level. How does that fact justify a doubling of the stock market?"

The salesman's face turned a pasty white. "I, uh, are you sure? Those things sound wrong."

Despite Jake's efforts, conversation at the table had fallen off to nothing. He looked around, embarrassed. Everyone stared at him.

From her seat opposite, Jean waved at him. "Oh, Jacob, you're always so negative. Father's made a killing in the market."

The salesman nodded at her, grateful for the support. "Well, I ah, I don't think Mr. Eastland's right, either. I don't specialize in rural markets, though."

At that moment, Jake experienced an epiphany. There *was* no rural market for stocks.

Jean's father and men like him, in big city offices far from the heartland, they were the ones who'd pushed the stock market out of sight. How could they ignore the facts? In the last nine years, farmland had lost thirty to forty percent of its value. More than half the population lived at subsistence level. Only one in five families had incomes that could be considered middle class. Who would buy the automobiles and the products produced by all the new factories? No, the market had to fall.

Another thing he'd read in the New York Times was that banks were profiting by loaning money so people could invest in the stock market. He needed to have a talk with his bankers, be sure his money stayed safe. He smiled at the stockbroker.

"This has been stimulating, but I wouldn't buy stock for all the tea in China. If you have some, it'd be a good idea to sell it pretty soon."

Jean waved her dessert fork. "How boring! You're such a stick, Jacob. Even if you had any money, you'd never get ahead with such a defeatist attitude."

Jake's anger stirred. She was so sure of herself, so utterly confident, yet she didn't know anything. Maybe it was time she learned.

The next day, with Jean along for a lark, Jake drove to Syracuse and visited the First Trust and Deposit Corporation where they were escorted into a vice president's office. The rotund banker's name was Gunderland.

"What can I do for you today, Mister Eastland?"

"How much do I have on deposit at the moment, including earned interest?"

"Just a moment sir, I'll check." The banker left the office. A minute later he came back with Jake's account card. He studied it as he re-seated himself in his comfortable leather-bound swivel chair.

"Seven-hundred-sixty thousand and change with the most recent dividend of four hundred twelve dollars," Gunderland pronounced, smiling happily.

Beside Jake, Jean gasped.

"Good." Jake returned the man's smile. "Mr. Gunderland…"

"Sir?"

"How solid is this bank?"

"Oh, my. We are as solid as any bank anywhere." Gunderland glanced at Jean, then back at Jake. "Our earnings have been fabulous over the past three years."

"How heavily invested are you in the stock market?"

"Totally. The way the market's been performing, it makes perfect sense."

"And would you be willing to loan money for the purpose of investing in the market?"

Gunderland said, "Certainly. I could arrange it at once, Mister Eastland."

Things were worse than Jake imagined. "I'd like to buy U.S. Treasury Bonds with my funds. Please arrange it at once."

"All of it?" Gunderland asked. "Is it something we've done to offend?"

"I'll continue to do business with you. Up to this point, I've been satisfied."

"Then, why is it necessary…?"

Jake held up his hand. "You can require up to ninety days' notice. Is that your intention?" His voice cracked like a whip.

Gunderland scrambled to recover, "Oh, no! Not at all! We can have the Bonds here next week. Will that be soon enough?"

"I'll need a safe deposit box to keep them in."

"Certainly. One will be made available at no charge."

Jake stood. "I'll be back next Friday. Please have everything ready."

He offered his arm to Jean and they left, leaving a very perplexed banker staring after them.

The moment they reached the sidewalk, Jean stopped him. "God in heaven, Jacob. How in the world did you get so much money? A person would never guess to look at you."

Jake squinted at her in the bright sunlight. There was satisfaction at seeing the change in her, but at the same time a sense of something lost. Now, if their relationship should blossom into something more, he'd never know if she wanted him or his money.

Estelle's face came to him, the way her eyes flashed that first night as she said, "Some other time we'll see about you and me, Jake-a Eastland."

No thought of money at all.

"There are ways like your father's, Jean, and there are other ways." He nodded toward the car. "Come on, we've got a few more stops to make."

He asked the same questions at every bank he visited. Where the answers were similar to Gunderland's, he converted his capital into treasury bonds and closed the accounts. Where they were more conservative, he left half his money on deposit and converted the other half to bonds.

From that day until she left a week later, Jake noted a change in Jean's regard. Now, he became the one who stood off and she the eager supplicant. She had position, culture, and upbringing, all assets he coveted, and he had mystery, strength and secrecy, facets that clearly excited her. With a little effort, he could have bedded her—but he wasn't ready to make his personal life into just another business deal. Not until the deal became a good deal sweeter.

Summer came and went. Jake began to think his ideas were wrong.

The market continued to spiral upward. At last, in September, when he was about to admit his mistake, the tremors began.

On October twenty-fourth, Black Thursday, the bottom fell out and the stock market crashed. Word reached Oswego the same day, but details were sketchy. When the New York papers reached town the next day, the headlines were dire.

Jake read of men committing suicide, once proud and wealthy, now paupers. He read of middle class people who had mortgaged their homes to invest in the market, and would now be losing them.

It was fortunate that only a million and a half of the hundred-twenty million Americans were investors. The unfortunate part was that those million and a half were also the businessmen, the factory owners, the entrepreneurs whose creativity and daring had for generations resulted in jobs for the multitudes.

There would be hell to pay now.

The New York Times

Thursday, October 24, 1929 Page 1, Col. 1

PRICES OF STOCKS CRASH IN HEAVY LIQUIDATION

TOTAL DROP IN BILLIONS

PAPER LOSS $4,000,000,000

2,600,000 Shares Sold In the Final Hour in Record Decline

MANY ACCOUNTS WIPED OUT
But No Brokerage House Is In Difficulties,
As Margins Have Been Kept High

ORGANIZED BANKING ABSENT
Bankers Confer On Steps To Support Market—Highest Break
Is 96 Points

"What about Jean's father? Did he lose everything?"

Laurel seemed to have forgotten her own troubles for the moment. Jake felt the irony. So far he hadn't gotten to any of the ugly parts. She wouldn't be so eager if he had.

A knock on the door interrupted. A waiter rolled a meal cart into the room.

While he set the table, Jake answered. "Reggie lost everything. Millions. But I didn't know any of that until later. Her mother had a little family money, not much from what I gathered, but they didn't lose their home."

"With her in New York City, and you here, how did you get together again?"

"That happened in, let's see, thirty-one, I think. I'd had some dealings with a young New York City agent, and I wanted to meet him. He brought me to a night club and I ran into Jean there."

She clapped her hands. "Great! You must tell me everything. Did you fall in love right away?"

Jake frowned. Love didn't enter into it. He'd run out of parts to sugar-coat. All that remained were the bad. Did he dare start down that path?

"I don't remember. I'll have to think about it some." Knowing he'd sounded curt, Jake went to the table and slid her chair out, motioning for her to come.

She didn't miss a beat. The moment he'd taken the seat opposite her, she pressed the issue. "Don't remember? How could you forget something like that?"

He made a little grimace. "I told you before. Not all my memories are good. I'm not sure I should tell you, or even if I want to."

"Grampa Jake, please! You can't stop now. I'm getting so close..." She clapped her hand over her mouth.

Jake put his cutlery down. "Close to what?"

She stared at him, then a determined line came to her mouth and she reached across the table and put her hand over his.

"To what's causing you to be so sad. I knew the very first day. You looked at me like you were a million miles away. It hurt me to see your pain. I thought if I knew why, I might be able to help."

Was he that transparent? She'd been on to him from the get-go? Jake felt his eyes moisten. He hated it when women used emotion to attack. He blinked several times.

"It's all right, Grampa Jake. I'll help."

He didn't answer at first. It would be a big risk, her respect on the line. Did he dare take his own advice this one time?

"In that case, I guess I'll have to keep going."

BROOKLYN, 1931

Jake stood in front of angled viewing mirrors. Beside him, Izzy the tailor did something with the shoulder of the suit, then brushed an imaginary piece of lint away.

Howard Spelnick said. "I told you Izzy was the best, Mister Eastland. That suit looks great on you."

Spelnick was an attorney who'd found his niche as a business agent. Two years had passed since the stock market crash, but Jake had yet to find the right opportunity. He'd come to New York to meet Spelnick after hearing about him through a friend.

A short man in his thirties, Howard had receding hair and a small paunch. He also had a sharp mind and good business instincts, and he knew his way around the city. He'd insisted Jake stay at his home during his visit. In private they were on a first name basis, but in public Howard kept it formal.

The tailor was Howard's cousin. He owned a stylish haberdashery in Brooklyn.

"A man with a suit like yours deserves a place to show it off," Howard said as they left the store. "I think we should take the train to Manhattan and have a few drinks at the classiest joint we can find."

Jake felt like a different person; the suit, muted accoutrements, soft leather shoes buffed to a glow, belt buckle gleaming. "If that's your official advice, Howard, I think it'd be wise to take advantage. A classy joint it is."

"Jake! Jake Eastland! Is that you?" The speakeasy was crowded, and the band loud, and Jake didn't hear his name at first. An arm waved above the crowd then the crowd parted and a girl slipped through and came toward them. She threw her arms open. "I can't believe it's really you! What are you doing in New York?"

Jean. And she looked terrific. "Holy mackerel! Jean, how are you, kid?" They exchanged big hugs. He held her at arm's length. "You look better than ever. What are you doing these days?"

Jean's face fell a little. "Not an awful lot. Things have been hard since the market…"

"Oh, I'm sorry. Did your father…?"

She slipped closer and let her head rest on his chest. "He lost everything. Bankrupt." She hugged him again. "Oh Jake, how many times I've wished I'd listened to you. You didn't lose your money, did you? I knew the second I saw you dressed like a millionaire."

What did she have in mind? They'd never been close. Still, it was nice with her pressed close.

Her friends watched, standing a few feet off. Two were men, stylish yet casual, and the third a girl Jean's age. He wondered which of the men Jean dated.

Beside him, Howard put his mug on the bar. "Want another, Jake? How about the young lady?"

Jean's gaze touched Howard, then flicked away toward her friends. "Jake! Come meet my friends." She pulled his arm. "This is Randy Whittlesy, and Jessica and George."

As she finished introducing him, the one named Randy let his hand rest on Jean's shoulder. His eyes expressed no pleasure at meeting Jake, only an amused tolerance. Jake knew the type: arrogance born of old money.

"You must join us, Jake." Jean seemed oblivious.

Jake declined. "I'm sorry, I don't want to interrupt your evening. Besides, I'm with a friend, too."

This time, Jean didn't even favor Howard with a glance. "Then you can escort me to the Herald party tomorrow evening. We can go with my parents. It'll be a chance for you to meet my father. Please! Say you will, Jacob."

Jake hesitated. He'd planned to leave for home, but this was a chance for an introduction in society, something Jake coveted and that Howard had been unable to facilitate. "Well… I guess that'd be nice. It'd give us some time together."

"Goodie! It'll be *so* much fun. I can't wait." Jean dug around in her purse and found a card. "This is our address. I'll meet you in the lobby and bring you up. How's 6:30 sound?"

Jake took her card. "I'll be there. Are any of your friends going?" He indicated Randy and the other couple.

Jean laughed, "Of course not. They wouldn't be caught dead at a stodgy old party like that." She stepped closer, went up on tiptoe and smooched him on the lips. "Besides, I want you all to myself afterwards."

Her breath smelled of mint. She'd always been arrogant, but now she seemed different, much more open, not the same girl he'd known in Oswego at all. The change intrigued him. He felt the familiar stirrings. Could she be interested in more than conversation? She left, waving, leaving him staring after her.

"That little Shiksa sure liked your suit, but she doesn't like Jews much."

Howard's matter-of-fact comment broke the spell. Jake put his foot on the footrest and his elbow on the bar and faced Howard.

"What makes you say that?"

"She looked right through me, like I wasn't even here. You get so you're sensitive to things like that."

"I wonder how she knew."

Howard pushed a fresh mug of ale Jake's way. "That's one of the things I like about you, Jake. I don't buy for just *any* Goyim, you know."

Jake lifted the mug, but before drinking he said, "I've decided to retain you, Howard. We'll sign the papers when we get home."

They touched glasses.

"In that case, I'd better start by calling Izzy. You'll need a tux by tomorrow night. He'll have to get going right away."

Jean's mother extended her hand, fingers curled downward "It's a pleasure to see you again, Jacob." She had a cultured voice and demeanor. Jake took her hand, bowing slightly, smiling but feeling awkward the way he always did in the presence of people who possessed what he thought of as "finish."

"Watch it there, young man, that one's mine," a gruff male voice said from somewhere inside, and its owner came into view, smiling as he approached. He was Jake's height but thinner, with long brown hair parted at the middle. He stepped up to Jake and stuck his hand out. "Call me Reggie," he said as they shook.

Jake liked him on sight.

Jean's family lived on the fifteenth floor of an exclusive building in Manhattan. From the foyer, Jake could see the living room. It was large, bright and expensively furnished.

"Why are we standing here?" Jean said. "Give me your coat, Jake."

Jean's mother showed him in and the four of them relaxed in the living room. The natural division took place, the men talking shop, the women about people they knew and what they were doing.

Reggie asked, "What are things like upstate, Jake? Business-wise I mean."

"We were pretty lucky up to last fall. Two hydro plants were being built on the river. They're just about finished now, though."

Reggie's eyes appraised Jake.

"Tell me, how do you manage to get along yourself? You don't work, do you?"

"I… started a small business a few years ago." Jake made sure his face gave nothing away. "Import export. Things have worked out well." He did plan to be forthcoming with Jean's father, when the time was right.

"Interesting. What did you import?"

Before Jake could deflect the question, Jean saved him the trouble.

"Are you men ready? We have to leave right away if we want to be on time."

Two hours later, in the smoking room of the Regency Hotel, Reggie lit Jake's Lucky and his own panatela, then waved the matchstick in the air to extinguish the flame. A trail of blue smoke traced a momentary "Z" in the air.

"Now then, Jake, you were about to tell me about your little import-export business."

The men's smoking room was a high-ceilinged space, well ventilated, with a bar stocked with dozens of colorfully labeled bottles of liquor.

Jake pulled at the cummerbund of his new tuxedo and leaned toward the man whose daughter he planned to seduce as soon as possible.

"Whisky. I imported whisky."

His words had the anticipated effect. Reggie straightened as if prodded from behind, and his jaw fell open. "But... but whisky is illegal," he sputtered. "You *can't* import it."

"I did. It paid well, too."

Reggie clapped his hands together. "Well I'll be... I think you really mean it. Of course! What could be more natural if you live on the border?"

He corralled Jake with his arm, looping it over his shoulders. "Come with me, young fellow. There's someone you must meet." He pulled Jake across the room, stopping in front of a blocky, serious-faced man. The man had close-cropped steel gray hair and hard-looking eyes of the same color.

"Jake, I'd like you to meet Harry Hatch." Reggie beamed. "Harry, this is my daughter's friend, Jake Eastland. You two have something in common." He watched the two strangers shake hands, eyeing one another.

Harry Hatch's voice was gravelly, a good match for his face "I wonder what that might be." He sported a large diamond ring on the third finger of his right hand. The diamond flashed as they shook.

"Import-export, Harry," Reggie supplied. "He's from Oswego, on the eastern end of Lake Ontario."

A calculating gleam appeared in Harry Hatch's eyes. "Ever hear of the McKean boys, Jake?"

"Are you saying there was more than one McKean? Bruce and I had a run-in with a Marvin McKean of the Coast Guard," Jake said.

Harry Hatch jabbed his cigar toward Jake. "Three of 'em. Brothers. Every one of 'em a tough buzzard. This 'Bruce' you mentioned. That wouldn't be Bruce Longley?"

Harry knew Bruce. That surprised Jake. "One and the same. I worked for him before I bought my own boat. I had an idea I wanted to try out."

"What was that?" Harry asked.

Jake described the way he had operated, keeping it simple.

Reggie joined the conversation, "Tell me, Jake, how many cases did you—import—altogether?"

Jake took a drag on his Lucky. "Sixty thousand, give or take."

"Sixty *thousand?*" Reggie's voice squeaked. "*Cases?*"

"Yes sir."

Harry stepped closer and placed his hand on Jake's right shoulder. "There must have been quite a profit. Did you invest it?"

"Uh huh," Jake nodded.

"In the market?"

"You're asking me if I still have it?"

Harry laughed. "Right."

"The answer is no," Jake said. "I put it into Treasury Bills."

Harry Hatch grinned. "And of course, T-bills were just about the only investment that held or even increased in value while everything else went to hell, right?"

It was a rhetorical question. Harry didn't wait for the answer. Instead, he changed the subject.

"Tell you what, Jake. You had a good idea. Now, you're looking around for the next one. Am I right?"

After a beat, Jake nodded.

"War," Harry said, his voice gruff.

"War?"

"Yeah. Within a few years, five or six, tops."

Jake didn't get it. "But why? We just finished a big war."

"The first war didn't settle anything, Jake. Germany is already beginning an arms buildup."

Harry checked again to be sure they were not overheard. He waved his hands as if to push the thought away. "Never mind all that. Ask yourself what it is that's worthless now, but will become valuable if there's another war."

Jake visualized masses of ships, machines, planes, guns, and bombs. "Just about any raw material I guess."

"Of course, but you're missing it." Harry exhaled a stream of smoke. "Listen, Jake. Right now, right this minute," he jabbed his finger at Jake, "the war has already started. Japan has invaded China to secure its supply of oil. If we weren't floating on an ocean of the stuff, we'd be going to war for it ourselves. We've got plenty of oil. What don't we have enough of, Jake?"

When Jake didn't answer, Harry held his hands out, palms up as if showing Jake something. "It's the metals, Jake." He ticked them off, one by one on his fingers, accelerating as he went along. "The gold, the silver, tin, mercury, lead, nickel, copper, iron, aluminium. That's where the supply won't meet the demand if there's a war."

He stopped abruptly.

"Now. Where could a person get his hands on those things without needing to buy them at market value?"

Jake thought about that. Nothing came to mind. Who would be foolish enough to sell for less than value? A person who thought what he had was useless?

And then he had it. Near the family home at Mexico Point, an abandoned farm tractor sat rusting in a field. It had a steel frame, copper in the windings of its generator, lead in its battery, aluminum in its radiator.

"Scrap?" he said, half asking.

Harry crowed like a carnival barker. "Give that man a fat cigar! If a person was to start buying up scrap now, by the time war comes he'd be in a very strong position." He stood there, his eyes fixed on Jake. Finally he made his last point.

"Know how I caught wind of this, Jake?"

"I have no idea."

"I was in San Diego last month. I happened to be on the waterfront. I saw a huge ship being loaded with crushed automobiles, tractors, old freight cars, every kind of scrap you can imagine went into that boat."

He waited, allowing Jake to wonder why for a moment. "Know where that boat was headed?"

Jake shook his head.

"Japan. It was going to Japan." Harry followed the word "going" with a hint of a pause. "The Japs are buying our scrap. It's costing them next to nothing. Why, Jake? Why are they doing that?"

Jake shook his head again.

"They're already fighting in China, Jake. They know the big war is coming. They're getting ready now."

UPSTATE

The trip to New York changed Jake's life. Reggie Gamble came aboard as a consultant, and the relationship with Jean developed into marriage, giving Jake a valuable entrée to New York society.

Harry Hatch's ideas had a profound effect as well. Without fanfare, Jake began to acquire scrap metal. The first thing he learned about the business was that though scrap could be cheap, often free, handling it was expensive. He had to transport it, identify it, separate it, and store it. Labor-intensive work.

He and Jean were just married when he set up his first yard in a field near a railroad spur east of Syracuse. Soon, many of his trucks hauled junk rather than produce.

Within five years he had seven yards scattered throughout the state. He bought wrecked or otherwise unserviceable automobiles for fifty cents each. He was paid to remove huge monolithic machines from defunct factories. He bought worn-out rolling stock from railroads, the wheel castings alone weighed two and a half tons each. He dismantled oil storage tanks, cut them up and hauled away fifty thousand tons of steel plate.

Huge old motors and generators, each with miles of copper windings, outmoded telegraph and telephone cable, thousands of miles all with cores of solid copper, Jake took it all.

He hired a metallurgist to identify the rare metals, the silver or gold contacts in switching mechanisms, the mercury, the zinc, copper, lead, chrome. He hired an engineer to figure out how to dismantle and store the stuff, and he hired men, hundreds of men, to strip and separate.

He worked as if pursued by the Devil, but loved every moment of it. By early 1936 he'd invested more than half his fortune, and owned nearly three million tons of iron and steel, not to mention the other more valuable metals.

He had competitors by then. The idea that war was inevitable had gained adherents. Hitler rampaged in Europe. Others could now see what Harry Hatch had seen years earlier. Scrap prices moved up.

Seven years after he started, on February 16, 1938, Jake received an offer of five million dollars for his yards, more than three times what he had invested. He thought hard about selling, then didn't equivocate. He turned it down flat.

"Not for sale at any price," he told the buyer's agent. Of course he didn't mean that. Everything had a price. He just hadn't heard *his* yet.

Unfortunately, not everything in life was as crystal-clear to Jake as the way to make money. He had a beautiful house built in Oswego's best neighborhood and gave Jean carte blanche to furnish it. Immediately, he began to experience the inevitable result of the way the privileged few raised their children, and this was not an altogether pleasant process.

"Wait just a minute, Jake. You spend so much time away, I hardly know you any more." Jake and Jean were in the kitchen where Josie, their cook-housekeeper, worked to prepare dinner. Early on, he'd realized the need for a household staff. Jean had never so much as boiled water. Housekeeping? Laundry? Out of the question.

Jean squeezed her hands together, almost wringing them. "You promised, Jake. Please! It's the biggest social event of the year."

The following Friday, the annual Firemen's Ball would be held downtown. Jean enthusiastically mocked every local organization's attempt at cultural and social events, but when it came time to attend, she considered her presence essential to the event's success.

She deserved a yes. He *had* been away a lot, but dammit, the ball had come at exactly the wrong moment: his level of excitement was at its highest peak ever. Just this morning, Howard Spelnick had called to tell him about an auction to take place in New Jersey. Sixty ships would be sold. Sixty in one lot.

It was the opportunity he'd been waiting for since he quit smuggling rum ten years ago. Plans to leave for New York were already complete.

"I'm sorry darling, but this won't wait. It's big, very big. I don't know if I'll be home by Friday."

Her voice tight with anger, Jean said, "You told me the same thing last year. I'm sick of it. Sick of being left alone in this awful house, sick of going everywhere by myself." She whirled and stalked to the sink. Her hand shook as she filled a glass with water and took a swallow.

Josie slid toward the door, experience having taught her that absence was the better part of valor when the storm flags flew.

It was hard to tell, given her present mood, but as far as Jake knew, his wife was happy with him. She'd never given him cause to believe otherwise. For his own part, he didn't love her. He'd told himself it would come with time. On the other hand, he knew from Estelle how painful total commitment could be if things went wrong, and something kept him from letting those last bars down, the ones that kept him safe— and kept Jean just that little bit away.

On occasion, it crossed his mind that the traumatic end of his affair with Estelle might be at the root of his inability to let Jean in. He lived with a sense of discontent, an incompleteness amplified whenever he entered his home.

Love hadn't come with time

Now, in the spring of 1938, his wife had grown more beautiful than ever, yet there was a peevishness about her when they were together. He'd taken a strong dislike to it, but she resisted fiercely whenever he suggested it was a problem for him.

With him gone so much, it was only natural for Jean to focus on beginning their family, hoping maybe to bring him home more often that way.

The fresh rush of enthusiasm at the beginning faded, increment by increment, as each monthly arrived, signaling another failure to conceive their first child.

She experienced bouts of depression, during which she would not allow him to touch her. God knew she reminded him of her sacrifice for him often enough, as if he could forget, but having a family had become central to her image of herself—so far they'd failed and to that extent, so had their marriage.

She spent months at a time in New York, staying with her mother and father, immersed in "social work." There, she circulated in the same circles as always. Her friend Randy popped up in conversation on occasion, but she pooh-poohed Jake whenever he questioned her about him.

Now, she waited by the sink, glass in hand, the light behind her.

"I know I said I would. I promise to make it up to you. Why don't you go shopping? Buy whatever you want. You'll have fun."

Her reaction was dramatic. She screamed, "I don't *want* to go *shopping*," then drew her arm back and threw the glass at him. Water sluiced everywhere as the container tumbled through the air. He managed to duck and it slammed into the curved glass front of the antique china closet behind him, smashing it to pieces.

"I *want* to go to the goddamn *ball*, goddamn you," she screeched and ran from the room, sobbing. A few seconds later there was a loud "bang" from upstairs as the bedroom door slammed. The curtains over the sink moved.

Jake wiped water from his face with a dishtowel. He picked his way through the swath of broken glass, left the kitchen, and moments later pulled the door of his home closed behind him.

When he came home the following night to prepare for his trip to New Jersey, Josie informed him the Missus had left that morning for New York.

She hadn't said when she'd be back.

Two days later, Jake bought the ships for a high bid of four hundred and twenty-five thousand dollars. It was the single biggest coup he'd ever pulled off, and he was on top of the world. Later that afternoon, he entered the offices of Reginald Gamble, his father-in-law. He hardly had time to put one leg over the other in the waiting room before the door burst open and Reggie came out.

"Jake! Son! How are you? I didn't know you were in town. Come on in. Jean's visiting us again. What's the matter with that girl?"

Jake followed Reggie into his office. "I came in day before yesterday. I need some legal work, Reggie. I just bought sixty ships."

Reggie fell backward into his swivel chair, nearly upsetting it. "You did *what?*"

"I bought them at auction, for four hundred twenty-five thousand. They're what's left of the old Continental line that went broke a few years ago."

Reggie leaned forward over his desk, his hands on its shiny surface. "I heard they were going up for auction. I thought it was supposed to be next month some time."

"It was today. I need a company to own the ships. I don't want to have to explain where I got the money."

Reggie nodded. "What do you want to call this company?"

"How about 'The Big ONE'?"

"As good a name as any," Reggie shrugged. "I'll have it up and running, titles to the boats switched over, everything all nice and legitimate, by day after tomorrow. How's that?"

"Good. By the way, there are some other assets the company would be interested in."

"Namely?"

"The Eastco Scrap yards. There are seven of them scattered around New York and New Jersey. I'll want the company to purchase them as well."

"For how much?"

"One dollar ought to do it." Jake smiled.

"Consider it done, son. Consider it done." Reggie came around the desk and looped his arm over Jake's shoulders. "Jake, I owe you a debt of gratitude for what you did to get me on my feet again." He halted, seemed nervous suddenly. "I don't want you to think I'm prying, but I want you to tell me why my daughter spends more time at the Continental Bar with her fancy friends than she does at home with you."

It was a serious question that deserved an honest answer.

Jake shook his head. "Heck, Reggie. After seven years, the only thing I can say for sure is the longer we're married, the less I understand her.

It's almost like the sunlight isn't bright enough in Oswego, or the days warm enough. We haven't been able to get a family started. That might be part of it."

He couldn't tell Reggie the truth. The man would never forgive him for failing to love his daughter. Was not telling an act of kindness, or the act of a coward?

Estelle hadn't been good enough. Jean was too good.

Reggie patted Jake's shoulder. "I know what you mean. I'm just worried she... might be doing things she shouldn't. She's drinking too much. That I know for sure."

"Are the women home now? Maybe we can all have dinner?"

Reggie let go of Jake and went to his desk. "Get me my home, please," he said into the intercom.

"There's no answer, Mr. Gamble." The receptionist's voice was tinny through the intercom. "Should I keep trying?"

Reggie's face took on a resigned expression. "Let's eat at my club. We'll catch up to them later."

By 9:30, there was still no answer at the Gamble apartment. Reggie went home. Jake found his way to the Continental Bar. Maybe he'd run into her.

Jean and her friends arrived at 11:30.

There were three couples, all attired in splashy clothing, all very merry, very loud.

Jake recognized Randy Whittlesy. Jean was draped on him and Randy half-carried her. He should make his presence known right away, but some deep foreboding stopped him.

The group passed right behind Jake, not seeing him, oblivious to anything other than themselves. Only *they* were animated, only they colorized—everything and everyone else black and white, still-life props on their stage.

They fell into a large, partially-shadowed booth at the end of the room. A waiter scurried over, removed the 'Reserved' card and took drink orders. Jake felt sick to his stomach. Jealousy? Fear? He decided to wait until after their drinks arrived. A minute later, when the waiter went toward the booth with the round of drinks, Jake followed.

The couples paid no attention to the waiter.

Jean and Randy were in the midst of a deep, mouth-open kiss. Her hand moved below the table. Randy had Jean's breast out of her blouse, in his fingers.

Jake froze. His wife. Jean whispered into Randy's mouth, then did something beneath the table. The day's thrilling business victory crumbled to nothing and Jake became the wall, invisible, but seeing everything.

She had a lover, maybe more than one. What did all the money in the world mean if his wife cared so little she could do such a thing?

He didn't love her, no, but he *had* been faithful, treated her as though he did, always given her everything.

So here it was, in front of him, and he could no longer deny the thing he'd known about himself from the day he married her. He would do anything to get what he wanted, including destroying the lives of others. He'd married her for the things she could do for him.

And Jean, being the person she was, had turned the tables on him by doing exactly the same thing. She didn't love him, either. She'd married him for his money.

Laurel jumped to her feet and paced away. He'd married his wife knowing he didn't love her. What did he think he'd get in return? She didn't want to know these things about him. Not any of them. She *had* asked, but that didn't mean she'd wanted to learn *this*.

If this was where his pain rooted... Christ. How could she possibly have seen herself helping? She had her own screwed-up mess of a life to deal with. She couldn't even hold a job, couldn't handle a simple friendship without doing something stupid and ruining it. What was she going to do about that?

Movement helped some of the anger slip away. Why had he revealed such a sensitive thing about himself? Obviously, the hurt he'd caused still troubled him. Was there some lesson there, some thing or point he was trying to get over to her?

As if reading her thoughts, he started again. Although he did not speak loudly, the room's acoustics carried his words along the shining sand-colored wood of the floor, past the wall of windows looking west, through the hesitant air to the far corner where she stood.

"Remember I said learning the truth about yourself doesn't necessarily make you happy? That was the day I finally admitted what I'd known all along. I didn't like myself very much after that. Not for a long time."

She'd retreated as far as possible, couldn't evade further through the device of distance. She let her shoulders slump. She didn't like herself very much either, only in her case she didn't know why. She didn't want to, but she would listen. Maybe there'd be a grain, a germ of some truth to help them both. His story happened half a century ago, but the things that mattered had to be pretty much the same as now.

She clamped her jaw closed and nodded to him, arms hugged to her abdomen, inviting him to go on.

Very soon, he did. "What I did on my wedding day, I did because I thought in some way it would make me acceptable, one of *them*. I didn't see the enormity of my mistake until the last instant."

He mumbled. She moved closer to hear.

He looked up at her, his eyes pained. "I should have stopped it then, as soon as I realized what I was about to do. But I was afraid to let myself disappoint them, afraid to dare to be the person I really was. I loved Estelle Zaia, not Jean, and nothing could ever change that."

He stared up at her. "Do you see? I was so caught up in the idea of who I thought I needed to become, I denied who I was, and that meant I couldn't love anyone, and no one could love me."

Zaia? Estelle's last name? There was value, real insight in what he'd conveyed, but she couldn't focus on it. He *had* said it: it was Estelle *Zaia* he loved. Very strange, both of them having bad experiences with someone with the same last name.

"I don't remember you mentioning Estelle's last name was Zaia."

The look that came over his face was so bittersweet she would willingly have let it drop, but he gave her a half smile.

"Yes. I might have forgotten that."

Laurel stared into his eyes. Somehow all of this connected to her. Now she *had* to hear the rest, and at the same time some gate deep in her psyche pried itself open. Grampa Jake might as well have been describing *her*; her conviction that she was flawed, her need to make up for it, the resulting single-minded way she approached every task, including relationships. Just as he had, she'd put the wrong things first throughout her life.

The leap of comprehension stunned her. When had she lost sight of what was important? Had she ever even known what it *was* before now? What would she need to do to change herself?

The long term seemed too hard to contemplate. But one thing she could do right away. She leaned closer to Grampa Jake. "I've been thinking it over, Grampa Jake. Mike McKean played it square with both of us. I think we owe him for that." She pushed her hair back, off her forehead. "*I* owe him. I think I should try to find him, tell him I'm sorry, and ask him to come back."

A smile hid around the corners of his eyes and he nodded agreement.

"Besides..."

"Besides?" he croaked, exhaling.

She gave a little grimace, "...I like him."

Grampa Jake grunted, then dug into his pocket and pulled out a folded slip of paper. "You'll be needing this."

She unfolded it. "Mike McKean, 16 Brook Terrace, Apt 423, Rochester, NY.

OSWEGO

At four A.M., Romy Zaia drove north on West First Street toward the grain elevator pier. A half block before he reached it, he turned into the short drive that led to the cement silo on the river where there were no streetlights. He parked and turned the engine off.

He'd only seen a few cars since entering the city. The cops were probably parked somewhere, catching up on their sleep. Getting out of his pickup, he closed the door as quietly as he could and walked out to First Street then north toward the Eastlands' boat tied up on the pier. He'd brought only a flashlight and a few simple tools.

He kept close to the water's edge as he neared the *Bruce B. Longley*, which lay shrouded in shadows. To his left across the way the Coast Guard station showed lights only on the ground floor.

The *Longley* didn't move under his weight as he stepped down to the gunwale and aboard. He went directly to the equipment lockers on the port side, just behind the pilothouse, and knelt in front of the largest one. Leaning close, he clicked the light on for an instant. The locker had a hasp closure, secured by a brass padlock.

He lifted the padlock, a Sesame combination lock, with four thumb wheels of numbers, and held the light on its base. Romy smiled in the darkness. Holding the lock so the combination wheels were toward him, he flashed the light one more time. The numbers 5-2-6-8 showed. He almost laughed. The *Longley's* registration number was 6-2-6-8, right there on the bow in six-inch numbers. Whoever'd closed the lock changed only one digit.

Romy rotated the first wheel so the six showed and squeezed the lock. When he released the pressure it clicked open. Fuckin' morons! Didn't they know every crook in the world knew to try the digit to either side of the ones left displayed? If that didn't work, the combination 0-0-0-0 did the trick the other half of the time.

He lifted the lid, shielded his light and clicked it on. Four identical closed-circuit re-breather systems were stored inside. The dive gear. Exactly what he'd come looking for. Big bucks, four or five grand apiece. He itched to swipe one. No sense alerting them though. Maybe later, after he dealt with the woman.

He placed his flashlight in the bottom of the locker and checked the adjustment of the harnesses. Two of the units had never been used. Of the others, he saw at once which one Laurel Kingsford used. The harness was adjusted for a much smaller torso. He pulled a pencil and paper from his pocket and wrote down the manufacturer, model, and serial number of the re-breather. For good measure, he made a note of the combination to the Sesame lock, too.

Romy turned off the light, closed the lid and replaced the lock, careful to leave it just as he'd found it.

Less than fifteen minutes after he first parked his truck, Romy was back behind the wheel, ready for the next step. Tomorrow he'd contact the manufacturer of the re-breather equipment and locate the nearest dealer. He needed to learn as much as he could about that dive gear.

The next afternoon, Romy entered a dive shop in Syracuse. The place didn't look too prosperous. He had it all to himself. He could have walked out of there with anything he wanted. After four or five minutes, a toilet whooshed somewhere and a tall man with a chesty build entered the display room.

"Yes, may I help you?"

The guy had an accent. Was it German?

"Maybe. I'm thinkin' about buying a SCUBA outfit. I want to get back into diving."

The clerk gave him a once-over. "You are experienced OC diver?"

"Huh?" Romy said. What the heck was OC? The salesman spoke terrible English. He reminded Romy of somebody.

The German tried speaking more slowly. "Open circuit… you know, air, bubbles. You have experience?"

"Yeah. But now I'm thinking about a re-breather. I hear they're the hot item these days. I like the CCA2000 by Western Diving." Romy dropped the name of the company. "They still make them in Sacramento, right?"

The salesman's upper lip twitched. "That model costs twenty-five thousand US. And we can only sell them to trained divers."

Romy whistled. Twenty-five thou. If he'd known that, he'd have pinched at least one outfit last night. He pointed at his groin. "Train this. How hard can it be?"

The guy looked at Romy like he doubted he could raise twenty-*five* dollars, let alone twenty-five thousand.

"You are open circuit diver, trained to the feeling that all is well as long as you can breathe. When riding a re-breather, that is very bad habit. A re-breather might deliver a gas that is not what you need to survive. You need training."

Schwarzenegger. That was it. The guy sounded more like Arnold than Arnold. Romy lifted a face mask from a display and inspected it. He put it back down. "You guys put out that crap because you want to teach some bullshit course and rake in the extra dough. I'm wise to that scam."

Schwarzenegger put one hand on his hip then he pointed at Romy and scolded, "When you breathe a gas that by mistake contains not enough oxygen, you will faint. When you breathe a gas that contains too much oxygen you can get spasms similar to epilepsy, which can be extremely dangerous while you are being underwater breathing through a mouthpiece."

Arny's English got more fractured as his zeal increased. His mission in life was to convince Romy of the need for training. "And then there is the CO_2. When you breathe…"

"You mean like in Carbon Dioxide? That CO_2?"

Schwarzenegger stopped, blinked then spoke again, more slowly, enunciating each word. "Right. You breathe out CO_2. A chemical, usually calcium hydroxide, cleans it from the air. If you breathe too much CO2, or retain what you exhale by wrong breathing, you can get cramps, visual problems, nausea, twitching, or any of the CNS-Tox symptoms, and then you die. A re-breather can kill you and you don't even know it's happening."

Romy was almost convinced. The fucking things *did* look complicated. "What's 'CNS' mean, anyway?"

"Central Nervous System. It operates the suction device the re-breather needs to function."

"Huh?"

Schwartzy laughed. "Suction device. The person. You. You're the suction device. You have to suck on it to get the system going before you dive."

Romy took a half step back. He didn't like the sexual connotation of that. "Calcium hydroxide, ain't that the same as lime?"

"Cal..." Arny stopped then he raised his eyebrows. "Lime, yes, slaked lime."

"You mean these things use lime to kill the carbon dioxide? That's all there is to it?"

"Basically, yes. If you breathe ten percent mixture of carbon dioxide, it wouldn't matter how much oxygen in the mix. It'd kill you right now."

He went behind the counter and slid the display case open. He showed Romy a small canister about the size of a soup can. "This is a two-pounder. Our units use two at a time. Together, they'd be good for about six hours at three atmospheres."

"Lime. Isn't that pretty mean stuff?"

"Oh yes, caustic, and it reacts with water to form lye. You breathe lye too long, goodbye."

"How would I know if the CO2 levels got too high?"

Arny shrugged. "Sucking and blowing; it gets hard to breathe: hypercapnia. There is no way to tell, actually. Problem with most of the things that can happen is they affect your judgment and physical strength before you realize. The only sure way is to make sure you have fresh canister every time you go down."

"So if I dove with a used-up canister..."

"It would be a very short dive. You'd have to operate the manual bypass and breathe directly from your diluent supply."

"Dy what?"

"Di-luent, the compressed gas the system introduces into the breathing mixture to compensate for the effects of increased bar."

Romy didn't have a clue what the guy just said. His expression must have reflected as much, because the salesman motioned him closer and pointed out the small tanks on the CCR2000 the shop had on display, one for the pure oxygen, the other for the diluent. He showed Romy the valve that could be manually operated by the diver if he needed to breathe the diluent directly in a bailout situation.

That was when Romy knew how he'd do it. He had things in his mind, ideas. He thanked the clerk and left the shop.

LAUREL

Laurel gripped the steering wheel of the Twice Told's Blazer and stared through the windshield. After sunset, lights showed in many of the windows of the apartment complex at 16 Brook Terrace. She was in the parking lot. Had been for fifteen minutes. People passed, paying no attention, coats pulled close in the chill of early evening.

He probably wasn't home. No, that excuse wouldn't fly. She could see his pickup from where she sat.

Try another. What if he wouldn't talk to her?

No good either. She still had to try.

The longer she procrastinated, the harder it got to do what she'd come for. Steeling herself, she left the Blazer and crossed the parking lot to the building entrance. In the vestibule, she scanned the intercom panel until she came to his name. Apartment 423. She took a deep breath and touched the corresponding numbers on the keypad, then the pound sign as per the instructions.

After half a minute a voice said, "Yes?"

An obstruction appeared in her throat. "Mike?" she croaked.

"Right. Who's there?"

She cleared her throat. "It… It's Laurel Kingsford. May I come up and talk to you?"

Two people entered the vestibule and stopped behind her, waiting for her to finish.

"Talk about what?" His voice sounded gruff in the closed area.

The couple stared at her.

"I… there are people waiting. Can't I come up? I won't stay long." She hated being reduced to pleading. Behind her, the woman made an impatient sound.

The inner door buzzer sounded, releasing the latch. Laurel darted through, then made sure the door closed behind her with a solid click.

On the fourth floor, she rang his bell. He opened the door but didn't invite her in. "What's this about?"

Laurel remembered Grampa Jake telling her about the salesman who tried to sell him stock just before the stock market collapsed. Now she knew how the poor guy must have felt. She made herself stand straight. If she went down in flames, she'd do it with élan. "I came here to apologize, and ask you to come back to work for us."

"Why didn't your old-timer friend come? Why'd he send you?"

"Grampa Jake didn't fire you. I did. He didn't know about it."

His eyes narrowed, and he frowned at her. "You? Why?"

Laurel held herself rigid. How could she tell him, when she didn't quite know the answer herself? Or did she? Yes. She did know. She needed to tell the truth now, for herself more than anything.

"I... saw you with that woman from the Coast Guard. Going home with her. I got angry. It was none of my business. I just thought... I had no right to be angry."

He was still for a time, measuring her, then he said, "Go ahead. I'm listening."

"Go ahead what?"

"Do what you came to do."

Hadn't she already? Oh! This was *so* awkward. She bit her lip. "I'm sorry for what I did, Mike. Will you come back and finish the job with us?"

There. She'd done it. She felt a weight come off and heaved a sigh of relief.

"That's it?" he said. "Nothing else?"

"Yes. That's it."

"Sorry, but no, I won't. I don't think I can work with you anymore." Without saying another word, he stepped back and closed the door, leaving her standing in the empty hall.

Laurel felt giddy.

Lady, lady! My steamroller just ran over your daughter.

Oh, I'm in the bathtub right now. Could you slip her under the door?

The silly old joke brought a giggle to her lips as she stared at the closed door, feeling somewhat steamrolled herself. At last, breaking free of it, she turned and went to the elevator.

Back in the Blazer, she stared at nothing. It was perverse. The harder he made it for her, the more she wanted him. Did she dare go back up there and try again? She'd already just about begged. Hell, what more was there to lose?

She climbed back out of the Blazer, marched into the building, and tapped in the 4-2-3 number. This time, he didn't answer the dialer. Steaming, she let it ring fifty times before putting the phone down, off the hook, still ringing his apartment, and left the building.

The forecast for the thirteenth of October was for cool and breezy, but when Laurel stepped aboard the *Longley* at 5:30 that morning, it was dark and downright cold. She had a stiff neck after a mostly sleepless night. Though her effort to apologize to Mike had been rebuffed, that didn't mean it wasn't the right thing to do and, all in all, she felt better about herself than she had in a long time. They'd need Mike, or someone with his skills if they found the wreck, but there were still things she could handle on her own. Today's search was one of them.

She shivered while Sheik lit the small propane heater. It emitted a hissing sound, its corona turning bright red.

When they left the pier, the air temperature was forty-six degrees. By contrast, the water temperature at the surface was fifty-five. Sheik took the helm while Grampa Jake helped Laurel set up the sonar towfish. He wasn't that much help. Nobody said a thing about Mike not being along.

The prediction called for fifteen to twenty knots of wind from the southwest. This meant the northeastern end of the lake would see good-sized waves and they could expect rough conditions. Within minutes the *Bruce B. Longley* surged through four footers, running with them, making excellent time.

By sunup, they'd reached the eastern end of the lake, a few miles from the site. Even though being aboard the *Longley* evoked strong memories of Mike, Laurel kept focused. She would zero in on her plan, no matter how much she missed him.

"We'll set up and look for anything metallic along the projected course of the *Ontario*. After we make a few runs over here," she pointed to the chart. "We'll go up the lake and see if we can spot the *Ontario*. We know she's there, and today is the day we put our finger on her."

When they approached the coordinates of their earlier find, Sheik slowed and Laurel deployed the sonar. When the fish streamed behind them at the correct depth, she went into the pilothouse, where she perched on the slide-out seat at the Nav station. With deft movements, she adjusted the settings.

"Okay, Sheik, three knots on the first heading."

Sheik moved the wheel, frowning at the GPS. He adjusted the throttle. The boat lost a little speed.

They hadn't traveled a quarter of a mile before she had one. It registered as a faint mark, just as the lone cannon find last week.

"Bingo!" She pointed, so Grampa Jake could see, and pushed a small button to lock in the coordinates.

"I knew we'd find more," Sheik said. "That Mike is a smart cookie."

Mike's name dropped like a rock onto ice. Into the resulting silence Laurel said, "I believe it was *my* idea, not his."

The moment it was out, she regretted her pettiness. "Never mind. Stay on heading. Let's see if there are any more."

In the next minutes, they recorded three more possibles.

"We see about your other idea next, right?" This time Sheik took care to attribute the correct source.

Laurel favored him with her highest-powered smile. "Stony Point, here we come."

The land mass behind Stony Point was formed mostly of rock and rose to a height of several hundred feet. The southwest face abutted the lake. The *Longley* made her way past the three small bays and rounded the point.

Here, the land sloped down more steeply, and after a distance, ended in sheer cliffs fifty feet high. The water had undercut the rock somewhat and waves broke at the base of the cliffs.

Laurel indicated a direction parallel to the cliffs. "We'll start in a hundred and fifty feet of water. Then we'll move a hundred yards closer to shore each run, until we're right on the beach."

Sheik's arms broke out in goose pimples. "Christ, Laurel. Look at it in there. There ain't no beach. You can make *that* run by yourself. I'll wait for you out here." His voice had a quivery note.

Laurel felt it too, something ominous about the cliffs. A chill stirred the hairs on the nape of her neck. Death waited here. She could feel it.

They made the first pass without incident. The bottom was no longer smooth and flat. Huge rectangular blocks of rock lay beneath them now, marked by deep chasms and vaults. On the second pass in twenty fathoms of water, the picture remained the same.

The bottom shoaled as they made the third pass. This one she made twice, once from each direction. Something half-hidden behind a steep, slanted rock shelf turned out to be nothing, another rock formation.

By 1:30, they were two hundred yards off the cliffs. Even today, in fair weather, the place gave Laurel the creeps. Anyone in the water along this shore would be in danger no matter what the weather.

They raised the fish to work in the shallower water while Sheik executed the wide circle to position it directly aft for the next run.

The run began. Laurel stifled a yawn. Maybe they'd missed it. Seconds later, she spotted something on the bottom, a long, angular projection, curved, like a rib.

Carefully, she made copies of the image. The angle was low, the sensors almost on top of it. She hadn't been able to see it until now because two giant pillars of rock were positioned in such a way as to almost guard the place, like sentries.

"Sheik, there's something back there," she called. "Let's make another pass. Twenty-five yards further in."

"Okay," Sheik said from the helm. "By the way, there's a stiff current along here. Every time I head south, I need twice as much throttle to hold my speed up."

Laurel didn't like hearing that. Diving in current was not easy. She had zero experience. Mike would know…

As if reading her thoughts, Grampa Jake put his hand on her shoulder and squeezed. "We'll cross that bridge when we come to it." His voice still hadn't come all the way back after all the talking he'd done the other night.

They watched the contours of the bottom pass in slow motion. "Man, it's torn up down there," Grampa Jake said after several minutes. "I've never seen anything like it on the lake before."

"We're coming up on the place now." Laurel concentrated on the screen, but from their new position closer to shore they passed directly over the object, and the sonar couldn't create an image.

"Darn," she fretted. "We're going to have to get right under the cliffs on the next pass in order to get a good angle."

"Not today. No way. It's too rough," Sheik's watery blue eyes were much rounder than usual. "We're already closer to them cliffs than we should be. There could be all kinda rocks and shelves in here. We need a super flat day—one with the wind blowing off the shore. Maybe we'll even need to use the Whaler."

Grampa Jake nodded, "I don't feel that safe either. I'm with you, Sheik. Let's head for deeper water."

Sheik needed no urging. He rotated the wheel to port and the *Longley* angled away from shore.

Outvoted, Laurel didn't protest. If Mike had been with them, they'd be starting the run she suggested. But he wasn't, and who knew how long it would be before the weather cooperated and she could find out what it was she'd seen down there?

Laurel spotted Mike's pickup the moment the Blazer entered the parking lot behind the Hotel.

Sheik pointed. "Hey. Ain't that Mike's ride?"

Grampa Jake croaked, "Laurel's road trip might have done the job after all."

Her stomach lurched. What *was* Mike doing here? She didn't know whether to be glad she'd see him again, angry, or relieved.

Laurel tapped Grampa Jake on the shoulder. "If he wants to come back, do we let him, after the way he practically slammed the door in my face?"

"I'd say the two of you are almost even. What do you think, Sheik?"

"Hard to say. By him showing up here like this, I'd have to give Mike the edge on style points."

"Okay, you two. Twenty thousand comedians are out of work. It's not a good time for you to be breaking in as a comedy team. When we get inside, I want you to make yourselves scarce. I started this mess. I'll finish it alone."

She found Mike in a booth near the back of the bar. He was watching a small boat enter the river from the lake when she slid into the seat opposite him.

His face was unreadable. "After you left, somebody rang my call number a hundred and fifty times. You wouldn't know anything about that, would you?"

Laurel's face burned. She couldn't answer.

His eyes found her cheeks. "I came back because I wanted you to know I... we... I mean, nothing happened between Char and me. I'm sorry I was rude to you the other night. Seeing you right there at my door made me so lightheaded I couldn't think straight."

Nothing had happened! He cared for her. More than as a friend. In the space of a few instants, her latent feelings blossomed.

He leaned closer. "Is the offer still open? Can I come back and help finish the job?"

Her voice trembled. "I couldn't finish it without you."

Mike smiled and covered her hand with his. Then he sat straighter, looking over her shoulder. "Hey, here come Grampa Jake and Sheik."

Her barriers were down. They'd come back into the bar after an excellent dinner. Several glasses of good wine later, Grampa Jake and Sheik tactfully off to bed, Laurel swirled the liquid in her half-empty glass. Everything fine, except for one thing.

All Mike seemed to want to do was talk shop.

"Assuming we can pinpoint it within a few days, I think we'll have time to dive, get our provenance, maybe even look for the ship's papers if there's a chance they still exist."

She nodded, unable to concentrate. A few couples swayed on the small dance floor in the back, just behind the booth where they sat. There was no band, only the juke box, but the sound system was good.

"…supposed to clear up for Thursday. Let's plan to go for it then."

"Okay." Only half tuned to his words, she glanced toward the dancers. She'd been hoping he'd ask her, but he sailed along, his mind on business, thinking about entirely the wrong thing.

She took a breath. "I like this song. Let's dance."

He stopped in mid-sentence and gaped. "D—Dance?"

"Yes. You know, we stand together, we put our arms around each other, we move in time with the music. Dance."

"Oh, *that* dance."

He slid out of the booth, reaching for her hand, and they walked back to the dance floor. It was darker there.

She raised her arms and he stepped up to her, taking her right hand. She rested her left hand on the front of his shoulder and he wrapped his free arm partway around her waist. Their hips just touched as they began to move.

He smelled of the outdoors, with a faint overtone of aftershave. His arm felt good, very good, where it rested.

His mouth grazed her ear. "This was a good idea."

She tipped her head back and let her eyes close. As they relaxed with one another, they moved closer until their abdomens touched. Her breasts brushed his chest. Oh my. This could get out of control.

The song ended too soon and she stood there, wanting more.

"Want to do another one?" He glanced at her lips.

For an answer, she leaned further into him. The next song began. They moved less now, joined in a virtual embrace.

He whispered. "I've been wondering… what it would be like to kiss you."

Laurel's belly and chest tingled. Her ankles quaked a little as she stood on tiptoe and tilted her lips toward his. "Why don't you try it?"

His lips touched hers, moving until her lips parted. They swayed to the music, pelvis to pelvis.

"Laurel…"

"Hush," she put her finger on his lips. "Don't talk. Let's try it again."

Five minutes later they were both out of breath. The song had ended minutes ago. Laurel was filled with the most wonderful lightness, but at the same time a little afraid. The morning-after blues had sounded the death knell for too many friendships with men.

"Your room or mine?" His voice soft. "Mine's closer."

Laurel shivered. "Not…"

"Not tonight? Not my place?"

Laurel buried her face in his neck while she tried to decide what to do.

The weather changed. On October twenty-first, a late-season low slid up the Atlantic seaboard, bringing wet snow to New York and Boston and a chilling northeasterly wind to the east end of Lake Ontario.

"This is what we want," Laurel said while she and Mike stood on the veranda of the hotel and watched waves break along the shoreline that morning. "As long as the wind holds from the northeast the eastern end of the lake will be flat."

Mike checked his watch. "Why don't I collect Sheik and get the *Longley* fired up? We'll meet you and Grampa Jake there at 10:30."

Tall waves battered the east breakwall as the *Bruce B. Longley* cleared

Oswego harbor and the area of confused seas just outside. Sheik headed east, skirting the shore.

By 12:15 they'd rounded Stony Point. In the lee of the land, Sheik pulled the throttles back, the engines in neutral. Except for their wake, the water lay flat calm. The *Longley* slowed, drifting closer to the cliffs.

The wall loomed, layered horizontal slabs of black-tinged slate. Lichens grew in dashes of green and brown. Otherwise, the face seemed devoid of life, beautiful in its raw wildness. And yet something more, some darker tension seemed compressed within, as if the place held its breath and waited.

Waited for the right moment. For fools to venture too close, or linger too long, and then it would crunch them in its stone jaws, and steal their souls from among the living. Overhead, a lowering sky cast brooding shadows over the desolate cliff, adding to the somber mood.

The *Longley* drifted ever closer, into the shadow of the high walls. Tinted by the reflected rock, the uneasy surface of the water turned a darker green there, almost black. Except for the sigh of wind high above and the steady drip, drip, of water from the rock, there was no sound.

A hundred yards offshore, puffs of wind swirled down, fanning out, making cat's paws on the surface as they left the land above and began their long journey down the lake. Laurel crossed her arms over her chest, shivering. She had come to steal its secret, but this place would not surrender it easily.

The low rumble of the *Longley*'s engines echoed from the undercut walls as Sheik put them in reverse and nudged the throttles, breaking the spell that held her.

Mike swung his arm, indicating a path along the face. "I think we should make a pass to see if there are any points of rock or shoals in close." He looked at Sheik. "Afterward, we can stream the fish and have a look at that hole where Laurel spotted the rib."

"Can do," Sheik nodded. "Why don't you go forward and keep a lookout. Laurel can give me the depth soundings."

Mike went to the bow, pulling his gloves on. The *Longley* transited the base of the cliffs with only a few small scares. The water averaged between sixty and seventy feet in depth before shoaling right under the cliffs themselves. They finished the pass and headed for deeper water while Sheik made another wide loop, planning to tow the fish along the same path they'd just completed.

They began the pass. Laurel stared at the screen. "It should be right about in here," she muttered, half to herself. An instant later, it was. The screen changed and she saw HMS *Ontario*.

"My God! There she is," she yelled, punching the "record" button several times more than necessary. Mike leaned over her back, straining to see.

The ship lay on her port side, bow and stern unmistakable. Much of the stern area appeared to be intact, but the starboard side of the hull, from the bow to near the after deck, was missing. All that remained were two or three broken ribs protruding from the bottom, one of them probably what Laurel had first spotted.

Another image replaced the ship as the towfish moved beyond the wreck. Laurel trembled with excitement as she stood and put her arms around Mike. "I can't believe it, we've found it."

He pulled her to him and lifted her feet off the floor, twirling her around like a doll.

"Congratulations, Laurel! You sure made the right call on this one."

Ontario lay less than a hundred and fifty feet from the base of the cliffs. They triangulated its position with shore references. Towfish aboard and stowed, they set an anchor and Mike dropped a small float to check for current. A puff of wind caught it and scooted it away.

He turned to Sheik. "Not much current today."

"Yeah, I see that. But it was screaming the last time we were here."

Laurel grabbed Mike's sleeve. "Hold it. Look there." She pointed.

The wind had carried Mike's float a hundred yards out into the lake. Now, against the wind, it surged back toward them, arrived and was swept past. At once, *Longley* tried to follow, coming up against her anchor with a jerk. Her bows turned into the flow.

"Cripes," Sheik said. "That's showing up as ten knots on the Sumlog."

Mike indicated the heavens. "The only thing that could cause water to move like this is air pressure. I've read about the phenomenon, peculiar to the Great La—"

"'Came the fearsome devil Seiche,'" Laurel said, watching the water stream past.

"What was that?" Mike asked.

"Oh, just something I read somewhere."

Mike came to stand beside her. "Well, we better pick a day when the atmosphere is stable. These have been known to raise harbor levels several feet in minutes. There must be a major disturbance somewhere nearby."

She'd studied up a bit herself. "Thanks for the confidence booster but I think you overlooked something."

His brows knitted. "What's that?"

"Low pressure to the southeast, the weather system that gives us the offshore wind and makes it calm enough to dive in here, is also the system most likely to spawn a seiche."

Mike looked unhappy, but after a pause he said, "You might have a point. We'll rig safety lines and tether ourselves to them."

Laurel shivered. No wonder Joshua's inscription ended, "and now the secret ever keeps". Diving here would be dangerous as hell.

Mike's teeth flashed as he smiled. "It's an incredible stroke of luck, though. If we stay lucky, we'll only need a few minutes on the bottom to get inside her and find our provenance, something to prove she's who we think she is."

Romy Zaia lay in the deep brush at the top of the cliff, less than two hundred yards from the place where the black boat had anchored. With Joey pretending to be fishing but really watching the Eastlands, Romy knew they'd left the harbor before they cleared the breakwalls.

Below, they'd upped anchor, turned away from the shore, and now headed toward the open lake. He lowered his binoculars. They wouldn't have anchored if the wreck wasn't right there.

"X" marks the spot.

They'd been so busy down there they hadn't noticed him watching. Good. With all their fancy equipment, they'd done the work for him. All he had to do now was drop a monkey wrench into their plans and help himself to the goodies before they had a chance.

First things first. He decided to pay another visit to the black boat tonight. As far as Miss Fancy Pants was concerned, next time she got around to diving, he had a nice little surprise in store for her.

OSWEGO HARBOR

Char Stone sat at rigid attention at her desk, listening to the person on the other end of the line. It was 0700 Thursday, October 24.

"...and let me tell you something else, Bosun's Mate Stone. The next time I hear about an incident like the one that took place aboard that private vessel, which by the way happens to be owned by the largest shipping conglomerate in the fucking *world*, we will be making a change at Oswego. Do you understand?"

Two weeks earlier, Char had stopped and boarded a vessel inbound down the St. Lawrence and searched it for contraband. Nothing had been found, and the vessel's captain had promised her she'd be hearing about it from her superiors. Actually, she had dragged her feet on the operational report, hadn't sent it in yet.

"Aye, sir!" Char said into the telephone.

The caller, her boss, was in Washington D.C. but her back was still ramrod stiff. Several minutes had elapsed since his call came in, during which they talked, or rather he talked and she listened.

"Good. Now listen up. I want that fucking report in my hands no later than 1700, before I lose my goddamn job over it."

"Aye, aye sir. Right away, sir."

"One more thing. Canadian Customs has been in touch with us again regarding smuggling activities on your end of the lake. Someone is still bringing cigarettes into Canada. They have their eyes on a suspect in Collins Bay, near Kingston, but haven't been able to identify the source from our side. I'm faxing the file to you. Put this one on the front burner, Chief. Get me results. Make me look good for a change. Got it?"

"Aye, aye sir! We'll put it on the hot sheet."

The reward for her obeisance was a click from the other end. Her fax machine beeped into action. She studied the first page, a grainy picture of a dick boat, the kind guys with tiny dicks liked to buy and run around in. Big, pointed phallic symbols, that was all they were. Most were unmuffled, noisy, blatant, and offensive, just like their mini-dick owners. Dangerous too. Whenever the waves were higher than the length of the owner's dick they could be completely unmanageable at anything faster than three knots.

This was a big one, around thirty-five or forty feet, with twin engines. If it was in the water, she'd find it.

The second page came through. This suspect looked like a cross between a tug and a lobsterman. Talk about contrasts. The tortoise or the hare. Which one should she concentrate on? She decided on the workboat. The guys with the dick boats could slip them onto trailers and store them out back of the barn. Hard to find with the forty-four-footer they gave her to work with.

She pushed the faxes aside and glared at the half-dozen printed pages in a neat stack on the otherwise empty desk. Her report of the boarding. She had to send it in now. There was no choice in the matter.

Across from the station, activity aboard the black workboat caught her eye. She pulled her binoculars out of their case and looked. Mike McKean. That bastard! He'd dumped her right when she was most hopeful, and for what? Probably for that little bitch who spent her time following him around, checking on him.

He went into the deckhouse. A minute later exhaust belched from the boat's transom. They were going out.

She leaned back in her chair and put her feet up on her desk. What would a deep-water diver and a mechanical engineer with a marine background be doing, in October, with a boat filled with state-of-the-art equipment? Could it be government money? The black boat was almost too modern to be private sector. No. It wasn't a government project. She'd have been informed if it was.

They had to be doing something marginal, or maybe even outright illegal, something involving diving and engineering. Otherwise, why sneak away before sunup every time they went out? In a flash of insight, the answer came. Her feet hit the floor with a bang as she sat bolt upright.

Treasure! They're searching for treasure.

She knew she was right. She also knew that on the Great Lakes even the smallest artifact retrieved from a wreck site remained the property of its owners, or in their absence, the people of the United States.

That made it her duty to stop them and seize any contraband they brought up. Char went to the windows overlooking the harbor and the black-painted boat there.

Time for a little payback.

STONY POINT

When the twenty-fourth of October arrived with the exact conditions they wanted for the first dive on the wreck, Laurel decided to go for it. The lake at Stony Point lay flat under a pale sky, high clouds in cornrows aligned north to south, and virtually no wind.

Shortly after nine, she finished the startup of her re-breather. From the water, Mike lifted his facemask. "The safety line is rigged. I ran it from bow to stern, along the exposed ribs. Clip on when we get down. All set?"

Laurel nodded. She wished she could be somewhere else, anywhere but here and about to dive to the bottom directly under the menacing cliffs. But she wasn't. She checked her gauges and looked over the side. Her image wavered up at her from the uncertain mirror of the surface. Below the sheen, the black-green water made it seem like she'd be stepping into darkness.

She'd be okay. The foreboding always passed. This would be a red-letter day for them. Mike depended on her. She couldn't let him down.

He smiled and called up. "This is the big one. Gonna make history today." He positioned his facemask and sank below the surface.

Laurel took one last look around, gave Grampa Jake and Sheik a wave, and stepped off the platform into the water.

Mike waited by the guide rope. "Ah, let's…" he made the vowel sound first to activate the com system.

"Go," she bent to begin the descent.

They didn't need the guideline. The current was slack, and the water so clear she could see the wreck from sixty feet above. At the bottom, they clipped their harnesses to the safety line Mike had rigged and split up. She went toward the bow to search for the ship's bell, or anything with a name on it, Mike headed toward the stern. The bottom was tan rock, slime-coated but devoid of any other kind of aquatic growth.

Mike rounded the stern. Four dark openings appeared. Once they'd probably housed the windows of the captain's quarters. He swam up to one and peered into its pitch-black interior. Unhooking the light from his belt, he directed the beam inside. Tiny bits of silt sparkled in the gloom. He stuck his head inside. There were no obvious pitfalls, so he wiggled through the opening.

In its normal position, the chamber wouldn't have offered sufficient headroom for him to stand erect. Now, the floor rose to his right and the ceiling to his left. Everything that had been on the floor, except for one table, which remained bolted in place, had to be underneath the deep layer of muck below his feet. His fins had already raised a thick cloud, reducing the visibility in the chamber. If he wasn't careful, he'd end up doing it all by feel, a Braille dive.

He scanned the mire. No shapes were visible beneath the surface. He had no idea how deep the mud was, or what it concealed. Their provenance could easily be beyond reach without more equipment and manpower.

Above him, in the cul-de-sac formed by the transom and the starboard planking up near the underside of the deck, a slime-coated box, like a humidor or a jewelry box, lay on a shelf, upended. He let himself drift up. Metal adorned its curved lid. He lifted the box and brought it closer to his mask. In the poor visibility he couldn't read the lettering on the lid but imagined it must be the personal property of a passenger or somebody important, probably in the captain's cabin for safekeeping. Maybe the box would give them their provenance, maybe not. He shoved it into the net at his side.

The water just above the shelf glittered, reflecting light from his lantern. Curious, he poked a finger into the shiny area. Air. He'd found an air pocket. How could air be present after so long? The air pocket seemed fairly broad, covering the entire corner formed by the transom, side and underside of the deck above, but less than six inches in depth.

Could a diver using compressed air have been here before him? That was probably it. Then again, the jewelry box had been in plain sight. Any diver would certainly have seen it just as he had.

He secured his find to the retrieval line and sent it on its way to the surface.

And then the seiche came. It built so quickly he just managed to catch hold of the hull before the full force of the current snatched him.

Laurel felt the first symptom less than a minute after she and Mike separated. It came in a broad stroke as she hung inverted over a metal object she'd found. Her vision went into a tunnel. Then she couldn't focus for a few seconds, and then it passed.

She checked her Oxy gauge. The partial pressure, or percentage of oxygen in her mix, was fine. Now that her senses were alerted, she realized her mixture wasn't flowing easily. She had to suck to inhale and blow to breathe out. Not too hard, but enough to be noticeable.

Just as she realized this, the second wave came, the blurred vision accompanied this time by an uncontrollable twitching of her eyelids. Toxic symptoms! Fear jump-started her pulse. She felt it accelerate. She had to stay calm. PpO2 was still okay. She had to be taking a CO2 hit. Something was wrong with her chemical.

The dive was over.

She had to flush her system immediately, then get the hell to the surface. Hypercapnia could kill you in a hurry. She reached over her shoulder for the bypass valve that would introduce nitrox from her diluent bottle directly into the breathing loop so she could breathe open-circuit and bypass the re-breather apparatus while she went to the surface.

It was then, the moment her fingers found the lever, that she felt the first flood of the seiche. Oh Jesus, not now! Not the very thing about this horrid place she feared most. Nausea snuck up her throat. She rotated the lever, opening the valve, anticipating the flood of fresh air.

The lever came off in her hand.

She stared stupidly. Another, deeper, wave of dizziness swept her. She had to work for her next breath.

The current carried her away from the wreck, twirling her like a leaf in the wind. Her heart thudded in her ears. She'd been on the verge of backing out all morning. Terror welled, threatening to blot out reason.

She came to the end of the slack in her safety line, and it brought her to a stop with a jolt that dislodged her face mask. Water flooded in, blinding her and cutting off all air. Somehow, she kept a semblance of control. The seiche pressed against her, physical, taking liberties with her person, pinwheeling her at the end of the thin safety line while she struggled to clear her mask of water.

Only three small strands of nylon kept her from being carried off, into the dark void.

She saw the loose terminal of the jack that connected the microphones in her facemask to the transmitter on the back of her head, but didn't understand that it had pulled loose when her mask was dislodged. After several seconds, she was able to clear the mask and get a full breath of the tainted mixture.

"Mike! Mike! Help me," she choked out.

Silence.

With her exertion, a hard wave of dizziness swam up her spine toward her head, threatening to overwhelm her. She grasped the safety line. Trembling from a full dose of adrenaline, she pulled herself hand over hand toward the guideline leading to the boat above. It was too much. She managed only a few feet before the excess waste in her mixture overtook her and she slipped back to the end.

Before her eyes, her safety line popped a strand where it turned at a sharp angle around one of the ship's ribs. Mother of Jesus! It must be chafing on something sharp. Her eyes saw only the safety line, as if she and it were at opposite ends of a glass tunnel. Another strand let go, twisting as it unwound itself. Then, slowly at first, the final strand stretched and let go.

With a victorious jerk, the seiche claimed her.

Confusion and dizziness swarmed. This place hated her. She should do something but didn't remember what. The current swept her between two tall pillars of brown rock, then down, away from the rock face, into the deep. She could no longer see the wreck.

A million burning hornets swam up the nape of her neck and spilled over her forehead, over her ears, taking her, taking over. Then they had her, and everything went black.

On the cliff above the wreck site, Romy Zaia watched Jake Eastland and his friend pull something aboard. Miss Smarty Pants hadn't seemed all that confident as they got ready to dive. To him, she'd looked tentative, as if she was afraid and being brave. Not many women were like that; afraid and strong too. Her name was Kingsford. What if she wasn't even related to the old bastard down there? Romy experienced a twinge of conscience. He almost wished he knew a girl like her.

Too late now. She and her boyfriend had been down ten minutes.

Beside the larger boat, their seventeen-foot Whaler, swung on the line tying it to the bigger vessel. Romy studied the water. A current had come up.

Romy grimaced. She had to be feeling it by now. He'd put those canisters in a bladder and bled CO_2 into them from a bottle of compressed gas, the kind used to power draft beer systems. He was pretty sure they wouldn't be able to absorb much more of the stuff. As a finishing touch, a little ten-minute epoxy took care of her emergency valve.

A popping noise disturbed his thoughts. Down on the water, Eastland and his buddy heard it too and turned to look at the sky. Right away, one of them jumped down into the Whaler and started the engine. He cast off and took off like a bat out of hell toward the north.

Romy got to his feet and tried to see what was up, but the headland blocked his view. Then he spotted the flares high overhead, at least a mile away. Somebody must be in trouble over there. Well, it wouldn't be long before the Eastlands had trouble of their own.

Romy brushed his hands on his jeans and began the climb up to where he'd left his truck. He couldn't afford to be observed near the scene of a fatal "accident." He'd watch TV tonight to see if it worked or not. Besides, he wasn't so proud of what he'd done any more.

Mike rounded the stern of the wreck in time to see Laurel's safety line part. "Don't panic, Laurel," he said, but he could see she had. The current carried her off, spread-eagled, stiff as a board, not answering or responding to his voice in any way.

An image of Mary's body, haloed in a carmine pool of her own blood, came to him. He'd known the right thing to do instinctively, but he'd followed the book. Now, it was happening again. He unclipped himself from his safety tether and swam toward her. He could just see her at the far edge of his range of visibility. The current sluiced her between two pillars of rock and down, out of sight. Deeper water waited over there. A lot deeper.

His pulse hammered. He swam toward the pillars as fast as he could.

Don't lose her. Don't lose her.

When he reached the pillars, the current swept him through. Nothing but blackness lay beyond. Which way? No time to think.

He swam in total darkness for more than a minute, saw nothing, pushed on for another minute, exerting himself to the limit. His re-breather couldn't keep up at this pace. The water was much deeper, colder, draining him. Still, he saw nothing.

He kicked through the dark, spurred by yet another shot of adrenaline. It drained away quickly. There was nothing there.

Then he glimpsed something, a flicker of white—her safety line! The frayed ends undulated as they streamed through the water. But where was she?

With the last of his strength he captured the line. Thank you,

God. He exhaled with relief, resting for a moment, letting the seiche carry them along. As he rested, he saw the gunman ducking behind the superstructure of the *Sea Angel*, heard his maniacal howl and the gunshots. Not this time. No. Never again.

When he caught his breath, he tied her line to his harness ring and began to reel her in. Even now, while they drifted out of control in the cold bowels of Lake Ontario, he knew she represented his salvation. He was not saving her; it was the other way around.

She drifted five feet away, upside down, unconscious. Her facial muscles twitched, her eyes fixed and dilated. Toxic symptoms! There was no time to decompress, he had to get her to the surface. He reached over and activated her ABLJ. As it blossomed and filled, her body righted itself and the ABLJ carried her upward. He activated his own.

When he broke the surface, he looked around, disoriented. Laurel bobbed beside him. He pulled her mask off and put his spare mouthpiece in her mouth, holding it there with his hand.

She breathed on her own. Relief waved through him. He pulled a flare from his vest with his free hand, held it out of the water and discharged it. The flare arched several hundred feet above them, throwing off red sparks. He pulled the other one out and set it off too.

Less than a minute later, the high-pitched whine of an outboard motor prop came through the water. The Whaler was coming, in a hurry.

THE BRUCE B. LONGLEY

By mid-afternoon, Laurel felt better. She had a splitting headache, but at least she could think straight again. Outside, the wind had come up and the *Longley*, still at anchor over the wreck, rose and fell in small waves.

Her interest in Mike's find was a strong factor in her fast recovery. The small box sat on the table in front of her.

"Do you think it'll work as provenance?"

He shrugged. "Don't know. All I know for sure is by bringing it up we've now broken the law for the first time. We get caught with this, it'll be the end of our search."

Grampa Jake listened from the foot of the steep stairwell. "Mike, why don't you sit. I want to talk to you before we up anchor."

"I've been thinking," Grampa Jake said when Mike settled himself opposite Laurel. "If the Coast Guard finds out what we've got, they'll give us a hard time."

Mike nodded. "A very hard time. And mess up our timetable. As it is, we might only get a few more good days before the bad weather hits."

Grampa Jake's wide blue eyes sparkled.

Laurel tugged on his arm, pulling him to the seat next to her. "What's on your mind?"

"Well, Mike, maybe you already know this from your grandfather, but there were a bunch of different ways rumrunners hauled booze during Prohibition. For instance, if the boat was big but slow, they'd load a couple thousand cases or so into two big nets and hang them off either side. Submerged, the booze didn't weigh much, and they'd just plow across the lake in broad daylight, pretending they were fishing. They'd deposit the nets on the sandbars along the shoreline and later, when the coast was clear, the buyers went out and retrieved the nets and that would be that."

"Cool," Mike said. "Did the authorities ever catch on?"

Jake fixed his eyes on him.

"After a while. The night runners were the ones who got all the press. The Coast Guard focused on them."

Laurel pulled her legs up on the cushion and beneath herself, and slid her arm through Grampa Jake's. "That's how you did it, wasn't it?"

"Actually, I was the first. If the Coast Guard came close, I'd attach a salt buoy and let the nets go to the bottom. The salt buoy sank in the water but later, after the salt dissolved, the cork inside would work loose and float up to mark the spot."

"Hey, I found a sinker just like that where we found the whisky!"

"Sure. There was a salt buoy tied to that load."

Mike laughed, "No wonder my grandfather didn't catch you. That's pretty slick."

"I rigged up a small net. I think we should put the box Mike found in it, hang it over the side, and transport it that way. Then tonight, you can go out and get it."

"Oh, Grampa Jake. You're so melodramatic." Laurel pulled on his arm again. "We don't need to do that."

Grampa Jake smiled. "No? Okay, it's your call, hon. But I have a feeling trouble is just around the corner. Why don't you humor me?"

Mike stood. "I think he's right. It never hurts to have an ace or two to pull out of your sleeve. I've got an idea of my own. I think I'll give Jake a hand."

USCG 44-FOOTER

Chief Bosun's Mate Char Stone leaned against the aftermost wall of the pilothouse and listened to the drone of the forty-four footer's diesel. They'd searched every nook of Fair Haven Bay for the boat suspected of running cigarettes to Canada. Now they were off Oswego, on the way east to check the Salmon River at Selkirk.

"Chief, radar's showing a contact thirteen miles east and north."

There were few recreational fishing boats on the lake this late in the year. The big salmon had made their spawning runs and were stacked up in the rivers and tributaries. "Probably some Fishhead too dumb to know the fish are all in the rivers."

"No. This guy's bigger. Heading toward Mexico Bay."

Char stood straighter. The black boat hadn't been at the pier when she and her crew left Oswego.

"Let's take a look. Set a course to intercept."

"Aye, aye, chief."

Char caught apprehensive glances from several of her crew and the tension in the pilothouse increased noticeably. They probably remembered the boarding up on the St. Lawrence. This time it would be different.

Five minutes later, Whaley, field glasses at his eyes, said, "I think it's the vessel *Bruce B. Longley*, Chief, headed toward Mexico Point."

Char almost shivered with anticipation. "Maybe they have something aboard they don't want to bring to Oswego. Maybe they plan to transfer it to a smaller boat. We'll board them and conduct a safety check."

If they had so much as an ounce of contraband, she'd shut them down so tight the mice on board would die of malnutrition. "Full ahead, Whaley, I'll be boarding with your team. Get me a sidearm and a handheld VHF."

The twin diesels had almost lulled Laurel to sleep when Grampa Jake leaned into the companionway from the deckhouse.

"You'll want to see this."

"What is it?" Laurel rubbed her eyes.

"Come on up."

She climbed the three steps to the deckhouse. Mike stood outside, at the starboard rail looking west.

Grampa Jake pointed. "What did I tell you?"

A mile off, the Coast Guard cutter steamed toward them, a large bone in her teeth, and a broad plume of diesel exhaust behind her.

"Are they coming for us?"

Mike came inside in time to hear her question. "No doubt in my military mind," he said. "Look at that bow wave. That boat can't move any faster than it is right now, and at the moment we're the only other boat out here."

When they were within hailing range, Char said, "Okay. Let 'em know we're coming."

The signalman picked up the hailer handset and spoke into it. "Attention *Bruce B. Longley*. You are ordered to heave to and prepare to be boarded. Please have your papers ready for inspection."

Char turned to Whaley. "Run their registration number."

"Aye, aye." Whaley bent over his keyboard to type the numbers into the system. A few moments later his computer beeped and the screen flashed the owner's name. "It belongs to some company called The Big One, Inc," he said, "out of New York City. Oh, hey. Get a load of the address. It's lower Manhattan." He pointed at the screen, eyebrows raised. "We're not really gonna roust these guys, are we?"

Char leaned closer until her jaw was inches from his. "If there's the smallest particle of contraband aboard that vessel, we're seizing them.

You understand, Whaley?"

Whaley stiffened. "Aye, Chief!"

Aboard the black boat, the bitch who was after Mike stood by the rail.

She called across the narrowing gap. "Why are you boarding us?"

"We are boarding you to..." Eyes questioning, the young signalman turned to Char for an answer. Char snatched the handset from him. She had no problem whatever in allowing the hate she felt for this woman, for all women who found it easy to attract men, to color her response.

She let contempt drip from her voice. "The vessel *Bruce B. Longley* is suspected of illegal salvage. We intend to seize any illegal objects or substances aboard. If you resist, you will be arrested."

The two boats came together with hardly a bump, and Whaley's five-member team boarded the *Longley*. Char went over last. Whaley had already asked for and received the documentation papers. He handed them to Char.

She glanced. New documents, clean. As she did, Mike came out of the deckhouse. He looked so rugged, so in his element, his presence made Char feel weak and out of her own by comparison.

"Char. Why are you doing this?" He made an effort to keep his voice low. "You know I'm no smuggler. What's going on here?"

Char's resolve threatened to melt. She took one step backward. Every ounce of her anger, her frustration over her inability to communicate her value as a woman, went into her voice.

"Bosun Whaley, if this man says another word, arrest him for resisting a legal search operation."

Mike nodded and turned away. She took a deep breath and let it out, still trembling inside.

After fifteen minutes of search, they had nothing. Char fumed. Goddamm it! There *had* to be something.

"Find something, damn you," she hissed as Whaley passed.

One hour later he hadn't. The *Longley* was clean, the only thing even mildly suspicious, a bottle of whisky. An unusual bottle, shorter and a little wider that usual, and rather than labeled, the glass was molded with the maker's name and city. Perfectly legal. She dismissed it from her mind.

Then she spotted it. Back near the transom, a thin nylon tether extended overboard. None of her team had gone anywhere near it. Damn! They were trained to look for things suspended overboard. That trick was old as the hills.

Char clenched her fists. "Whaley!"

Whaley's head appeared from inside the *Longley*'s cabin. He scrambled up the steps. "Aye, Chief."

With the index finger of her right hand, Char pointed to the tether. She smiled as Whaley's eyes grew big as cue balls.

Mike McKean had been watching in silence. Now he moved and Char looked his way. He pointed to the tether. "It's our bait bucket, Chief. You've been aboard more than an hour. It's time to give it up."

"I told you to shut up." Char turned to Whaley. "Haul that object out of the water. Then we'll see who's giving up."

Every eye followed Bosun Whaley to the rail near the stern. He reached overboard and began to pull the line up hand over hand.

A round bait tin appeared, galvanized, two-gallon capacity, with small holes cut so water could circulate. Perfect for concealing a small item.

Whaley lowered it to the deck and watched as the water drained. "Open it."

When he looked up at her, his eyes showed dark pleasure.

"Empty, Chief."

Five minutes later one of Char's red-faced seamen handed Sheik a citation for failing to have a required sticker advising against the discharge of oil overboard. The boarding team left much more quietly than it arrived.

When the Coasties were back aboard their boat and had cast off from the *Longley*, Laurel turned to Mike.

"I don't get it. Where's the box?"

"Oh that. I put it overboard."

The frustrations of the day, almost dying, feeling sick and confused, being boarded and searched, all swelled to a crescendo in Laurel. "Jesus, Mary, and Joseph! You jettisoned what might have been our provenance? There must be two hundred feet of water here. How the hell are we going to find it?"

Her ears were hot and Laurel knew her face must be bright red. In the shade of the deckhouse behind her, Sheik chuckled. Laughing at her? She wheeled about. Sure enough, Sheik looked like a cat who'd just had the cream.

When he saw her glaring, he snapped to attention and tried to wipe the smirk off his face. "Don't look at me. I dunno nothin.'"

Laurel turned back to Mike. "Okay. What's the joke?"

Mike checked the Coast Guard cutter. It was a mile away and moving fast. He held up a small transmitter.

Laurel squinted. "What's that?"

"I tied the box to a PFD, the inflatable type. Then I disabled the auto inflation device with one of these." He held up a jaw-like device. "It's a neat little tool the Navy uses. You can operate it by radio. The second it lets go, the jacket will switch back to automatic and inflate. In just about a minute, that sucker is gonna pop up to the surface and deliver our little secret right back into our hands."

Mike opened the radio and pressed the appropriate button. "And, that's all there is to it."

Grampa Jake laughed. "It's a salt buoy, nineties style."

The direction finder in the deckhouse beeped. Sheik leaned over it. "Hey, it worked! We got a signal."

Mike threw his arm around Laurel and gave her a hug. "Come on. This'll be our big discovery. Let's go get it."

They decided that the sooner Laurel went ashore, the faster she'd recover, so she and Mike boarded the Whaler for the run in to the hotel, leaving Sheik and Grampa Jake to bring the *Longley* to Oswego.

"This isn't helping my head much," she said from beside Mike as the Whaler bounced around on the waves.

Mike pulled back the throttle, slowing so the boat rode more smoothly. "Thank God you're all right. Did you know your canisters were used up? You should have changed them."

"I did. This morning. I've taken CO2 hits before. I made darn sure they were fresh. God, even my eyeballs hurt." Laurel covered her eyes with her palm.

"What happened to your bypass? The lever was missing, looked like somebody twisted it right off."

"That's the funny part. I dreamed I did that. I tried to flush but I was so strong I broke it right off."

Mike growled, "Some dream. No way you're that strong. The valve must be defective. That's brand new equipment, top shelf. Jake should send that unit in for inspection. You could've been killed."

He leaned closer until his nose touched hers. "Don't *ever* do that to me again."

"Don't worry. I'll never go near the water within ten miles of that place again." Laurel's head cleared just for a second, and she imagined him inside the wreck. "By the way, did you see…?"

She stopped in mid-sentence. He didn't know about the treasure. Didn't she owe him the truth? Laurel wavered. She'd been dumped on so many times. Did she dare throw herself into the flames again?

Grampa Jake's words came. "Do the things you think will make you happy."

Laurel thought she knew how, but proving it to herself meant letting go, trusting.

"Mike. There's a treasure aboard the *Ontario*."

Mike did a double take, his mouth falling open, then pulled the throttle all the way back. The Whaler settled in the water and stopped.

"What?"

"I've seen the documentation. Very obscure, but accurate. It was aboard, a box so heavy it took six men to carry it, the proceeds of a tax levied on commerce to help finance the Revolutionary War. It'll be worth millions today."

Mike's face first questioned, then reddened. "Okay," he said. "I guess I didn't need to know. I don't like it, but I do understand."

Relief. He'd reacted like a mature, sincere person. She'd done it, and it felt wonderful.

"It would be a good-sized chest. Did you see anything like that?"

"No. It was a mess in there. I didn't see it."

Her hopes receded.

He nudged the sack holding the box he'd recovered. "If it's there, we'll find it. The silt had to be half a dozen feet deep. Right now, I'm more interested in learning about this."

She nodded. "I'll talk to Aaron. He mentioned an archivist by the name of Genevieve Degas. She's an expert on the period. Maybe we can get her to help us."

TWICE TOLD HOTEL

Genevieve Degas not only agreed, she and Aaron arrived at the Twice Told less than twenty-four hours after Laurel called with news of the find.

"And best of all," Aaron told Laurel after introducing Genevieve, "she's unaffiliated, doesn't have a commitment to a major museum or organization. That means she isn't afraid to bend some of the rules they like to surround themselves with to make the examination of artifacts seem more complicated than it needs to be."

Genevieve lifted an eyebrow in Aaron's direction, then stepped over to Laurel, extending her hand. "I don't know about this bending of rules. Pleased to meet you anyway, Ms. Kingsford." She was in her forties, trim and attractive, with a light French accent.

"Call me Laurel. Welcome to the Twice Told."

"Is it here? The little discovery you made?"

"It's upstairs, in Grampa Jake's safe. Should we go have a look?"

Grampa Jake seemed unusually reserved. He took Genevieve by the elbow and escorted her to the cocktail table between two facing sofas. "There you are, Genevieve." His pronunciation had the French inflection just right and he offered her the position of honor directly in front of the artifact.

The box they'd found was of wood, twelve by fourteen inches and half a foot high, and stood on short legs. The lacquer that must once have been present was long gone, leaving the surface dull grey.

Genevieve knelt and touched one of the elegantly formed corner reinforcements. The metal was black with grey highlights, every surface engraved. She studied the engraving work, her fingertip tracing the seam where lid and base joined.

"It is a safe box, designed to be airtight. The most skillful craftsman could not make a dozen in a career."

Laurel said, "Is it possible it's still airtight?"

Genevieve regarded her. "After two hundred years? Possible, yes. But not likely. Still, it would be staggering if the contents were intact. Is it not so?"

The room was silent as Genevieve used a magnifying glass to inspect the metal letters on the domed upper half of the box.

"The letters are PDD," she said, folding the tool and putting it aside. "They're formed to the curve of the lid, attached with tiny screws. Look at the detail of the engravings, how deeply embossed in places and shallow in others. The work is exquisite, nearly three dimensional."

"How does it open?" Laurel said.

Genevieve frowned. "Minus the key, impossible without destroying its value. Perhaps we can find this 'PDD.' and he or she will lead us to a key that will open it for us."

The letters were initials. It made sense.

Mike said, "The locking mechanism is probably rusted solid, anyway."

Genevieve turned to him, eyebrows lifted. "Non. There will be no rust. All the metal, and the initials too, is silver. The key would be silver as well, almost certainly engraved with the same initials."

Laurel sat back on the sofa, eyeing the mysterious box. "What if we can't find the owner?"

Genevieve considered the question and shrugged. "Perhaps an expert in the field could fabricate a key. I would have to think about who to approach."

She paused, taking in each of them in turn. At last, she tapped the surface of Mike's find. "Only rich and influential people owned boxes like this. For it to be aboard this ship is a contradiction. The fact that it was tells me there are things, important things, we have yet to learn about the last voyage of His Majesty's Ship *Ontario*."

OSWEGO HARBOR

Char sat at her desk in the deepening darkness. Her reaction to the other woman's presence in Mike's life had been visceral, produced by years of frustration. She'd acted like a complete fool.

Two things were sure. First, as long as he didn't see the light, Mike McKean wasn't going to be safe from her. Second, neither would that twat Laurel Kingsford.

2100 hours. Time to go home. As she crossed the office, her intercom buzzed. She ignored it, closed her door and went down the stairs.

At the duty station, Whaley looked up, phone in hand. "Chief! I just buzzed you. There's someone here to see you." He pointed to her left. Ten feet away stood a short, dark-complected man with a mop of black hair and striking eyes. He was dressed like a hobo, sagging pants held up by a strand of rope, dirty t-shirt filled with holes, the one under his right arm huge. He leered at her while she studied him.

She moved closer. "What can I do for you, sir?" The rank aroma of unwashed human reached her.

"Ahhh! It's what I can do for *you*, chief." His leer widened, became conspiratorial, and he worked his bushy eyebrows in a campy way.

She was in no mood for baloney, especially from some lowlife. "Look. I'm busy. Please get to the point."

He fixed his stare on her. Up close he was a fierce-appearing little guy. He opened the burlap sack on the floor, reached inside and withdrew a bottle of whisky. With a flourish, he presented it then stood it on the counter.

He pointed toward the *Longley*, which could be seen through the window of the day room. "This is why that big aluminum job is tied up over there. It's bootleg whisky, from Prohibition. Illegal as hell, I imagine. No federal tax stamps, ya know?" He grinned, his white, even teeth flashing. "I found this on a site they excavated."

Whaley said, "Hey, I saw a bottle like that this afternoon."

Char's pulse accelerated; she'd seen the bottle too. Maybe this guy wasn't such a creep after all. It *was* illegal to possess untaxed whisky, to say nothing of the murky legality of removing it from the bottom. If there was a sunken boat involved on site, a definite misdemeanor.

She had Mike by the balls now, the bastard.

She tried to keep excitement out of her voice. "Whaley, have somebody get the 'off-limits' tape and the chains. If I find a drop of this stuff on that boat, I'll lock it to the dock so tight the tourists'll think it's another frigging museum."

Cheeks warm with anticipation, she let herself gloat a little as she turned back to the hobo. "You stay here. I'll be back in a few minutes."

She steamed out of the station. Two seamen followed close behind, lugging the box containing the chains and locks.

Romy let go of the air he'd been half-holding. The woman's face had run the gamut from irritation to predatory to fervent malice, all in the space of a few seconds. He smirked. It had been sheer luck the kid behind the counter spoke up. The tall broad wouldn't have to look too hard. He'd planted a second bottle of the stuff practically in plain sight.

When they were gone, he took the bottle of whisky from the counter, slid it into his sack and eased himself out the door. He was pretty sure he'd have time to find the treasure and be long gone before the Eastland bunch got their boat out of hock.

As he slipped away in the failing light, he saw the expression on the chief's face again. What was her name, Stone? Christ! If looks could kill, somebody out there should just go ahead and lie down now, before two yards of bitch came along to help. But oh, what a lay she would be. He shuddered as he imagined her on top of him, forcing him to give it to her. Whew! In his dreams, but only there. That chief was too much woman for any one man, and he didn't need a bitch like her on his tail.

Mike stood beside his pickup and stared. Yesterday the boarding, now this. What could be going on in the woman's head?

The Longley lay behind a barrier of yellow plastic tape with black letters, the kind used at crime scenes. Armed Coast Guard seamen stood on either side of the gangplank, eyeing him.

Mike shut the door of his pickup and walked over to the guards. He held himself straight, like an officer. The stance came naturally, even after several years.

"Morning men. What's going on here?"

"This vessel has been seized under conditions set forth by United States Coast Guard Regulations," the taller of the two said. "Contraband was found aboard."

Mike knew the "zero tolerance" policy well, having enforced it many times himself. He also knew if this incident got to the lawyers it would take time to sort out, time they might not have. Winter weather could arrive any day now.

He nodded. "Is the chief over at the station?" Better to deal with it in a calm logical manner.

"She was there when I came in an hour ago, sir. She might still be there," the taller of the guards said.

"Thanks, men. What'd they find anyway?"

The guard responded without thinking. "I think contraband alcohol, sir."

That little slip would have been good for a reprimand in Mike's command. "Anybody bring coffee out yet?"

"No sir."

"I'll see if I can remind them for you." Mike gave a wave and went back to his truck. He drove around to the parking lot of the station and stopped. Char's car was in the spot designated "Chief."

He parked and entered the station. The interior smelled of paint and brewing coffee. He approached the duty station, to his left.

The young woman behind the counter stood. "Good morning, sir. How can I help you?"

"The men on guard duty could use some of that coffee, and I'd like to see the chief if she's in."

The woman picked up her phone. "We'll get it to them, thanks. Your name sir?"

"Mike McKean."

The rating touched three numbers. A few moments later she said, "There's a Mr. McKean to see you, Chief." She listened, then her eyes scanned him and she nodded. She placed the receiver on its cradle and pointed at the stairs. "She said for you to come right up. It's at the top and straight to the back of the building."

Mike went up the single flight of stairs to the second floor. From there he could see Char working at her desk. He went to the entrance and tapped on the doorframe.

She motioned for him to enter. "Close the door," her voice was hard. "You're here about the boat."

The harsh tone surprised him. He approached her desk, wondering why she was so angry.

"What's all the fuss, Char?"

"You salvaged illegal artifacts. We had probable cause to search, and we found illegal alcohol. The policy is zero tolerance. We seized the evidence and the boat."

He stopped opposite her desk. "That's not quite accurate, Char. I'm sure you know that in the Great Lakes, title to lost property remains with the owner. We were hired by Mr. Jake Eastland of Mexico Point to search for, locate, and possibly retrieve property he lost in 1925. We succeeded. There's nothing illegal about it at all."

He wasn't changing her mind. She'd covered herself this time.

"Possession of whisky with no tax stamps is a federal violation, Mike. So is the importation of whisky without paying the duties. And selling it is illegal, too."

He was too calm. She didn't like it at all.

"Chief, I assure you the duties will be paid, as soon as we can determine how much of the load survived. So far, we've recovered around two hundred bottles."

Char felt the first niggling tendril of doubt. Was he fucking with her head? If so, she could return the favor, no problem. "How much whisky was there, originally?"

If he didn't know, or even stumbled, it would weaken his argument. The rightful owner would know exactly how many bottles were lost.

He didn't skip a beat. "Twelve hundred. That's a hundred cases."

Shit, the bastard could charm a water moccasin out of its skin. She clung to her anger. "That still doesn't get you off the hook. The federal taxes have to be paid in advance of shipment." Despite her outward show of confidence, the twist of doubt pulled at her harder, and she forcibly stilled her breathing.

He sighed and shook his head again. "I'm afraid you're a little off on that one too, Char. You see, when those bottles were lost, whisky was illegal. There were no laws on the books taxing it. After Prohibition was repealed, taxes were levied, but they were not made retroactive."

Was he right? Judas Priest, what if she'd fucked up again? What if they were completely legit?

"The sale…" she couldn't even make it all the way to the question mark. It sounded too hopeful.

He waved her off. "Mr. Eastland has no intention of selling it. He's a multi-millionaire. Do you have any idea how much money is sitting at that dock behind your tape? I'll tell you—several million at least." He leaned toward her. "Mind if I sit?"

He'd backed her into a corner. Despite her anger, and her frustration at his all-too-obvious lack of response to her charms, her heart raced as he came closer. She hated him for his male assuredness, truly hated him, but why did she feel like hugging him and never letting go?

Mike moved to the chair at the side of Char's desk. Seated, he leaned forward and studied her eyes, reading the hurt and confusion there. She had the makings of a fine leader, could be a credit to her sex and to the Coast Guard. She possessed a stronger will than many men he knew.

Strong or not, she'd overmatched herself. He hadn't risen to the rank of captain by accident. He knew the laws cold. He toyed with the idea of confiding in her. Maybe she could become an ally, rather than an enemy. She'd find out about the cannons soon enough anyway. He decided to tell her.

"Char, I'm going to tell you something. Something more important than the whisky." He had her full attention. "We found other abandoned property on the bottom, right there beneath the load of whisky."

"What did you find? Is there a wreck? If so…"

He cut her off with a quick shake of his head. "There's no wreck on the site. We found three old cannon. We've raised them. They're in storage at Mexico Point. We are claiming them under the Law of Finds."

"In order to do that you have to prove they were abandoned."

So, she knew some law. Still, it wasn't grounds enough for her to confiscate the ship.

He nodded. "We've identified them as being from the British warship *Ontario*, which was lost at the end of October, 1780. They must have been thrown overboard to lighten ship in a storm. Their position only a few thousand yards from the end of the lake makes that logical."

He gave her a questioning look. "Did you get the key words 'thrown overboard', Char?"

She rewarded him with an exasperated, do-you-think-I'm-stupid? expression.

"Right. Abandoned. I think that will stand up in any court. As I said, there is no wreck on the site."

Char's tormentor sat back in the chair and crossed his legs. He rolled a pencil back and forth a few times on the surface of her desk with his finger, as if offering her the next move.

After they stared at each other for several seconds, he said, "So. What else have you got, Char?"

Char didn't respond. She'd fucked up again, no doubt in her mind.

His voice became almost friendly. "Let me tell you, then. You've got one reprimand for boarding the *Longley* already."

She jerked erect. This she hadn't heard. "How do you know that?" she demanded.

"I told you, my employer is a powerful man. He has friends in very high places. And he was innocent, Char, innocent."

The word brought bile to Char's throat. She swallowed, feeling it burn.

He wasn't done. "Okay. You've got one reprimand already, and now this." He waved his arm toward the *Longley*. "Look. Nobody knows about it yet. It could just as easily go away and no one would be the wiser. See what I mean, Char? No incident, no report. No egg on the face."

She had to say something, anything, to hide her desperation.

"Reprimand? I don't know anything about a reprimand. Maybe you're pissing in my face and trying to tell me it's raining."

"Char, we have an archaeologist from Woods Hole here for this dive. We'll have a representative of the Naval Academy. The cannon will be donated to their museum. This will not be a little mistake for you. This will be a great big mistake."

He covered her hand with his and leaned still closer, his face inches away. "I like you, Char. I really do. Take my advice on this one. Please."

He liked her. She took a big breath, trembling a little as she let it go. Inside, she willed him to keep going, willed him to say those things that made her quiver when she let herself imagine them. This was a man who could understand her, who knew what the service meant to her, who could complete her. He would know there was more to her than just a drive for success. With him there could be love, even family, kids.

The truth broke through her fantasy with the force of a slap, stinging. She let the breath go. She would not have those things with him—and if it could not be with him, then it would be with no one.

Her life—her life and her career—were over. All those secret hopes she'd harbored all these years, kept alive while others called her "ape girl," "fatty," all the names she hated, were slipping away, fading fast, lost.

She nodded, her last ounce of strength going into her words. "Very compelling. Only one thing's wrong."

"What's that, Char?"

"I sent the sonofabitching report in last night."

She held her breath as the words echoed in the sudden silence that followed, and she gained no satisfaction when his face collapsed. He'd been a captain, knew as well as she did she couldn't back down after the initial report had been made.

He stood, frowned down at her for long moments without speaking, then left the office.

Chief Petty Officer Char Stone sat motionless. She'd stopped him, but victory wrung from him at the expense of his friendship, and perhaps even of her career, had no value whatever.

When he'd gone, Char laid her head on her desk and cried.

STONY POINT

Romy pulled his exhausted body onto the swim platform of his boat and lay flat, panting.

His crew, Tony, stood above him, at the transom. "You okay, boss?"

They were at Stony Point. It was the twenty-eighth, two days since he'd dropped his little surprise at the Coast Guard station. How they got their boat out of hock so fast he'd never know, but they'd done it, and he'd been forced to run up here and dive right away with practically no planning.

Bad decision!

Still panting, Romy sat up and slipped the SCUBA tank off his back.

"I never saw so much fuckin' current," he gasped. "If I hadn't grabbed the anchor line and clipped myself to it, I'd be halfway to Sacket's Harbor by now." He flopped onto his back on the platform. "Gotta catch my breath."

He'd found the wreck, even swum inside, but the mud was so thick he didn't find anything. He really needed one of those sand guns like the Eastlands had. Outside the cabin, he picked up a few trinkets, but nothing like the big score he hoped for. Then, just as he reached for something sticking up through the gravel, the fucking current came from nowhere and he'd just barely managed to catch the anchor line as the current swept him past.

He understood now what happened the day the girl dove. The flares had been for her and her boyfriend. That current had grabbed them and taken them to hell and gone down the lake.

There'd been nothing on the news, but she had to be dead. Nicky would be tickled pink, but for himself he wasn't happy. He wished Nicky hadn't asked him to do it. He wasn't some piece of trash.

Damn! He just didn't have the equipment he needed to make the one big score that would set him free. That left only one alternative. Keep watching the Eastlands, and when they recovered the treasure, relieve them of it at gunpoint. He already had everything he'd need for *that* job.

After, he'd be more than just another bum with a boat. He'd be able to face that woman from the Coast Guard like an equal. He'd dreamed about her last night. Boy, oh boy. If he only had the coupons he'd show her the time of her life.

Jake put his hand over the receiver and waved the waiter in, pointing toward the kitchen. When the man left carrying the dinner trays, he continued the call.

"That's good news, Allie. Fast work. Your people are damn good." He could feel Allie's smile through the phone line.

Allie's voice boomed into his ear. "I still can't believe it, Uncle Jake. Did that chief have any idea who she was dealing with? She must have a death wish or something."

"I'm old, Allie, not deaf. Stifle it a little. See? I told you, sometimes sugar works better than vinegar. On this project, time was money. We had NOAA here, we had the Naval Academy here, we had a fancy French Archivist here…"

"Jesus, Uncle Jake, what the heck is going on up there?"

"Never mind. You take care of your end. I'll take care of the Roosevelt doctrine."

"Roosevelt doctrine?"

"Speak softly, but carry a big stick."

"Oh, *that* Roosevelt. Very cute. God damn, Uncle Jake. NOAA? Annapolis? I hate being left out."

"What time are they supposed to call and let us know the boat has been de-commandeered?"

"According to the boys over at Ampanco, the *Longley* was released as of five o'clock yesterday."

Jake changed the subject. "What've you got for me on the Zaia character and his buddy Rob?"

Allie laughed. "Zanzibar was as far as I could arrange to send Rob. I hear an old enemy will suddenly discover where he is, and he'll need to leave town fast. We'll offer him something there."

"What about Zaia?"

"If you want, we can have him fired without notice. He'll find it tough to find work with the recommendation we'll give him."

"No. Don't do anything there yet. The guy tried to hurt Laurel, but I haven't decided how to handle it yet. I want you to look into his performance; how the guy he promoted is doing; how their project is progressing. If Laurel is right, the person he moved up hasn't got a chance of handling the job. Let me know the second you have anything."

"Uncle Nicky, it's me, Romy." Romy shouted over the noise of an engine revving out at the gas pumps. It was the morning after he'd tried to dive the wreck.

"You didn't have to tell me, Romy. Nobody else calls me from a gas station."

Uncle Nicky's voice sounded far off. Romy raised his voice. "I took care of your little problem. She's dead as a doornail." Romy flinched as he realized the engine noise was gone. Out at the gas pumps, a woman turned and stared at him. Romy stared back until she looked away.

"Are you sure?" Nicky said. "It looked like an accident?"

Romy turned away, in case the nosy bitch pumping gas could read lips. "Yeah. She tried to dive on… tried to dive with bad chemical I put in her SCUBA gear. I saw the flares go up. She's history."

Uncle Nicky practically purred. "Excellent. My roommate's a lawyer. I'll have him start collecting the documentation that'll prove my father's paternity."

"Paternity?"

He heard rustling noises as Uncle Nicky put his hand over the phone. Someone laughed in the background as Uncle Nicky said, "Never mind, Romy. I'll get things like my father's birth certificate, copies of the hospital records and physician's statements. Then there are his school records, and his Navy records. I mean the guy's middle name was Eastland. There's bound to be plenty there. I'll have a good case."

"You mean anybody could track down information about you, or even about me?"

"Sure. It's all public record."

Romy growled, "I ain't so sure I like that."

Uncle Nicky laughed. "Never mind, Romy. Nobody gives a shit who *your* father was."

Romy didn't have a college degree, but he knew when he was being mocked, and he didn't like it. He held his tongue. He had plans of his own. Nicky was a selfish jerk, anyway.

"Okay, Uncle Nicky. I just wanted to let you know my part is done. Let me know when I can help with something else." Romy waited, but the line clicked and the dial tone came on.

TWICE TOLD HOTEL

November 1. Laurel woke to low scudding clouds and showers. The significance of the date was not lost on her, but no one else seemed to notice, so she kept the anniversary of *Ontario's* day of destiny to herself. Last night's forecast said the winds would be from the northeast today, but only for a few hours, after which a new low would arrive, bringing with it a chance of severe thunderstorms.

Five days had slipped away while they waited for the right conditions. After almost a week, both Aaron and Todd were out of time. The decision to attempt the dive had been made because if it didn't happen today, it might not happen at all.

They'd left the harbor at first light and by eight-thirty were on station over the wreck.

Mike, Aaron, and Todd would go down. The plan was simple: bring the sand gun inside, blow the silt out into the open water, and let the current carry it off.

The divers went over the side. Laurel stood by at the com unit, listening as the team worked to position the sand gun. Progress was slow because they raised so much silt everything had to be done by feel. On the *Longley*, time dragged.

"It's a lockbox!" someone yelled. The sound was tinny, coming from the small speaker, but they all heard it.

Laurel's heart flopped. Beside her, Grampa Jake sat straighter. "I think they might have found Jacob's gold," he said, pointing toward the stern. "Look, they're taking more line."

"Hello, the *Longley*." Mike's voice came through the speaker. "We've got a small chest. Looks like we're not the first to find it, either. Aaron is coming up to talk with you."

A small chest. The treasure had needed six men to carry it.

Aaron surfaced, swam to the dive platform and pulled himself out of the water. "We've found a strongbox. It's hooked up but it's still inside the wreck." He stopped to catch his breath then motioned for Sheik to come closer. "Go slow at first, so they can maneuver it into open water. There's a big hole in the top. We don't want to spill whatever is inside."

"No problem," Sheik said too loudly. "I'll move that sucker so slow they won't be able ta see it happen." He went to the winch, took three turns of the retrieval line around it, and pushed the tail into the self-tailer. "Here we go," he pulled the lever.

Mmm, mmm, mmm, the electric winch rotated. The line tightened. Sheik reached over the side and grasped it. "Yup. Somethin' down there's movin.'"

While they waited, Aaron held up an object. "Look what I found!"

Sheik's brows flew up. "Holy moly, a flintlock pistol."

Todd and Mike broke the surface together. Mike slipped his mask up. "It's clear of the hull. You can bring it up."

Laurel caught his glance. He shook his head in a silent "no." He hadn't found the treasure. Where was it, then? Somewhere along the line she had to have miscalculated.

On the cliff above the *Longley,* Romy Zaia crept into position. When he saw slack water, he snorted. Sure, where was the fucking current now that *they* were diving?

Jesus H. Christ! Laurel Kingsford was down there. A wave of relief began at his head and flowed out into his body. He hadn't killed somebody after all. Uncle Nicky would be royally pissed, and he'd made a total chump of himself, crowing about how she was dead when she wasn't. How had she managed to survive that son-of-a bitch of a current?

He forgot about the girl as he watched a small chest come awash. His pulse quickened. This was it, his big score. After this, there'd be no more running cigarettes for pennies. Who needed Uncle Nicky's pie in the sky when he could put his hands on real dough like this?

Romy backed into the overgrowth until he was out of sight from below, then stood. His boat was tucked away at Henderson, in a little hiding place he knew, loaded with cigarettes for the last run of the year. Here was a golden opportunity to make two scores on one trip.

But first things first. He needed to get going now if he wanted to get out to them before the black boat upped anchor and left for Oswego. He had to take them while they were anchored. He stood his motorbike up and straddled it. Moments later he was on the way.

The chest came aboard, streaming water as Sheik lowered it to the deck. Laurel stared. Few things she'd seen in her lifetime were as significant as this. In the world she knew, reality could shift like the desert sands, but this was real in a fundamental way. The chest's very existence proved irrefutably that the history she "knew" had actually taken place. It wasn't the creation of someone's speculation written down later, and therefore a fantasy like so much else people believed. In the most sincere way possible, this physical visitor from a time long past said, "You are real, because I exist."

"Looks like someone paid the wreck a visit at one time," Aaron said, feeling the edges of a triangular hole at one end of the lid. "These look like axe marks." He kicked off his swim fins and bent over to examine the bronze padlock, then fished through his duffel bag until he found what he needed. A few minutes later there was a double-clicking sound and the two-hundred-twenty-year-old bronze lock rasped open.

"I think Laurel should do the honors of opening it. After all, if it wasn't for her we'd never have discovered it."

Suddenly, Laurel felt just a little short of breath. She knelt in front of the strongbox, lifted the lock out of the hasp and swung the lever up. She tested the lid. It would move, but she'd need to use all her strength. Determined to do it herself, without help, she set herself and in one smooth motion powered the lid up and open.

Below the hole near one end, the chest was filled with silt and water.

She checked with the experts.

"What next?"

"Maybe you should let us take it from here," Aaron suggested.

"Sure. I do the 'wet' work and you get the glory." She shook her head. "I've come this far. I'm ready to go the rest of the way."

"What do you think, Todd?" Aaron exchanged looks with his counterpart.

"It's only fair."

Aaron nodded, "Make your hand flat." He showed her his open hand, palm down. "Now push downward."

Laurel pushed her hand into the muck. Right away, her fingers touched an object.

"Okay. There's something long and flat just under the surface, like a book," she said. "I'll see how large it is." She moved her hand under the silt. "Scoop off some of the crud, Todd."

Todd pushed a bait can into the muck, slid it along, dumping a dozen cans full before the outline of the object came awash.

"It is a book." She grasped a corner and lifted. With a sucking sound one corner came above the surface. It looked like a log, bound by stiff leather covers.

"This is fabulous, but we can't open it." Aaron's voice was apologetic. "If we do everything just right, there's a chance an expert will be able to dry it enough so the pages can be read."

Laurel sank her arm in the silt. She touched something, knew what it was even before she lifted it out of the water. A yellow coin. There were more, too.

She held it up, not minding that water ran up her arm.

"Whoa!" Sheik coughed. "I think that's gold."

"No doubt about it," Aaron agreed, grinning ear to ear. "We should get this chest to the hotel where it'll be safe. Then we can get a closer look at the goodies."

Everyone aboard the *Longley* that afternoon had spent years on the water. But during the last half hour, engrossed in the treasure chest, no one noticed the change.

Laurel's senses told her: too dark.

She looked up. The cliff had stilled. Water forgot to drip. Insects fell silent. Nothing moved. At a primal level, she knew before any conscious thought: the place was about to try again to kill her. Hardly able to breathe, she leapt to her feet and scanned the horizon to see what it was, trembling even before she saw.

"Holy mother!" she cried, pointing. "Look!"

Every eye followed her finger.

Less than a mile away, a squall bore down on them from the west, its base a horizontal black line. Above it, a roll-cloud churned, miles long and thousands of feet high. She could see the rotation, bottom to top, seething with yellow-gray energy. From the base of the cloud to the water's surface, a black wall swept before it.

Beside her, Mike whistled. "Man! Look at that sucker. Get rid of the stern lines. Hurry! Cut them."

They'd placed four anchors. They'd be swamped in no time if they weren't able to cast the stern lines off.

Mike grabbed her by the arm. "Cut the bow lines. No time to haul the anchors. Hurry!"

He turned to Sheik.

"Sheik, fire her up, but whatever you do, don't make any turns until we're clear of the anchor rodes. They'll need time to sink. We can't afford to foul a prop."

Jake watched from his seat at the port helm station as Sheik ran into the pilothouse. Just as Sheik slammed the door behind him, the howling wall struck the *Longley*.

"*Oh Mama!*" Sheik yelled, his legs nearly letting go beneath him. He grabbed the console for support and stared at the controls, unmoving.

"You heard Mike. Start the engines, Sheik. Get them running."

"Gotta get the hell out of here," Sheik howled.

The *Longley* rolled hard to starboard, away from the initial blast, and Jake held on as hard as he could.

"Oh God, we're goin' over," Sheik screamed.

Laurel cut one of the two bow lines before the squall laid the *Longley* over on her side. Freed at the stern, the boat swung her bows toward the wind.

A fusillade of golf ball–size hail bracketed her, bouncing as high as her shoulders. The boat vibrated under her as the engines caught. The bow lifted and fell in six-foot waves that appeared from nowhere.

An ice ball struck her square on the forehead, turning her legs to jelly. In rapid succession, two more hit her and a third drove her to her knees. Her head rang and she saw red. What was it she had to do? Something important. What was...? Yes, cut the lines. She struggled to her feet. She had to cut that last line. Had to...

In her confused state, Laurel failed to perceive that they would be safe swinging at a single anchor for the minute or two it would take the anchor lines they'd cast off to sink. Instead, she did as she had been told and cut the second line.

Jake felt the jerk as the bow line went. Damn! Freed, the *Longley* presented her port side to the wind and drifted toward the cliffs at an alarming rate. In seconds the deadly wall loomed directly overhead.

At the active helm station, Sheik's entire body shook. Jake heard him mumble. "Do something... something."

Sheik's hands went to the shift levers.

"No! No, Sheik! Not yet!" Jake screamed.

But Sheik kicked the props into gear anyway, and then, eyes glazed, he jammed both throttles forward. The transom squatted as the *Longley* moved, her ribs less than a dozen yards from the rocks.

No one aboard could see, but beneath them the port propeller sucked the tail of the easternmost anchor line upward. At the last instant, a large wave lifted the transom, almost allowing the tail end of the line to slip past, just below the rotating prop.

Almost, but not quite.

The prop snagged the line, and within a dozen revolutions the shaft was choked with wound line: the engine stalled.

Jake heard the engine rev down, labor and stall and knew they'd fouled an anchor. Now they were caught fast with no escape. At the controls, Sheik didn't understand. "Noooo!" he screeched, and jammed both throttles to their stops. The remaining engine roared, but the *Longley* stayed put.

Seconds later, a huge wave lifted the black boat as if it were a toy and slammed her into the face of the rock.

Jake lost his grip. The force of the impact careened him across the pilothouse toward Sheik. He might have caught himself, but his fingers slipped at the last second, and his leg gave under him. A bulkhead seemed to reach up and hit him on the head. He slammed into the far wall.

Everything went white. He looked up at the ceiling. It tilted at a crazy angle. Laurel's face looked down on him, her short hair glued to her head. Water dripped from her face. He tried to make out her words.

"You don't have the seed. You can't make a baby."

Why did she say that? He was very dizzy.

"You have a daughter, Jake."

His head swam. Everything spun. He was so very dizzy. Why would she say that? Who would want to say awful things like that, right when he was least able to defend himself?

Tony, one of Romy's deckhands, grumbled when his boss stepped aboard. "I don't like th' looka that sky."

Tony wasn't very bright, but he knew a storm when he saw one. Romy was upset. The weather might get in the way of his plan.

"Yup. We're gonna get pounded for sure," Joey said. Joey was a small, thin man with several days' worth of patchy beard. At twenty-one he was already as accomplished a thief as Romy, who was thirty-five. They worked well together.

Romy wasn't worried. Their anchorage was protected on all sides. They'd be snug as a bug in a rug.

Minutes later, the squall struck and the sound and fury of it enveloped them. The three of them went below, buttoned the boat up, and played a few hands of Pitch while they waited for it to blow over.

Laurel's head rang and her eyes refused to work together, but at least she was awake. A yard from where she'd fallen between the raised bow plates, the rain-black slate of the wall glistened as the *Longley* beat against it.

She struggled to her feet and moved along the pilothouse to the door. Mike appeared beside her.

He yelled over the maelstrom, "We've got to get out of here. Those rocks will slice us up in a hurry."

Laurel's headache pounded harder. Nausea gripped her. "Let's get inside. I can't hear you."

Mike grabbed the door handle and fought to open it against the pressure of the wind and horizontal spray. She ducked inside and he followed.

Sheik stood frozen at the wheel, staring straight ahead, both hands pressed against the throttles. Grampa Jake lay on the floor, a large gash on his head pouring blood.

Laurel snapped to full consciousness. "Grampa Jake!" she screamed, and rushed to him. "Can you see me? Are you awake?" Grampa Jake looked confused then his eyes rolled up and closed.

Mike pulled her away. "Laurel! Get the helm. Back off that engine before it burns up. I think we've fouled a prop."

Laurel came back to herself. She had to close one eye to focus.

"Damn!" Mike swore. "I told Sheik not to put the engines in gear until we were clear."

Laurel elbowed Sheik aside and took the wheel. "The port engine's stalled," she yelled.

Mike tried to think while the *Longley*'s starboard side ground against the rock face, buckling against the sharp outcroppings as wave after wave heaved her against the wall. He forced his mind to clear. Sound and fury, that's all it was. Sound and fury. He was alive, in one piece. He could still function.

"Which engine?" He had to be sure.

"The outboard port, furthest from the rocks."

He knew what he had to do. "Throttle back the other engine, take it out of gear. I'll go over the side and cut the line we're hooked on."

Laurel screamed, "Jesus Christ! Those rocks'll grind you into mincemeat!"

Mike glared at her for a second, his teeth bared. "Do it, Laurel! While we still have a fighting chance."

Slowly, the fight crept back into her face. Her lips formed into a grim line, she nodded.

"While I'm down, try to get the port engine re-started. Maybe you'll be able to use it to pull the nose off the rocks once I get rid of the fouled line."

"Okay," she yelled, "but once you cut that line, get back aboard in a hurry, cause I'm taking us the hell out of here!"

While he watched, Laurel pulled the throttle back to idle, and put the engine in neutral then pulled the stalled engine out of gear and cranked it. Maybe, just maybe, she'd be able to make turns with it after he got rid of the fouled line.

Mike left the deckhouse and worked his way to the stern. Big waves slammed them, breaking right over the aft rails. The backwash had the water roiled, confused, the surface white with foam. He stepped down to the dive platform and pulled his knife from its scabbard. Then, without allowing himself time to consider what he was doing, he stepped off into the water.

Irresistible force grabbed his body and swept him beneath the boat. His hand found the fouled line and he caught hold an instant before the suction smashed him into the rocks. He worked his way up to the propeller shaft, just managed to grasp it before the backwash of a wave sucked his feet the other way, away from the black rock toward the deep water. This time, he both heard and felt the *Longley* grind against the wall as it sank into the trough of the receding wave, making tearing noises, agonized groans as the tortured aluminum structure flexed.

Holding firmly to the shaft where it passed through the support strut a foot in front of the bound-up prop, he waited for the next wave to lift the boat and cause it to strain against the line that held it captive. As the line went taut, he placed the blade on it and sliced through with one firm stroke

The line parted with a pop. He let go of the knife. That was the easy part. Now for the real trick, getting back to the platform and aboard.

The wave that had lifted the boat reached its crest against the rock face and began to fall away. Its backwash sucked his lower body away from the wall. He let go of the prop shaft and tried to control his slide along the hull so he could surface close to the side of the boat, but the suction swept him out too quickly, and at the same time rolled him head to foot in the soup of bubbles and debris. Flotsam swirled every which way in the dark, turbulent backwash.

He didn't know which way was up. Then, just as he located and started to swim toward the surface, the butt end of a large piece of driftwood lanced down from above and before he could fend it off slammed square into his head.

⤛⤜ ⤝⤞

Laurel felt the change as the *Longley* came free of her bondage, but the oncoming waves still held her hard against the wall.

She peered through the window. Thank God! They'd thrown a rescue ring. The storm hid Aaron and Todd from view again. Did they have Mike? She watched and waited, her heart almost forgetting to beat, until Aaron appeared out of the storm, yanked the cabin door open and came in, water pouring from every part of him.

"The undertow took him," he yelled. "Down that way." He waved toward the south, toward where the land curved westward at the point. "He never even got his life vest inflated."

No! It couldn't happen, she wouldn't let it. Laurel ran to the controls and kicked the starboard engine into forward and the port into reverse, hoping it wasn't too bound with anchor line to make turns. At once, the port engine labored. She gave it more throttle. It didn't stall, but something would have to give there, and soon. She wouldn't need it for long. Too bad if the transmission burnt itself up.

Now, or never. The *Bruce B. Longley* fell into the trough of a wave and another loomed. She pressed both throttles forward, right to their stops.

Propelled forward on the right but kept from moving by the reversed port engine, the bow drew away from the rock, far enough clear to allow her to throttle back on the port engine and slip it out of gear. Seconds later, driven by the good engine, the bow lifted to meet the next wave and they were off the face and moving away.

She had to search for Mike, but visibility was zero and she had only one engine. To present either side of the *Longley* to the weather would invite disaster. She had to keep the boat driving into the oncoming waves, away from the death cauldron they'd just escaped. Searching for someone in the water here was not possible. The good prop was damaged too, maybe even a bent shaft because the entire hull vibrated. She reduced the number of turns. A minute later, they were in deep water, safe for the moment, but the storm had nowhere near spent itself.

Mike had saved them, but now he was out there alone. Who would save him?

The temperature gauge of the port engine tilted deep in the red and she shut it down, then let herself sag into the seat. She'd forgotten something. What? Her head ached worse than it had after the dive, and she still couldn't focus her eyes, but everything, all of it paled beside the rest.

Todd came into the cabin, took one look at the scene and went directly to Grampa Jake. God! She'd forgotten all about him. Aaron bent over him, pressing a towel to the scalp wound. Sheik came to her, his rheumy blue eyes apologetic.

"I'll call the Coast Guard. Okay, Laurel?"

Laurel's stomach swirled. That was it. What she'd forgotten to do. "Yes. Right away. Then can you take over, Sheik? I can't see straight and my head is throbbing."

"That why you got one eye closed?"

"Yes. I got hit by hail. I have a terrible headache, and I'm seeing double."

Aaron came over and surrounded her with his massive arm. "You have a concussion, Laurel. It could kill you. You need to lie down and stay very still until the symptoms disappear. Come on, brave person, let's get below. Sheik and Todd can take over."

He grasped her by her armpits, lifted her like a doll, and carried her below just as a new batch of hailstones pelted the cabin top.

The anchorage Romy had tucked into was so tight his boat hardly moved even during the worst of the storm.

The rain stopped. Almost at once, a stiff breeze from the north stirred the trees on the rocks above them. The lake would get rough now. Taking on the Eastlands in rough water wasn't his idea of doing the job right.

They'd heard the distress call during the storm. The black boat had lost somebody overboard. Tough luck, but it was one less person he'd have to contend with. The Coast Guard would be all over the place real soon. That was all right, too. They were tucked in nice and tight on the harbor side of the hill, sheltered from the search area, and hidden from all but the most determined boater.

Tony pointed. "Hey, ain't that the boat you been watchin'?"

Like a gift from the gods, the black workboat had just rounded Association Island to the north and headed toward them.

"Hey, hey. This is our lucky day." Romy clapped his hands. "It's gonna work out fine. They must have decided to stay at Henderson overnight." He grinned at his cronies. "They brought up a big chest today. We'll wait till dark then relieve them of it. No sense them worrying over how to divvy it up when we can do it for them. Meanwhile, let's find a spot up on the hill so we can watch every move they make."

～～～　　～～～

Since 0700, 1 November, Char had inspected every anchorage and marina from Cape Vincent to Chaumont Bay. She was determined to find that smuggler. She needed to put points on the board in a hurry after that fiasco with the *Bruce B. Longley*.

"Radar's showing an intense squall fifteen miles west, Chief," Char's radioman reported. "It's headed our way at thirty-one knots."

"Very well," Char said. "Let's get her battened down for heavy weather." She leaned forward and studied the chart. "We'll duck into Sacket's Harbor while the squall goes through. Helm, make your course one zero zero."

"Aye, aye, making the course one zero zero," the helmsman announced, one "aye" for "I hear", the second for "I will obey."

Sacket's Harbor was deserted, all the recreational vessels out of the water and on cradles for the winter. Many were covered with protective membranes of blue shrink-wrap.

They tied the forty-four-footer up at the small municipal dock while they waited for the squall to arrive.

"And now, heeeeere's Johnny," the radioman said. Moments later, the squall roared in overhead. Visibility dropped to zero in an instant. Even in the total protection of the harbor, the boat rolled to one side as the wind pressed against her.

Char checked the time. It was 1300, one P.M. They had about five more hours of daylight. If the squall passed them soon, there was still plenty of time to check Black River Bay and Henderson Harbor before they ran back to Oswego.

The radio crackled to life. "Mayday, Mayday, Mayday. This is vessel *Bruce B. Longley* off Stony Point. We have lost a person overboard. Repeat. Lost a person overboard. Request immediate assistance from any vessel in the area. Please respond if you are able to assist."

The electricity of the message brought everyone in her pilot station to full alert, but no one more than Char. Her man was aboard that boat. It couldn't be him they'd lost.

"Respond. Give them our location and tell them we'll be underway the second this weather lets up. Plot our ETA to Stony Point. It can't be more than half an hour. Get in touch with Rochester Air. See if the rescue bird is available."

Mike was lucky in one respect. The bat-sized branch hit him square but on the thick bone of his forehead and didn't knock him out. He saw stars as he fought his way to the surface, gasping when he reached it. He couldn't see the *Longley*. Before he could so much as look the other way a side-wave broke right on top of him, pushing him beneath the surface again and he breathed water. Choking, he tugged at the valve of his PFD. It didn't release. He tried again. Nothing.

Then he knew why. He'd grabbed the same PFD he'd used to hide the box from the Coast Guard. Its CO_2 cartridge was empty.

Up to now he'd been functioning on pure momentum. Now the skin behind his neck tightened as the first tingle of dread triggered the last of his body's adrenalin. He bulled his way to the surface, this time from sheer fear. He coughed hard when his head cleared the water. He had to get air, but the water was deep in his air passages and prevented him from getting a full breath. Working hard, he managed to cough enough out to breathe. With a good lungful of air at last, he got hold of the fear, subdued it and looked around. In the slashing rain and wind he could see only a dark area to leeward where the cliffs had to be. A strong sideways set towed him south, toward the point.

He took several more deep breaths, consolidating. He'd need to inflate his PFD by mouth. But did he want to? Now that he was able to assess his situation, one thing stood out: he had to stay away from the immediate area of the cliff face. If he inflated the vest, the wind might push him back in there. Of course, if he didn't, he'd have about twenty minutes of full function left. Never had he been in a worse situation.

He could no longer see the wall or anything else. The storm had grown more intense and the water was cold, very cold. Already he could feel it sapping him. He lay out on his back, spread his arms and legs, and tried to use his natural buoyancy to get a rest. It was not easy in the steep waves and the irregular cross-waves that kept sneaking up on him. Maybe he could get away with inflating his vest just a little, enough to keep him awash but not enough for the wind to get hold of. He grabbed the stem, took a breath, and blew into it. One. Sound and fury. That's all it was. He took another and blew again. Two. Sound and fury.

An hour after Laurel took them off the wall, Jake stood on the dock at Henderson, supported by Aaron Hoenig, somberly examining the damage to their vessel. He had a severe headache, and his body felt like it'd been run through a trash compactor, but for once his heart had decided to keep working the way it ought to.

They'd done everything possible. The Coast Guard had been notified, as had the state police and sheriff. They'd already heard a helicopter making passes on the far side of the headland, the side that abutted the lake.

"She looks like she just won a Demolition Derby for ships." Aaron didn't quite make it to levity. "This is one hell of a boat, Mr. Eastland."

Jake agreed, on both counts. Along the full length of her starboard side the *Longley*'s plates were either pushed in, gouged, or partially ripped open. There was damage below the waterline, too, but nothing like that on her flank.

"The van will be here in a few minutes," Sheik called down. "Better get your gear ashore, Aaron."

Laurel had a concussion, was partially sedated, and under orders not to move for the rest of the night. That meant she'd be staying aboard with Sheik to look after her. The rest were going back to the hotel to await news from the searchers.

The odds of Mike's survival decreased with every minute that passed. One hour, tops. That was the longest a person could hope to survive in this water on November 1. There were always extenuating factors though. It had been a warm fall. You never knew. Some people were tougher than others.

Jake was weakening. He was hardly hurt at all by comparison to Laurel with a concussion, except he didn't really feel *in* himself. It was a strange sensation, one he'd never had before. He'd almost be willing to trade what little time was left to him if it would bring Mike back for Laurel. Me for him, how's that, Big Guy? He smiled. It was a crummy trade and the Big Guy upstairs would know that.

By ten minutes after three, the hotel van arrived and everyone who was going was aboard. Jake waved to Sheik from the front passenger seat. "We'll see you tomorrow around noon. There'll be somebody here first thing tomorrow to clear that shaft."

Sheik nodded and waved, and Jake closed the window. Tires crunched on gravel and the van backed away, bumped up onto the pavement, and in thirty seconds they'd left the *Longley* behind.

Despite the early presence of air support, the MOB was not sighted. Once Char knew for sure who'd been lost overboard, she drove her crew hard, ordering them to bring the forty-four in close to the cliffs where the incident had taken place. Even well after the storm passed, the water there remained dangerously turbulent. If anybody could survive in there, Mike McKean would be the one, but deep down, she feared no one could.

Whaley spoke up, "I've been noticing a north-south set in here, Chief. Why don't we move south, closer to the point. If a swimmer could stay away from the cliff face, he might get swept past them and find a way to the beach down there."

Char stared at him. Whaley had never volunteered anything before but this was a good idea. Damn good. Her face must have conveyed a different message, though. Whaley shrank like she'd just struck him, and looked away.

"Helm! You heard the man. Move south. We'll search the area off Stony Point, and watch the depth sounder. There'll be less water off that point. Great idea, Whaley. Next time, speak up sooner."

This had to be what it was like to be dead—no sense of feeling at all, floating, awash in warmth, everything white. Hardly a need to even breathe, that was how perfect it all was. Or would have been, if something hadn't kept bumping against his side, over and over and over, until at last it penetrated the haze and began to annoy him. It had his foot, too, keeping it from floating free.

And that, at last, was why Mike opened his eyes. He lay in water, partly afloat, a big black slimy rock next to and above him. Each time a wave came it pushed him against the damn rock again. His heels had to be on the bottom, his knees flexed with each wave. He couldn't feel a thing, on any of his surfaces, anywhere except those two places. If only that stone would stop bumping him he'd be able to sleep.

A commotion came from somewhere, unusual sounds through the water. Droplets splashed his face. Was it rain?

"He's alive, awake too. We did it, chief. Let's get med evac in here, pronto."

Full dark at last. Romy moved to spring his trap. "Quiet now. We're almost there."

They eased alongside the black boat. He turned to Joey. "This should be a piece of cake, but if any shooting starts, back me up."

There wouldn't be. The setup was perfect. He'd watched all afternoon from right across the harbor. Everybody who'd been aboard, except one guy with white hair, had gotten into a passenger van and left three hours ago.

He hadn't seen the Kingsford woman all afternoon. Could she be the one they'd lost overboard? It would be all right if she was. Either way, with only one guard aboard, the job would to be too easy.

Fifteen seconds later, silent as a cat, he stepped up to the rail of the *Longley* and down to the after part of her deck. A moment later Joey let Romy's freaking boat bump the *Longley*.

"Hey, stupid," he hissed into the darkness. "What are you trying to do, send 'em a telegram?"

Sure enough, he'd just finished speaking when a light showed in the control room and someone came up from the cabin below, "Who's there?"

Fuck! No time for stealth now. His element of surprise was lost. Romy pointed his pistol and pulled the trigger. He was rewarded by a cry, and the head disappeared. He stormed forward, into the cabin. The old man he'd seen with Jake Eastland lay unconscious on the floor, his shirt quickly staining with blood.

"Sheik. Sheik! What was that?"

Fuck! It was a woman's voice. Romy jumped down the steps and barged into the cabin. She was there, the Kingsford bitch, on the settee, blinking at him.

He grabbed the blanket covering her and jerked it away. Oh, Jesus. She had on little undies and a half bra, her skin was white, smooth as cream. He could see the bunching of her pubes through the flimsy cloth as she drew her legs up. Her tits squeezed halfway out of the bra. His heart hammered and his blood stirred at the raw sexual charge of the situation. It was just the two of them. She was helpless, so dizzy with fear her eyes weren't even focusing. No one would ever know if he threw a fuck into her. Why not? He couldn't let her live now, not after she'd seen his face.

Romy undid the top button of his pants. Forget what he'd thought before. She'd already be dead if his first plan had worked. He might as well enjoy that sweet pussy before doing the job right this time.

"Get away!" she screamed as he jerked her leg straight and snatched at her panties, ripping them off in one quick movement.

～∽～   ～∽～

The station at Oswego reported twenty-five knot winds, gusting to forty, and large waves on the lake. Char was an emotional mess as the forty-four approached the central marina in Henderson, where she planned to tie up and lay over for the night. Mike McKean would make it, maybe. The medics said his pulse was strong and his blood pressure coming back, but even if he made it, he'd still belong to Laurel Kingsford. She'd saved the only man she'd ever wanted for another woman.

Whaley had the helm. The change in him was amazing. One pat on the back and he opened right up. "Chief, the *Bruce B. Longley* is tied up at the central dock. There's another boat rafted alongside her. We'll have to raft off of them."

Char peered forward. It was dark, but lights on shore made the situation clear. Whaley had a way to go yet. The two boats would have to move.

"Hold your position, Whaley. Radio, give them a growl, put the small light on them to let them know we're out here."

A second later, the radioman touched the hailer button to emit an attention signal, and spoke into the hailer, "Ahoy, the dock. This is the Coast Guard. We will need the end of the dock overnight. Prepare to adjust your position."

Romy almost swallowed his heart it jumped so high in his chest when the lights came through the window and the bullhorn roared. He scrambled off the settee, pulling his trousers up. Another second and he'd have been stirring the honeypot, not that the bitch would have noticed. She was out of it, on drugs or something. Rich people were all alike. Weak.

He rushed up to the control room, stepped over the guy... Oh, shit! He'd shot the guy.

"Boss! It's the fuckin' Coasties. What do we do?" Joey held the rail of the *Longley* and was half aboard.

"Make tracks, that's what," Romy hissed. He stepped out of the control room and stumbled into the treasure chest. "Help me with this. Hurry!"

"Ahoy the dock!" The second hail from the Coast Guard boat was more strident. "Show yourself, or prepare to be boarded."

"Tony," Romy called. "Give the assholes something to think about."

From aboard Romy's boat, Tony's rifle banged away, quickly nailing the small spotlight.

He and Joey pushed the treasure up onto the railing and let it drop, only to be greeted by a loud splash. Tony had let the boat slide forward while his attention was on the Coasties and they'd missed with the chest.

"Oh shit. Leave it. Get back aboard. We're gettin' the fuck outta here." They jumped down. Romy elbowed Tony off the helm, threw the throttle all the way forward and swung the wheel hard to port. The diesel faltered, given too much fuel all at once, then revved. The boat ripped forward, grinding against the side of the dive boat until at last, they were clear. The prop bit deeper then, and they rushed past the Coast Guard vessel.

"Light them up," Char commanded, grabbing the hailer handset. Two powerful spotlights clicked on, bathing the fleeing boat in light.

Char smiled inwardly. This was what she'd been born for.

"Hot pursuit," she said, her voice calm. She knew exactly how to deal with this kind of situation. It was the personal ones she had trouble with. "Report from the fifty."

Seconds later, the intercom crackled. "Fifty manned and ready."

The workboat couldn't outrun them under ordinary conditions. But on a night like tonight they'd be even or better in the big waves out on the lake.

She slapped Whaley on the shoulders. "Let's reel em in before they hit the open water."

"Radio. Call the station. Get a report to headquarters. Tell them we've been fired on and are in hot pursuit of a vessel we've observed attempting an armed hijacking."

Hot stuff. Five minutes later she had the go-ahead.

"Put a few rounds over his bow. One burst only."

The fifty opened up and a long, graceful stream of tracers arched out and over the bow of the boat ahead. It turned hard to starboard but did not slow.

"He wants to play. See how frisky he is with a few rounds up his tailpipe."

The gun spoke again, this time the elevation lower. As the stream of tracers walked over and found their mark, bits of wood and pieces of metal flew off the boat ahead. Dust from the impacts, illuminated by their spotlights, made the boat appear to be smoking. Then in rapid succession a plume of smoke blossomed and three men leaped into the water. The hijacker veered to port and slowed. There was a fire aboard.

"Launch the inflatable and pick those swimmers up. And prepare to extinguish that fire."

This would look good, very good, on her record. It might even outweigh the two bad moves she'd made in the name of love. She admonished herself for the hundredth time. From now on, she would keep control. She had to. It hurt too much the other way.

"Chief," the report came from the firefighting team aboard the disabled boat. "We've hit the jackpot here. This boat is chock full of cigarettes. Cases of them."

Char took it as her due. When things went right, they went right. Suddenly, she felt more like her old self. The question was, what would she do for an encore?

One by one, her crew fished the swimmers out of the water. When they were all aboard, she left the helm station and went out to the afterdeck. The creeps were all shivering, bent over for warmth. She put her flashlight on them, starting with the nearest. Not prizewinners, any of them. When she reached the third man, she started with surprise.

"Hey, Chief," Whaley said. "It's the guy who brought the whisky bottle to the station."

He was right. It was the little man with the strange eyes and the wild mop of black hair. This night would be good for a commendation for sure. Maybe two.

"Get blankets for the prisoners, Whaley. Bring them below. Then call the state police. Have them meet us back at the dock. I want to check on the *Bruce B. Longley*."

"What do we do with the evidence boat?"

"Have the inflatable tow it in. Let's get moving. And Whaley."

"What, chief?"

"I want to see you in my office first thing tomorrow."

Whaley had more potential than she'd seen at first.

BRUCE B. LONGLEY

"You people. Out of here, right now."

It was a woman's voice. Laurel opened her eyes. The Coast Guard weightlifter towered over her, shooing people out of the cabin. What was her name? She couldn't remember. Laurel watched as the woman spread a blanket over her, acting like some kind of mother hen, of all things.

She realized she was naked. How had that happened? She only vaguely remembered a man with eyes like Grampa Jake's and black hair, but nothing had happened. She'd know if it had. She was very confused.

The woman perched beside her at the edge of the settee, her crisp blue uniform crinkling as she did. She smelled of oil, and machines and smoke, but her blouse was spotless. A patch over her breast said STONE. That was it. Her name was Charlene Stone.

"We found your diver, Miss Kingsford. Alive. He'll be at the hospital in Syracuse by now. I thought you'd be anxious to know."

Laurel's heart missed a beat. Mike! They'd lost him. She'd completely forgotten him. Had Charlene just said what she thought? She'd found him?

"Found him? Okay?" was all she could manage.

"Yes. He's quite a guy, you know. How he made it out of there I'll never know, but he did."

The woman's voice was not like Laurel imagined it would be. She sounded normal, not like a hormone case at all.

"Thank you, Chief, for finding him. You'll never know what he means to me."

The woman looked down at her. "I might have an idea."

THE SECRET EVER KEEPS ■ 285

TWICE TOLD HOTEL

On the afternoon of November 8, Genevieve Degas returned. A week had passed. Sheik was home but still confined to bed. Grampa Jake was better, but Laurel fretted, he didn't seem to be gaining his strength back as fast as he should.

They met in his living room. Grampa Jake had yet to make an appearance today, so only Genevieve, Laurel and Mike were present.

Genevieve began, "I've found the owner of the box, Laurel, and it is very strange. Very strange," she repeated herself. "A French officer aboard an English ship, while the two countries were officially at war. Most unusual."

"Who was he?" Laurel asked. She should have been more anxious to know, but after everything that had happened it was hard to imagine anything of importance still to come. They'd located the chest in eight feet of water, and its contents were now safely tucked away for study by all the proper, boring authorities.

"Baron Pierre Dubois D'Avangere. He was among the French officers sent to America to help train your armies. He and the American Commander were confidantes."

The level of tension in the room increased. Everyone knew who that could mean. No one said anything for many seconds.

Genevieve reclaimed the stage. "What I can't comprehend is what he was doing on his way to Carleton Island at the mouth of the St. Lawrence River."

Mike touched the crescent-shaped wound that outlined the crown of his forehead. "Maybe he was a prisoner." It was healing nicely, but looked awful.

"No. The passenger list mentions an unnamed French Officer traveling incognito under the protection of Colonel Bolton, Commandant of Fort Niagara."

"What about the box itself?" Laurel asked.

Genevieve smiled, "Ah, yes! It's French in origin. At least the engraving was done there. That's how I picked up the Baron's trail. We'll probably find the maker's mark somewhere inside. Fortunately, I've located an expert in the field. He's in London, but I've been assured that in less than a month he will be available to assess this find."

"We won't need him."

The words came from behind them. Grampa Jake stood in the entrance of his bedroom, leaning on a cane. The small white bandage on his temple made him seem frail.

"I might have an idea," he said. "Why don't we keep it here a few more days while I look through a few things?"

Some time later, Jake closed his safe and spun the dial, locking the French-made jewelry box inside. Mike and Genevieve had left to freshen up before dinner. "Come on, Laurel, I'll show you how to open it. Just in case."

"Are you sure you want me to have the combination to your safe, Grampa Jake?"

"Oh, I think I can probably trust you by now. We're getting to be friends aren't we?"

Laurel moved closer and gave him a hug. "Yes. More than that."

Warmth spread through Jake. Laurel's eyes were a little misty as she embraced him. He liked that. It would be safe to tell her the truth now. If only his heart would quit jumping around, he'd do it right now.

It was a miracle he hadn't broken something last week. As it was he felt truly old today. His body ached everywhere.

He patted her on the back. She'd held her own in some pretty rough moments. He held her away, at arms length. "Come, let me show you."

For the next several minutes, Laurel practiced opening the safe. He showed her where the combination was hidden, in case she forgot. While she practiced, Jake went into the next room and punched in

Allie's phone number. It rang four times before an operator answered.

"TBO, Incorporated. How may I help you?"

He'd dialed Allie's direct line. What was an operator doing answering? "Jake Eastland calling. Put me through to Allie King."

A hesitation. "I'm sorry, sir. There's no one in the building."

Jake had injured his shoulder in the fall. Holding the phone to his ear hurt. "Why the hell not? What am I paying you people to do?"

The operator remained courteous. "But sir, it's almost six o'clock Sunday evening."

Jake jerked. Was it really? What was wrong with him? "Oh! Yes, of course. Everyone is gone for the weekend. I'm sorry to bother you." He hung up and snuck a look at Laurel. Damn, his shoulder ached. Thank God she hadn't been able to hear the other side of the conversation. What had possessed him to react like that? Could that whack on the head be affecting him more than he thought?

He lifted the phone again and tried Allie's home. This time he reached an answering machine. He identified himself and left a message for Allie to call.

A minute later, Allie called back. His arm ached, and instead of holding the phone, Jake put him on the speaker.

"Crying out loud, Allie. Doesn't anybody down there answer their phone anymore?" Jake knew he sounded peevish. He was definitely a little off his pace today.

"Sorry, Uncle Jake. Family obligations. Know what I mean?"

Allie didn't sound at all upset to be called at home on Sunday night. In fact, he sounded glad. "Uncle Jake. I've got to tell you something. There's been a development in the background check you had me initiate on that Nicholas Zaia character."

Damn! Through the doorway, Jake saw Laurel stiffen at the mention of Nicholas Zaia. Jesus! It was too late to turn the speakerphone off. Jake could almost hear the wheels turning in Laurel's head.

Allie rushed on, "I already told you about his connection to Laurel's ex-fiancé, right? Well, it seems this guy's birth father was a man named Julian E. Zaia. He died during World War Two at the age of seventeen, but not before he had our boy Nicholas with one Carmella Zaia, a first cousin, and out of wedlock." Allie took a breath. "Listen to this, Uncle Jake. I checked into the middle initial. Guess what the father's middle name was?"

Jake didn't need to guess. At the first mention of Julian's name, his skin had prickled and he'd broken out in a cold sweat. Julian's middle name was Eastland.

Christ! Laurel was listening, but right now he didn't care about that. He felt sick. The man he'd given a leg up, thinking it would be a good-will gesture to the Zaias, the man who'd schemed against Laurel, set her up to be ripped off by a predator, and who was now undoubtedly poised to come after Jake himself and everything that was his, was his own grandson, his illegitimate grandson.

"Never mind. I figured it out already," he said. "But I had no idea there was a son." Jake's heart took off on one of its hop, skip and jump routines, and he waited while it flopped around in there, just slightly dizzy from it. A sudden thought occurred to Jake. He turned to Laurel and made a gesture at the phone. "Would you excuse me for a minute, Laurel? I need a little privacy."

She nodded, her face white and her expression serious. She went into the living room. Jake picked up the receiver and switched the call. "Allie," he hissed, "I need to change my will again. Laurel isn't in it anywhere. Jesus, Allie. How'd you let me forget to do that?"

"But I…"

"Never mind. Jesus! Get that damn paperwork to me."

"Uncle Jake, you…"

Jake felt his control slipping. His head ached and his damned heart wouldn't quit the flip-flops. He couldn't leave his entire fortune vulnerable to some opportunist.

"Allie. Never mind me being grumpy. I'm sorry. I got a bump on the head. The headache won't go away. I've got to lie down. Take care of it, Allie. I'm relying on you on this one."

"Okay, Uncle Jake. Meanwhile, you take care of yourself, I'm very worried about you."

Allie did sound worried. Jake smiled. Allie was a good kid. He put the phone down.

If he'd hoped to gloss over the part of the conversation she'd overheard, she wasted no time disabusing him of the idea.

She stood square in the middle of the room, her chin thrust forward as if ready for battle. "Who the *hell* gave you the right to go investigating my ex-boss? And what in the world could his father's middle initial possibly mean to you?"

She seemed to take up every inch of available space, and most of the air, too.

He stopped a safe distance away. "I... I thought you might have a case. Sex discrimination..."

"Bullshit! There's a connection to the woman Estelle. I've heard that last name around here too many times for it to be some kind of dumb co-incidence. Now I want to know what's going on, and I'm not leaving this room until I find out."

The force of her will rode over him like a shock wave, swaying Jake on his feet. She would guess the truth. He might be instants from losing her. He had to take a full step back to balance himself.

She was at his side in a flash. "Grampa Jake! Are you all right? I'm so sorry. Here, sit."

The mercurial shift in her demeanor rocked Jake a second time. He felt his knees wobble. Jesus, he couldn't fall down right here in the middle of the room. He let her help him to his favorite chair.

She sat on the armrest, an arm around his shoulders. "I'm sorry. I had no right to yell like that."

She hadn't made the leap yet. Jake took a deep breath then picked up the small album from the lamp stand beside his chair. He opened it and flipped through the pages. After the last page, between it and the cover, lay a five-by-seven photo, a head and shoulders shot, black and white, very well worn. He held it up.

"This is Estelle."

Estelle stared at the camera with the no-nonsense expression he remembered. Her hair was long, full of curls.

Laurel's breath brushed Jake's cheek as she leaned closer, and her head touched his. "She's very pretty. She looks older though. I thought you were both very young when you met."

"We were, the first time. Neither of us knew anything. You already know what happened that time."

She slid off the armrest until she was beside him in the chair. He made room.

She took the picture from him and studied it. "You said there was more between you. Was this after you and Jean broke up?"

Jake thought about it, about how to put it. Ah, hell. Might as well tell it the way it was, and take the lumps when they came.

"No. Not quite. Jean and I were still together when we met again, by chance, early one morning near the end of 1939. Funny, I still remember how thrilled I felt the moment I first saw her again after all those years."

1939

The locomotive rumbled to a stop several hundred feet beyond the station, a plume of steam hissing upward from the relief valve atop its boiler. A conductor stepped down to the platform from the passenger car, one hand on the bronze handrail.

"Okay to board, watch your step," he called to the handful of waiting travelers.

Jake Eastland made himself smile at his wife of nearly eight years. "I'll get the bags, you go ahead and get aboard."

Jean did not comment. She seemed pale this morning. He gathered her hand luggage and followed her up the short stairwell into the car.

"Tell your mother I'll be coming for the holidays for sure," he said as she settled herself in the open car—she would have a suite in a Pullman after the change of trains in Syracuse.

She sniffed, "I still don't see why you couldn't come along this time. You know I hate traveling alone."

He'd heard the petulant note in her voice one time too many. He shut the words out. It was an excuse, anyway. She didn't want him to go and she knew he knew. He glanced at her familiar luggage. For someone who hated traveling alone, she sure did a lot of it. He'd had more hands-on time with her luggage the last few years than he had with her.

A year had passed since that night in New York City when Jake came face to face with the fact that theirs was a marriage of convenience. His knowledge of her infidelity colored their relationship in dark tones. He continued as before, using the veneer of social acceptance she lent, but whatever warmth had existed in their relationship had gone.

Of course, she used him as coldly as he used her. She spent so much time away it was no wonder another year had passed with no sign of the children she claimed to want. He gave her credit; at least she was discreet about her affairs.

They hadn't made love in months. On those occasions when biology overcame him, and he made an overture, she would turn him away. Intercourse with him hurt, she claimed. How much did it hurt when one of her fancy New York fops balled her? Did she pull away from them like she did from him? These questions never passed his lips, but they were there, between them like a barrier.

He forced another smile and leaned forward to give her a goodbye kiss. "We've been over it and over it. I don't want to start again." He gave her a hug and straightened.

Jean's lips pinched together and she sniffed, focusing on something outside. He was dismissed. Another of her mannerisms he detested. He frowned as he left the train. Although his house would be empty, he was relieved she was gone. On the platform, he waited by her window, giving her reassuring waves whenever their eyes met.

"All aboard!" the blue-coated conductor called, signaling the engineer. Shortly, the engine chooched several horizontal gouts of steam in rapid succession and its drive wheels did a few quick revolutions, spinning on the steel track as the engineer built pressure too fast. Then gradually they bit, and the train moved forward onto the trestle that spanned the Oswego River gorge. A minute later, the caboose was across the river and out of sight in the tunnel.

Jake's mind wandered as he passed through the open gates into the station, headed toward the parking lot on the far side.

"Jake-a Eastland."

A woman's voice, vaguely familiar.

He slowed, looking around. A woman stood to his left, ten feet away, a cautious look on her face. At her feet were two large baskets of flowers, and she carried two others.

Estelle Zaia.

In that moment of first recognition, some long-sounding dirge in him fell silent. Immediately, the day seemed brighter, the air clearer.

Had he lived with the hurt so long he'd forgotten life without it?

Possibly. Whatever had gone, its absence was like a drug.

"Estelle!" He went to her, holding out his hands. She put the baskets down and took them. Her hands were rough, work-hardened. Still, her touch was good in a way Jean's could never be. "It's wonderful to see you. How've you been?"

Surrounded by flowers, she seemed the wildflower to Jean's hothouse blossom, sprung from the earth unplanned, uncultivated, all the more hardy and beautiful for it. No longer the slim girl of his mind's eye, she'd filled out, matured, but her hair still shone the way he remembered, and although small wrinkles pulled at their corners, her eyes were the same. In them he saw summer nights, declarations of love, unrealized dreams.

"Okay," she said, interrupting his reflection. "How about you?"

Suddenly, he felt shy. "I keep pretty busy."

"Married?"

He nodded.

"Kids?"

"Not yet. How about you?"

She smiled, "Which, married or kids?"

"Both, I guess."

"I have a thirteen-year-old son." A hint of defensiveness crept into her voice, and her eyes seemed darker. "I'm not married."

Jake tried not to show how happy her words made him. Was she divorced? Widowed?

"Gosh, Estelle, I'm glad to hear that… I mean, about your son."

He still held her hands. She seemed to notice and pulled hers away.

Old memories, feelings he thought had died long ago, clamored for more time with her. "Do you have time for coffee? We could talk a while."

"I wish I could," she said, "but I have to finish my deliveries. Maybe some other time?" She stooped to pick up the baskets of flowers.

She was right. They both had to go. He tried to still his sense of disappointment.

Estelle straightened. "I have a small florist shop on the east side. We live in the apartment over the store. Why don't you come for dinner tonight? I'd like you to meet Julian. We could talk then."

Could there be a hint of ulterior motive in her invitation? Seeking the favor of the wealthy Eastlands? Impossible. He'd been around Jean too long. Estelle was the least complicated, most open woman he'd ever known.

Jake still floated on the high of seeing her again. Dinner would give him a few more hours to be near her.

"Okay. I'd like that very much. Just this once, for old times' sake."

Estelle's expression changed. This one he couldn't decipher. Second thoughts? Had she asked just to be polite, not thinking he'd accept?

"How about 7:30?" she said.

He nodded, and she gave him directions.

That afternoon in her shop, Estelle clipped the stem of a rose without really seeing it, and positioned it in the bouquet. She remembered the first time she'd seen Jake Eastland, the summer she'd turned sixteen, how madly in love she'd been.

She didn't want to remember him that way. Life had been difficult since, and he a big part of the reason. Better to hold onto her anger. Tonight was for Julian, the supper invitation, all for her son.

She checked the time. The clock seemed frozen at 2:30. Five more hours. She felt unsettled, jittery. She shouldn't be feeling so eager. Her hands shouldn't be shaking. Tonight would not be for her.

Not for her.

At exactly 7:30, Jake knocked on the door at the top of the stairs. A boy, about five feet tall and slim, opened it. They stared at one another, the light behind the boy threw his face in partial shadow.

Estelle hurried toward them, wiping her hands on her apron. "Jake. Welcome, come-a in." She stood behind the boy, her hands on his shoulders. Jake stepped in and closed the door. Cooking aromas filled the apartment.

"This is my son, Julian. Say hello to Mr. Eastland, Julian."

The boy offered his hand. "Hello, sir." He had dark brown hair and a fair complexion. His eyes were blue.

Jake gave the lad's hand a firm shake. "It's a pleasure to meet you, Julian. How old are you, son?"

"I'll be fourteen in February." Almost nine months away. Julian's voice was changing. Jake remembered being that age, always in a hurry to grow up.

"Oh, so you must be in what, the first year of high school?"

"No. I'm in eighth grade."

Estelle put her hand on her son's shoulder and motioned to Jake with the other. "Come on, you two. Dinner's on-a the table."

"*On* the table, *On* the table," Julian corrected.

Estelle's eyes showed her pride. "*On* the table," she said, exaggerating the pronunciation. "He's helping me learn." She patted her son's shoulder.

"I noticed. Your English is very good."

Estelle served greens tossed in a garlic-flavored dressing, then veal covered with melted cheese in a thick tomato sauce. Squash, and a few vegetables he didn't recognize, steamed in their containers. She leaned close from behind. "You like zucchini?"

"I've never had it."

"You try. You'll like."

"I hope I never get too old to learn something new every day."

She laughed, and so did Julian, but when her eyes touched Jake's, they questioned.

They ate. Jake reflected on the difference between this table and his own. Here were warmth, caring, closeness; there, cool politeness, courtesy, and long silences.

Julian put his milk glass down. "Momma said you have a boat." A white moustache outlined the pale hairs of his upper lip.

Jake glanced at her. "Not any more, I'm afraid."

The boy's face fell. "Oh."

"Why'd you ask?"

Estelle touched her son's wrist. "Julian loves the water. You should see him swim. He's like a fish."

Julian tittered, sneaking a glance at his mother. "Mom says I'm gonna come back in the next life as a fish. But what I'd really like to do is learn how to sail. Sailboats are so neat."

"I had a sailboat when I was about your age. I sailed it all over the place," Jake said.

Julian' eyes widened and he sat forward, forgetting to wipe his mouth with his napkin. "Honest?"

Jake nodded. "Yes. We lived out past Nine Mile Point. The easiest way to get here to Oswego was to sail. In the summers, I sailed over to Selkirk, up to Sandy Pond, west to Little Sodus. Maybe I'll get a boat some day and we'll go sailing."

The boy's eyes glowed as he glanced at his mother, then back at Jake. "You mean I really *could* learn? Someone like me?"

Jake stopped, his brows furrowed. "How come you say that? 'Someone like you.'"

Julian flushed and his eyes fell. "We… we don't have a lot of money, and… and the other kids…"

Before Julian could finish, Jake reached over and grasped the boy's wrist. "Let me see. One, two. Yup. You've got the right number of arms." He pretended to check under the table. "And two legs. Amazing! That's the exact number you need. So Julian, that means you could learn. You need to know the secret, though."

Julian sat stock still. "What's that?"

Jake tapped the boy's chest with his finger. "Right in here is where it is, Julian, inside you. And here's the secret: you can do *anything*. All you have to do is believe you can, right in here, and then put your mind and heart into trying."

"Is it really that simple?"

"Yes. It's that simple, but simple isn't the same as easy. If you're willing to try very hard, nothing in this world can stop you from becoming who you want to be."

Julian turned to his mother. She nodded without speaking. He sat straighter in his chair. "Then I will. I will learn to sail."

Jake slapped the table, making the silverware jump. "Darn right you will." Then, each energized by the other, they forget their food and began to talk about sailing.

Estelle took a deep breath. Neither had the slightest notion, yet they'd taken to one another within minutes. She couldn't have hoped for a better beginning.

She hated Jake Eastland from long habit. He'd spurned her, and because of him her father was dead, her brother a hopeless drunkard, and her family mired in hopeless poverty. Blood was thicker than water, and she was a Zaia.

All the same, how could she blame him for not standing up if he'd never had the chance to do right? Her brother Emilio was a born liar, and a coward. Ambush was *his* style, not Jake Eastland's. Maybe the papers were right. Maybe none of what happened was Jake's fault.

Puta her father had called her. *Whore*. The word still made her burn with resentment. It hadn't been that way. Julian was a child of love, not a bastard, not the son of a whore. He had a birthright, a father, and now she would see to it his father did the right thing by him.

She'd seen Jake a few times over the years, but always from a distance, never up close like this morning. Her plans hadn't considered how his presence would make her feel. God, he was still the most beautiful man she'd ever seen. She hadn't forgotten the way they *were* together, either, but neither had she forgotten the hurt. It still hid in her, alongside the secret she'd kept from him, feeding her determination.

But *did* she hate him? The sensation when she first saw him this morning, joy that peeled away the petals of her hatred until she could scarcely remember it. No other man had ever affected her like that. Other places within her were warmed by his presence too, allowing the lovely weakness she'd almost forgotten to rise.

No. Her hate and anger would carry her. She was no foolish girl now. She could give her body, bind him to her, assure their son's future without losing her heart again. She could.

But would he even want her? He hadn't shown the slightest sign. He was married. Maybe he didn't want her at all. Maybe their son would never have his chance. An ache filled the back of her throat as she remembered Jake's words: just this once, for old times' sake. She only had this one chance.

"Eat your dinner men, before it gets cold. Dessert is yet to come." She caught Jake Eastland's eyes and made herself smile at him.

Julian off to bed, it was time for Jake to leave. He lingered. Estelle felt it too, the weight of things unsaid, but there seemed no way to begin.

They sat on her sofa, arm's length apart, in the orange-yellow glow of the streetlight outside the windows.

"Julian seems to have taken to you. He's usually shy around men."

"He's a fine boy. I'm hoping I'll have a son like him some day."

Tears rushed to her eyes, forcing her to turn away. "I'm sure you will." She blinked until they were gone.

"What happened to us, Estelle?"

Her throat refused to allow a response. Who was she trying to kid? She'd been wrong. She didn't hate him enough. If he pursued that question, she might lose control. She wanted to, didn't want to, didn't know what she wanted.

Jake slid off the sofa to his knees, facing her. He took her hands in his. "Every day I spent away that summer, I missed you more. You told me you would show me what love was. I didn't believe you. But you did, you showed me. Then, the night I came to tell you—you were with another man, kissing him. He touched you." He squeezed her hands.

"Seeing you like that broke my heart into a thousand pieces."

Madre di Dio! She'd turned him away just as she was about to win him forever.

She couldn't stop herself. It all happened again in her mind; her anger at him for disappearing for so long; the worry over missing her periods; the buzz of alcohol; Tony on the dance floor, embracing him, kissing him, all to make this man jealous…

She sat forward on the sofa and gripped his shoulders. "You din't call for so long. I was sure you forget me. I din' care about him. I was angry, hurt. I wanted to make-a you jealous!"

He whispered, "What did we do to each other, Estelle? What did we do?"

She felt a letting go inside, opening, out of all control. She pulled him up, inches from her. She had to, had to say it, the words burned in her soul.

"I love you, Jake-a-Eastland." Then, full of urgency, she embraced him and they kissed.

For many seconds afterward he hugged her harder, then released her and sat back on his heels, reaching in his pocket. He took out a small box and opened it, held it up so she could see. It held a gold heart-shaped locket on a thin gold chain.

"I brought this for you that night." His voice was husky. "Open it."

Estelle touched the locket nestled in the white cotton as if not sure it was there at all, then operated the tiny catch.

To EMZ With all my love JE 1926

Everything he'd said, true, really true. The locket proved it.

His lips were beside hers. "I could never make myself throw it away, even after I married Jean. God help me, Estelle, I've never stopped loving you, and now I love you more than ever."

She slid to the floor and knelt beside him. "Make love to me Jake-a-Eastland. I can't lie to myself any more. I've dreamed of you too many times."

Two wonderful weeks flew past, but time would soon run out and they both knew. The night before his wife was to return, he finally said the words she longed to hear. They were together, in the darkness of her room.

"I've decided to leave her. I'll tell her as soon as I can." His lips touched Estelle's hair as he spoke.

She lifted her face to him. "Are you sure, darling? I hate the thought of hurting her... but at the same time I need you so much."

"It'll be all right. It's been over between us for quite a while anyway."

"I love you, Jake. Hurry home to me."

The nerve of the man. I leave for a well-earned visit to civilization, and he jumps into another woman's bed the moment my back is turned.

Several days after arriving in New York, Jean had called home to make sure Josie had everything she needed. When she asked after Mr. Eastland, Josie told her she'd only seen him once, the morning after she left. He hadn't been home since. Should she keep preparing his dinner each day?

Forty-eight hours later, the Syracuse-based private investigator her father's office retained on their behalf reported that her husband spent his nights in the apartment of one Estelle Maria Zaia, thirty-one, owner of a florist shop which occupied the ground floor of the building where she lived.

That had been more than a week ago, but nowhere near long enough for the humiliation of his public betrayal to subside. Her mother had consoled her, urged her not to return to Oswego alone, but Jean had it in her mind to confront him and bring him to heel once and for all.

He greeted her at the train station, hugged her dutifully, as if nothing had happened. She imagined she could smell the other woman on him.

"Hello darling, you look much better. It must be your mother's home cooking."

She sniffed. Her mother hadn't been near a kitchen in forty years, except to pass through.

"Yes, must be. My bags are right up there." She pointed to her luggage. Jake grabbed two, and a porter the remaining three, and they delivered it all to the car.

She stewed all the way home while Jake brought her up to date on events in the city since she'd left. Not that there was much to tell. At their house, she had the bags brought up to the bedroom. Moments later, she went up the stairs, following them.

Half an hour later, Jake stood at the bottom of the stairs and listened. Hearing nothing, he went up and stopped in the entrance of their bedroom. She was on the bed, her bags on the floor inside the door. A new suitcase, one he hadn't seen before, lay open at the foot of the bed, half filled.

She hadn't uttered a dozen words since getting off the train. The signs were clear, she was miffed at something. He waited. She'd never been good at curbing her emotions.

When she saw him, she stood, parking her hands on her hips, another of her warning signals.

"Have fun screwing your hussy while I was gone?"

The directness of her question startled him. While he thought about how to answer, she said, "Never mind. I know all about her. She's a piece of Eye-tee trash from the east side."

"No. She's a good woman. An old friend."

She gave a snort of derision. "Friend! Filthy floozy is more like it. I hear she has a bastard son. Typical Eye-tee slut. Well, let me tell you something. You're finished with her. You see her again, I'll sue you for adultery so fast your head will spin."

In the year since stumbling on Jean with her lover, he hadn't allowed himself to feel anything, suppressed all reaction, sacrificing to keep things on an even keel. Now he remembered the way she'd clung, how she'd allowed herself to be fondled in public. The powerful surge of rage surprised him. With a supreme effort he quelled it.

Through a veil of red, he faced her. "I'm leaving you, Jean. It's over between us. It has been for a long time, we've just been going through the motions. Estelle and I will start a family together."

"You're a fool! You won't be able to," she shrilled, her voice a physical assault. "You don't have the seed to make a woman pregnant. My doctor said there isn't a thing wrong with me. It *has* to be you. *You're* the weak one."

Her words stung, inflamed him, and this time he lashed out. "Maybe if you hadn't shut me off for so long, things would have been different. Maybe we'd have kids. Maybe I would have been able to forget you fucking your fancy boyfriends one by one, or do you take them all at once?"

He took two steps toward her, gut trembling, anger boiling over. "I'll tell you this, you cold bitch. She's twice the woman you are in the daytime, and ten times the woman in bed."

She slapped him. The sound echoed in the room. His face stung.

"Bastard! If you weren't so weak, if you were more of a man, I'd have been pregnant long ago." Her voice trembled with contempt.

"Weak? Not a man?" Tipping over into a deep rage, Jake gripped her arm and threw her backward onto the bed. "I'll show you a man, you arrogant, spoiled little shrew." He grasped her skirt and ripped it from her body, then pressed her legs apart and back.

"Jake! No! Don't," she screamed, her eyes round with terror. Then his pants were open and he'd ripped her undergarments off and pushed himself against her.

"No! Oh God, Jake, it hurts. Stop! Please!"

But he did not stop. He pushed, hard, without regard for her readiness, sinking deep into her, taking what she had withheld for so long. Then, his movements rapid with rage twisted into lust, Jake Eastland coupled himself to his wife.

Long moments later, when she had quieted and even begun to respond in an involuntary way to the furious pace of his thrusting, his body rose to the climax point and he moaned, panting, as his seed was propelled into her.

Finished, he withdrew and stood beside her supine form. A deep wave of remorse flooded him, followed by pain, and then sorrow.

"I didn't mean for this to happen." His throat was so raw he hardly made a sound. "...didn't want it to end like this."

A pained sob came from the bed, his only answer.

"I'll send someone for my things." Spinning on his heel, he left the room, went downstairs and left the house.

PENTHOUSE

Jake was almost grateful when Laurel pushed herself forward and stood, her face white. He'd carried the weight of that memory like a cross for almost sixty years. His throat ached the way it had that night, only this time from the telling.

Laurel strode away toward the den.

"Laurel."

She stopped and glared back at him. No warmth showed in her face. She spun on her heel and stalked out of the room, much as he himself had done all those years earlier.

Jake felt confused and a little sick. He stared at the doorway then shook his head and shut his eyes. What he'd done was cruel, violent. He deserved this kind of reaction. What did he expect? The trouble was, he'd just started to work up to the really *bad* part, and she'd already freaked. He didn't want to lose her now, he had too much more to tell.

Laurel wished, fervently, that Grampa Jake hadn't told her. Bristling, she paced the den. The first time he told her something like this at least there'd been a moral to his story, and in a strange way, after curbing her anger, knowing how he'd made mistakes helped her get her own head straight.

He'd married the woman without even liking her. Ugly, but not all that unusual in those days. Then he'd made things worse, kept his wife at arm's length, practically driven her away, and destroyed what little chance their marriage might have had. With him so young, and still hung up on Estelle, she could see that happening, too.

But not rape. Not that. Yes, his wife goaded him, drove him to it, used words she knew would cut him in his most vulnerable place. Words could be ugly, hurtful, but they weren't the same as actions. Actions had weight, they were real, physical, and their effects lasted, especially if they were violent, as rape was violent.

Damn him! If she could go back, will him to have been a better person when he first entered that bedroom, she would have done it gladly.

The picture she was building of Jake Eastland as a young man disturbed her very much. Coupled with the news about her former boss, it was enough to knock her flat.

Laurel made an effort to put the pieces together. She'd overheard Allie saying Nick Zaia's father's name had been Julian. And Julian Zaia was Jake's son by Estelle. Okay, Nick Zaia was Jake Eastland's illegitimate grandson. How could Jake not have known that? More important, what did it all have to do with her? Apparently, Nick Zaia hated her enough to try to destroy her life. Why? Because she and the stranger in the next room were friends? That didn't make sense. She hadn't even met him until well after the meltdown at Forrester.

And why had he felt the need to tell her in such detail about that awful night? She ached from listening, like her insides had been pulled out, rendered, and then jammed back in any old which-way.

Unanswered questions, each a discordant note in her head, clamored for resolution.

Her pacing brought her to the entrance of the living room. She peeked in. Jake stood by the windows, staring out, even though it had grown dark outside. She felt sick, let down, her image of him unalterably changed. He might have been a stranger standing there.

There had to be a reason why he'd led her to this point. Laurel squeezed her eyes closed and went over it again. Nick Zaia hated her. He was Jake's illegitimate grandson. But no lights went on. Only the frail old man by the windows knew how the facts fit together. The story she'd interrupted by leaving the room had been leading to something she couldn't see yet.

There was only one way to find out, but she wasn't sure she could take much more. Laurel closed her eyes and steeled herself, then, taking a breath, she went back into the living room.

He turned to face her, and the light came on in his face, but quickly faded again when he saw her expression.

"That was rude of me, Jake. Tell me the rest."

He came to her, and, though she held herself stiff, put his arm around her shoulders. "I'm sorry about disappointing you." He hugged her tighter. "Maybe telling you the rest will help me forget, a little."

He paused for a moment or two, his arm slipping lower, toward her elbow, then he said, "Jean sued for divorce. It was a mess. They tied me up in a knot of lawyers. We got to the end of it after several years, but it wasn't pretty. She sued, I countersued. All that."

"What about Estelle and the boy? When did you learn he was your son?"

"We stayed together..." His eyes shifted to hers, then away, rapidly. "In my usual self-centered way, I was the last to know."

Grampa Jake fell silent again, collecting himself. It showed in the way he stood. This would be it. No matter what he said next, it couldn't possibly be worse than what she'd already heard.

She tried to help him. "It's okay. You can tell me. I'll understand."

His chest jerked in his familiar silent ironic laugh. Then he turned and went over to his chair. This time when he began to speak, his voice was almost a monotone.

DECEMBER 1940

Jake stood at the top of the hill, leaning into the wind, one foot behind the other for support, and watched the northeasterly storm batter the stone breakwall that guarded the mouth of the Oswego River.

Mid-December. He'd been with Estelle seven months.

The damp wind chilled him and he shivered, burrowing his hands deeper into the pockets of his three-quarter-length sheepskin coat, one of the few carryovers from his rum-running days.

Twelve years since his last smuggling run. He thought of stormy nights on the water as he watched row after row of wind-driven combers rear and smash themselves to froth on the breakwall.

He loved to come here when the wind was up. The high ground was perhaps a hundred feet above the water. At his feet, the land fell sharply away, exposing a panoramic view of the harbor.

Men had kept vigil here before, built signal fires here to guide ships to the safety of the harbor. Had they felt the same?

Just as a particularly strong blast of wind sucked the breath from him, making it hard to inhale, an automobile purred to a stop behind him and the horn beeped. He recognized the sound. It was his new Chrysler.

Estelle motioned from behind the wheel, holding onto her hat against the wind that whistled through the open window. "Jake! Jake Eastland! You come inside where it's warm right this instant." He smiled. She was beautiful, so beautiful.

"I don't know what it is about this place," she said once he settled in the passenger seat and she'd rolled her window up. The car vibrated beneath them as she held it there, one foot holding the clutch down, the other on the brake. "Every time it storms, I know right where to find you."

"It's the lake, and the wind." He leaned toward her and gave her a smooch. "There's just something about it."

She put the car in gear and let the clutch up. They accelerated, rolling down the incline toward the river. "You told me already. That's why you're building a hotel at Mexico Point, right on the water. So you can smell seaweed every day." She feigned exasperation. "For a man with such a good business head, I just don't understand. The place will never make money."

"It's not the money. I don't care if it makes money. It's a beautiful spot, and my family has owned it for a long time. Besides, I sleep better when I can hear the lake." He rested his hand on her thigh. High up.

She glanced down, then back up at him.

He squeezed, "There must be something in the seaweed."

"I swear. You'll wear me out."

"Fourteen years is a long dry spell. A man can get thirsty."

She laughed and swatted him. "Calm down. It'll still be there later. Right now we've got to get home. Dinner is cooking."

That night, the three of them played cards. Outside, the storm had abated, but the building still creaked under an occasional gust. Jake didn't notice Julian's agitation until the boy dropped his cards on the table in the middle of a hand.

"Hey, the hand's not over," Jake said.

Julian's voice cracked, going from bass to alto in mid-sentence. "Are you my father?"

The question came so totally without warning, Jake could only gape at the boy.

"I look like you, and our eyes are the same color."

Jake focused on the boy's eyes. His heart forgot to beat. Julian was right! Their eyes were the exact same shade of blue. And his hair... Julian had sandy brown hair, just like Jake's, and a fair complexion, not dark like his mother's, or her father's.

He looked just like Jake. Stricken, Jake turned to Estelle.

She gave a little nod. Something sparkled in the corner of her eye. Julian, his son. He put his hand over Julian's.

"Yes. I'm your father. Can you forgive me for not knowing?"

The boy's eyes narrowed. "Why didn't you? Where've you been? Mom works from dawn to dusk to support us."

Estelle rested her hand on top of Jake's, which still covered the boy's.

"Julian. I didn't tell. He don't know until just now."

"But why?" Julian's eyes shone with moisture. "I've had to go without a father all this time. It's not fair."

Estelle leaned closer. "I'm sorry, darling. We were young, very young. We made mistakes." She covered their hands with both of hers now. "Jake and I love each other. The first time, it didn't work. This time it's different. Please let us have this chance. We need it very much. I promise, someday you'll be glad."

Julian gazed at his mother, silent, then he nodded and his hand came over and he let it rest over his mother's, and they were joined then, one, a pyramid of hands, a family for the first time.

Later, Jake lay facing Estelle in the silent darkness of their bedroom. Her fingers were in the hairs of his chest and her leg over his. She kept her voice low.

"It's like a dream. I can't believe it's true. The three of us together."

He pulled her closer. "I'm so glad you stopped me that day in the station."

"I was all shaky while we talked." Her voice quavered a little. "You know, scared and thrilled and hopeful."

"The moment I saw you... I knew I had to be with you. Nothing else mattered. I would have come looking if you hadn't asked me to dinner."

"Really?"

"Yes."

"We're meant to be together?"

"I think that's it."

She lay still, her breath stirring the hairs on his chest. "Jake?"

"Mmm?"

"What would you do if you wanted something very much, but it would cost every dollar you had and all the businesses you owned to get it?"

Jake smiled in the darkness. There was no such thing. Money could buy anything, if you had enough of it. But he knew the game she liked to play and went along.

He kissed the top of her head, "Couldn't happen. The really important things in life are all free."

"Come on, teaser, say it. You know I love hearing you say it."

"Okay." He kissed the outer corner of her eye. "If it was your love, I'd do it in a second. We could live here. I could deliver flowers, wash the windows..."

She gave him a playful shove. "Never mind." She slid her knee up his leg. "You know what? All of a sudden I feel like letting you do it again."

He pulled her against him in the darkness. "We just did it fifteen minutes ago."

Estelle lay facing the window with Jake curled against her back, asleep. Something bothered her. She couldn't pin down what. He was hers, she knew that. No woman could come between them now. Still, the little grain of foreboding wouldn't go away. It lay back there on the edge of her awareness, waiting for the moment when she let her guard down. Keep him close, Estelle. Keep him close, her heart said.

MAY 27, 1941

"You have a daughter, Jake."

Jake and Estelle had been together a year. He'd gained several pounds. Business was fantastic, he'd just sold his scrap yards for more than he dreamed possible. He had the world by its ear.

He didn't want to hear those words, not at all.

But he had, and it was the twenty-seventh of May, 1941, and Jean's father Reggie stood in front of him, on the veranda of the Twice Told, blocking his view of the lake.

The somber voice of Franklin D. Roosevelt came from the radio on the table.

"...We are placing our armed forces in strategic military position... Therefore, with profound consciousness of my responsibilities to my countrymen and to my country's cause, I have tonight issued a proclamation that an unlimited national emergency exists..."

The president's gravelly voice caught Reggie's attention as well, and they both listened as if Reggie hadn't just appeared without the slightest warning, hadn't uttered the words that had Jake's nerves jangling.

"...I repeat the words of the Signers of the Declaration of Independence, that little band of patriots, fighting long ago against overwhelming odds, but certain, as are we, of ultimate victory: 'With a firm reliance on the protection of Divine Providence, we mutually pledge to each other our lives, our fortunes and our sacred honor.'"

The voice on the radio fell silent.

Evening shadows stretched, the sun just touched the surface of the lake off to the west.

"I said, you have a daughter, Jake." Reggie's voice had less patience now. Inside the hotel, dinner hour was in full swing. It was almost time for the drive back to Estelle's, and dinner with her and his son.

Jake stood and faced his father-in-law. Since the breakup they'd confined their conversations, after one short, unpleasantly acrimonious discussion early on, to business.

"No. You're mistaken. The woman I'm with has a son. I have no other children."

His father-in-law's voice carried no inflection as if he couldn't care less. "You have a daughter with Jean. Her name is Saundra."

What about Jean's fancy lovers? The words were in his mind when Jake's breath caught. It *was* possible. It could have happened that last night. The night he...

At that moment, the full weight of Reggie's words crashed down. Jake stared at his father-in-law, stricken.

Reggie said nothing. After a moment, he motioned for Jake to follow and walked away.

"You mean... Jean's here?" Reggie did not answer, and Jake felt compelled to follow. This was happening too fast. Clearly, Reggie had not come of his own volition. He didn't slow his pace. Jake followed him to the far end of the veranda and down the steps.

In the parking lot a black Cadillac limousine idled, headlights off. Reggie led the way to the back door on the passenger side. As they approached, the driver reached up and switched on the dome light.

Jean appeared in its glow, dressed in white, smiling up at him. Her gaze shifted to the infant cradled in her arms. When she turned back to him, her eyes said, "look what we did."

"Jean..." The rest jammed in his throat.

"Shhh, she's just about to go to sleep."

He opened the door and sat beside her. The interior smelled of talc. The baby's eyes were scrunched closed, one hand beside its face, tiny fingers flexed, each one perfect. While he watched, the eyes opened wide, gazed directly into his, then away, fearful, and the baby began to cry. Jean shushed, calming her.

"Her name is Saundra."

Out of breath, Jake absorbed the image of this new woman, his wife. Her face had filled out, she glowed with health. The baby's eyes were Eastland blue. There could be no doubt: he had a son—and now a daughter—by different women.

"I hated you for what you did that night." Jean said in little more than a whisper. "Then, when I missed my monthly and the doctor told me I was pregnant, in spite of my anger, in spite of everything, the only thing I cared about was telling you…" Her voice broke.

"But you were gone, and mother wouldn't let me travel, and it all felt so wrong. I began to think about the way I acted, the things I said, how horrid they were…"

"Jean…"

She placed her hand on his arm, stopping him. "Come back to me, Jake. We can start over."

The idea rendered him incapable of expression. He'd committed to Estelle, to Julian. Now, this other duty. He couldn't do both. He couldn't.

Jake forced himself to take a deep breath, felt his throat tremble. "I'm sorry. I have to go. Right now." He pushed the door open.

"Jake! Please."

Outside, he closed the door and stooped to face her. "I…I need to think," he said, then turned and went into the hotel.

In his Penthouse, Jake lay on the bed. For the next hour, his mind grappled with what had just happened. He checked the time. Estelle would be worrying. He went to the phone and called her.

"Ah-loo," her cheerful voice came.

"Hi. Say, something's come up. I have to park here for the night."

"I drive out? Julian likes some time alone."

"Better not. The truth is…" His voice tailed off.

Her voice changed. "Now you make me worry, Jake Eastland. Are you okay?"

"I'll see you tomorrow."

"'kay, love you." Her voice wobbled just a bit, and it pained him to have caused her to worry.

"I love you, too." He put the receiver down.

He couldn't sleep. In the small hours just before dawn, the time when each soul is most alone, Jake felt more empty than ever before. Jean was his wife. He'd made vows, oaths of honor. Now he had a daughter, and heir. His responsibility. His.

Estelle didn't sleep either. He wanted to be alone. It had to be something about his wife. The grain of foreboding lodged deep in her heart stirred, and her mind began adding layers, one by one, until it became a pearl. She fingered the locket that lay between the swell of her breasts, her most prized possession, a gift from him, bought for her the summer she was seventeen, but never hers until fourteen years later.

She hadn't had it for her own anywhere near long enough.

The next morning, he stood by the window in her living room and looked down at the street below. On the corner cabinet, among plants and curios, a clock tick-ticked: 9:30.

His wife had come back.

The pearl was a thousand times larger now, and her heart caught somewhere inside.

He turned and came to her. "She knew all about us, called you names. Then she slapped me, and accused me of being too weak to father a child. It was too much. I lost control. I… I took her." His eyes fell, then rose to meet hers again. "I made her pregnant."

Another dagger stabbed her, this one the worst of all: a child. This had all happened the night he left his wife and he'd never said a word.

"It's a girl."

Did he throw his wife on the floor and do it to her, fresh from her bed? The thought first angered, then stung, and then cut. None of it mattered now. Now, her problem was much larger. Through the ache in her throat, she knew the truth, the sure and certain truth: his wife had used her body in the one way Estelle could not defend against. She'd given him a child.

She would lose him now.

She shivered as certainty crept toward her secret place, the place hope leased from despair that wonderful day they found one another again, the place where all impossible dreams, like hers from the very beginning, lived.

"I don't want to live without you, Jake-a Eastland."

The words, now that she'd said them aloud, agonized, and her chest ached with their weight. Then there was no containing it, no holding it in. She bent forward, on the sofa in the living room of her home above the flower shop, put her elbows on her knees, and wept deep racking sobs, handkerchief pressed to her mouth.

He came to her, knelt, and wrapped his arms around her. "I'll stay, darling. I'll stay. I can't bear the thought of not being with you. I just need some time to work it out, think it over. A few days." His voice broke. She felt his tears drop onto her hair.

She wiped her eyes and looked at him, so earnest, so loyal. He didn't even know yet. He had to go back to her, he wouldn't be able to live with himself if he didn't.

"I promise, darling, only a few days to think it over," he said again.

If only it could be true. If only he would think it over and choose her. But he wouldn't. She saw it with perfect clarity.

He wouldn't.

He left. To think it over.

The few days passed. He didn't come. Estelle couldn't sleep. A few days, he'd said. She forced herself to function, but her head filled with thoughts of him and her work suffered.

After ten days, her druggist mixed her a sleeping powder. By now her pain was a dull, empty ache but still it reverberated from every movement, every thought.

That night, a thick fog moved in behind a day-long rain. It came in waves, visible in the diffused yellow light of the street lamp outside, deepening until the brick face of the building across the street lost definition.

At 2:30 in the morning Estelle lay on the sofa, knees pulled up, a thick wool blanket over her. She should take the powder and go to sleep, but her mind wanted to dwell on him, wanted to remember their times together. Each waking memory of having him for her own now became more precious than the most priceless gem, and she wanted to examine each one, revel in it.

Across the street, a light glowed in an upstairs room. The shade was not drawn, but no shadow could be distinguished within the yellow rectangle. The fog was the thickest she'd ever seen. On the clutter of utility wires, water droplets clung to the undersides, growing, accumulating until each drop's weight caused it to tremble and fall.

In those few shivering instants before the fall, the street light reflected just so through each quivering droplet, making it sparkle for her eyes, blue-white-orange fire lancing out through the billion suspended molecules of fog, a starburst brighter than any diamond.

Never had she witnessed such a magical thing.

An hour passed. The droplets fell less often. Was it the same for people, moving until the right amount of resistance stopped them, and then collecting life, accumulating until, in the end, life's sheer weight pulled them loose?

Had she become heavy so soon?

Their son was fourteen. Helping him grow to manhood was a father's job.

She wondered if she would be one of the lucky ones, if the light would be *just so* for her. Would another soul somewhere be brightened, just a little, by her sparkling last moment?

She pushed the blanket down and sat up. The floor cold under her bare feet, she took the packet of powder from the end table and tipped it toward the glass of water, tapping it against the rim until some powder slipped in and dissolved. She swallowed half of it.

I forgive you darling. I know how much you love me.

Fifteen minutes later, she still didn't feel sleepy. She sat up and tapped more of the powder into the water and swallowed it all down. Now, she began to get groggy, but sleep evaded her. The druggist must have mixed a very weak powder.

Frustrated, she tipped the remainder of the white grains into the glass, added water from the small pitcher and forced herself to swallow all of it. It left a bitter taste in her mouth.

She lay back and rolled onto her side again, gazing through the window into the light, but seeing nothing now. After a few minutes she turned away from the light and closed her eyes.

She decided she would wait. Wait for him forever.

At last the pills worked, and she dropped off to sleep.

Jake parked across the street from Estelle's shop. Even though he'd made his decision the first night, he hadn't told her yet. News of an urgent problem in Newport News had arrived, demanding his immediate attention. He'd been away two weeks. He smiled, imagining her face. He had good news and couldn't wait to beg forgiveness for staying away so long without calling.

Strange. He checked his watch. Mid-morning, but her shop was dark. He crossed the street and went up the steps to the entrance. A small handwritten sign inside said, "Closed until further notice."

Jake went back down the steps and around to the apartment entrance. The downstairs door sat ajar and he entered. A black wreath hung from the apartment door at the top of the stairs.

He ran up the steps and knocked on the door. They had to be all right. Had to be. He heard movement inside.

"Estelle! Open up. It's me, Jake." He banged on the door this time, his imagination flying off in wild directions. What if it was Julian? He had to know.

Footsteps approached, the door unlatched and swung open. A man stood there, his shabby black suit shiny with wear. One of his hands... Jake did a doubletake. Emilio Zaia, Estelle's brother. He'd cut the man's tendon and now the hand had become little more than a withered claw.

Emilio scowled, "Whatta you want, bastard? Can't you see this is a wake? Get out!" He made a fist and stepped toward Jake.

Julian appeared from behind and pushed Emilio aside. He wore his best suit, the one Jake had bought for him. His face was pale, wide blue eyes dark with emotion.

Jake caught his breath. His son, okay. "Julian! Thank God. Where's your mother?"

Julian stepped closer, his eyes afire. "Don't you think you've done enough to hurt my family?"

"Julian. What are you saying?"

The boy cut him off with a wave. "My mother's dead. She killed herself. Because of you! You *bastard!*" Tears poured from the boy's eyes, and he trembled violently. He drew his hand over his eyes, throwing the tears aside. "Ever since you came into her life you've hurt her and hurt us. My uncle told me everything. Well, you can get out. Get *out*. I'm not your son! If I ever see you again, I swear I'll kill you."

Julian raised his fists and hit Jake on the chest as hard as he could. Hit him again and again until Jake had to push him away.

Emilio grabbed Julian from behind and dragged him away where Julian collapsed in a heap, screaming, pounding his fists into the floor.

Jake and Emilio faced one another from a distance of ten feet. Emilio's expression slowly became triumphant. Jake understood why. The man had used his lies well. He'd stolen Jake's son from him.

He turned and went down the stairs. He went directly to the cemetery on the bluff east of the city. Although the burial ground bordered the lakeshore, her grave was in the low ground, away from the overlook. The fresh-turned dirt made a low mound. Only a few flowers marked it.

One month later, Jake ordered and paid for a good headstone.
Everything went on as before. He went to work. He functioned, but
one part of him was no longer animate, suspended until the day when
he'd be able to approach his son again, lay down the first new stepping
stones that would lead to the restoration of love and respect.

The money poured in. No one saw his despair. No one knew he'd
killed the only person who'd ever been able to find a way to love him. He
became very, very good at hiding it.

Two years later, in his new home in Georgetown, Jake picked up
the week's mailing of the Oswego Palladium. Unrolling the package of
newspapers, he scanned. Obituaries always caught his eye, especially
now, during the war.

Julian Eastland Zaia, 17, while serving aboard the USS Mervin in
the South Pacific. Lost with all hands, 15 July 1943.

He let the pages fall to the floor.

Now his son was dead.

His failure was complete.

Laurel sat cross-legged on the carpet and listened. This part was
different, not ugly or hateful, but heartrending. When Grampa Jake
stumbled over the reading of his son's obituary, the sound of his voice
reduced her to the point of tears and she rose, wiping her eyes with the
back of her hand. She went around behind him, leaned over the back of
his chair and embraced him.

"That's so tragic, Grampa Jake. You were only trying to do the right
thing. How could you know what would happen? You mustn't blame
yourself."

But he did. That much was evident in the droplets easing down
his cheeks, and by the silent spasms that racked him with each breath.
She clutched him tighter, as if holding him might infuse him with her

strength. At the same time she noticed he seemed diminished, almost physically smaller than she remembered, if that could be possible.

He gathered himself, tried to continue, "I should have gone back the next day... Never could... for letting business..."

He didn't finish, but she didn't need him to. He'd shared with her. It was a start, and a beautiful compliment. She couldn't let him give up now.

"Now, now. It'll be all right." A strong sense of déjà vu came with the words, as if something had come full circle, and in some earlier existence she'd said the words before. "It'll be all right."

She patted his chest. "You're different now. If I can see that, you ought to be able to."

After a minute, her comforting began to have some effect, and Grampa Jake breathed more evenly. She let go and sat on the armrest again, glad he was beyond the backwash of his emotions.

He stirred. "I never told anyone that part of the story, not even Allie's father. Thanks for being such a good listener." He had his voice under control again.

She made light of it. "It's all part of the service, sir. By the way, I wouldn't mind meeting this Allie character. He sounds like a good guy."

He laughed. "He's been badgering me to let him come up here to meet you."

Grampa Jake pushed his way to his feet. "Darn, my stomach's growling. Where the heck is my dinner? It's almost seven."

His stories left Laurel feeling drained, almost as if she'd participated in his anguish instead of only listening. "Guess I'll go down to the bungalow."

"Why don't you stay, have something to eat?"

She gave him a last hug. "Next time. I'm developing a little headache."

It was only after she left him that she realized what had happened. His story had so overwhelmed her she'd completely overlooked the fact that she still didn't know how she fit into the big picture. Laurel sighed.

They'd find a chance to sit down together again, and he could spell it all out for her. It didn't seem that important right now.

To her surprise, Mike was perched on the front step of her porch. He looked up at the penthouse. The windows glowed with light. "I thought you'd be having dinner by now."

"And I thought you were keeping Genevieve company for dinner."

"I begged off. I wanted to talk about something."

Laurel felt her tiredness deepen. "Can we talk some other time? Right now, the only thing I want is to lie down and close my eyes."

"That sounds nice. I could lie down myself. Want some company?"

So far, he'd waited for her to make the first move. She gazed at him. If it happened, it would be okay. "I'd like that. Let's…"

"…go," he finished for her.

They spent two hours on her bed, dressed, her comforter pulled over them. At first they talked, then he urged her over on her side and began to stroke her back and neck.

When he said it, he spoke so softly she almost didn't hear him. "I've been thinking about asking you to marry me."

Laurel's heart froze in place. She rolled over to face him, tried to keep the tone light. "Was that some kind of progress report? Are we in the concept stage here?"

He took it just right, smiling. "Oh, I think it's well beyond the conceptual stages."

"Mike. I… I don't think I'm ready for that question. Not yet."

"Okay. How about, 'I love you, Laurel.'"

She pulled him close. "Could you put that in the form of a question?"

Laurel opened her eyes. Light flooded her bedroom. Crystals of frost laced the corners of the nearby window. She yawned as she checked the time out of habit. Eight-fifty. Was it Monday? Who cared? She was still drowsy.

The air in the room was cold on her face, a breath of it reached in and touched the base of her neck. She shivered under the warm blankets. Rolling onto her side, she pulled them higher. She smiled as she remembered the events of the previous night.

Next to her, the source of her contentment slept. His mouth was open a bit and he breathed up at the ceiling, a slight rasping sound accompanying each inhalation. The corners of her mouth pulled as she remembered his face at the moment they first joined their bodies in the act of love, the way his eyes filled with ecstasy while at the same time tears of joy trailed from their corners. He loved her. She knew for sure.

The second time, an hour later, it was better for her. By then she began to see how she needed to move with him to enhance the contact of their bodies and give herself pleasure.

After that, the lovely tremors began. One by one they lifted her higher and higher, until at the peak of it her insides locked on him for long moments, while releasing a flood of the most delicious sensations she'd ever experienced in wave after wave. She held on to each as long as she could, bracing herself as the next loomed.

She knew when he reached his own peak. It happened to him a lot sooner the second time than it had the first. Something about that pleased her.

He was beautiful. His hair was mussed, and his face carried the stubble of a day's growth of beard. None of it mattered. She was in love, her heart filled with him.

Even now, as she thought about it, her body sent little tremors of anticipation, little reminders. Stop it, Laurel, she scolded herself, it's only been one night and already you're getting to be a little sexpot.

But she didn't want to stop. She snuggled closer, pressing against him. She wished he'd hurry and wake up. She moved her leg over his under the warm covers. He didn't react. She slid her toes up the inside of his calf. He still didn't respond.

Holding her breath, she let her fingers touch him.

That woke him up.

"He loves me, Grampa Jake." Tears came as she entered Grampa Jake's apartment later that morning. "It's all because of you, all because you helped me."

He held his arms open and she ran toward him, the friend she had come to love, and threw her arms around him, nearly knocking him over.

"Careful sweetheart, you'll break something," he laughed, struggling to remain standing under the assault of her happiness. "Well, that is the best news, the best news a grandfather could ever hear." He pulled her closer. "I knew you'd find the right one. We Eastlands don't give up so easy."

She leaned back and looked at him, puzzled. "We Eastlands?"

He smiled at her, nodding. "Sure. Eastland. Why not?" He thumped her on the back. His eyes had a funny gleam to them.

He looked at her. "When you two decide to make it official, make sure your daughters learn how to bait a fish hook, and take them to dive off the cliffs at Nine Mile."

"I will, Grampa Jake. You can be sure I will."

It was after eleven. Jake rarely stayed up so late, but tonight his favorite movie, Mr. Roberts, had aired and he'd stayed up to enjoy it again.

Laurel had her man. He was happy for them both, but worried because he'd been playing phone tag with Allie all day.

He still didn't have the paperwork to make Laurel his beneficiary again. In retrospect, it seemed foolish to have changed his will the second time. He'd left it all to her in the first change. Why hadn't he left well enough alone?

He went into his bedroom and disrobed, thinking how sweet it was to finally have something worth living for. Life was good. Before kicking off his slippers he went to the window overlooking the lake and cranked it open a few inches. Fresh air, carrying with it a hint of the beach, seaweed, the shore smells he'd known all his life, gushed through the vertical slot.

He lay on the bed and pulled the top sheet and covers over himself. He adjusted his pillow and closed his eyes. He could hear the lake. Always loved this place. His heart gave an extra beat, then three or four more. He ignored it.

He seemed to be smiling a lot these days, and did again as he remembered Laurel when she first arrived after quitting her job, how down she'd been. He was proud of the way she'd gotten back up again, and found her man. They would be happy together.

The long string of years drifted past as he hovered between wakefulness and sleep. The last thought that entered his conscious mind was that dying was a part of life. Funny, he'd never thought of death that way before, just another part of living. There in the darkness he appreciated the bittersweet irony of it for the first time.

He slept.

Two hours later Jake's heart made a series of extra beats and another longer series until it began to fibrillate. He dreamed he was standing on his favorite rise in Oswego, looking out over the harbor. It was blowing up a storm from the northeast.

Behind him Estelle Zaia called, "Jake! Jake Eastland. You come inside where it's warm right this instant."

He took one final breath of the fresh lake air and went to her.

Grampa Jake's funeral was out of all proportion to the life he'd led at Mexico Point. Services were extended an extra day for the more than five hundred mourners who came from all over the world. Many times that number sent telegrams or floral arrangements.

Very quickly, Laurel realized she knew next to nothing about Grampa Jake's business life. She knew everything about his most secret failures, had learned and grown in the knowing, but nothing of his successes. His life, the bulk of it, had taken place in a different time.

She was astounded when representatives of governments attended, along with Arab princes, Texas oilmen, European art dealers, German automakers, representatives of dozens of charitable organizations, and various and sundry dignitaries, and banks, many, many banks.

Not quite understanding why, the Syracuse television stations were all in attendance, and the newspapers carried articles speculating about who this man was, why he was so loved everywhere, yet unknown in the United States. They came up with few answers. Most of those interviewed would only say Jake Eastland had helped them at one point or another along the path of life. He had always been a private man. His death changed nothing.

The guests departed, the hotel quieted. Todd Pike took the ship's log and the Captain's chest and its contents to Annapolis for restoration and cataloging, and Aaron left for Woods Hole. Plans were being made for a full-sized expedition next summer. Only Genevieve remained. She would leave tomorrow.

Cold reality set in. Grampa Jake, her friend, was gone. Soon she and Mike would leave the Twice Told, too.

"We'll come back every summer for a few weeks." He held her hand as they rode the elevator to the penthouse.

She nodded, a lump in her throat. It'd never be the same without Grampa Jake. Thank God she had Mike. He could never take Grampa Jake's place in her heart, but she knew Mike had loved him too. She pulled him closer, leaned up and kissed his chin.

They sat on the sofa in Grampa Jake's penthouse, her head against his shoulder. The silence was oppressive. To have something to do, more than anything else, she went into the office and opened the safe, intending to remove the French nobleman's jewelry box. An envelope lay atop it. Her name was scrawled on it.

"This is strange." She brought the letter over to the sofa and sat next to Mike. "Grampa Jake left me some kind of a note."

As she removed the single sheet of paper in the envelope, a small key on a thin chain slipped from between its folds into her lap. She picked it up. It was old, very old. She could just make out a hint of engraving on the wide part.

Mike sat straighter. "Hey, let me see that." He held out his hand and she gave it to him.

She unfolded the paper and read. "My dear Laurel," it began.

"*During our short time together I have come to love you very much, as befits a grandfather for his granddaughter. I have not always acted in the best ways a man can, but in the time I've known you my life has been immeasurably enriched, and I've found real peace and happiness at last.*"

Tears welled in Laurel's eyes.

"*I assure you that as you read this I am with my true love, united once again, so don't feel remorse for me. I hope you will think of me as your 'grandfather from the Twice Told' and not the man I was when I did those terrible things I told you about.*

One last thing. Sometime in the next day or so, a man will be contacting you. He will have another letter for you. That one will concern my estate.

Good bye my darling granddaughter.

Have a wonderful life."

It was signed, Jake Eastland.

Laurel fell against Mike. "I don't want him to be gone. I want him the way he was." Tears flowed, words from the past reopening the wound.

He comforted her, held her tight, rocking a bit. When she had control again, she handed him the letter and went to the kitchen for a tissue.

"You know, it sounds as if he might have put you into his will."

She stopped short, halfway across the room. Her eyes overflowed again and she sobbed. This time, she fell to her knees, put her forehead on the floor, and drummed her fists into the polished wood. "... don't want money... want Grampa."

Mike went and knelt behind her, stroking her back. "Yes, I know. I'm sorry, honey."

A minute later he yelled, "Whoa!"

Laurel jerked her head up. He held the small key. "This engraving. I think I've seen it before. It's so worn its hard to tell. Someone must have worn it around their neck, or carried it in their pocket for a long time." He paused and stared at her. "Get the box out of the safe, Laurel. I think this might be the key."

Laurel gasped. The key? Had Grampa Jake found it? But how? She got to her feet and went into the office, returning with the box, which she placed on the cocktail table in front of Mike.

He held the key close, comparing the initials on the key to those on the box. They matched. Slowly, with ever-so-careful movements, Mike placed the key at the opening of the lock and inserted it to the hilt.

Laurel could hardly breathe. The key fit like it had been made for the lock. She let her eyes meet Mike's. His were wide, as solemn as she'd ever seen them, awed by what might be about to happen.

"Where would Grampa Jake get it?" he said. "It can't possibly be the right key."

As if some magic wand had been waved, Laurel knew the truth. Grampa Jake in the cemetery, telling the story, Joshua swept overboard. The key had to have come from him. Grampa Jake had insisted he had proof. And here it was.

The feeling she'd had that day in the graveyard, that the treasure existed for her, was there only for her. That had been destiny calling her, and if it hadn't been for Grampa Jake, she'd never have learned how to see through life, never have given herself the chance to go ahead and become the person she needed to be.

"Yes." Laurel reached over and nudged his fingers aside. "It is the key. The right key." She grasped it between her thumb and forefinger. "He had it all along."

She turned the key with a firm, clockwise movement.

The lock released with a sharp hissing sound and a small jet of mist escaped from the joint between the lid and the box itself.

"It's pressurized," Laurel breathed. "How in the world could they have done that?" The dry odor of decaying paper, a little like the inside of an old attic trunk, drifted to her nostrils.

"I don't think they could have. It's probably just part of the natural process," Mike speculated. "Paper making was pretty crude then. Maybe it gave off some kind of gas as it aged."

"See if you can open it." Laurel urged.

Mike grasped the lid and lifted. It moved. The fit between the two halves was so perfect air hissed in as he lifted the upper half.

There wasn't much inside. On the surface lay a piece of blue cloth that Mike lifted and folded away. Beneath was a piece of paper folded into thirds like a letter.

"Call Genevieve," Laurel said. "Tell her we found the key to the box."

Three minutes after Mike reached her in her suite, Genevieve ran from the elevator into the penthouse. "Wait! Don't touch anything," she cried. "Especially not with your fingers. I have the special gloves." She pulled several pair from her briefcase then bent over to study the paper. Her breathing came in gasps, as if she had just run a marathon. "It seems robust, not dried out at all."

Laurel knelt next to Mike and leaned forward. "Could we pick it up and put it on the table?" she asked Genevieve.

"I think it will be all right. Put it on the cloth. Flip it over when you do so we can see the other side."

Laurel pulled on a rubber glove and picked up the letter. The paper was brown on the ends. She turned it over, revealing a dark wax seal and placed it on the coffee table beside the box. The seal was blackened, but there were hints that it might once have been plum colored.

"Let me see," Genevieve produced a magnifying glass from her case. For several seconds she studied the impressions in the wax. Then she pulled her head away and abruptly sat up, the color gone from her cheeks. The hand with which she held the magnifying glass trembled.

"This document must go immediately to a proper laboratory."

"Why? What's so important all of a sudden?" Laurel couldn't keep impatience from coloring her voice.

"This is the seal of the Commandant in Chief of the Continental Army," Genevieve whispered.

They stared at one another. The folded paper on the polished surface of Grampa Jake's coffee table took on an aura, a life force of its own. This was no housewife's shopping list, or someone's letter to a lonesome spouse. It could be from the hand of the first President of the United States, a historical figure and national hero.

History waited for them to recover from the shock of discovery, waited for them to get on with it.

Laurel was first. "It's for you to say, Genevieve, you're the expert."

Genevieve stood and backed away. "But you are the discoverer, Laurel. I think it is proper to examine this under controls."

"It looks very solid," Laurel said. "What if we open it and see what it is. Then we can decide what to do with it."

Genevieve shook her head. "I am sorry, but…"

Mike said, "Come on, Genevieve. Where's that 'devil take the hindmost' spirit Aaron swears you're so famous for?"

The Frenchwoman sniffed, hands going to her hips. "Ah, yes. The trouble that man has made for me in the world of archaeology. Do not think I have forgotten." In spite of her best efforts, she was unable to hide the élan that came into her eyes. "Very well, then. We shall do the best we can with what we have. We'll need photographs, many photographs, and good light. Then I'll try to remove the seal and we'll see what we have."

After Genevieve had taken pictures from every angle, she left to get her tools. Laurel slid closer to Mike. He put his arm around her.

"I'm half afraid to touch it, let alone open it," she admitted. "Somehow, it gives me the shivers."

"I know what you mean. It's come across such an unimaginable void and now it's here, in front of us, for us alone to know, to judge."

Laurel considered. There were two possibilities. The letter would either alter their vision of the man, or it would not. If there was something there, something that hadn't been known, some piece of dirty laundry, it would be a huge discovery.

Genevieve returned with the tool. Her fingers were deft as she slid the razor knife beneath the dry wax, freeing it little by little. After a half hour of painstaking work, she had the seal loose. Keeping her movements slow, she unfolded the document.

She leaned over it, positioning a pair of reading glasses on her nose then read aloud.

To the Honorable Lt. General Sir Frederic Haldimand, Governor

Greetings Sir,

Allow me to introduce the Baron Colonel Pierre Dubois D'Avangere, who has graciously agreed to carry this to you and carry your reply to me, should there be one.

Your recent appointment as Governor pleases us in that we have previously had the privilege of meeting in person and I feel that we have in common many things.

We have concern over the future state of relations between our governments. No doubt word of our recent successes both in New York, and elsewhere has reached you. May I assure you our commanders are urging us to proceed against Fort Niagara and points north at the earliest possible moment.

We find ourselves hesitant to come to the point but here we must. We seek reaffirmation of the land grants given the Virginia Company by Charles II, which as you know were abrogated by the Quebec Act of 1774, namely those interests of the Ohio and Vandalia Companies.

Your intervention on our behalf with George III would be well received here. In return for a favorable response, we are prepared to reposition our offensive forces in New York, namely those that threaten Fort Niagara and Montreal, leaving them and all between them forever in your hands. We very much prefer the current state of affairs to further westward expansion from New York, preferring that expansion to take place from within the Virginia Grants in their stead.

We trust this will arrive to find you well. We await your reply.

Yours truly,

"And it's signed and dated August 15, 1780." Genevieve finished, putting the letter on the table.

Mike scratched his head. "I don't quite get it, but it sounds like he's asking for a favor of some kind in return for pulling his army out of Western and Northern New York."

Laurel addressed Genevieve. "How well versed are you in the Revolutionary War?"

"Well I wasn't there, if that's what you think." Genevieve primped her hair at the back of her neck then became serious. "I've not made the study of the war, but I have the idea of the politics involved."

"What did the Ohio Company do?" Laurel said.

"Let me think. Virginia formed the Ohio Company before the war, yes? It was to survey and administrate the sale of lands in the Northwest Territories, what the states of Ohio, Indiana, Illinois, Michigan and Wisconsin now have become. The company was privately owned through shares."

"How did Virginia get the right to control those lands?" Laurel asked.

"Royal grants from the King, of course. All authority came from the Kings. Charles II made the grant to Virginia during the seventeenth Century."

"So Virginia had the right to sell those lands to settlers."

"Yes," Genevieve nodded. "A lot of money is at stake, no? Both George Washington and Patrick Henry, governor of Virginia, had substantial investments in the Ohio Company. The history books hint that one of the little-known reasons for the Revolutionary War came from the fact that King George III decided to cancel the grants."

"Would that have been the Quebec Act of 1774?" Mike asked.

"You have been doing the study of history, no?" Genevieve nodded.

"Very good. Yes. In it, George III ceded all of the Northwest Territories to Quebec. It meant the Ohio Company shares were worthless."

"So here, the owners of the Ohio Company—who happen to be highly placed in the Continental Army—make an appeal to the governor of Canada to intervene with the king on behalf of Virginia."

Genevieve squinted at him as she thought about it. Her eyes narrowed even more as she leaned closer. "The entire matter will revolve on whether or not the—how do you say—inducement, is offered." Her voice was measured, calm, but her eyes glowed with excitement.

"That's exactly what was done," Laurel said. "He offered to back off and leave Montreal and Fort Niagara alone. That'd be considered an inducement wouldn't it?"

Genevieve shrugged. "It is clear, the answer. An inducement, and contrary to the interests of the union at the least, and at the most, an act of treason."

The chilling word was pronounced in a matter-of-fact way, her slight accent making it all the more ominous.

"Does this mean the letter has value?" Laurel said.

"Oh, my word yes. This letter, properly authenticated, it will be worth millions."

Late that afternoon, the phone rang. Laurel stirred. Since Genevieve's pronouncement she'd felt as if she was under water and everything happening in slow motion. It was on her to decide: what should she do with the letter?

Mike answered, listened for a moment then spoke into the receiver and put his hand over the mouthpiece.

"There's someone to see you. A Mister King."

Laurel sighed. Grampa's note had said there would be, but she wished she didn't have to deal with it so soon after the burden of the letter had fallen on her shoulders.

"Tell him to come up. Please stay. I might need your help."

Their visitor strode toward them as he left the elevator, a tall, rangy man in his late fifties and very fit. He held his hand out to Laurel. "My name is Albert A. King—Allie to my friends. You must be Laurel."

Laurel shook his hand. "Yes. Please come in. This is my frieind, Mike McKean."

"I'm president of The Big ONE, Inc.," Allie went on, "a holding company owned by Jake Eastland. I've been operating the company for Jake since 1987."

When they were seated, Allie addressed Laurel.

"If you don't mind, I'd like to establish certain facts if I may."

"Go ahead."

"Your full name is Laurel A. Kingsford, and you were born on December 12, 1969."

Laurel nodded. "That's correct."

"Let's see. Your mother's name was Saundra F. Gamble, and your grandmother?"

"Her name was Jean Gamble."

"Yes, that was her maiden name, which she reverted to upon her divorce from your grandfather."

"I didn't known that." She slid closer to Mike and grasped his hand. Almost as if from outside herself, she heard herself ask, "And what was her married name?"

"Why… Eastland, of course."

Laurel's mouth fell open. She didn't, couldn't breathe. She cried out and fell against Mike, sobbing.

"Oh, God, no! Why didn't he tell me? I never even had a chance to tell him how much I love him."

"I'm truly sorry, Ms Kingsford. I thought you knew."

She nodded, daubing at her eyes with a tissue.

"May I take a minute to tell you about my experience with your grandfather?"

Laurel sniffled. "Yes. I'd like that."

"My father and Uncle Jake, or rather Mister Eastland," he looked at her, his eyes warm, "became friends just before World War Two. I grew up hearing stories of their wild exploits in Europe and Africa, and later in Asia, so it was natural for me to want to follow in their footsteps. It was hero worship, plain and simple. I wanted to be just like them."

He stopped and shook his head, remembering. "I let it all hang out, so to speak, and I was this far," he held his thumb and index finger about an inch apart, "from a permanent jail cell in Morocco when Uncle Jake found out and came to my rescue. Over the next few years, he managed to convince me that the way he came up wouldn't work anymore. I needed education, lots of it, and morality. He kept harping on that. I didn't listen very well at first, but thank God I finally did, because I was able to step in when we lost dad and keep things going."

He stopped and pulled a handkerchief from the pocket of his coat. "I swear, working for Uncle Jake is the best experience I've ever had. I'm going to miss him."

He fell silent and his mouth worked at smiling, but the corners of his eyes were shiny.

"Thank you for that," Laurel said. "I know how you feel."

After a moment, Albert straightened, smiling, his expression a bit sheepish. "About now, Jake would have told me to quit blabbering and get on with it because he didn't have all day."

Laurel laughed. "That sounds just like Grampa Jake."

Allie reached into his briefcase and pulled out a legal document bound in thick blue paper. He dropped it on the table in front of them.

"About six weeks ago, on the twentieth of September, Uncle Jake called me at home and told me he was changing his will, leaving everything to you. He told me to get the papers right out to him. If I'm not mistaken, that was a few weeks after you arrived at the Twice Told Hotel. I remember being surprised, because I didn't even know you were alive at that point."

Allie touched the document. "Naturally, I made sure the papers got to him right away. He signed and the notary notarized, and that became his official will." He gave it a little push away from him. "Then, a few days later, things started getting interesting."

"What do you mean, Mr. King?" Laurel said.

"Call me Allie, let's not be formal." Allie smiled. "He called me again and told me he'd changed his mind and ordered me to change the will back. You were no longer to be the beneficiary."

"I wonder why he did that," Mike said.

Allie lifted his eyebrows. "Hey, with Uncle Jake you don't second guess. You do what he says. Anyway, at the same time, he asked me to investigate Laurel's ex-boss, a guy named Nicholas Zaia." Allie leaned closer. "Now get this. This is where it gets interesting. This Zaia guy turns out to be the son of one Julian E. Zaia, who is..." he paused for dramatic effect, "nothing less than Uncle Jake's son by a woman named Estelle Zaia."

"Grampa Jake told me about that."

Allie blinked. "I'm surprised. We just found out about it a few days before he died."

"I was there when you called. He had the call on speakerphone."

Mike said, "That would make your ex-boss Nicholas Zaia an heir. If the estate is anything sizeable he'd probably try to claim it if he knew."

"Oh, he knows all right. Take it from me." Allie paced to the windows and back, as if overloaded with energy. He stopped in front of Laurel and leaned forward. "If you know about him, you probably also know it was Nick who sicced that vulture on you, the one who stole your savings. Then he maneuvered to discredit you and your boss, pushed you into a corner and forced you to resign from G.A. Forrester. And I've learned he's getting ready to go after Uncle Jake's estate."

His words pounded on Laurel, making her head throb. Even now, the coldness of Nick Zaia's plot disturbed her.

"Where'd that information come from?" Mike asked.

"Can't tell you," Allie smirked. "Wiretaps are illegal." He waited until Mike smiled. "Uncle Jake called me a few days before he died. I'd just received the final report on Zaia, with all the stuff I told you about. He told me to change his will back. He wanted Laurel back in as beneficiary.

We discussed it, but Uncle Jake became confused. I think that head wound affected him. Anyway, he ended up telling me to take care of things for him."

Laurel had trouble breathing. Allie'd said Grampa Jake owned the "The Big ONE". Did he have more money than they thought?

"Did you get the new documents to him?"

Allie shook his head. "I didn't have time. I was in the field for three days, running down some important stuff." He patted his briefcase. Then he put his fingers on the document he'd put on the table earlier, turned it so it faced Laurel.

"*This* is the last will and testament of Jake Eastland. It's all nice and legal. You, Laurel Kingsford, are the principal beneficiary. He left his entire estate to you."

He stopped, waiting for her reaction.

Had she missed something? "But I thought…"

"I never changed it back the first time. He yelled at me once, but then he forgot."

"Why?"

"He was my favorite person in the world. I loved him. I was happy to see him showing signs of life again. Besides, he trusted me to take care of things for him."

Allie reached into his briefcase and removed several documents. "By the way, Nicholas Zaia won't be bothering you with any claims on the estate."

"He has a legitimate claim, doesn't he?" Laurel felt a step behind again, Allie sure seemed like a ball of fire.

"Oh sure, but without these he'll never be able to prove he is who he is." He tossed the documents on the table.

Several were quite old. Laurel leaned forward and lifted the top item, a packet of microfilm strips. She looked at Allie, puzzled.

"Those are film cards from the archives of the local newspaper. Julian's birth announcement is in there, so are the reports of Nick's birth and Julian's death." He picked up the next item. "This is his birth certificate. And this…"

The birth record was a yellowed page that had been sliced from an official record book. Laurel was aghast, "But, you can't steal records. They're public property."

Allie's eyes narrowed, and he leaned closer. "This man plotted to kill you, Laurel. He almost succeeded. We've got it all on tape. They doctored your SCUBA gear. Do you think for one second he would hesitate over some dumb thing like a public record?"

He straightened and smiled. "He had his bird dog on the road looking for this stuff. We had to get to it first. I took care of it in person. Tell you what. By now, he knows we've beaten him. He won't be a happy guy right now. The estate is all yours."

"Wh... What does Grampa Jake's estate involve?"

"Well, it means you're the new owner of the Twice Told Hotel, for one. Don't you wonder how much it's worth?"

"No. Not really. I mean, I never thought about it. Which, the Twice Told, or the estate?"

Allie chuckled, "Both, I guess." He consulted his briefcase. "Let's see here, the Twice Told Hotel. Yes, here it is. Oops, there are shoreline parcels attached. Apparently you own two miles or so of lakefront to the east of here. It's all valued as a package. Yes, that works. Two point five million."

"M... Million?"

"You better hold onto something, honey. The Twice Told was one of Uncle Jake's toys. His estate is worth fifteen billion dollars. And it's getting bigger every second we sit here."

Hot darts pricked the back of Laurel's neck, made her feel as if she would pass out. Someone said, "hold your head between your knees."

Bit by bit she fought the darkness off, re-gained control.

Rich beyond all ability to measure, but money with blood on it.

"I don't want it. I won't take it."

His voice was gentle. "Think how much good you can do with it. Why do you think so many people came to Uncle Jake's funeral? For the last several years, he's given every penny he earned to charity, and to worthy people. Think of the good things *you'll* do with it."

Laurel thought for a moment then turned to Mike and squeezed his arm. "We'll set up a foundation. Allie will run it. We'll put the entire estate into it."

"You'll need to keep some for yourself," Allie said.

She shook her head. "No. I don't want any part of it. I'd rather find my own way."

Allie stared at her. Slowly a different expression took over his face.

"That's probably what he would have said." He gave her shoulder a hefty squeeze. "I think I'm going to like working for you, Laurel Kingsford. You won't need to chain *me* to my desk."

Chain… Chain him. A chest padlocked into chains, six men to carry it, a length of chain for each.

Thys man spent his life avain, searching for six legs of chain.

She'd seen chains. Where? Where had she seen them? The answer came and Laurel laughed. She laughed from the wonder and irony of it. She'd turned her back on her grandfather's riches and now, almost in the next breath, she knew where to find her own.

Except, money no longer meant as much to her. She turned to Allie. "Know what? If I ever need some money, I know right where to look. Meanwhile, let's see how much of Grampa Jake's we can give away."

In front of her, Mike smiled and opened his arms. She stepped into them.

EPILOGUE

Laurel and Mike sat on the sofa in Grampa Jake's penthouse. Allie was on his way back to New York.

"We need to decide about the letter."

He sighed, a slow exhale, his mouth curved down in a frown.

"Why can't we leave it alone, let things stay the way they've always been?" Laurel said. "Do we have the right to destroy him after everything he did for our nation?"

He considered that, his face serious. "I guess you could let Genevieve make it public. That way you'd be off the hook. But I couldn't do it. I'd never feel right about having broken my oath, not ever."

"What oath?"

He studied her, his face almost ready to smile. "The oath Grampa Jake had me take, remember? I swore to God I'd keep the secrets you shared, and promised never to reveal them, or any others that I might learn in the course of my work with you."

He sat up and leaned toward her. "Anyway, I don't think making it public would do any good. It'd just be one more bad thing, make people that much more jaded and disillusioned about America. Everything that happened will still have happened. The letter never made it to Haldimand. All we'd be doing is changing how people see one man."

He frowned at her. "I don't think that's important. Do you?"

She hugged him, thankful for his wisdom. "No, I don't. I think I know what to do."

She went into the office. There, she opened the safe and removed the letter.

She crossed to Grampa Jake's luxurious kitchen range and turned the valve. The burner clicked twice and ignited.

Then, looking Mike right in the eye, Laurel held the priceless two-hundred-twenty-year-old document by an upper corner and moved its bottom corner over the flame. It caught, a yellow tendril licked the side of the paper and quickly ran upward.

She held it over the sink and let it drop just as the flame reached for her fingers. Mike circled her with his arms from behind. Together, they watched as the sheet of paper in the stainless steel bowl blackened and shriveled.

In seconds it was no more.

ABOUT THE AUTHOR

Art Tirrell grew up in Syracuse, New York, and spent summers at Selkirk Shores State Park on Lake Ontario. In 1974 he founded a retail business in Oswego NY, which continues.

He's a respected competitive sailor with many seasons of racing experience in Lightnings and other types of sailboats, and a keen observer of wind and weather and their effect on the lake he loves.

He writes character-driven adventure. *The Secret Ever Keeps* is his debut novel and the first in the Eastland series. The second, as yet to be named, is well advanced.

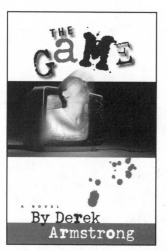

Provocative. Bold. Controversial.

The Game
A thriller by Derek Armstrong

Reality television becomes too real when a killer stalks the cast on America's number one live-broadcast reality show.
■ "A series to watch ... Armstrong injects the trope with new vigor." *Booklist*

US$ 24.95 | Pages 352, cloth hardcover
ISBN 978-1-60164-001-7 | EAN: 9781601640017
LCCN 2006930183

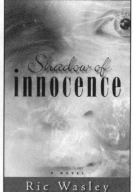

Rabid
A novel by T K Kenyon

A sexy, savvy, darkly funny tale of ambition, scandal, forbidden love and murder. Nothing is sacred. The graduate student, her professor, his wife, her priest: four brilliantly realized characters spin out of control in a world where science and religion are in constant conflict.
■ "Kenyon is definitely a keeper." STARRED REVIEW, *Booklist*

US$ 26.95
Pages 480, cloth hardcover
ISBN 978-1-60164-002-4
EAN 9781601640024
LCCN 2006930189

Whale Song
A novel by Cheryl Kaye Tardif

Whale Song is a haunting tale of change and choice. Cheryl Kaye Tardif's beloved novel—a "wonderful novel that will make a wonderful movie" according to *Writer's Digest*—asks the difficult question, which is the higher morality, love or law?
■ "Crowd-pleasing ... a big hit." *Booklist*

US$ 12.95
Pages 208, UNA trade paper
ISBN 978-1-60164-007-9
EAN 9781601640079
LCCN 2006930188

Shadow of Innocence
A mystery by Ric Wasley

The Thin Man meets *Pulp Fiction* in a unique mystery set amid the drugs-and-music scene of the sixties that touches on all our societal taboos. *Shadow of Innocence* has it all: adventure, sleuthing, drugs, sex, music and a perverse shadowy secret that threatens to tear apart a posh New England town.

US$ 24.95
Pages 304, cloth hardcover
ISBN 978-1-60164-006-2
EAN 9781601640062
LCCN 2006930187